THE GRESHAM SCANDAL

TRACY GRANT

The Gresham Scandal

Copyright © 2024 by Tracy Grant

Ebook ISBN: 9781641973236

POD ISGN: 9781641973342

NYLA Publishing

121 W 27th St., Suite 1201, New York, NY 10001

http://www.nyliterary.com

For Mark and Cindy

Love looks not with the eyes but with the mind;
    And therefore is winged Cupid painted blind.
        –Shakespeare, *A Midsummer Night's Dream,* Act I, scene i

DRAMATIS PERSONAE

*indicates real historical figures

<u>The Rannoch Family & Household</u>

Malcolm Rannoch, MP and former British intelligence agent
Mélanie Suzanne Rannoch, his wife, playwright and former
French intelligence agent
Colin Rannoch, their son
Jessica Rannoch, their daughter
Berowne, their cat

Laura O'Roarke, Colin and Jessica's former governess
Raoul O'Roarke, her husband, Mélanie's former spymaster, and
Malcolm's father
Lady Emily Fitzwalter, Laura's daughter from her first marriage
Clara O'Roarke, Laura and Raoul's daughter

Miles Addison, agent, Malcolm's valet
Blanca Mendoza Addison, agent, his wife, Mélanie's companion
Pedro Addison, their son

Valentin, footman

The Mallinson Family

Julien (Arthur) Mallinson, Earl Carfax, former agent for hire
Katelina (Kitty) Velasquez Mallinson, Countess Carfax, his wife,
former British and Spanish intelligence agent
Leo Ashford, her son
Timothy Ashford, her son
Guenevere (Genny) Ashford, Kitty and Julien's daughter

Hubert Mallinson, spymaster, Julien's uncle
Amelia Mallinson, his wife
Lucinda Mallinson, their daughter

David Mallinson, MP, Hubert and Amelia's son
Simon Tanner, playwright, his lover

William, footman
Teddy, coachman

The Davenport Family & Household

Lady Cordelia Davenport, classicist
Colonel Harry Davenport, her husband, classicist, and former
British intelligence agent
Livia Davenport, their daughter
Drusilla Davenport, their daughter

The Roth Family

Judith Roth, Malcolm's cousin
Jeremy Roth, Bow Street runner, her husband
Serena Derwent, Judith's daughter from her first marriage

Samuel Roth, Jeremy's son from his first marriage
Dorian Roth, Jeremy's son from his first marriage
Harriet Roth, Jeremy's sister

Cressida Caldwell Beardsley, Jeremy's first wife's sister
William Beardsley, MP, Cressida's husband
Vincent Caldwell, Cressida's son

The Southcott Family

Anthony (Tony) Southcott, Duke of Bamford
Désirée Clairineau, former French agent, his fiancée
Sophie, their daughter
Belle, her puppy

Prince Franz Stroheim, Désirée's nephew
Lisette Varon, his fiancée

Henrietta (Hetty) Southcott, Duchess of Bamford, his wife

Lord Lionel Southcott, diplomat, Tony's brother
John Southcott, foreign office, his son

The Delaney Family

Hara Delaney, Laura's childhood friend
Lizzy Delaney, his wife
Hal Delaney, Hara's son
Anjali Delaney, Hara's daughter
Laila, Hal and Anjali's nurse

Austrians and Russians

*Prince Metternich, Austria's chancellor

*Dorothea, Countess Lieven, wife of the Russian ambassador and Metternich's mistress
Count Karl Augustin, diplomat
Charlotte Augustin, his wife
Baron Josef Hauke, diplomat

In the British government

*Lord Palmerston, secretary at war
*Emily, Countess Cowper, patroness of Almack's, his mistress
*Arthur Wellesley, Duke of Wellington, Master General of the Ordnance
*Lord Fitzroy Somerset, his secretary
*Lord Castlereagh (now Lord Londonderry), British foreign secretary
*Lord Sidmouth, home secretary
*Sir Nathaniel Conant, chief magistrate of Bow Street

Others

Tristram Gresham, composer and agent
André LeFou, assassin
Danielle Darnault, opera singer and agent
Pierre Ducroix, journalist, her husband
Ilia, their daughter
Edmund Blayney, journalist
Pippa Blayney, his wife
Colonel Frederick Radley, soldier

CHAPTER 1

July 1821
London

*R*ifle shots pinged off the rocks. Mélanie rolled to the ground, sneezing at the dust. How could the shooter have reloaded so fast? Rifle fire whizzed overhead again before she could get more than a few feet to the shelter of trees. She ducked, then pushed herself up against the rocky ground, only to come awake and feel smooth linen and a soft pillow beneath her fingers.

She was in her bed, in Berkeley Square, not in the Cantabrian Mountains. But the pinging sound hadn't stopped. Not rifle fire. Gravel thrown at the window.

Before she even turned her head, she knew her husband Malcolm was awake beside her. She exchanged a quick glance with him in the dark, more sense than sight, then grabbed her dressing gown from the foot of the bed and ran to the window.

Berowne, the cat, sat up on the bed and gave a yowl. Malcolm stumbled to the window beside her. They pushed up the sash together. The moonlight glanced off the pale stone of the house and the white window moldings, and lit the upturned faces of the man and woman who stood below in the garden. The man's unruly shock of dark hair and the woman's tumble of dark gold curls. Jeremy Roth, friend, fellow investigator, and Bow Street runner. And Judith, Malcolm's cousin, and Jeremy's wife of less than a year.

"Come to the front door," Malcolm called.

"Get Raoul and Laura," he added to Mélanie as he struck a flint to a candle.

Malcolm ran out of the bedroom and down the stairs. Mélanie rapped on the door of Malcolm's father, Raoul, and his wife, Laura. "It's Jeremy and Judith," she called.

Raoul and Laura emerged, wrapped in dressing gowns, with a speed that said they'd heard and had merely been waiting to see if they were needed. In a family of former spies, no one slept soundly. Their gazes flickered across her face.

"I don't know anything more," she said. It was not wholly unusual for Jeremy to come to them with a case at unexpected times of day. It was more surprising for Judith to be with him. Though Judith had been managing to work her way into his investigations with admirable tenacity.

The door creaked open in the hall below. By the time Mélanie, Laura, and Raoul hurried down the two flights to the entrance hall, Malcolm was ushering in Jeremy, greatcoated but bareheaded, and Judith, wrapped in a blue velvet cloak.

"I'm sorry," Jeremy said. His voice was level, but his face was set with worry.

"No need," Malcolm told him. "But why the dramatic arrival?"

"You answer your own door at night," Jeremy said, nodding to Mélanie, Laura, and Raoul. "Admirable, but it occurred to me it makes middle of the night visits complicated. I wasn't sure whom ringing the bell would wake, and in truth we wanted to keep this quiet."

"I told him picking the lock would be better than throwing gravel," Judith said.

"Not necessarily," Malcolm told his cousin, moving to open the library door. "Screams of shock have a way of waking people."

"Oh, stuff." Judith moved past him into the library. "Julien used to break into your house all the time. I imagine he still does."

"He has a key, actually," Malcolm said. "We'll get you one."

"We don't all have to hear whatever it is," Raoul said from the base of the stairs. "Depending on what it is."

"No," Jeremy said. "That's appreciated. But we'll need all of you." He turned to face them as they moved into the library and Malcolm lit the lamps by the fireplace. The warm light sharpened his face and caught the fear in his eyes. "It's Harriet. She's disappeared."

Mélanie cast a quick glance at Malcolm and then at Laura and Raoul. Harriet was Jeremy's sister, who had lived with him and helped care for his sons when his first wife left him and now continued to live with him and Judith. Quiet, ironic, stylish, she had been on the edges of so many investigations, but never at the heart. Not even their investigation into the death of Jeremy's first wife.

"She didn't leave a note?" Mélanie asked.

Jeremy shook his head. He was pacing before the unlit fireplace. "We all had dinner together. Serena woke with a bad dream, and Judith and I got up to sit with her. Harriet's door wasn't latched and it swung open. I went to close it and saw she wasn't in her bed." He paused, cheeks flushed in the lamplight. "I wouldn't intrude on my sister's privacy. But when I saw the bed was undisturbed, I glanced in. There was no response when I called her name, so I went in." He hesitated. "In the life we lead, one worries."

"Understandable," Malcolm said, gaze steady on Jeremy's face. Mélanie could hear the echoes of the night Jeremy had summoned Malcolm to the tavern where Allegra, his first wife, lay knifed to death.

3

Jeremy inclined his head, gaze filled with ghosts. "Her reticule and cloak were gone. Nothing else. From what I can tell from physical evidence, she left the house by the front door."

"Jeremy." Mélanie chose her words carefully. Harriet was a friend, but they were hardly confidantes. "Harriet is a grown woman." Mélanie wasn't sure of Harriet's precise age, but somewhere in her late twenties or early thirties, she suspected. "Could she—"

"I said as much." Judith jumped up from the Queen Anne chair where she'd plopped when they came into the library. "Just because Harriet has devoted her life to Jeremy and the boys doesn't mean she has no other interests. Gentlemen can be so obtuse when it comes to their sisters."

Jeremy's gaze clashed with his wife's. "You know perfectly well Harriet doesn't—"

"That's just it, Jeremy," Judith said to her husband. "We don't know what Harriet does with her spare time. And it's really no concern of ours."

"No—" Jeremy sucked in his breath.

"For a Radical," Judith said, "you're ridiculously old-fashioned about your sister, dearest."

"It's all very well," Jeremy said, "but as we often say, however much we may want to change the world, this is the world we live in. And you know what would happen if people realized Harriet—"

"Had a lover?" Judith said. "No one's going to realize it if we don't make a fuss."

"Do you have any reason to believe Harriet was involved with anyone?" Raoul asked in a quiet voice, leaning against the back of the settee. "While I would not want to intrude on anyone's personal life, I also know better than to assume the obvious reason for anyone's disappearance."

"No," Jeremy said. "There was never the least hint—"

"Don't be silly, darling," Judith said. "You know perfectly well she'd shut her door for hours on end and she was always scribbling away—"

"All of which anyone may do without having a secret lover," Laura said.

"Well, yes," Judith acknowledged. "But now that she's missing—"

"A point," Malcolm agreed. "But there's more than one reason a person can disappear. And given the attitudes of her family, I find it hard to believe Harriet would elope. She'd have no need to fear disapproval." He held Jeremy's gaze for a moment. "What did you find in her room?"

Jeremy gave a faint smile that did not touch his eyes. "You know me well enough to know I searched."

"I wouldn't do you the discredit of thinking otherwise."

Jeremy's mouth twisted. "I'm not sure it's to my credit. But the only significant thing I found was this." He reached into his coat and pulled out a rectangular calling card on heavy cream laid paper. He held it out to Malcolm.

Mélanie moved to her husband's side and started at the black print on the card. A name that suggested much and explained nothing. A noted roué. A known Radical. A brilliant composer. A man whose life was cloaked in secrets. The former lover of Jeremy's first wife.

Tristram Gresham.

CHAPTER 2

October 1818
Normandy

rees overhung the cottage, making it appear smaller than it probably was. Creamy yellow stone softened by vines with a timber roof and wood-framed windows painted a slate blue. Not the place one would imagine an agent who had been feared across the Continent hiding from the world. But then, as she had learnt from her Bow Street runner brother's investigations, sometimes the most dangerous people were the most deceptive.

Harriet Roth hesitated in front of the blue-painted front door. For all the risks she'd run recently, it seemed absurd to cavil at this one. Yet at the same time it felt a significant step. A move into the unknown, from which she could not return.

She rapped at the door. Light footsteps on a stone floor. The door opened to reveal a tall woman in a moss green gown, brown hair caught up in a disheveled knot, a small girl of about three or close to it clinging to her skirt.

"You must be Harriet," the woman said with smile that was quick and disarming. "This is Sophie. And I'm Désirée."

Harriet must have started. Somehow it was a surprise to hear the woman speak the name.

Désirée gave a full-throated laugh. "Did you think I'd use another name? I've used so many through the years. I'm more myself here than I have been anywhere for the past two decades."

Sophie tugged at her mother's skirt. "In a minute, *petite*." Désirée touched her daughter's hair. "We don't have a lot of visitors. She's very excited."

"We made cookies." Sophie stretched out a hand and grasped Harriet's fingers.

"She may want to go up to her room first, *petite*," the woman said.

"It's all right. I can't refuse cookies." The child's smile was infectious and made Harriet miss her nephews Samuel and Dorian. But more than cookies, Harriet was eager for information.

Désirée smiled and took Harriet's valise. Sophie pulled Harriet into a sun-splashed sitting room with dark wood mellowed by age, a huge stone fireplace, and tapestry furniture. A plate of the promised cookies and a pot of coffee sat on a table before a sofa strewn with comfortable cushions.

"You had no trouble getting here?" Désirée asked as she poured coffee.

Harriet shook her head and took a cookie from the plate Sophie was holding out. "The carriage met me at the dock. And I made sure they let me off in the woods as instructed."

"Thank you." The woman held out a cup of coffee. "I know the instructions were a bit circuitous. But we find it best to take precautions."

Given her past and the current conditions in France for anyone connected to the Bonaparte regime, it seemed a massive understatement. Harriet accepted the coffee and stirred in milk.

Désirée sat back in a chair, her own coffee cup cradled in one hand. "You're quite daring."

"Not really. Not at all, compared to you."

Désirée took a sip of coffee. "I've been doing this for far longer. And I was trained for it."

"You must have started somewhere." Harriet took a bite of cookie and smiled at Sophie in approval. Sophie, halfway through her own cookie, grinned.

"There is that," Désirée acknowledged. "Difficult to remember the start now."

"I may not be an agent," Harriet said. "But I'm no stranger to keeping secrets."

"No. According to our mutual friend you're brilliant at it." Désirée took another sip of coffee. "Are you sure about this?"

Harriet set down her cup. "Why else would I have come all this way?"

"I don't doubt your daring. Or your commitment. I don't doubt the lure of adventure. But there's no shame in facing a risk and deciding to walk away."

"Are you advising me to do that?"

"By no means. But I'm suggesting you consider the risks. I'm a dangerous collaborator."

Harriet sat forward in her chair and met the gaze of the agent who had been feared across the Continent. "Let's get to work."

CHAPTER 3

July 1821
London

Mélanie met Jeremy's gaze over Tristram Gresham's calling card. The fear roiling behind his eyes made a great deal more sense now. "I didn't know Harriet knew Tristram Gresham," she said.

"Nor did I." Jeremy's voice was tight.

"We don't know that she does," Judith said. She bit her lip. "All right, even I admit that strains belief. But they've been at the same events. Gresham could have given her his card."

"Why?" Jeremy rounded on his wife. "Why on earth would he have done so?"

"Don't be obtuse, darling. Gresham isn't just a noted composer. He's a man. A man known to be—"

"A rake. In fact, he rivals Lord Byron. But Harriet—"

"Is a very attractive woman."

"She's never—"

"Been one for flirtation? Just because you don't know about it—"

Jeremy scraped a hand over his dark brown hair. "You're right." He looked from Mélanie to Malcolm to Raoul to Laura. "Do any of you know of any connection Gresham might have to Harriet?"

Malcolm shook his head. "Like Mel, I didn't know they were acquainted."

"Nor did I," Raoul said.

"They've certainly been at the same events, as Judith says," Laura said. "But I can't remember ever seeing them speak together."

"I'm going to Gresham." Jeremy took a step towards the door. "I probably should have started there. But I was hoping—"

"That we'd know something?" Malcolm said. "Or that we'd come with you?"

"Both, I think. To the extent I've been able to think at all."

Mélanie glanced at the clock on the mantel, then exchanged a look with Malcolm. "No. Let us go on our own. Tristram keeps irregular hours, so we can show up at his rooms late at night. But we're likely to learn more this way."

Jeremy grimaced. "I may be an overprotective brother, but I won't plant him a facer."

"It's not that," Malcolm said. "But imagine if you were confronted by the brother of a girl you'd run off with."

"I wouldn't—"

"Yes, I know." Malcolm met Jeremy's gaze, his own steady. "But Gresham's likely to say more to us if you aren't there."

"We'll go with Raoul," Mélanie said. "Stay here with Laura. Drink some coffee and start making notes of what we'll need."

"Darling—" Judith stretched out a hand to Jeremy.

"I know." Jeremy jammed his hands into his greatcoat pockets. "I'm being managed." He drew in and released his breath. "And I know you're all right."

≈

"WELL?" Mélanie looked between Malcolm and Raoul as they walked down Berkeley Street towards St. Martin's Lane.

Malcolm slanted a look at her. "We've all learnt not to assume the obvious."

"No." Mélanie gripped her hands together beneath the cloak she'd thrown on over a midnight blue sarcenet dress that blended into the shadows and she could scramble into easily. "Harriet always struck me as eminently sensible. But I never quite felt I knew her. She holds her feelings close. Even more so than Jeremy."

"She's spent over a decade taking care of her brother and his children," Raoul said. "I can see her wanting adventure."

"Which could mean a number of different things," Malcolm said.

"So it could," Raoul agreed.

"Allegra Roth is the only connection we know of between them," Mélanie said. Now that they were away from Jeremy it was easier to talk about his first wife, who had been Gresham's mistress.

"Allegra and Gresham's affair was over long before she married Jeremy," Malcolm said.

"But Allegra knew Jeremy and Harriet from childhood. She might have written to Harriet about Gresham. It's hard to see how that would have created much of a bond between Gresham and Harriet, though. If anything, one would think it would have prompted Harriet to run a mile."

"Whether or not she knew about Allegra and Gresham in the past, she certainly knows now," Raoul said. "Which at least accounts for her keeping the relationship secret from Roth and Judith."

Mélanie looked from Raoul to Malcolm. "Gresham isn't just a composer and a rake. He's a political Radical. As is Harriet. Or at least her family are, and her own feelings tend that way, to the extent she's shared them."

"But she hasn't acted on them," Malcolm said.

"That we know of."

"Quite."

"Are you suggesting Harriet might have been working with Gresham on Radical causes? Or fallen in love with him because he's a Radical?" Raoul asked.

Mélanie glanced at her former spymaster. The gaslight from a passing lamp lit his gaze, but it was always difficult to read his expression. "What do you think?"

"I'm not sure. Though I think it's an interesting question."

"Gresham's work has mostly focused on allies in France and Italy," Malcolm said. "Difficult to see a connection to Harriet, who's never left the country, so far as we know."

"Not leaving the country doesn't mean she doesn't have interests beyond its borders," Mélanie said. "I may be wrong, but I always had the sense that Harriet had more that engaged her that went beyond the confines of what we saw of her life. Or perhaps it's just that I hate to see any connection between a man and a woman reduced to romance."

"Not a bad instinct." Raoul flashed a smile at her.

"Either way, she's always struck me as very careful of her family. The very fact that Jeremy and Judith are so shocked by her disappearance supports that. Which makes the fact that she didn't return home tonight all the more concerning."

MALCOLM PAUSED in front of a red-painted door in St. James's Place. A gas lantern on the wall cast warm, flickering light over the yellow stucco. "There'll likely be a porter on duty," he said. "It's typical in rooms like these that cater to well-heeled bachelors. There always was one—there's always one in my experience."

Mélanie cast a glance at her husband and felt Raoul do the same. Malcolm had once had fashionable bachelor lodgings in

London himself, in the Albany in Piccadilly, after he came down from Oxford. He'd been living there when he'd slashed his wrists, and his valet Addison had saved him with the help of his friends David and Simon, who had also lodged in the Albany. She could only imagine the memories behind her husband's contained gray gaze. And what they brought back for Raoul, who had been living abroad and hadn't been able to openly acknowledge Malcolm as his son at the time.

"Good to know," Raoul said, voice cheerfully neutral.

Malcolm rang the bell. There were times, Mélanie had to admit, when the calling card of an established Mayfair family was an inestimable help. The porter admitted them, after a discreet colloquy and a flash of Malcolm's card, and they were on the second floor, rapping at the door of Tristram Gresham's rooms.

No answer came. They tried again. They had brought picklocks, but when Malcolm turned the handle, the door gave with surprising ease. They stepped forwards into a shadowy sitting room. The only light came from a lamp and moonlight streaming through the window. Malcolm took a step forwards and stumbled. Mélanie and Raoul both caught him by the arm or he'd have fallen. A dark mass was sprawled on the ground just beyond the door. A shadowy figure stood to the side. Another bent over the mass on the floor, distinctive fair hair picked out by the moonlight.

Mélanie tightened her grip on Malcolm's arm. "Julien. What the devil are you doing here?"

CHAPTER 4

*J*ulien Mallinson, Earl Carfax, former agent and assassin, sat back on his heels and looked up at them. "I suppose I should have known. Did Hubert send for you too?"

"Why on earth would Hubert have sent for us?" Malcolm, balance recovered, took a step closer to Mélanie, gaze fixed on the form on the ground. "Is that Tristram Gresham?"

"No." Julien looked down at the dark shape beside him, which now that Mélanie's eyes had adjusted to the dark was quite clearly a body. "It's the man Uncle Hubert sent me here in search of."

"Explanations." Julien's wife Kitty stepped forwards out of the shadows, tawny hair catching the light from the windows. "Hubert contacted Julien tonight. He had someone tailing André LeFou." She glanced down at the body on the floor. "Do you know him?"

"By reputation," Raoul said. "And I heard rumors he was in Vienna during the Congress, though we never met. He's an agent. More specifically, an assassin."

"Almost my equal, but not quite," Julien said. "Speaking with due modesty. But of course I don't do this sort of work anymore."

"And Hubert hired LeFou?" Malcolm said. That wasn't as surprising as it might have been. Hubert Mallinson, Malcolm's former spymaster, Julien's uncle, and the unofficial head of British intelligence, had engaged the services of assassins more than once that Mélanie knew of. And probably untold other times as well.

"No." Julien pushed himself to his feet, gaze still on LeFou. "At least, not as he tells it. Uncle Hubert said he had someone tailing LeFou because he'd got wind LeFou was in London and was worried about what he might be up to. Hubert's agent saw LeFou go into Gresham's rooms tonight. When LeFou didn't emerge after over an hour, Uncle Hubert sent for me and asked me to investigate."

"Trusting you more than his agent," Malcolm said. "That's plausible."

"I thought so. Enough that Kitty and I came here."

"Was there any sign of Tristram Gresham when you arrived?" Mélanie asked.

Julien shook his head. "The rooms were dark. The door was unlocked. No sign of Gresham's valet or any servants either. We haven't had a chance to search. You came here to see Gresham?"

"Yes," Mélanie said. "Or rather, to question him. Harriet Roth disappeared tonight. And Jeremy found Gresham's calling card in her room."

"Interesting." Julien looked down at LeFou. "I suppose Gresham could have been his target. And Gresham killed him and ran. Though one would rather think Gresham would have simply sent for the authorities."

"Unless he had a Bow Street runner's sister with him," Kitty said.

"A point. But surely he could have smuggled Harriet out if that was the case." Julien cocked a brow at the others. "Is that the case? I never had the sense there was anything going on between Gresham and Harriet Roth, but I've certainly been known to miss things."

"If that's the case, we all missed it," Mélanie said. "We still aren't sure of the connection between them. Or if Gresham has anything to do with Harriet's disappearance."

Raoul had advanced into the room and was studying LeFou. "You can't tell me Hubert didn't know more about what he was doing in London."

"No," Julien agreed, gaze on LeFou. "My thoughts exactly." He glanced from LeFou to the corner of the room. "He was shot. One bullet, through the chest."

Mélanie could see the bullet mark now, and the dark congealing blood on the floorboards beneath LeFou. The bullet had gone through his chest.

"If I'm right about the angle, the shooter was standing in the corner by windows," Julien said. "Not an easy shot to make and precisely delivered. It looks like the work of another professional. Not something delivered in the heat of an argument."

Mélanie cast a quick glance round the room. "Have you looked—?"

"We haven't had time," Kitty said. "The door was unlocked when we got here."

Malcolm was already at the window. "No sign it's been forced open. I suspect LeFou and the killer both came in the front door. Assuming the killer came in."

"You mean assuming the killer isn't Gresham?" Kitty said.

"We have to consider it." Malcolm picked up the lamp.

Of one accord they moved to the door to the adjoining room. Malcolm held up the lamp. A bedchamber. A four-poster bed. The covers disarranged. Which didn't necessarily mean anything—Gresham seemed the sort not to be tidy. Two glasses of burgundy on a pier table.

Julien cast an eye over the bed. "It doesn't look as though two people were in it. Hard to be sure."

Kitty bent down and picked up something from the floorboards. Shimmering white dangled from her fingers. A moon-stone earring, set in silver. Mélanie crossed to her side and met Kitty's gaze. "Harriet has an earring like this, as I recall," Kitty said.

Mélanie nodded. "They're the earrings she wears most often. Of course plenty of people have moonstone earrings. But given that Harriet is missing—"

Raoul was at the door to the back stairs. "Scuff marks. It looks as though someone's gone out this way."

Malcolm gave Raoul the lamp. Raoul ran lightly down the stairs.

Malcolm moved to the wardrobe. Mélanie studied the wine glasses. "No traces of lip rouge. But Harriet doesn't wear it."

"No hair on the pillow cases except what looks like Gresham's," Julien reported. "And no sign of anything else on the sheets."

"Nothing obvious missing from the wardrobe," Malcolm said.

"His shaving kit is on the dressing table," Kitty said. "Whyever he left, I doubt it was planned. What man leaves without his shaving kit?"

"The door's unlatched at the bottom." Raoul ran back up the stairs. "A few threads caught on the door frame. Dark blue cloth. Could be from a coat or a cloak."

"So Harriet and Gresham ran that way?" Kitty said.

"Or the killer did," Julien said. "But in that case, where are Harriet and Gresham?"

"Or LeFou attacked one of them, the other shot him from across the room, and they ran." Malcolm closed the wardrobe drawers. "I know Julien said it looked like the work of a profes-sional, but we don't know that Gresham isn't a crack shot. For that matter we don't know that Harriet isn't. I'm quite sure she has hidden talents."

"You think Gresham was LeFou's target?" Kitty said.

"Given that LeFou was here? Gresham has links to Radicals

abroad. Hubert had Allegra Roth—Allegra Wainwright—spying on him years ago." Malcolm looked at Raoul.

"Don't look at me," Raoul said. "I hardly know the activities of every Radical in London. Besides, I'm retired, don't forget."

"Define 'retired.'"

"Gresham is involved in a lot," Raoul said. "I'm not surprised he has enemies. I'd be a bit surprised someone hired an assassin of LeFou's calibre to go after him. But anything is possible."

"Of course, it's always possible Harriet and Gresham left first and then LeFou broke in and someone else killed him," Mélanie said. "Possibly mistaking him for Gresham."

"How many people do you think are targeting Gresham?" Malcolm asked.

"Well, if LeFou is, it's possible someone else is as well."

"A point," her husband conceded.

"What did Hubert think?" Raoul asked Julien. "Did he take it for granted LeFou was after Gresham?"

"No." Julien was frowning. "He seemed surprised LeFou had gone into Gresham's rooms. I assumed he thought they were allies —Hubert's quick to assume the worst of any Radical mostly. But that didn't seem to be the case."

"We need to see him," Malcolm said.

Julien sighed. "I was afraid you'd say that."

KITTY CAST a glance up at the elegant facade of the building where Tristram Gresham lodged in St. James's Place. Mélanie, standing beside her, met her gaze for a moment, but it was Julien who spoke first.

"What?" he asked.

"I'm just wondering about our just leaving him there."

Julien smoothed his coat sleeve. "He wasn't our problem to get rid of. We don't know what Uncle Hubert would want. And we don't know if we'd want to go along with whatever Uncle Hubert wants. If it seems it's better for Harriet and Gresham we can go back and move him."

Kitty cast a glance at Malcolm. "Not pretty," Malcolm said. "But I agree. Besides, we'd be tampering with evidence."

"Assuming we agree with the authorities about not tampering with evidence," Julien said. "Such distinctions are relative."

Malcolm met his gaze. "A valid point."

"We'll see what Uncle Hubert says. God, I can't believe I'm saying that. Though what Uncle Hubert says may prompt me to want to do the opposite."

"All the more reason we need to see him," Raoul said.

"I was afraid you'd say that." Julien slouched forwards, out of the range of the gaslight from the lodging house.

Then he went abruptly still.

Mélanie, a few steps behind, caught it seconds later. Hard to say if it was a sound or sight, but something broke the pattern of the night. Julien sprang and nearly caught a dark form that darted towards St. James's Street. Kitty grabbed a handful of gravel and threw it. The fleeing form stumbled.

Malcolm, closest to the corner, sprinted and caught the figure in a flying leap. As Mélanie ran with the others, Malcolm sat back and she heard him say, "Stroheim?"

CHAPTER 5

Mélanie and the others arrived to find Malcolm helping Franz Stroheim to his feet. The lamplight bounced off Stroheim's wide eyes. His gaze swept the crowd. An accomplished diplomat, he knew better than to play his hand too quickly. Even with friends. Perhaps especially with friends.

"Sorry," Julien said. "We didn't know it was you."

"I didn't know it was you," Stroheim said. "Or I wouldn't have run. Obviously."

"Not obviously at all," Raoul said.

Stroheim grinned, suddenly looking more like a schoolboy. He was about Mélanie's age, but she always thought of him as younger. "That would depend on what we were all doing. But in this case, I think we were all tailing the same person. I know none of us likes to be the first to use names. So can I say I assume we were all after André LeFou?"

Mélanie felt the stillness that ran through the others.

"Do you know LeFou?" Malcolm asked.

"I met him once," Stroheim said in a level voice. "On a mission." He drew a carefully calibrated breath. "It wasn't my decision to hire him on that occasion."

"You'd be close," Julien said. "In thinking we were all after him. We started after him. Actually, Uncle Hubert sent Kitty and me to look into why he'd gone into the house in St. James's Place. Mélanie, Malcolm, and Raoul went there in search of Tristram Gresham."

"And LeFou was there?" Stroheim's gaze darted among them.

The silence that followed was only a few fractions of a second. But in those fractions they all made the inevitable calculations. How much to reveal. To a friend who might or might not be an ally, depending on circumstances.

"In a manner of speaking," Malcolm said.

"I'm sorry," Stroheim said. "I realize you could have a hundred reasons not to share with me. I don't know how much you know. But I have reason to believe LeFou poses a grave danger. Possibly to people we care about."

Another fractional, weighted silence.

"At the moment he doesn't pose a danger to anyone," Julien said. "He's dead."

Stroheim went still. "You—"

"None of us killed him," Mélanie said. "But someone killed him. In Tristram Gresham's rooms. There's no sign of Gresham." No need to bring Harriet into it at this point.

Malcolm put a hand on Stroheim's arm. "You were searching for him?"

"You must know who LeFou is," Stroheim said. "And what he does. I don't say this lightly. I've left the employ of my country, but I'm still an Austrian. I have friends and family who work in Austria's service. It's difficult to sort where one's loyalties lie. You know that as well as I. If not better." He drew in and released his breath. "I have reason to believe LeFou was in London because he'd been engaged by someone in my delegation. That is, the Austrian delegation."

"To kill someone?" Malcolm said.

Stroheim met his gaze steadily. "Given what LeFou does—did

—that would seem the logical inference." He glanced at Julien. "Is that why your uncle Hubert wanted you to follow him?"

"I wouldn't know. Uncle Hubert rarely gives me an explanation for why he wants me to do anything."

"Who hired him?" Malcolm's gaze was steady on Stroheim.

"I don't know," Stroheim said. "That's the honest truth. I went to dine with a friend tonight in a tavern off Golden Square. One frequented by Austrians. My friend had to leave early, and I was paying the reckoning; I glimpsed LeFou at a table in the corner. Talking to Karl Augustin. You must know him."

"Since Vienna," Mélanie said. "I've had the misfortune to dance with him a few times."

"So have I," Kitty said. "He has wandering hands."

Julien quirked a brow at her. "You never said."

"I can look after myself."

"Count Augustin is pugnacious across the negotiating table," Malcolm said. "But I wouldn't think he was the sort to bring in someone of LeFou's calibre on his own."

"No," Stroheim said. "Nor would I. He doesn't much care for me, and he looked as though he was in a temper over whatever LeFou was saying to him. In fact he stormed out of the tavern. I wasn't sure how much I'd get from him in that mood. So instead of confronting Augustin, I followed LeFou when he left the tavern."

"I'm impressed," Julien said. "He's not an easy man to follow."

"Believe me, I was aware of the risk if he turned on me. I kept my distance. But I didn't have to follow him far. He stopped in a coffee house in Piccadilly. A gentleman engaged him in conversation and it appeared to me he had trouble extricating himself. When he left at last, he walked as though somewhat hurried. And came here."

"What time was that?" Malcolm asked.

"Just past eleven."

Julien nodded. "That fits with what Uncle Hubert said. You've been watching the house since?"

Stroheim nodded.

"And you didn't see anyone come out?"

"No. But if they'd gone through the back entrance I wouldn't have seen."

Which was what they thought Gresham and Harriet and, likely, the killer had done, based on what Raoul had discovered. "Do you know anything about LeFou's connection to Augustin?" Raoul asked, without alluding to his own investigation of the back stairs.

Stroheim shook his head. "I'm hardly at the center of things anymore. There are things afoot no one wants to talk to me about. Everyone seems to be scrambling for an inch of advantage. Against the British and the Russians. But also against each other. It could be a rogue agent trying to improve their own situation." He drew another hard breath. "Or it could be a target action of the Austrian government. I no longer feel certain of anything."

"How does Tristram Gresham fit into this?" Kitty asked.

"I don't know. Honestly. I hadn't heard anything about him. But Metternich considers Gresham an enemy. His actions in Naples had Metternich apoplectic."

"You're saying Metternich hired LeFou to kill Gresham?" Raoul asked.

Stroheim met Raoul's gaze. "No. I'm saying I could imagine Metternich doing so. Which says a lot about why I am no longer in the employ of the Austrian diplomatic corps."

"You've risked a great deal," Raoul said.

"We all run risks. The question is what and whom to run them for. I hope I'm getting better at making that judgment."

Raoul touched Stroheim's shoulder. "You impress me, Stroheim. But then you always have."

"If your people hired LeFou," Kitty said, "the question is still who killed him. And why."

Stroheim nodded.

A carriage rumbled down St. James's Street. They all sprang into the shadows on instinct. Matched bays, crest on the door, though Mélanie couldn't make out the details.

"We need to talk to Uncle Hubert," Julien said, when the carriage had rattled on. "Which I have been resisting doing. And it seems you should come with us, Stroheim. My commiseration."

WILLIAM, THE MALLINSONS' footman, greeted their late-night arrival without surprise and indicated Hubert was in his study, where he was usually to be found at all hours of the night. But he was not alone. Another man sat in a chair beside Hubert's desk, swinging a foot against the chair leg, fingers taut round a glass of brandy that looked little touched.

"Harry," Mélanie said as she and Kitty preceded the three men into the room. Not their friend Harry Davenport, but Harry Palmerston, the secretary at war. Which was almost as surprising. He and Hubert were not particular allies.

Palmerston's gaze shot to her and then took in Kitty, and Malcolm, Julien, Raoul, and Stroheim behind them. "Thank goodness. You know something?"

"What do you have to do with this?" Malcolm asked.

"Hubert brought me in. And I take it the Carfaxes brought you in?"

"Not precisely." Malcolm closed the study door behind the others.

"Just as well you're here," Hubert said, brows taut above his spectacles. He'd always reminded Mélanie of an eagle, circling, ready to pounce. "We're in the devil of a mess." His gaze shot to Stroheim. "What's he doing here?"

"Prince Stroheim," Malcolm said, "is kindly assisting us with our inquiries."

"I was also following LeFou," Stroheim said.

"Also, LeFou's dead," Julien said. "Which solves one of your problems. But probably creates others."

"Christ." Hubert's fingers tightened on the edge of his desk. "Did you kill him?"

"No. He was dead when we found him. Were you expecting me to kill him?"

"No, I wanted him alive. Gresham?"

"He's missing. Possibly along with a lady." No need to bring Harriet's name into it at this point, they'd all agreed.

Hubert sighed. "You'd better sit down. All of you. Julien, pour everyone some brandy. They're likely to need it."

Julien raised a brow and moved to the decanters on a table by the window. Kitty handed the glasses round. Malcolm and Raoul dragged a settee from the fireplace to the desk and Stroheim and Palmerston pulled over two more chairs.

"What was LeFou doing in Britain?" Malcolm asked when they were seated.

"I'm not sure." Hubert grimaced at this admission of lack of knowledge. "But it seems fairly clear he was targeting someone."

"Could it have been Gresham?" Raoul asked as he took a glass of brandy from Julien.

Hubert tugged at his earpiece. "I wouldn't have thought so. But one never knows."

"You've seen Gresham as a threat for years." Julien set down the decanter.

"So I have. He's a dangerous man. But I wouldn't think of killing him."

"A number of husbands would like to challenge him to a duel," Palmerston said. "But hiring an assassin seems a bit unorthodox." He looked round the company. "Are you saying Gresham killed LeFou?"

"That's one possibility," Malcolm said. "It's also possible Gresham left first."

"Why?"

"Why indeed?" Julien perched on the arm of Kitty's chair with the last glass of brandy. His gaze moved to his uncle. "How long had LeFou been in London?"

"Five days as best I can tell. I got word from an agent in Southampton at first."

"Clever of you to have him followed."

"I'm not entirely without resources."

"By no means." Julien swirled his brandy. "What aren't you telling us?"

"What makes you sure I'm not telling you anything?"

"Because I know you. And because the pieces don't add up."

"If it's because you're worried about an international incident," Stroheim said, "I've already told them I'm quite sure someone in my—the Austrian—delegation hired LeFou."

"What?" Palmerston clunked his glass down on Hubert's desk, spattering brandy on the polished wood and tooled leather blotter.

"That's not what you thought?" Malcolm said.

"Not precisely." Hubert adjusted his earpiece again. "What have you done with the body?"

"Left it for now," Malcolm said. "We'll need to summon Bow Street."

Hubert pushed himself to his feet. He wasn't tall but he could command a room. "No."

"It's a straightforward investigation," Julien said. "Someone killed him. Bow Street might come up with information. Unless you don't want to know who killed him? Unless you killed him?"

"I told you, I wanted LeFou alive. "

"Then why—"

"Because Bow Street report to the home office." Hubert's fingers tightened on the edge of his desk. "And I think LeFou was hired by someone in the British government."

CHAPTER 6

*M*élanie stared at her husband's former spymaster. She felt Malcolm's utter stillness on the settee beside her. And Raoul's. And Julien's and Kitty's.

Malcolm broke the silence. "You think someone in the British government brought an assassin to London?"

Hubert sank back into his chair and reached for his brandy. "Does that surprise you? I thought you were all too ready to believe the worst of our government."

"Usually that meant plots you were involved in running," Julien said. "If you're trying to stop this one, it's intriguing."

Mélanie cast a glance at Palmerston. "I take it this is why you're here?"

Palmerston smiled, but his gaze remained unwontedly serious. "I noticed something amiss in some payment ledgers. Actually, in point of fact, John Southcott did."

"Frowny-faced Southcott?" Julien said. "Good god. He looked disapproving at the age of eight. Which is about what he was when I left Britain."

"He's at the foreign office now," Palmerston said. "And quite convinced the entire government is run inefficiently and he could do much better. Can't say I can argue with him on the first, though I'm not sure about the second."

"His father and his uncle, the Duke of Bamford, are chief among those I suspect he thinks are hopelessly outdated," Malcolm said. "I went to Harrow with John. He's not stupid, by any means. But he does at times lack imagination."

"So he does," Palmerston said. "When he came into my office, I was ready for a lecture on reforms for the commissariat. Instead, he told me he wasn't sure but he thought there was something out of order in the ledger he'd borrowed. And it was precisely because of his lack of imagination that I took it particularly seriously."

"What did he notice?" Malcolm asked.

"Payments that didn't add up. He said he couldn't make sense of them but something seemed amiss, and I'd know more than he did what to do. Actually, I think that was Southcott being typically disingenuous. He's not stupid. He knew perfectly well something was wrong. I thanked him and said I'd take a look. When I looked at the accounts it was quite clear someone had been hiding a payment to an outside source."

"Like with the business with Warkworth and the Argentine mine," Mélanie said.

"Precisely. Amazing what can hide in accounts."

"Uncle Hubert hides all sorts of things in accounts," Julien said. Then went still. Because those payments had been to Malcolm's brother Edgar. And that investigation had led to Julien's killing Edgar to save Malcolm. Kitty reached for her husband's hand.

"Yes, that occurred to me," Palmerston said without batting an eyelash. "I decided the best course was to reach out to Hubert. If he were behind the payments, I thought I might be able to detect something in his response. So I shared the intelligence with him."

"Accused me, more like," Hubert said in a mild voice.

"It wouldn't be the first time you've hidden things in accounts, as Julien points out."

28

"No," Hubert agreed. "Fair enough. It led to an interesting conversation."

"That's one word for it." Palmerston grinned, though his gaze still showed the gravity of the situation. "Suffice it to say, Hubert convinced me he wasn't behind the payments. I realize the rest of you may not share my view."

"Julien may disagree, but I'm inclined to agree with you," Kitty said. "Because Hubert roped us in and he knew that would eventually mean involving Malcolm and Mélanie and Raoul."

Julien settled his shoulders against the back of the chair he was sharing with Kitty, arms folded across his chest. "As usual, my wife makes eminent sense. For the moment, I'm willing to give Uncle Hubert the benefit of the doubt. What did you and he determine?"

"Someone appears to have been sending money to LeFou through war office accounts," Palmerston said. "We haven't been able to determine who."

"But if they had access to those accounts, it's someone fairly highly placed," Malcolm said.

Palmerston gave a curt nod. "Quite. But there's still nothing to tell us who."

"Or whom LeFou was hire to target?" Raoul asked.

"Assuming he had a target. Though it's difficult to imagine why else someone would have been paying him to come to Britain." Palmerston looked at Stroheim. "I don't know how much comfort it is at this point, but this lets out the Austrians."

"Unless someone in our government was working with the Austrians," Julien suggested. "One can't deny the possibility," he added under a crossfire of looks.

Stroheim had been sitting by in silence, watching the back-and-forth exchanges like someone observing a particularly fraught tennis match. Mélanie could sympathize. "Whoever hired LeFou, he was in a pub off Golden Square with Karl Augustin tonight," Stroheim said.

His words landed like a particularly effective serve.

Another crossfire of glances shifted across the room.

"I don't know the connection between them," Stroheim said. "As I told the others, I followed LeFou to a coffeehouse in Piccadilly, and then to St. James's Place. I was hanging round outside, waiting for him to reappear."

"Could Augustin be working with the British?" Kitty asked.

"Theoretically, just about anyone could be working with just about anyone," Malcolm said.

"Quite." Hubert grimaced.

"So you were watching LeFou," Raoul said to Hubert and Palmerston.

"It seemed the prudent course while we gathered data," Hubert said. "This all unfolded very fast."

"You must have ideas," Malcolm said.

"About who is behind it? Or who the target is?"

"Both."

"Any number of people could hide payments in war office accounts," Palmerston said.

"Castlereagh's been increasingly secretive lately," Hubert said. "I wouldn't put it past him. Or Sidmouth, if either or both of them thought they had cause."

"Are you sure you wouldn't agree with the cause?" Julien asked. "Or are you just miffed they left you out of it?"

Hubert reached for his brandy. "It's dangerous hiring a man like LeFou. One never knows where such things will lead."

Julien fixed his uncle with a gaze hard as the flat of a blade. "That never stopped you in the past."

Hubert took a drink of brandy. "Perhaps I've learnt prudence. Or did you assume I was too old to change?"

"I'd never assume you were too old for anything, Uncle."

Kitty shifted in the chair and laid a hand lightly over Julien's own. "If whoever is behind this is working with someone in the Austrian delegation, one would think the motive is international."

Hubert nodded. "It's the same suspects we had with the situation in the spring. Russia's doing their damnedest to get Austria and France on their side." He cast a glance at Stroheim.

"I don't deny it," Stroheim said. "And Austria is eager for the ability to interfere on the Continent where they see revolution threatening their position. Where Metternich sees revolution threatening his position. Or Austria's position. I'm not sure how well he differentiates the two. I make no secret of the reason I am no longer formally in the employ of my country."

"You think killing anyone could interfere with an alliance between Austria and Russia?" Malcolm asked.

"It might if someone else took the blame," Julien said. "Nothing like an international incident to shake the playing field. Though that seems a bit devious for Castlereagh. Londonderry. I can't get used to his new title."

"I don't think he can either." Malcolm took drink of brandy. The foreign secretary, Lord Castlereagh, under whom Malcolm had served in Vienna, had recently come into the title of Marquess of Londonderry on his father's death, though everyone still tended to refer to him as Castlereagh. "Castlereagh's fully capable of being devious."

"More than fully." Mélanie leant against Malcolm's shoulder. She remembered with chilling clarity the British foreign secretary standing by when Malcolm was arrested for murder. Of course, he might have believed Malcolm was guilty. She wasn't sure if that made it better or worse.

"There are plenty of other options," Hubert said. "Including your other former employer."

Malcolm clunked his brandy glass on a table beside the chair he and Mélanie were sharing. Brandy droplets spattered on giltwood. "You think Wellington—"

"I'm not ruling him out."

"No." A host of thoughts flashed through Malcolm's gaze. Among them disillusionment. "I wouldn't rule him out either."

"Or the PM." Hubert shot a look at Raoul. Surprisingly, given his politics, Raoul had been friends with Lord Liverpool, the prime minister, decades ago in France.

"Liverpool wouldn't be where he is if he couldn't be ruthless," Raoul said.

"Speaking of ruthless." Julien twirled his glass between his fingers and regarded his uncle. "Possibly the most ruthless person in the British government is in this room. You'd be quite capable of inventing this for your own purposes, Uncle Hubert."

"You think I hired LeFou, hid it in the war office accounts sloppily enough that John Southcott could find it, and then sent you to check on LeFou?"

"You might have sent me to discover him if you'd had him killed. Which you could have done without hiring him. In fact, you're more likely to be behind his murder if you didn't hire him."

"His being killed makes a complicated situation more complicated."

"It's presumably stopped him from attacking his target, though. Hard to imagine a more effective way of stopping that."

"You haven't answered the other part of the question." Kitty leant forwards, glass between her hands, tawny ringlets falling about her face. "Who do you think his target was? Could it have been Gresham?"

Hubert went silent. For once, to Mélanie, he appeared to be genuinely considering. Though one could easily forget Hubert had once been a field agent himself. One never knew what hid behind his seemingly blunt plain speaking.

"Castlereagh certainly finds Gresham challenging," Hubert said. "He seems to be connected to every Radical movement on the Continent. And Sidmouth could be worried about Gresham's work at home."

"Metternich finds Gresham a thorn in his side," Stroheim said. "He's been very effective at aiding the Italian revolutionaries."

Kitty twisted in her chair to look at Stroheim. "You think

Metternich and someone in the British government allied to get rid of a troublesome composer?"

"A troublesome composer who is also a noted Radical," Stroheim said.

Kitty nodded. "A point."

"You said Gresham left his rooms with a lady," Palmerston said. "Any idea who?"

Mélanie looked at Malcolm and then quickly exchanged glances with the others. The consensus was clear. Sometimes withholding information could be more dangerous than sharing it. "Harriet Roth," she said.

"Good god." Hubert's glass tilted in his fingers.

"Odd," Palmerston said. "Miss Roth's quite lovely. But Gresham usually confines himself to married women."

"We don't know that that's what's going on," Mélanie said.

Palmerston raised a brow. "I'll own Gresham can do the unexpected, but usually not when it comes to his relationships with women."

Hubert leant forwards, hands curled round his glass. "What's interesting is whose sister she is."

"A Bow Street runner's?" Palmerston asked.

"A member of the Levellers." Hubert looked at the others. "Surely you realized I knew."

"No comment," Malcolm said. The Levellers, a Radical organization, had been started by their friend Simon Tanner.

"Could LeFou have known Gresham?" Palmerston asked. "Perhaps they met abroad."

"An interesting idea," Raoul said.

"Gresham traveled abroad. He had connections to all sorts of people."

"All sorts of dangerous people," Hubert said.

"Any number of people can be called dangerous," Raoul said. "But it might offer another explanation for what LeFou was doing there."

"The point," Hubert said, "is that for now we can't trust anyone. Including Bow Street. I'm an outsider when it comes to the government these days."

Julien snorted.

"I always have been, to a degree, and certainly now." Hubert took a drink of brandy. "I'll confess to asking for your help more than a bit in the past."

"A bit?" Julien said.

"But if I ever needed it, I need it now. And I can't protect you."

"You protected us?" Julien said.

"Probably far more than you realize. Though not all the time."

"We could use Bamford," Raoul said. Anthony Southcott, Duke of Bamford, a diplomat and agent, was theoretically retired, but he still had connections in the government that none of them shared.

"Yes, I thought about that." Hubert grimaced. "I've already sent an express to him. He's at his villa in Richmond now with Désirée Clairineau and their daughter. I'm sorry to interrupt what one might call his honeymoon, though his divorce isn't final yet, but I imagine he'll understand. We could use Mademoiselle Clairineau too."

Palmerston frowned. "Bamford's mistress? Wasn't she a French agent?" He looked round the group. "I may not be an agent, but I'm not entirely lacking in intelligence. In either meaning of the word. I've heard rumors about Mademoiselle Clairineau. Who is a beautiful woman, by the way."

"She's also my aunt," Stroheim said.

"My word," Palmerston said. "Though perhaps I shouldn't be surprised. You're an adept family."

"She's retired from the intelligence game," Stroheim said. "To the extent anyone does. But I do think she wants a life with Bamford and their daughter."

"You don't think she's LeFou's target, do you?" Malcolm looked from Hubert to Raoul.

Hubert's brows drew together. "Interesting thought. But except for Sylvie St. Ives, I don't think a number of people are worried about Désirée Clairineau just now."

"Sylvie works for Castlereagh," Julien pointed out.

"So she does. I don't think Castlereagh would hire an assassin because of her, though."

"Not just because of her. But she could have influence."

Palmerston blinked. "You've lost me. Sylvie St. Ives works for Castlereagh?"

Julien took a long drink of brandy and set down his glass. "There's too much at stake for me to spend time defending Sylvie —which I've wasted too much time doing as it is. Sylvie's been an agent for years. Lately she's working for Castlereagh. She used to work for Uncle Hubert."

"She's Bamford's daughter-in-law," Palmerston pointed out.

"Yes, that's the source of much of her dislike of Désirée Clairineau."

"Whom no one is apparently worried about anymore." Palmerston looked round the room.

"Well, I'm not," Julien said.

Palmerston looked at Hubert. "You claimed Mademoiselle Clairineau was one of the most dangerous women in Europe."

"Did I?" Hubert tugged at his spectacles. "Yes, I suppose I did. And I suspect I was right. But that was before she and Bamford retired to the country. They seem genuinely happy raising their daughter. Of course, perhaps I'm a sentimental fool."

"Ha." Julien took a drink of brandy.

"You of all people should realize people can change," Hubert said.

"Meaning you, or Désirée?"

"Perhaps both of us." Hubert settled back in his chair. "I've always had a healthy respect for Mademoiselle Clairineau's understanding. That hasn't changed because she's about to

35

become the Duchess of Bamford. But it may make her more of a —" He broke off.

Julien stared at his uncle in fascination. "Were you about to say ally?"

Hubert settled his shoulders against the back of his chair. "I've always taken my allies where it was most useful to find them." He looked round the group. "You're going to have to investigate carefully, as we can't be sure who in the government can be trusted. Palmerston can get files, if needed."

"We'll have to tell John Southcott something," Palmerston said. "He was polite about leaving things in my hands, but he obviously has questions."

"He might be a help," Malcolm said. "Southcott has some keen instincts, for all he can be ponderous. And he's close to a lot of powerful people. Tony Bamford is his uncle, so perhaps—"

He broke off at a rap on the door. Not the door to the hall, but a side door that opened onto the back garden. That was specifically there to be used by people who wanted to speak with Hubert without coming in off the street and past the servants. Mélanie had used it more than once with Malcolm. And once or twice on her own.

Hubert frowned, got up from his desk, moved to the door, and peered through a small hole in the wood. He went still for a moment, a rare sign of surprise, then eased open the door. "Countess. This is unexpected."

The cloaked woman stepped into the room. Even in the shadows, the candlelight revealed the elegant features and glossy dark hair of Dorothea de Lieven, wife of the Russian ambassador and patroness of Almack's.

CHAPTER 7

*D*orothea put back the hood of her cloak. The velvet lay against her shoulders, framing her high-cheek-boned face. Pearl earrings shimmered through her dark ringlets. The folds of a peach satin gown showed beneath her cloak. She surveyed the company, dark eyes steady beneath her finely arced brows. "I didn't expect to find such a crowd."

"Would you like some of us to leave?" Raoul asked without irony.

Dorothea met Raoul's gaze, gave a faint smile, and shook her head. She was a confirmed monarchist, opposed to everything Raoul stood for. "No. Perhaps it's as well you're here. I suspect this is all connected." She moved into the room and turned to Palmerston. "I've had the devil of a time tracking you down. I've left word at all your usual haunts. I'm sorry. I fear Emily won't be happy with either of us."

Palmerston waved a hand. Emily Cowper, his longtime mistress, was a patroness of Almack's Assembly Rooms, along with Dorothea "Emily will forgive both of us. She's less prone to jealousy than I am." He moved to the drinks table. "Let me pour you a brandy."

Dorothea sank into a chair Malcolm pulled up, accepted the drink, and gulped down a sip.

"Are you sure you aren't going to ask us to leave?" Julien said.

Dorothea returned his gaze. They had met on the Continent. Not for the first time, Mélanie wondered exactly what had passed between the two of them there. From Kitty's expression, she appeared to be having the same questions, though she didn't seem perturbed by them. But then Kitty was rarely perturbed when it came to Julien.

"No," Dorothea said. "All things considered, I think we may need all of you." She folded her hands round her glass. "There's a very dangerous man in London." Her fingers tightened. "I'm guessing that may be why you're all here."

"A good guess," Julien said.

"I don't know who hired him," Dorothea said. "Or who his target is."

"Nor do we," Malcolm said.

Dorothea nodded. "Not that I can't be sure anyone in the Russian—or Austrian--delegation hired him—"

For once, the group went silent. Even Hubert.

Julien, not surprisingly, recovered his voice first. "We are talking about André LeFou?"

"Of course."

"And you think someone in the Russian or Austrian delegation brought him to London?"

"I'm afraid so."

"To do what?"

Dorothea took another quick drink of brandy. "To kill someone in the British government."

This time the silence was even more deafening.

"You think LeFou was hired to kill someone in the British government?" This time it was Palmerston who spoke.

"That's the rumor I've heard. I'm assuming you heard it as well." Her gaze darted among them. "Otherwise, why on earth—"

"We heard someone in the British government hired him to assassinate someone else," Julien said.

Dorothea stared at him.

"Quite a conundrum," Julien agreed. "Of course, Stroheim thought he was working with the Austrians, but we'd begun to think someone in the Austrian delegation was working with someone in the British government."

"Not that we have proof," Hubert said.

"I'd be the first to admit that," Palmerston said. "Though the accounts are certainly suggestive."

"But that's why you're all here?" Dorothea said.

"No, we're here because LeFou was murdered tonight," Julien said.

Dorothea sat back in her chair, sloshing the brandy in her glass. "By?"

"We don't know," Mélanie said. "That's why we're here."

Dorothea stared round the group. "Where was LeFou killed? In the street?"

A quick crossfire of glances flashed across the room. Mélanie looked at Malcolm, then Raoul, then Julien, then Kitty. Hubert sat back in his chair, looking half intent, half almost amused. And yet, if Dorothea had information…

"He was found in Tristram Gresham's rooms," Malcolm said.

"Tristram Gresham's—" Dorothea repeated the name, faltering over it. "In St. James's Place?"

"Not so far from where I used to live myself," Malcolm concurred.

"Dear god. Are you saying Gresham—"

"Not as far as we know," Mélanie said. "Gresham is missing. We're not sure if he disappeared before or after LeFou was killed."

"We did wonder if Gresham was the target," Julien said.

Dorothea's spine straightened. "Gresham can be challenging. But he's hardly enough of a challenge Metternich would hire an assassin."

"Meaning he'd hire an assassin to go after others?" Mélanie asked.

"No comment," Dorothea said.

Julien swung his foot against the chair leg, saying nothing.

"Tristram Gresham angered a number of people," Dorothea said. "Here and abroad. Not in the least being angry husbands."

"Angry husbands don't usually engage assassins," Palmerston said. "They issue challenges for pistols at dawn."

"Someone could have been angry with him on both counts," Kitty said. "Or it's always possible there's a coward who wanted Gresham gone and didn't want to fight him. Or a former mistress who wanted him gone. But it's difficult to work out the ties to the British government and Austria and probably Russia, in that case."

"What makes you think Austria or Russia were involved?" Julien asked.

Dorothea took a careful drink of brandy. "I've heard rumors. I'm sure you'll all understand when I say I can't say more at present." She folded her hands round her glass. "I know mysteries fascinate all of you, but I can't claim to be very concerned over who may have killed LeFou. If LeFou is dead, the problem would seem to have been solved."

"Save that whoever hired him presumably still wants whomever he was hired to kill dead," Raoul said. "So someone is at risk."

"And apparently we can't trust anyone in the British government," Malcolm said.

"Or the Russian or the Austrian delegation," Kitty added.

"Well, that's different," Julien said. "I'm used to trusting all of them."

"Meaning you're going to have to investigate on the outside," Palmerston said.

"Even though Uncle Hubert asked us to," Julien said. "An unusual situation."

"This is a fragile time on the Continent," Dorothea said. "Tempers run high. It would be all too easy for things to tip in a direction from which it would be difficult to turn back." She cast a glance from Mélanie to Raoul. "And for once I don't mean revolution. We may disagree about a number of things, but in this I think we are all allies."

"And the only allies we have in this investigation are the people in this room," Palmerston said.

"Go carefully." Hubert's voice was even but his gaze held surprising tension.

"Don't we always?" Julien said.

"I mean it," Hubert said. "We're dealing with someone dangerous. And powerful. And we don't know where this ends. Palmerston took a risk bringing me the information he did. Stroheim took a risk talking to you and then to me. Countess Lieven took a risk coming here. We don't know how complicated this may get. We don't know who is being targeted. Or how far whoever is behind this will go."

Julien stared at his uncle. "I don't know that I've ever seen you so worried."

Hubert pushed his spectacles up on his nose. "This is unlike anything we've faced before."

"You're not used to being an outsider."

Hubert grunted. "In this government? I'm an outsider more often than not. But there's more uncertainty to this than usual."

Dorothea looked at Stroheim. "You must have heard the rumors about the Russian or Austrian delegation hiring LeFou, if you're here."

"Not precisely rumors. Though I made that assumption. Because I saw Karl Augustin meeting with him."

Dorothea went still. "I didn't know Augustin was involved. Though that doesn't necessarily surprise me. But if he's working with someone in the British government—given what happened tonight, that changes things."

"How?" Mélanie asked. "You already suspected the Austrian delegation might be involved—"

"Because Augustin's wife Charlotte had an affair with Tristram Gresham."

Julien whistled.

Palmerston raised his brows. "I hadn't heard. But surely you don't think Augustin hired LeFou to kill Gresham?"

"It does seem odd," Dorothea agreed. "Augustin is fearfully proud. I would think he'd want to confront the problem himself, so to speak."

"Perhaps he simply wanted to make the problem go away," Kitty said.

"I suppose stranger things have been known to happen," Palmerston said. "But then what on earth did I find in the war office accounts? LeFou was definitely getting paid with funds funneled through the British government."

"Perhaps LeFou was here to do two jobs," Kitty suggested. "Hard to see a man like LeFou coming here simply for a personal revenge quest."

"He might if he'd been paid enough," Julien said. "But it might make more sense if he were already here."

"Augustin would have to have known about it though," Mélanie said. "Is he close to anyone in the British government?"

"He's colleagues with all of them," Dorothea said. "But that hardly means they'd confide such secrets."

"How long ago did the affair end?" Mélanie asked.

Dorothea shrugged. "I'm not interested in following every detail of Tristram Gresham's affairs. They never seem to last long. When I first heard about it was last winter. I doubt it would have lasted so long."

"We have a number of things to investigate." Julien said. "It seems we should get to work." He looked at Dorothea. "Do you have a carriage?"

She shook her head. "We were dining with the Esterhazys. I

slipped out and walked, then sent my husband a message that the Thornfields had taken me home."

"We'll get you a carriage," Hubert said. "Julien—"

"On it." Julien moved to the door.

"Thank you." Dorothea drew her cloak about her. "It may be challenging getting into the embassy without detection."

"I'll go with you," Malcolm said. "I can make sure you get in safely."

"Thank you, Malcolm. But I'll be quite—"

"I can pick the lock on a side door for you to get in without detection."

Dorothea's face relaxed into a smile. "Thank you," she said again, with genuine warmth.

Hubert looked at the others. "I'll order coffee. We can talk while you wait for Malcolm to get back."

CHAPTER 8

*D*ésirée Clairineau pushed herself up in bed and looked across the room at her lover. Her betrothed, a word she still had trouble with, though when his divorce went through the House of Lords, they'd be married and she'd be Duchess of Bamford. Something that had seemed impossible when they first met over twenty years ago on a spy mission, as spies for opposite sides. She'd had a knife to his throat.

Tony, otherwise known as Anthony Sebastian Aloysius Southcott, Duke of Bamford, was at the door, loosely wrapped in his blue brocade dressing gown, a paper in one hand, a lit taper in a pewter candleholder in the other. Both probably handed to him by whoever had knocked on the door and woken them.

Désirée pushed her tangled hair back from her face. "What is it?"

"An express. From Hubert Mallinson." Tony was still studying the paper, brows drawn. "Apparently there's a situation in Whitehall involving a foreign agent. And possibly a connection to Tristram Gresham. He can't put more in writing." He crossed back to their bed and handed her the paper.

Désirée scanned the express. And nodded. Because she

couldn't do anything else. And she didn't trust herself to meet Tony's gaze with the thoughts racing through her head.

"I should go," Tony said. "However much I may disagree with Hubert, he wouldn't ask if it weren't urgent. And he says he's called Julien and Kitty in, which inevitably will mean the Rannochs and Raoul as well."

"And you can't resist the call of adventure."

"I didn't say that."

"You didn't need to, my love." She managed a playful smile that wasn't wholly feigned.

Tony sat on the edge of the bed. "You can't think I'm bored in the country."

"Of course not." Désirée smoothed the blue velvet coverlet and glanced round the ridiculously luxurious bedchamber—all damask furniture and inlaid tables and delicate walls in ivory and robin's egg blue that made her think of macarons—which nevertheless had become home. One of their homes. Tony had so many she hadn't visited all of them. But wherever he was was now home. When she'd never really had a home her entire life. "But we've also never been idle for so long."

"I wouldn't quite say that. There were times in Normandy—"

"We were still looking over our shoulders."

"And we aren't doing that here?"

"Not precisely. The biggest drama is meeting with lawyers." About the divorce which was going to free them to marry. And make her Duchess of Bamford, which she still hadn't quite come to terms with.

"I'm sorry. A tiresome necessity."

"You needn't apologize." Désirée fished her dressing gown off the bedpost it had got tangled round when Tony had unlaced it. "But I'm going to London with you."

Tony grinned. "I thought as much. And I can't tell you how pleased I am."

Désirée smiled back and pulled the frothy rose silk and lace round her shoulders. Because of course there was no way she was going to send him off without her. That would have been true in any case. And it was doubly so when the news in the express meant she was going to have to investigate on her own. Before Tony learnt the truth without her and wreaked all sorts of havoc. But then they'd always known a little thing like divorce and marriage couldn't change the fact they'd always be lying to each other.

"THE CARRIAGE IS READY." Julien poked his head into Hubert's study. "Malcolm's waiting with it in the mews. More discreet than having you go out into the street." He held out his arm to Dorothea. He couldn't refrain from an ironic smile as he did so, but Dorothea had always been the sort of woman who brought out courtly formality.

"Thank you." Dorothea got to her feet and lifted her hood over her carefully dressed hair. Despite the strains of the evening, she looked as immaculate as if she were on the way to a dinner party. She'd always had that knack.

She nodded to Hubert and then to the others. "It seems we are allies. Unlikely allies, perhaps, but I hope you realize that as a diplomat's wife, I take alliances seriously."

"I'd never doubt it, Countess," Hubert said.

Dorothea's fingers closed round Julien's arm. "At the risk of being open to misinterpretation, it's good to see you again," she said, when they had moved into the privacy of the hall. "It seemed prudent to keep a polite distance, and you seem to be avoiding society, in any case. But I always suspected our paths would cross again."

"They've crossed more than a score of times, for all I do my best to avoid Almack's. We saw each other at the Bamford musicale not so very long ago." In fact, Julien and the others had been involved in recovering a communication from Metternich to Dorothea that Tristram Gresham had intercepted. Which might be relevant to tonight's events.

Dorothea slanted a smile up at him. She had the knack of being at once charming and imperious. "Beyond the occasional encounter in society. I meant that I'd be pulled into another of your intrigues."

"I think you mean investigations."

"Is there a difference?" She watched him for a moment in the light from the candles in the wall sconces. "I used to think you were one of the most dangerous men I'd ever met."

"Has that changed?"

"Ask me in a fortnight. But I have come to you for help."

"I thought you came looking for Palmerston."

"I'd have come to you eventually. Which perhaps shows how desperate I am."

"Desperate times call for desperate alliances." He opened the door to the garden and moved back to let her precede him. "I'll try not to let you down."

Dorothea moved past him, holding her cloak against the night air. Even a July night in London could have a bite. "Surely that depends on what you discover."

"So it does." Julien pulled the door shut. "Mind the step. And have a care for thorns. Aunt Amelia is fond of roses." The garden was in shadow, though he could make out a faint glow from the mews.

"You always had the eyesight of a cat." Dorothea took his arm again and stepped carefully onto the gravel walk. "I'm sorry for Kitty. I don't know what she's heard."

"Nor do I, but she'll be fine. Kitty and I don't fuss about each other's pasts. You and Lieven don't seem to fuss about your presents."

"It's a bit different when one feels as Kitty appears to for you."

"Ah, there is that. Love can be a damned complication. The reason I avoided it for so long. But Kitty and I both are sensible enough to leave the past in the past."

"Not always easy to do."

"No. The source of many of our problems."

Dorothea paused to look up at him again, her gaze hard in the shadows "I pride myself on my judgment. But I begin to think I misjudged you."

"Not surprising. I carefully cultivated a reputation. It's useful to give off the air that one is much more dangerous than one is. It saved me no end of trouble that everyone thought I was lethal."

"Oh, I have no doubt that you're lethal. But you're not as entirely lacking in morals as I thought. I begin to think you're every bit as much of a romantic as Harry Palmerston."

Julien laughed. "I think that's the first time anyone's compared me to Palmerston."

"Palmerston may not be faithful to Emily, but he's quite incapable of loving anyone but her. In fact, I sometimes think he's only unfaithful in an attempt to get her attention. You're much the same."

"I'm not sure this is any of your business, but I'm not unfaithful to Kitty for any reason. Including to catch her attention."

"No, but you're quite single-mindedly devoted to her. And you're just as capable of believing in other things, like ideals, as your English friends. You're fully capable of stabbing someone in the back, but there are people you wouldn't do it to."

"Well, that's always a difficult distinction."

"Yes. Which is why I'm trusting you now. Which I fully realize may be a mistake."

"You realize, of course, that I am trusting you. At least as far as to work with you."

"And you're wondering if it's a mistake?"

"My dear. I can't claim that our association gave me intimate knowledge of you. But how could I not wonder?"

"You're a wise man, Julien." She watched him a moment longer. "And I can't believe how much you've changed."

"Oh, I haven't changed. At least, I don't think I have. But I have discovered my priorities."

"Did Kitty help you do that?"

"Kitty would clout me for saying so. But you could say she is my priority. Or at least one of them. Along with the children. But it goes beyond that."

"Meaning you've become an idealist."

"You say that with such disdain, my dear."

"Ideals are like romance. Very pretty in a story. But in real life they make tangles and get in the way of getting anything done."

"They can be the reason to get things done."

"My god." Dorothea twitched her skirt out of the way of a passing rose bush. "You are far gone."

"Hopeless."

"And happy."

"Oh yes." Julien rested a hand on the garden gate. "Not a word I use easily. And not anything I ever thought to be. But I am. I highly recommend it. Not that either of us has the luxury of thinking about such things at present."

"No." She wrinkled her nose. "My god, the stables smell."

"It's not glamorous moving in the shadows." He opened the gate and his hand to Malcolm who was standing beside the carriage with Hubert's coachman. "I'll do my best, Dorothea. My word on it. Not that the idea of my word means much to me. But it's something I was raised to say. A part of my heritage I haven't rejected. You can decide for yourself how much that means."

Dorothea stepped through the gate, then turned back to look at him, backlit by the carriage lamps. "Oddly enough, I find that comforting. I have no idea what that says about me."

～

"I'm sorry to have disrupted things," Dorothea said as she and Malcolm drove towards the Russian embassy.

"It's hardly your fault." Malcolm reached for the strap as they rounded a corner.

"You might make that sound a bit more like a joke, *mon cher*."

"What else could it be but a joke?"

Dorothea pulled the folds of her cloak about her. "Don't pretend to innocence, Malcolm. You're heroically chivalrous, but you're as keen a player in the game of political chess as my husband. Or Metternich."

"I'm hardly in their league. And Mélanie would clout me if I showed any inclinations to chivalry."

Dorothea settled back against the cream silk squabs, arms folded beneath her cloak. "I warned Metternich in Vienna that you were dangerous. That you'd see the pattern behind the most complicated maneuver. And that you couldn't be counted on to do what Castlereagh wanted, let alone what Metternich wanted you to get Castlereagh to do."

Malcolm smiled. He liked Dorothea. And for all their differing political views, he thought she genuinely liked him and Mélanie. But there were a number of things she didn't know. Notably, that Mélanie had been a Bonapartist agent. That would undoubtedly shake the bonds of friendship. To put it mildly. "You're right. That's why I left the diplomatic corps. I didn't like arguing a case I didn't agree with."

"Even before you left, you worked against it."

"Only a bit round the edges."

"Governments fall and rise round those edges. That's what we're risking now."

"You think LeFou's death could bring down a government?"

"I think this plot could," said the woman who was the Russian ambassador's wife and the Austrian chancellor's mistress. "Don't you?"

"Diplomacy has taught me not to discount any eventuality."

Dorothea's gaze glittered hard on his own across the carriage. "I told Julien I used to think he was the most dangerous man I'd ever met. But I think you're a close second."

"My dear Countess. You're far too shrewd a woman to think anything of the sort."

"I'm a keen judge of character. I wouldn't have survived this long otherwise."

The carriage came to a standstill. The coachman let down the steps and Malcolm handed Dorothea from the carriage. He'd had the coachman let them off a street over from the embassy, for safety. He took Dorothea's arm and led the way round the back, through the mews, the same way they'd left Hubert's. She wrinkled her nose at the smell of horses but made no comment. Malcolm opened the back gate. A few lights shone in the embassy, but the curtains were drawn. He gestured to a side door. "Can you find your way in through there if I get the door open?"

Dorothea nodded, though her eyes widened. For all her experience of intrigue, she wasn't accustomed to spy missions.

They crossed to the door, moving carefully through the shadows. Malcolm dug out the picklocks Hubert had lent him and had the door open in under a minute.

Dorothea's smile gleamed white in the shadows. "You're a man of many talents, Malcolm. Someday, you must show me how to do that. It could come in very useful. For any number of reasons."

Malcolm lifted her hand to his lips, then held open the door and watched her go into the embassy. He could make out the outline of stairs at the end of a passage and saw her start up them. He closed the door with care, made sure the lock was secure, and picked his way back to the gate. He opened the latch and stepped into the mews. And felt cold steel against his side.

"Don't try anything heroic, Mr. Rannoch." The voice was low and lightly accented. Austrian, he thought.

"I'm never heroic."

"Good. That will make this easier."

A whish of movement and splitting pain as something crashed into his head. Then the world spun black.

CHAPTER 9

*H*ubert clunked down his coffee cup. "Go carefully, talking to Augustin. And his wife. This could spill over. As Countess Lieven said, the balance between Russia, Austria, and Britain couldn't be more precarious."

"Which could be the very reason LeFou was hired," Kitty said.

"You brought us in, Uncle Hubert," Julien said. "You'll have to trust us."

Hubert raised a brow.

"All right, no." Julien reached for his cup. "Folly to suggest you could ever trust anyone in this group. But you'll have to at least trust our instincts. Or else you can find someone else to do your dirty work."

"If you thought this was dirty work you wouldn't undertake it, Julien. And you're going to investigate, in any case."

"I know Charlotte Augustin a bit," Mélanie said. "But Cordelia knows her better. I can enlist her help."

Hubert's brows drew together.

"Surely when you brought us in you realized we'd end up bringing in Cordelia and Harry Davenport," Mélanie said.

"I didn't bring you in," Hubert pointed out. "I brought Julien and Kitty in. But I take your point. Anything shared with any of you is going to be shared with the whole lot of you."

"Not necessarily," Kitty said. "I keep plenty of secrets from Julien. I'm sure he does the same with me."

"You make that sound like a point of pride," Palmerston said.

Kitty smiled. "It is, rather."

Hubert tossed down a swallow of coffee. "I just want to contain how far this spreads."

"Cordy and I can talk to Charlotte discreetly." Mélanie reached for her coffee and glanced at the mantel clock. Even allowing for some difficulties getting into the embassy, it shouldn't have taken so long for Malcolm to return. She saw Raoul watching her and met his gaze for moment. He gave a quick, reassuring smile. That didn't reach his eyes.

A rap sounded on the door. "Forgive me, sir." William, the second footman, poked his head in. He was always formal, but his gaze was unwontedly serious. "But Teddy's returned with the carriage. He has news."

Mélanie pushed herself to her feet as Teddy, the coachman, came into the room, red hair ruffled as though he'd been running his fingers through it.

Teddy cast a quick glance round the group. He was less used to being in the main part of the house than William, but Mélanie had driven with him more than once. "Mr. Rannoch had me pull up a couple of streets away from the embassy," he said. "He said it might be half an hour or so. But when it was getting on for an hour and he hadn't come back, I got out and looked about the street, but I couldn't find any sign of him. I'm so sorry, Mrs. Rannoch."

"It's not your fault," Mélanie said. Her hands had gone cold.

Raoul was on his feet and at her side. "Did you hear anything? See anything amiss?"

Teddy shook his head. "The streets were quiet at this hour. And I didn't even know which house they'd gone into."

"We'll follow the path they took." Julien was on his feet as well.

Palmerston had gone still. "Surely you don't think—"

"Difficult to know what to think," Mélanie said. "But Malcolm wouldn't simply disappear without reason. We'll look. At least I will."

"I'll go with you," Raoul said.

"So will I," Julien said.

Kitty hesitated. "I'd like to. But someone should be here in case he comes back."

Mélanie smiled at her friend. "Thank you."

MÉLANIE TOOK Raoul's hand and stepped down from the carriage. Teddy had pulled up exactly where he'd let out Malcolm and Dorothea. She glanced round the street. A rat scurried into a hedge. The lamplight washed over the pavement. Sand-scoured steps. Candlelit windows. Columns casting elegant shadows over porticos. A still, innocuous London night. And her husband had vanished into it. Raoul had been knifed on a street like this two months ago and nearly bled to death on the pavement.

She could make out the roofline of the Russian embassy. But she understood why Malcolm would have wanted to approach discreetly. "He was trying to protect Dorothea. They'd have gone round through the mews to get in with the least notice."

Raoul and Julien nodded. They made their way along the street, then turned down the mews, past the smell of hay and horse dung and the occasional whicker. But mostly all was still, and darker than the main street. It was Julien who pointed to the back gate to the Russian embassy. He reached for the latch, but Mélanie hesitated, gaze caught by something on the ground by the gate, bright in the moonlight. She bent down and scooped it up, fingers numb.

"What?" Raoul asked.

Mélanie uncurled her fingers and stared down at the silver button engraved with a griffin. "It's Malcolm's."

Julien turned. The moonlight gleamed off his hair and caught a flash of concern in his eyes. "It could have simply fallen off."

Mélanie shook her head. "It didn't come from anything he was wearing tonight. We keep buttons to drop as a signal in case of emergency. That's what this is. It's why he picked one with such a distinctive image. He left it as a warning. Because someone snatched him."

"THE WAITING'S THE WORST," Stroheim said. "I've felt it when Lis— people I care about are on missions."

Kitty flashed a smile at him. Lisette Varon, Stroheim's betrothed, was a former French agent. Not only had he spent years knowing she was on missions, much of the time they'd been on opposite sides. "We don't even know Malcolm's on a mission," she said. "He's simply disappeared." Which any agent did, at times. She'd done it herself and panicked Julien. He'd done it and panicked her. But it wasn't like Malcolm. Every instinct screamed that this was wrong, even as her mind scrambled for explanations.

"If someone pulled up with information, Malcolm might have climbed into their carriage to talk," she said. "Or walked away to speak with them. Any one of us would have done."

"Surely he'd have sent a note," Palmerston said.

"Julien didn't send one when he disappeared last month," Kitty said. In the company of Sylvie St. Ives, who was lethal and also his former lover. "Of course, Malcolm's generally more thoughtful than Julien."

"What if Miss Roth pulled up in a carriage?" Stroheim suggested. "Or on foot, wanting to speak with Malcolm. What if she had Gresham with her?"

"And you think he wouldn't have told us?" Palmerston said. "Wouldn't have sent word?"

"He might not have wanted to talk in front of Hubert." Kitty flashed a look at her husband's uncle, who inclined his head in agreement. "They might not have been willing to talk in front of Hubert. In fact, that's the best explanation I've heard."

"So it is," Hubert agreed. "Malcolm's very good at taking care of himself."

But Kitty detected a note of worry even in her former spymaster's voice. She folded her arms over her chest, gripping her elbows with tight fingers, and looked at Palmerston. "Do you think the countess could have set it up?"

Palmerston's eyes widened. "Good god."

"I'm not jealous," Kitty said. "I'm inclined to like her. But Malcolm left with her. And now he's missing."

"She risked a lot coming here," Palmerston said. "If that was an attempt to lure Malcolm, she was willing to go to extreme lengths."

"Not impossible, knowing the countess," Hubert said in an appraising tone. "She and Metternich both play a ruthless game. But for what it's worth, I don't think it likely."

"Nor do I," Stroheim said. "Mostly because if that were the goal, I don't think she'd have risked herself by coming here. She may be ruthless, but she also has a keen sense of self-preservation."

"So she does," Kitty said. "Perhaps—"

She broke off at a rap on the study door. "Forgive me, Mr. Mallinson," William said, poking his head in. "But the Duke of Bamford and Mademoiselle Clairineau have arrived. And their daughter. And a puppy. The little girl needs a place to sleep, so I've shown them up to the blue room. But then they'd like to see you."

Hubert inclined his head. "Show them in. Just as well they've arrived," he said to the others when William had withdrawn. "We need them now more than ever."

It was unusual for Hubert to admit to needing anyone. But then a great deal was unusual tonight. All things considered, it was very comforting to think of Tony and Désirée's expertise. And it would be particularly good to see Désirée, who would have a perspective on the night's events Kitty could share with no one else.

A short time later, Tony and Désirée came into the study. They were always a striking couple and unfailingly elegant, but both looked as though they had dressed hastily. Tony's impeccably cut blue coat looked to have been hastily pulled on, and Désirée's brown hair was slipping from its pins.

"Sorry," Tony said. "But we don't—"

He hesitated on the threshold, taking in the crowd, all still standing. "This is more serious even than we realized."

"A lot's happened since I wrote to you earlier tonight," Hubert said. "You'd best sit down."

"Sorry to descend upon you," Tony said as they moved to the settee, "but from your letter it seemed we should come at once. We don't really have a London home at present. Well, I'm sure Hetty would be happy to take us in at Bamford House, but it felt a bit awkward. And St. Ives and Sylvie are there. Not sure how much we had to worry about letting something slip."

Hubert nodded. "Your little girl's all right?"

"Tony carried her in, sound asleep," Désirée said. "Thank you for giving us a place for her."

"Thank you for coming," Hubert said.

"Of course." Tony smiled as he accepted a cup of coffee from Kitty.

"I'm sorry we had to interrupt your time in the country."

"Quite like old times." Désirée undid the ties on her cloak. She wore a simple gown of fawn-colored sarcenet that tied on the side over a silk slip, the sort of dress Kitty recognized as something that could be scrambled into quickly. She had many of the same herself. "Waking up in the middle of the night and hurrying to a secret meeting. Tony's thrilled at the call of adventure. To be honest, we both are. Which isn't in the least to question the delights of life in the country. But there's nothing like this to quicken the blood. Even Sophie was excited. Mostly because she knew she'd be seeing her friends, but I think she caught her parents' excitement. And, quite honestly, it's far from the first time she's been rushed somewhere in the middle of the night."

"I'm not sure I need to know how often that happened," Tony said.

Désirée gave her betrothed a dazzling smile. "No, my dear. Some things are best left secrets. Speaking of which, would you like me to leave?"

"Don't be silly," Tony said.

"You don't know what this is about yet. You may not want an enemy agent in the room. Our friends may not want an enemy agent in the room."

"We have agents from a number of sides in the room, regardless. And just about everyone present was an enemy of someone in the room, at some point."

"A point. But Mr. Mallinson may have different ideas."

"On the contrary," Hubert said. "We could use both your expertise."

Désirée raised her brows but took a drink of coffee without comment.

Hubert recounted the events of the night, with Kitty taking over when she and Julien had gone to Gresham's rooms, and Palmerston and Stroheim filling in bits.

Tony sat back in his chair, gaze intent.

Désirée cast a sidelong look at him. "You don't look as shocked as I'd have thought," she said. "Do people in the British government regularly hire assassins?"

"In London?" Tony passed a hand over his face and reached for his coffee. "Not precisely. But I'll admit I've suspected for a long time that there was a faction within the government working for their own interests. Thinking it might be better to ally ourselves with Russia and Austria than to try to get between them. Castlereagh's been distracted lately. Quicker to jump at shadows, but also less in control." He looked at Palmerston. "You must have seen it."

Palmerston nodded. "He's still a force to be reckoned with, but he's not the man he was."

Tony gave a contained nod. "That creates a vacuum someone else could move into."

"Who?" Kitty asked.

"I'm not sure. I've heard rumors. But nothing I can substantiate."

"And if whoever this is did hire an assassin, who would have been the target?" Stroheim asked.

"There you have me." Tony took a fortifying drink of whisky. "There are almost as many options as there are diplomatic representatives in London."

"Or it could be someone British," Désirée suggested.

Tony met her gaze. "So it could," he agreed.

"Assassination is the most direct way to shake up the power dynamic and rise to power oneself," Désirée said. "Back to Brutus and Cassius."

"Which didn't work out too well for them," Tony said.

"No. A point," she conceded.

"What about Augustin?" Stroheim said. "Or anyone else who might have been working with Austria or Russia?"

Tony frowned into his coffee cup. "As I said, there's a faction that would like us to ally ourselves with Austria and Russia as opposed to pushing the two of them apart. But I can't point to specific people. Not at this point. I can make inquiries, though."

"Thank you," Kitty said with feeling. "I know that's probably the last thing you feel like doing."

Tony stretched an arm along the back of the settee, brushing Désirée's shoulders. "I own to more than my share of regrets about my diplomatic work. But at least this lets me put it to use. And I can still be listened to." He took another drink of coffee. "I'm glad John brought the ledger to your attention, Palmerston. He has some good instincts, though I fear he sees me as a dinosaur who would be replaced."

"Oh, that's nothing," Palmerston said. "He's three years my junior and he sees me as hopelessly outdated."

"It's concerning about Malcolm," Désirée said. "You must all be very worried, and I can only imagine what Mélanie is feeling. Though he's certainly an able agent. And there are plenty of times both Tony and I have disappeared. Of course, Malcolm isn't on the opposite side from anyone."

"There are a number of sides," Hubert said. "As Malcolm himself would be quick to point out."

Désirée glanced at the door. "I should go up and make sure Sophie is all right."

"I'll go with you in case you need anything," Kitty said. "I know the house."

"Thank you." Désirée smiled. She had a wonderfully disarming smile. It was one of an agent's best assets. And gave no clue to the secrets they had to discuss.

CHAPTER 10

*K*itty uttered nothing but commonplaces to Désirée as they climbed the stairs. The house was quiet and Hubert's wife Amelia and youngest daughter Lucinda were seemingly asleep, but in a Mallinson house, one never knew. She liked Hubert's staff. She was also quite sure more than one of them collected information for him.

The blue room was a pretty room at the back of the house, hung with forget-me-not patterned paper. Sophie, Désirée and Tony's daughter, was asleep in a white-painted bed curved like a sleigh, her puppy curled up by her feet. Désirée touched her fingers to her daughter's fair hair in the glow of the tin-shaded nightlight. "She has a knack for sleeping through anything. Helpful in the child of agents."

"Mine are the same," Kitty said. "We've made more than one midnight escape. They tended to see it as a great adventure. Which helped me remain calm."

Désirée smiled, smoothed the blue-flowered coverlet, rubbed the sleeping puppy's head. Then she looked up and met Kitty's gaze. The weight of their shared knowledge hung between them in the shadows.

"Had you heard anything?" Kitty asked.

Désirée shook her head. "The last I heard from her was over a week ago, with no mention of anything that might have made her run. But as soon as Tony got the express from Hubert, I was afraid of a connection. No mention of her, but there was of Gresham."

"Yes, that's how I felt when Hubert asked Julien and me to go to Gresham's tonight," Kitty said. "I could feel it all starting to unravel. And I had a sickening sense I should have seen it coming."

"Have you told them?" Désirée asked.

Kitty shook her head. "I didn't want to in front of Hubert. I was going to when we went back to Berkeley Square. Then Malcolm disappeared. But they have to know." She didn't make it quite a question, but she held Désirée's gaze.

Désirée nodded. "I understand."

"I can keep you out of it."

"That's generous. And up to you."

"No, I think it's up to you what you share. Always a balancing act for any of us. Especially with spouses."

Désirée gave a faint smile. "Tony's used to me lying. I don't want to speak too quickly. I also don't want to get anyone in trouble. It's a more complicated calculus with Hubert involved. And even Palmerston, who seems likable but hardly shares the politics of the others."

"I flirted with him when I first arrived in England," Kitty said. "I needed his support in Spain. I thought about going further than flirting. That was before Julien came back into my life. Also before I realized how attached Palmerston is to Emily Cowper. I have no desire to get in the midst of a relationship like that, whatever rules they play by. He's agreeable. And a decent man. But I wouldn't trust him with this. Not unless we have to. Of course, Julien will keep quiet what I ask him to."

"And you don't think Tony will?"

"What do you think?" Kitty asked. She was very fond of Tony

63

but there was no denying he was a Tory diplomat and an English duke.

Désirée smoothed Sophie's hair. The emerald betrothal ring Tony had given her flashed in the glow of the nightlight. "Tony's shown remarkable flexibility lately. But these are his people. It's not so much that I'm afraid he'd betray me at this point as that I don't want him to close off options for himself."

"You want him to go back into politics?" Kitty studied her friend in the shadows.

"I want him to be able to do so if he wants it. Is that so surprising?"

"No." Kitty pressed her finger over a crease in her amber silk sleeve. She'd spattered something—brandy?—on the ruffled cuff at some point. "I want Julien to be able to achieve what he wants in the House of Lords. He'd say he won't compromise to get there, but I can't but know certain things we may do could stand in his way. So I try to make sure I don't cut off his opportunities, while not compromising my own. Always a balancing act."

"Indeed."

Kitty rubbed her arms. "It's difficult to think what to do until we get Malcolm back."

Désirée's gaze settled on Kitty's own. "I could say he's good at taking care of himself. And I'm quite sure he is, from what I've seen. I've also become absurdly fond of him—far more than I used to admit to being fond of anyone—and I can scarcely imagine what you're going through."

"It's just"—Kitty hesitated. "There's a part of me that went into an absolute panic. But I don't want to show it. He's not—I don't want to intrude."

"I'm quite sure Mélanie wouldn't think you were."

"No, I suppose not." In fact, she doubted Mélanie could think at all beyond the need to find Malcolm. The sheer terror in Mélanie's blue-green eyes was burnt in Kitty's memory.

"And I'm quite sure Julien wouldn't be jealous."

"No, I'm quite sure as well. We aren't, either of us. Or at least we don't admit to it. But that doesn't change that I'm not the one who has the right to be worried. Not anymore."

Désirée crossed the room and put an arm round her. She was less than a decade Kitty's senior, yet for a moment Kitty caught a whiff of the mother she had never known. "We all have a right to worry about those we care about, *chérie*. Never doubt it. I never shared Malcolm Rannoch's bed, and I'll own to being quite panicked."

"I'm not sure whether that comforts me or terrifies me," Kitty said. "But thank you." She drew a breath. "We should go down. Mélanie and Julien and Raoul should be back soon. Or at least send word."

~

MÉLANIE LOOKED ROUND the group gathered in Hubert's study. Which now included Désirée and Tony. A distinct relief. Not that they would know how to find Malcolm, but they were an asset in any crisis.

"Malcolm might not have been able to send word," she said. "He might well not have wanted to let all of us know if he were talking to Harriet and Gresham, for instance. But we definitely agreed leaving the button is a sign of distress. Even if he couldn't have sent word he was all right, he wouldn't have left the button if something weren't wrong."

Raoul's hand closed on her arm. They were all standing, and the others had risen when they came into the room.

Julien moved to Kitty's side. "We spent a long time examining the mews for clues," he said, taking up the story Mélanie had started to recount. "Difficult to be sure, with so many carriages going in and out, but from the mark on the pavement it looks as though a carriage pulled up not far from the Russian embassy mews."

"So they forced Malcolm into a carriage?" Kitty said. Her eyes were wide and dark. She was usually a model of calm self-control. She'd once stuck a knife in Julien to stop him from killing an opponent and sat by calmly as he was bandaged. She'd been terrified when Raoul's life was at stake but she had focused on comforting Laura and Mélanie. Mélanie saw Kitty marshaling all those resources now. But she also caught the stark fear at the back of Kitty's gaze.

"Probably," Raoul said in a steady voice. "Presumably because they wanted to get him to reveal information. It won't be the first time he's been in such a situation."

Mélanie looked up at him. "Tell me you aren't worried," she said, voice tight in her throat.

"I'm terrified." His gaze locked on her own, with no effort to disguise his fear. "But practicality says Malcolm can look after himself and there'd be little to gain and a lot to risk from anyone hurting him."

"I'm not feeling very practical just now," Mélanie said.

"Understandable. I own I'm not, myself."

"I don't think any of us is," Tony said.

"Malcolm can talk his way out of things," Julien said. "None better. And no, I'm not suggesting you not worry," he added, looking at Kitty. "I'd be climbing the walls if it were Kitty."

"This happens in the lives we lead," Kitty said.

"Sometimes. More to me than to him. We're used to it. We're supposed to be used to it. But I confess I'm on edge."

"You couldn't have predicted this," Raoul said.

"No. Probably not." Julien's hands fisted at his sides.

"It's the waiting that's the hardest," Désirée said. "And at this point, we have to wait."

❧

Désirée moved across the library and touched Raoul's arm. Resigned to waiting for more news on Malcolm's disappearance, the group had scattered to various parts of the house. She'd left Tony in the study to talk with Hubert and Palmerston about the sort of things they wouldn't say in front of anyone not in the government. Mélanie, Julien, Kitty, and Franz were at one end of the library, but she found herself alone with Raoul at the other, perhaps not accidentally. "How are you still on your feet?" she asked.

He met her gaze. His gray eyes were steady, but open as they seldom were. She and Tony and Raoul had been agents together when many of the others were children. Or not even born. "Because if I stopped in the slightest, I'd collapse," he said.

"I can't imagine—no, I can now, better than I could have before. Just now, I went to look in on Sophie and thought that I hadn't really known fear until she was born. But it will be a long time before she's old enough that I let her out of my sight."

Raoul scrubbed his hands over his eyes. "I used to lie awake at nights when he was a child. Because I was away so much. But there was no reason to think anyone would target him. So I told myself, and it was true. Then when he became an agent—he's been in danger more times than I can count. But never quite when I knew it so specifically as tonight."

Raoul didn't speak this way to many people. Much like Désirée herself. "Have you sent word to Laura?" she asked.

"There's no need to do so yet. Nothing she could do. And she'd only worry."

"She might be glad to share your worrying." Désirée was still trying to grasp the same about Tony.

"She's dealing with Jeremy Roth's worry tonight. Time enough to tell her—later."

Désirée cast a glance at the other end of the library. Kitty and Julien were sitting on either side of Mélanie. "She won't collapse just because you show your worry, you know."

"Laura?"

"Mélanie."

"Oh no. Of course not."

"But you're worried about her?"

"How could I not be?"

Désirée slid her arms round him. "Malcolm's sensible. Far better at taking care of himself than any of us were. And look at what we survived."

Raoul turned to look at her and gave a twisted grin. "Remembering what we went through, I'm not sure how comforting I find that. I sometimes think all three of us survived on luck alone."

"It's not just luck. It's instincts. And Malcolm's are probably better than all of ours."

Raoul watched her for a moment "Are you all right?"

"Of course not. I'm worried sick about Malcolm."

"I mean beyond that."

Désirée met his gaze with a look designed to appear to let her mask slip while holding it more tightly in place than ever. Deception was second nature to her. But it was always hard with Raoul. "Tony's been dragged back into his old world. I always knew that was going to happen. We're lucky, really, that we got as long as we did." She cast a glance at the study door. "And Hubert is being remarkably understanding about my involvement."

"Hubert thinks you can be an asset."

She drew back to look at him. "Good god. He didn't say so?"

"He did. Don't let it turn you against us."

"Perish the thought. But it does make me wonder what Hubert is plotting."

"Not a bad strategy to keep one's enemies close."

She smiled. "Why do you think I had an affair with Tony for so long?"

Raoul laughed unexpectedly. "The truth is Hubert recognizes your brilliance. And that at times you could be an ally. He's always had the flexibility to take his allies where he finds them. Often in unfortunate places. But he's learnt a bit."

"You like him."

"Well, yes, I suppose I do, in a way. We're veterans of the same war, after all. And I've seen what he's been through." His brows drew together. "He's worried. Even before Malcolm disappeared. More so than I've ever seen him."

"We've never confronted anything quite like this," Désirée said.

Which was truer than even Raoul could know.

CHAPTER 11

*M*alcolm forced his eyes open. He couldn't be sure quite how much time had passed, but he judged it had been long enough to show signs of waking up. In truth, he might have gone in and out of consciousness. It had been all he could do to fumble the button from the concealed pocket inside his coat as he slumped to the ground. He'd have been in no state to run or fight. And in any case, if someone was going to this much trouble to get him alone, he rather wanted to know what they were after.

He blinked across the carriage. The interior lamps were low but bright enough that pain sliced through his head. The shadowy form on the seat opposite would not quite come into focus, but it appeared to be a cloaked lady. Or possibly a man wearing a lady's cloak. "Was this really necessary?"

"We needed to talk to you, Mr. Rannoch." It was a woman's voice, lightly accented. Probably Austrian. Like the voice of the person who had hit him. But not the same voice. That had been a man. At least he thought so. "You will not be harmed if you cooperate."

Malcolm glanced at the carriage door. The woman's arm

shifted. The glow of the interior lamps and the moonlight coming through the carriage windows glanced off metal. A pistol.

"Don't worry," he said. "I'm in no state to jump."

Difficult to tell where they were, when he couldn't be sure how long it was since he'd been bundled into the carriage. The road sounded rough beneath the wheels. He thought he could catch a whiff of river air, but he couldn't be sure.

"Good," the woman said. "I've heard you're pragmatic but also have a tendency to be a hero."

"I'd never presume to be anything of the sort." Malcolm let his head flop back against the squabs.

The carriage came to a stop, sending pain slicing through his temples. The door jerked open and he caught a glimpse of a man in a dark coat and hat who let down the steps. "No sudden moves, Mr. Rannoch." The lady descended the carriage steps and turned, the pistol trained on Malcolm. Malcolm pushed himself up. The carriage swam for several seconds. In truth, it was all he could do to descend the steps without falling flat on his face.

They were pulled up in front of a narrow alley between two dark buildings. Definitely a smell of the river. Tar, brine, and the stench of waste. Always worse in the summer.

He could see a bit of the woman's face now. Thirties, probably. Dark eyes and brows, a bit of dark hair showing beneath the hood of a cloak that was black or possibly dark blue or green. She jerked her head down the alley.

Malcolm stepped forwards, on cracked pavement, between smoke-stained brick buildings.

"Stop," she said when he had taken a half dozen or so steps. "Go through that door."

It was an innocuous door with peeling brown paint. He turned the handle and stepped forwards. Possible, of course, that this was an elaborate ruse to kill him indoors, but it seemed unlikely. Easier to have left him in the alley or killed him there and then moved the body. But his senses were returning and he could put up a fight if needed.

The door gave on to a narrow passage, patchy wallpaper in some sort of floral pattern, the sour smell of damp.

"Third door on the left," the woman said.

Candlelight met him. He blinked and the pain shot through his head again. A table, a chair, a figure seated beyond the candle that burnt on the table. Malcolm moved forwards. The light cut into his eyes. But he could make out a bit of the person across the candle.

Malcolm moved to a chair across the table, picking his steps with care. The last thing he wanted was to betray he was quite as unsteady as he felt. "You could have just asked. You should know by now I'm always willing to talk to anyone."

The man across the table smiled, a smile that took Malcolm back to council rooms in Vienna choked with tobacco and snuff and the scent of brandy. "You might have been followed." He cast a glance towards the door. It clicked shut. The woman who had escorted Malcolm had presumably withdrawn.

"Not a lot of respect for my expertise." Malcolm pulled out a ladder-back chair and sank into it, relieved beyond all measure to have solid wood beneath him. "Though it's a fair point."

The man across the table smiled through the candlelight. "My apologies for it coming off as it did. But we need to talk to you. We need to explain."

Malcolm settled his shoulders against the hard back of the chair. "I didn't ask for an explanation."

"Didn't you?" Josef Hauke, one of the abler Austrian attachés at the Congress of Vienna, leant forwards across the table. Malcolm knew that posture. It said, *This is between us. I'm sharing the truth, whatever my superiors say.* It was effective. And sometimes it was even to be believed. "Listen. This is different. No one knows whom to trust. We certainly didn't. Anyone could be watching."

"Fair enough. But why me?"

"Aside from the fact that you reached out? We needed to make it clear this wasn't us. We needed to tell someone who'd be believed."

"I'm not a diplomat anymore."

"They'll listen to you."

"Hubert Mallinson and Castlereagh regularly accuse me of being a traitor," Malcolm said. "Castlereagh once was convinced I was a murderer."

"There are different ways to use words. They don't mean it the way they use it."

"You'll have to get them to explain that to me. Perhaps I miss the nuances."

"Don't be difficult, Malcolm. We both know what Hubert Mallinson thinks of you."

"I won't argue with you there. Precisely what he thinks of me is the question."

"They're looking in the wrong direction now."

"We've already received a great deal of information tonight."

"Countess Lieven is looking in the wrong direction. So is your friend Stroheim. I have a fair amount of respect for both of them. But they've got this wrong. Austria wasn't behind this."

Malcolm leant back against the hard slats of his chair. "Behind what, precisely?"

"Surely you know. Surely that's the question of the hour."

"I'm asking you to put it into words."

"Behind engaging André LeFou. They've jumped in the wrong direction and gone to the British authorities."

"Some of the British authorities."

"Fair enough. But if they persist, if they get Hubert Mallinson and others to believe them, we could be facing war. I don't think you want that. I certainly don't. And you're one of the few people I trust to stop it."

"That's placing a great deal of trust in me."

"As you say."

Malcolm shifted his shoulders against the hard wood. It felt slippery. "What do you want me to do?"

"Take the truth back. And get them to believe it."

"Get whom to believe it? And what truth?"

"Hubert Mallinson and Lord Palmerston, for a start. And Countess Lieven and Stroheim. The truth that whatever crazy game is afoot, Austria isn't behind it."

"That's asking a lot of me."

"If anyone can do it, you can."

"You flatter me."

"I don't think so." Hauke sat back in his chair. "Hubert Mallinson respects you."

Malcolm gave a harsh laugh.

"I'm serious. He may not trust you, but he respects you, as he respects few people. If you tell him, he'll listen."

"Oh, he may listen. Whether or not he'll take what I say remotely seriously is another question. I've been telling Hubert Mallinson things he doesn't take seriously for years."

"That's up to you." Hauke leant forwards, reached for a decanter on the table, poured two glasses of red wine, and pushed one towards Malcolm. "If you can't persuade him, ask Mélanie."

Malcolm's fingers closed hard round the stem of the glass. "Why would you think Mélanie would have more luck?"

Hauke dragged his own glass close and took a drink. "Surely I don't have to tell you how brilliant a woman you are married to, Rannoch?"

"I hope no one recognizes that more than I do." Malcolm kept his fingers easy round the stem of his glass.

"Well, then." Hauke set his glass on the table. The wine glowed blood red in the candlelight. "I'm serious, Malcolm. This is genuine. Countess Lieven and Stroheim are putting the wrong pieces together." He reached into his coat, tugged out a paper, and pushed it across the table. "If you question my sincerity, take a look at this. We've been watching Tristram Gresham for months. I'm giving you all our notes."

"Why?"

"As proof of our sincerity. Why else?"

"Any number of reasons. Including to mislead us with false information."

"Always possible. I won't insult both of us by asking you to take my word. But you'd be wise to look at the papers." He sat back, the stem of his glass tilting between his fingers. "The intelligence I gave you on Gresham is real. But false information is out there about LeFou. I don't think the countess or Stroheim realize it's false. But others will feed on it. Will twist it to their own ends. Before we know it, we'll be at war again. With the same players, if arrayed on different sides. And it will be a war no one can easily win. We disagree about a number of things. But I'm quite sure you don't want war. That was clear in Vienna, however much we disagreed."

"That should be obvious from everything I've ever said or written."

"Well, then." Hauke took a drink of wine as though sealing a pact. "I want to prevent further conflict. You do too. You're a sane man with an ear to power. You may not have the ambitions of most diplomats, but that makes you all the saner. If anyone can stop this from spiraling out of control, you can."

Malcolm took a drink of wine. To play for time. To prove that he could. And because, at this point, it couldn't make things worse. "It didn't occur to you that to snatch me off the street might have quite the opposite effect?"

"With anyone else. But you won't hold it against us."

"That's relying a lot on my good humor."

"I had months in Vienna to take your measure."

"And Hubert Mallinson? And the others?"

"My dear Malcolm. If we didn't trust you to persuade them, we wouldn't have snatched you in the first place."

CHAPTER 12

"The waiting's the hardest." Désirée crossed the library, Raoul at her side, to join Mélanie and the others gathered by the fireplace.

"It's hard to sit still." Mélanie curled her fingers into her palms. "I keep reminding myself it would do no one any good for me to run about the streets looking for him. There's nothing like one's family being at risk to send basic spycraft out the window." She looked at Raoul. It must have been good for him to talk to Désirée. He'd been trying so very hard to keep up a facade in front of the others. Probably her especially.

Raoul met her gaze and gave a quick smile in return.

"I couldn't be still during Waterloo," Désirée said. "Even though Tony was fighting for the opposite side. It made me an excellent nurse."

Mélanie nodded. "It was much the same for me. But at least I knew where Malcolm was. Even if where he was was the hell of the battlefield."

The study door opened. Mélanie turned round, ready for William with more coffee or a note that someone else had called, and found herself looking at her husband.

For a moment she couldn't move. Couldn't even breathe. Then she ran across the room, tripping over her skirt and nearly falling. She caught herself on a leather-and-mahogany table and ran into her husband's arms. "Malcolm." She slid her arms round him. "Darling." She pressed her face against his chest.

"I'm all right." His arms tightened round her. "They just wanted to talk to me."

"They?" She drew back, drinking in the familiar Celtic planes of his face. His dark hair was more than usually disordered. There was a mark on his forehead that was probably going to turn into a bruise.

"Josef Hauke." He drew back and looked round the room at the others. "And a very hard-headed and quite self-possessed woman who held a pistol on me."

"Why on earth did she think she had to—"

"So I wouldn't be followed, apparently. And they wouldn't be connected to talking to me. They apologized."

"Charming." Mélanie thought back to moments at the Congress of Vienna. "To think I used to think of Josef Hauke as a good waltzing partner."

"This doesn't cast any aspersions on his waltzing ability. And don't tell me you wouldn't have been quite as capable of forcing someone to go with you at gunpoint in similar circumstances."

"Well, yes." Certain past incidents echoed through her head, quick as rifle fire. "I admit I didn't think about people's families in those days. Amazing how one's perspective can change."

Mélanie dragged him over to a chair and pushed her husband into it. "Sit down. Do you want coffee? Or whisky?"

"I told you I'm fine, Mel." He grinned up at her. Making her heart turn over. Or it would, except that it was pounding in her throat. "You always accuse me of fussing."

"In circumstances like these, I wouldn't complain."

"Ha."

Kitty handed her a whisky and Julien brought over a coffee

cup. Malcolm downed a generous swig of whisky, then took a drink of coffee.

"What did they want?" Raoul asked.

"To convince me they weren't involved in hiring LeFou. Or in his death."

"Did they?" Julien asked.

"They strengthened my opinion. Hauke claimed Countess Lieven and Stroheim were reading things wrong."

"Did he say how?" Stroheim asked.

"Not in specifics. But he shared their surveillance notes on Gresham as a gesture of good faith. Or what he claims is their surveillance notes. Though I'm inclined to believe he was telling the truth."

"What's in the notes?" Kitty asked.

"I scanned them briefly. We'll need to look more. But a woman who matches Harriet's description was seen going into Gresham's rooms more than once."

"That doesn't prove why she was going in," Mélanie said.

"No," Malcolm agreed.

"Did they say why they chose you?" Désirée asked.

Malcolm reached for the whisky again. "They said I was fair-minded and could be trusted." He leant back as Mélanie brushed a hand over his head. "That and I reached out to him."

"You—" Mélanie sat back on her heels and looked at her husband. "That was clever."

"You asked them to kidnap you?" Kitty said.

"Not in so many words. But I sent him a message when we got to Hubert's. Through Sim, the bootboy, so don't blame the other staff for not knowing. I didn't have it in mind for it to play out quite as it did. But I thought talking could be useful."

"It usually is," Raoul said.

Malcolm met his gaze. "Yes. You taught me that."

"I'm always glad if something I taught you helps."

Malcolm reached for the papers about Gresham, but before he

could pull them out, Hubert, Palmerston, and Tony came into the library and they had to repeat the story all over again.

Malcolm looked at Stroheim as he concluded his account. "It's not that I didn't believe your story. But you aren't inside the Austrian delegation anymore."

"No, I quite understand," Stroheim said. "I had questions myself. All I knew was what I saw of Augustin." He hesitated a moment. "Countess Lieven's story is a bit more problematic."

"You don't trust her?" Hubert asked.

"Do you?" The candlelight bounced off Stroheim's steady gaze.

Hubert settled back in his chair. "I don't trust anyone."

"And you expect me to?"

"You're younger. And you claim to have ideals."

"Oh, I do. They make me wary," Stroheim said. "Of people out to remake the world. Like Metternich. Like the countess. Like you, sir."

"Touché."

"I have a great deal of respect for the countess," Stroheim said. "I'd go so far as to say I like her. But if you're asking if I think she'd have spun a story about LeFou for her own ends, or Metternich's, or both of theirs together—because she certainly wouldn't work for him if didn't benefit her, whatever their relationship—of course she would. Surely you can't think me so naive you'd ask me that."

"For what it's worth, Hauke thinks the countess is being manipulated," Malcolm said. "Of course, that might be his own self-preservation at not moving against her."

"Hauke's very worried about the repercussions," Mélanie said.

"This has international incident written all over it."

"Which raises the question—is someone trying to create an international incident?"

"Hauke was certainly afraid so." Malcolm leant back in his chair. Mélanie, perched on the chair arm, could feel the crackle of the papers about Gresham that Hauke had given him. Malcolm hadn't said anything about them since Hubert had come into the room. Understandably.

Kitty looked at Raoul. "Should you talk to the prime minister?" she asked.

"I've been wondering." Raoul shot a look at Tony.

"I haven't been round Liverpool much lately," Tony said. "But he's difficult to read. He likes you, though. That's always been clear."

"He takes personal loyalty seriously," Raoul said. "And he's a decent person. That doesn't mean he trusts me. Any more than I trust him."

"Oh, if we could only talk to people we trusted—" Julien said.

"Quite," Désirée agreed.

"Are you off?" Hubert crossed the library to join Raoul, while the others congregated round the fireplace, donning the coats and cloaks William had brought in.

Raoul nodded. "We'll be able to start making inquiries in the morning. Little more we can do tonight." And back in Berkeley Square without Hubert they could talk freely.

Hubert's gaze said he was perfectly aware of that and perhaps even welcomed what advances they might make on their own. "Bamford and Mademoiselle Clairineau are going to stay here. Their daughter's sound asleep. Foolish to disturb her again."

"Kind of you to take them in."

Hubert grunted. "I'm grateful for their help."

Difficult to tell what Amelia, Hubert's wife, would think of taking in a couple who were not yet legally married. Considering her and Hubert's marriage was currently strained by the affair Hubert had had with Malcolm's mother under cover of a mission, the issues involved were certainly fraught. "And I'm sure they're grateful for the shelter," Raoul said. He'd never forget that Hubert had been instrumental in his ability to get a divorce and marry Laura before their daughter Clara was born. "We're all going to need each other."

Hubert nodded, gaze uncharacteristically fixed on the medallions in the carpet. "O'Roarke?" he said.

"Yes?"

Hubert hesitated. "Keep an eye on Julien if you can."

Raoul suppressed the instinctive quip that Julien was hard to keep an eye on and excellent at keeping an eye on himself. "You're worried about him."

"He thinks he's invulnerable." Hubert risked a quick glance over his shoulder at his nephew. "Or perhaps that he should run any possible risk because he has some misguided sense he needs to make up for his past." Hubert adjusted his spectacles. "I blame you for that. Julien paid far too much attention to you and your ideals."

"You mean in and about the moments I was afraid he was going to stick a knife in my back?"

"Oh, well. You're used to people doing that." Hubert tugged at his spectacles again. "Probably shouldn't have said that, given the recent past. You'd think it would have made Julien cautious, but I don't think it has. He knows what he has to lose, but it doesn't stop him from facing down danger. And Kitty won't stop him."

"Kitty knows it would be pointless to try. He won't stop her either."

"No. They're well matched. They have an interesting future—providing they both manage not to get themselves killed. Julien's absorbed far too much of a conscience from you lot."

"Julien always had that, I think. He just hid it."

"Possibly."

Raoul watched Hubert for a moment. He knew the fear of a parent. Especially after tonight. He wasn't as accustomed to seeing it in Hubert. "He'd be bored. If he walked away from all of it."

"Are you bored?"

"No."

"Say it as though you mean it."

Raoul leant a hand against the paneled wall. "I'm older. And anyway, I haven't walked away. Not entirely."

"No. But you've got a bit more caution."

Raoul crossed to Hubert's side and put a hand on his shoulder. "I know what it is to worry about the younger generation. All the more so after tonight. Julien wouldn't thank me for keeping an eye on him. Even I find the idea laughable. But I'll do my best."

"You keep an eye on all of them."

"They keep an eye on me. Especially Mélanie."

"You're still the adult in the room."

Raoul felt himself smile. "I'm not sure they'd agree."

"Oh, they would. Except when Laura's about to be another adult."

"Oh, Laura's certainly the adult in the family." He was going to have a lot to explain to Laura when they got back to Berkeley Square.

"Along with you. They'd all admit it. Even Julien."

Raoul studied the face of his longtime foe. There were shadows in Hubert's face that had not been there a year or so ago. Or perhaps Raoul was better at looking behind the mask. Or Hubert allowed it to drop more. "In this game, we make decisions that impact our family. We set up situations that can seem unpardonable, looking back. That probably are unpardonable. I don't sleep well most nights. I probably never will. I'm quite certain I don't deserve to."

"Are you saying there's nothing you can do?" Hubert asked.

Raoul tightened his hand on Hubert's shoulder. "I'm saying I'll keep an eye on your nephew."

CHAPTER 13

"Stop prowling about, Jeremy, " Judith said. "It won't help us find Harriet."

"It may help him think." Laura refilled the coffee cups. Mélanie had sent a note saying only that they were well but had been delayed, and had no direct news of Harriet. Jeremy, of course, was chafing to be doing something. And Judith was chafing at her husband's frustration. The early months of marriage were both wondrous and fraught with unexpected challenges, as Laura recalled. Not that it had been precisely the same for her and Raoul, given that they'd been living together and raising Emily together for over a year, and had been about to have another child. Still, it took time to accustom oneself to another person's quirks, to taking them into account in one's planning, and at the same time not getting in each other's way. Because they'd had to flee Britain with Malcolm and Mélanie, she and Raoul had jumped into living together as a couple.

Jeremy paused on the hearthrug, scowling at the closed curtains. "If only I'd warned her—"

"What? About Tristram Gresham?" Judith added milk to her coffee. "I'm quite sure Harriet knows the sort of man he is."

"And that makes it better?" Jeremy spun to look at his wife.

"We don't know for a certainty that that's what's going on with them," Laura said. "You've certainly seen unusual explanations often enough in your investigations."

Jeremy frowned. "That's true. But—"

"You can't imagine another reason a lady would have a secret connection to a gentleman?" Judith asked.

"No. That is, yes, of course I can." Jeremy ran a hand through his hair. "It's just—"

A clang reverberated through the house.

Laura sprang to her feet. "Someone's at the door."

Jeremy moved into the hall beside her, Judith following. "Are you sure—?" he said as Laura went to the door.

"People are always calling at all hours. As you should know."

But she still eased the door open with caution. A dark figure lurched forwards and fell against the door, pushing it open. Laura stumbled backwards against Jeremy as the new arrival collapsed on the hall floor.

"Darling!" A cloaked figure ran through the door and dropped down beside the man who had collapsed on the tiles. She touched her fingers to his throat, then looked at Laura, Jeremy, and Judith. Her hood fell back from her cloak to reveal chestnut hair falling loose from its pins. "He's breathing, but I think he's fainted. I was afraid the knife wound was worse than he admitted."

"Knife wound?" Laura dropped down beside her.

"They caught us in a street just off the square. We—"

She broke off. Laura scarcely heard her words. She was staring at the man lying on the black and white marble tiles in a tangle of coat and booted feet. Disordered dark hair. Tawny skin, fine-boned features. A face that took her flooding back over a decade to blazing sun and air fragrant with spices. "Hara."

"Oh, I'm so sorry," the woman said. "I haven't explained anything."

"Explanations later," Laura said. "Where is he wounded?"

"His left arm."

Laura eased Hara's arm up and felt blood seeping through his coat. But not enough that he'd bleed out. He'd probably fainted from the shock. "Judith, can you get Mélanie's medical supply box? It should be on the chest of drawers in her and Malcolm's room." She looked from Jeremy to the chestnut-haired woman. "I think it's safe to move him to the library sofa. If the three of us work together—"

Jeremy already had his arms under Hara's shoulders. Laura and the chestnut-haired woman lifted his legs and the three of them managed to carry him through the library door to the closest sofa. Hara stirred and groaned but didn't fully regain consciousness. By that time, Judith had returned with Mélanie's medical supply box. They got Hara out of his greatcoat and coat. Laura cut away his shirt sleeve. The wound was not long, but it was jagged and seemed to have gone deep.

"Does it need stitches?" the chestnut-haired woman asked, gaze fixed on Hara.

Laura didn't quite have Mélanie's skills, but she'd tended a fair share of wounds at this point. One could scarcely live in this family without doing otherwise. "I think so. I'm not as experienced as my friend whose supply box this is, but I've patched my husband up more than once. I can stitch Hara's wound. If you trust me." She put the faintest question in her voice. About a number of things.

"Of course. Oh!" The woman's eyes widened. "You don't know who I am. For all you know, it might not be my business in the least to say who tends to Hara. I'm Lizzy. Lizzy Delaney. Hara's wife. Though I don't suppose you know about me. We got married just before we left India."

Hara's wife—first wife?—had died three years before. Laura remembered the letters vividly. He had never mentioned anyone named Lizzy. But then Hara wasn't quick to share his feelings. She hadn't told him about Raoul until Clara was on the way.

"It seems odd in the circumstances, but my felicitations." Laura smiled at Lizzy, seeing her properly for the first time. Level dark brows, clear brown eyes, a delicate face. Mid-twenties, she judged, though the older she got herself, the harder it was to tell. "You might hold his hand. If he wakes, that will help. Though, as I recall from childhood cuts and bruises, he was always stoic."

Once they'd both taken a tumble while playing tag in the street. She'd screamed bloody murder. Hara had carried her back to her father's house with no complaint about his own injuries, which had been worse. It had been years before she'd realized that that had probably had more than a bit to do with who they were. Colonel's daughter and son of a soldier and an Indian mother, who already knew that if he followed in his father's footsteps, he'd be barred in how far he could rise in the ranks.

Lizzy gripped Hara's hand between her own, brows drawn with concern.

Judith, who had tended more than one wound herself, brought over a decanter of brandy. Jeremy moved a lamp to give her better light. Laura cleaned Hara's wound with brandy, and then stitched carefully. Hara stirred a few times, but Lizzy murmured to him and he didn't pull away.

"Thank you." Lizzy stared down at the neat stitches in Hara's arm. "This isn't how we wanted to arrive to see you. That is, Hara was worried about coming to see you at all. But in the circumstances, he agreed we had no choice."

"Do you know who attacked you?" Jeremy asked. He had hero-ically held his tongue while Laura tended to Hara's injury, but Laura knew he was itching to investigate.

Lizzy shook her head. "They jumped on us in an alley off the square. Hara fought them off but took a knife to the arm."

"Much the same happened to my husband," Laura said. She looked from Lizzy Delaney to Jeremy and Judith. "Jeremy and Judith Roth. Judith is the cousin of my stepson, Malcolm Rannoch. Jeremy is her husband and a Bow Street runner."

She wasn't sure how Lizzy would react to this, but her eyes widened in relief. "Oh, thank goodness. We need all the help we can get." She cast a quick glance at the mantel clock. "We left the children at the hotel with their nurse. Our children. That is, Hara's technically, but now they're mine. A lot has changed in the past six months." She looked at Laura. "I understand why Hara couldn't write to you about our marriage. There really wasn't time, and it's difficult to describe an elopement." Her strong dark brows tightened. "Hara won't be happy with me for saying that, but there's no sense in pretending it wasn't an elopement when it was. Not that I wanted it to be an elopement, but my father obviously wasn't going to consent, so there weren't a lot of options. At least, that's what I told Hara. I threatened to simply move in with him and refuse to leave if he wouldn't agree to something more permanent."

"Brava," Judith said. "I had to do much the same with Jeremy. And it's worked splendidly."

Jeremy drew a breath.

"Argue at your peril," Judith said.

"I wouldn't dare."

"Well, then." She reached for his hand and folded it between her own.

"I'm sorry," Lizzy said. "For pulling you into this. But we didn't have a lot of options."

"Nonsense," Laura said. "I'm glad you came to us. We'd want to see you in any case, but it's clearly important. Assuming you were on your way to see us in the middle of the night before you were attacked, and you didn't simply decide to come here because you were in a crisis. Which I'd also understand."

"No, we were coming to you. Hara said we could trust you, though he hadn't seen you in years. And we weren't sure whom else to turn to."

Laura looked at Jeremy and Judith. "Hara and I were childhood friends. Best friends. We went everywhere together."

"Hara says you were much braver than he was," Lizzy said.

"I ran more risks, but that may have been because I was less afraid of the consequences if I were caught." Laura turned back to Jeremy and Judith. "Hara's father is a British officer who went out to India in the last century. In the days when it wasn't considered so scandalous for a British officer to marry an Indian woman. Hara's mother is the daughter of the Rajah of Kolmara. His parents lived near us and his father was my father's second in command. But by the time Hara grew up and followed his father into the army, the options for a half-Indian were limited."

"And it's only got worse," Lizzy said. "Things are appalling in India now."

"I was in the army myself," Jeremy said. "In the Peninsula. But I've served with men who were posted to India. I've heard enough to understand."

Lizzy looked at him for a moment. "Roth. I didn't make the connection. But Mrs. O'Roarke has written to Hara about you. Your sister is Harriet?"

"Yes." Jeremy's mouth tightened and his brows rose. "How do you know about my sister?"

"Mrs. O'Roarke wrote to Hara about all her family and friends. Hara shared the letters with me."

"Wellesley—Wellington now—and Hara's father were friends," Laura said, returning to the previous topic to spare Jeremy from having to talk about Harriet. "But he refused to promote Hara on general principles. No matter how many times my own father tried to intercede."

"How appalling," Judith said. "It makes me never want to speak to Uncle Arthur again."

Lizzy stared at her. "He's your uncle?"

"Honorary uncle." Judith sat back on her heels in a froth of pink tulle and ivory lace. "He's a family friend. My mother knows everyone." By which Judith meant everyone in the beau monde and Continental elite. "I remember him telling me stories about

India when I was little. It sounded quite exotic. But I never realized—I'm going to be very cross with him the next time I see him."

"That won't work, Judith," Jeremy said.

Judith looked up at him. "Why not? Don't you believe one
should speak out against injustice?"

"He'll tell you that you don't understand such things and
metaphorically pat you on the head."

"He'll get clouted if he does. Metaphorically speaking. Or not. I
know you think my family's position is quite appalling, but I don't
see why I shouldn't be able to put it to use."

"I quite agree," Lizzy said. "Through it's got harder and harder
to accomplish anything. I grew up in India, as you did," she said to
Laura. "My father was deployed to your father's old garrison two
years ago. That was where I met Hara. My father didn't notice our
friendship for the longest time. Hara was an officer in the
garrison and that made him unexceptionable. Until suddenly they
forbade me to see him. So something drastic was called for. Hara
took a lot of persuading."

"I can imagine," Laura said. Hara had always been cautious.
He'd grown up in a life balanced on a knife's point.

"He was planning a trip to England. His parents are settling
here and he's decided to leave the army himself. I told him I
couldn't bear for him to leave without me." She glanced down at
her husband, then round the group. "We'd already declared
ourselves, but then he had gentlemanly scruples. I suspect you'll
understand."

"All too well," Judith said.

"It was silly. It's not as though I'm a child in the schoolroom.
I'm three-and-twenty and perfectly capable of knowing my own
mind. So I had to tell him if he wouldn't take me with him I'd
simply run after him on my own." Lizzy looked down at her
husband and smoothed his hair. "That woke him up enough to
take me seriously. I slipped off and met him, and we left with the
children and were married in Calcutta. Really, for an elopement, it

wasn't so dramatic. Well, except for the part where Gerald came after us and threatened to call Hara out."

"Gerald?" Laura said.

"My elder brother. Who appears to think that gives him the same sort of dominion some countries like to claim over other countries. I must say Hara was splendid. He simply refused to fight Gerald. Gerald said, then, Hara wasn't a gentleman. And Hara said, no one in the garrison had ever thought he was, so why on earth should he follow some antiquated rules?"

"That sounds like Hara," Laura said. "The Hara I grew up with."

Lizzy met her gaze. "I think he found a bit of himself again. Gerald said I was lost to the family and I said I was quite happy to be lost, and in any case, Hara and I were already married and I might very well be with child. That shut Gerald up and we were able to get on the ship. It seemed as though we'd escaped, but that's when things really started to get complicated."

"Started?" Jeremy said.

Lizzy nodded. "The voyage was peaceful, mostly. Crowded, but we had each other. The children thought it was a great adventure and it was easy to get caught up in their excitement. Then, the night we docked, we stayed at an inn in Southampton. Hara heard something that changed everything." She cast a quick glance round the room.

"You can trust Jeremy and Judith," Laura said. "And if you were hoping to tell Raoul and Mélanie and Malcolm, they'll be back soon and we can update them. But they'd share this with us, in any case."

Lizzy nodded. "It was George Wilcox." She spoke quickly, but at the same time seemed to be choosing her words with care. "He'd been in the garrison, but he left India before we did. He was in Southampton to meet someone. Or so he said. He and Hara had never been particular friends, but he was eager to catch up. Soldiers will say things. Sometimes it's a boast to show how much inside information they have. And goodness knows drink loosens tongues. Still, Wilcox usually showed more sense. Not that he said it in front of me. He and Hara were drinking in the taproom after I took the children up. They hadn't spoken in a long time, and according to Hara, they'd consumed quite a bit of brandy. But usually there's a great deal of deference to Wellington among all soldiers. Of course, Wilcox said he knew Hara would understand because of how Wellington had treated him. Which isn't true, precisely. Hara's never denied Wellington's brilliance, whatever his personal thoughts. He's much fairer about him than I am."

"Wilcox said something about Wellington?" Laura asked.

"Hara can still scarcely credit it." Lizzy stared at her hands, then closed her fingers on her elbows. "Nor can I."

"We'll take whatever it is under advisement," Jeremy said.

Lizzy looked up at him and held his gaze, soldier's daughter speaking to a soldier. "Wilcox claimed Wellington was involved in a plot to kill one of his colleagues."

CHAPTER 14

"What?" Judith said on a note of disbelief. The disbelief of one who thought of the Duke of Wellington as a sort of indulgent uncle.

"Did he say why?" Jeremy asked.

Judith swung her head round to look at her husband. "You believe it?" she asked.

"I think we need to know the reasons behind the accusation before we can remotely begin to assess whether to believe it or not."

"Hara asked him," Lizzy said. "Wilcox would just say, who knew what went on in the minds of generals. Which made no sense at all. When Hara pressed him, he said he needed another drink and went into the coffee room. When he didn't return after twenty minutes, Hara went after him, only to find he'd left the inn. Hara told me in the morning. We could scarcely credit it. I mean"—she looked at Judith for a moment—"I don't know Wellington as well as you, but I met him when I was a girl. My father fought under him. Not that I agree with my father about everything. Well, not about most things. And when I realized how Wellington had blocked Hara's preferment, I was furious. But this was hard to accept. Of the man I'd met. Of the man I'd grown up hearing about. Hara said the same." Lizzy reached out and touched her husband's hair. "But we couldn't ignore it. Not if there was any chance it was true, or even if Wilcox said it for some other reason. We had to get to the bottom of it. In the end, we decided to come to you." She looked at Laura. "Hara knew the investigations you and your husband undertake with the Rannochs. He said we could trust you. We came to London and settled the children at an hotel with their nurse and then came directly here. We didn't want to waste a moment." She looked down at her husband. "I think we were both hoping we'd be reassured by whatever you said. Then, on the way, we were attacked."

"Which rather confirms your suspicions," Judith said.

"It confirms something," Jeremy said. "Certainly that you are in danger. Do you have anything to identify the men who attacked you?"

Lizzy frowned. Laura gripped her hand. "One was taller, not quite as tall as you, Mr. Roth, but taller than Hara. The other was an inch or so shorter than Hara and more stoutly built. They were both dark-haired, but the taller man's hair had a touch of gray. And the shorter man had a scar over his left eye."

"You have a keen eye, Mrs. Delaney. Thank you. That can't have been easy to recall."

"I can scarcely forget it." Lizzy looked from Jeremy to Laura. "I don't want to pry, but could this have anything to do with why your husband and the Rannochs are out tonight? I mean, given the hour, I assume it's—"

"A case?" Laura said. "It is. But it appears to be of a personal nature. One can never be sure, but I doubt there's a connection." She kept her voice steady and didn't glance at Jeremy and Judith. They'd protect Harriet's privacy as long as they could.

Lizzy's gaze moved round the group. "So you don't have reason to think Wellington is involved in anything?"

"No," Laura said.

"Though if he were, we likely wouldn't know," Judith said. She looked from Laura to Jeremy. "I mean, he's a friend of Mama's and Malcolm used to work with him on intelligence missions, but his politics are miles away from Malcolm and Julien and the rest of them. None of us moves in Tory circles, and even if Hubert Mallinson knew, I doubt he'd tell Julien." She gripped her hands together. "I'm not saying I believe it—I'm not sure what to believe. But I certainly don't think any of us would know if it were true."

"Well stated," Jeremy said.

"They'll know how to investigate, though," Judith said to Lizzy, with the conviction of one who had been on the fringe of numerous investigations without necessarily knowing the details. "If anyone can get to the bottom of this, it's Mélanie and Malcolm and everyone else. Including Jeremy, of course."

Jeremy smiled despite the gravity of the night. "Thank you, my love. Generally, I turn to the Rannochs and their friends when investigations tinge on politics. This will call for delicate inquiries."

"Is the other case very serious?" Lizzy asked.

"I'm not sure," Jeremy said. "But on a personal level, it feels serious indeed."

MÉLANIE UNLOCKED the door of the Berkeley Square house and opened it to let the others in. They had only been gone a matter of hours, though it felt like days. The sky was still dark. The children would have slept through everything—at least, she hoped they had —though Jeremy must be gnashing his teeth, and she suspected even Laura's usually iron calm was strained.

A candle still glowed on the console table in the hall and light showed from the library. Laura came through the door from the library as Mélanie and the others stepped into the hall. "Thank goodness." Laura cast a quick glance at her husband as though assuring herself he was unhurt. She smiled at Julien and Kitty but showed no surprise at their returning with the others. In their family, it really wasn't surprising. "No more difficulties?"

They'd sent word twice from Hubert's that they'd been delayed, though not about Malcolm's disappearance.

"I just took a slight detour seeing the Countess Lieven home," Malcolm said.

Laura studied him in the candlelight. "You have a mark on your forehead."

"He was knocked out and abducted at gunpoint," Mélanie said.

"Just a misunderstanding," Malcolm said. "Someone wanted to talk to me."

Jeremy and Judith emerged from the library. "What did Gresham say?" Jeremy demanded without preamble. And then frowned as he took in Julien and Kitty.

"We weren't able to talk to him." Mélanie took a step towards the library. "Perhaps we should—"

"We've had other visitors," Laura said. "A lot to explain, but perhaps you should tell us about Harriet first."

A dozen questions shot thorough Mélanie's mind. She cast a quick glance at Malcolm, then said, "We didn't find Harriet or Gresham, but we found a man dead in Gresham's rooms."

"*What?*" Jeremy said.

"Gresham was gone," Malcolm said. "There was no sign of him in the room. Or of Harriet." He hesitated a moment.

"But there was a sign she *had* been there?" Jeremy said.

"We found her earring," Kitty said. "She seems to have left with Gresham. But for the moment, the important thing is the dead man."

"He's a noted assassin for hire," Julien said.

"You know him?" Jeremy asked.

Julien gave a faint smile. "We've crossed paths. Not recently."

Jeremy stared at them. "An assassin was killed in Gresham's rooms and Harriet fled the scene of a murder with Gresham?"

"Not necessarily," Julien said. "We don't know it was the scene of a murder when they fled."

"They may have left St. James Place before LeFou was killed," Malcolm said.

"They being Harriet and Gresham."

"They appear to be together," Kitty said.

"And they could have gone anywhere." Jeremy's hands had curled inwards.

"We're looking," Malcolm said.

"Did you—"

"We collected evidence. Not as well as you'd have done, but we managed."

Jeremy's eyes narrowed. "I'm sure you did a damn good job. But—" He spun round and smashed his fist down on the console table.

"Darling." Judith righted the candle before it could tip over. "You can't do this."

He swung round to look at her. "You mean I can't be objective."

"I mean it's not safe. Not if what they say is true. And for now we have to assume it is."

"LeFou was after Gresham."

"Not necessarily," Mélanie said.

"What else was he doing there? You think Gresham hired him?"

"Unlikely, but possible," Julien said.

"He seduced my sister."

"We don't know that," Mélanie said.

"Why on earth else—"

"I've gone traveling with men I wasn't involved with," she said. That was probably a mistake. It might raise questions she didn't want to answer.

"So have I," Kitty said. "If they realized they were in danger,

96

they might well have decided to flee and that they were safer together."

"But why not come to us?"

"Perhaps they wanted to protect us," Judith said.

"*Us?*" Jeremy stared at his wife.

"Well, you can certainly be idiotish about protecting those you love. Perhaps Harriet follows the family trait."

"If they had to run, it would be risky to hide with any of us," Kitty said. "They may have thought their best course of action was to disappear."

Judith put a hand on Jeremy's arm. "I know it's hard to be sidelined. Believe me. Because it's usually what happens to me."

"Not if you can help it."

"A fair point," Judith conceded.

"No word from Harriet here, I take it?" Malcolm said.

"No," Laura said. "But our new guests have some disturbing news to share. Come into the library."

More lamps and candles were lit in the library than when they'd left. And a man now lay on the sofa nearest the door, dark hair showing above a blanket. Apparently asleep. Or unconscious? A chestnut-haired young woman sat beside him, holding his hand, back very straight, eyes dark with anxiety beneath dark brows.

"Hara Delaney," Laura said. "My childhood friend, whom you've heard me talk about. And his wife Lizzy. Hara was attacked in the street on their way here."

"Wounded?" Mélanie noted her medical supply box on the table by the sofa.

"He took a knife cut to the arm," Laura said. "I stitched it. He's still asleep, but he seems easier."

Lizzy Delaney pushed herself to her feet. "We're sorry to have pulled you into this."

Mélanie smiled at the younger woman. "Don't worry, people are always pulling us into things."

"When they hear the story, they'll be glad they were pulled into it," Laura said. She introduced the others and then suggested everyone sit. Odd, Mélanie thought, settling into a Queen Anne chair with Malcolm, on a night when they had been through so much, to feel as though they were bystanders about to hear something even more startling. Odd to think what it could be.

And then Lizzy recounted her story.

CHAPTER 15

"*W*ell," Julien said. "This changes things."

"To put it mildly," Kitty added.

"And yet you don't look shocked," Lizzy said.

"I wouldn't quite say that," Malcolm said.

"Are you saying you knew about this?" Jeremy asked.

"No." Malcolm cast a glance at Mélanie, then at Raoul. But at this point, it was difficult to try to keep anything secret from any of those in this room. "As we told Laura and Jeremy and Judith, tonight we went to see a man named Tristram Gresham. We didn't find Gresham, but we found a man murdered in his rooms. A noted assassin named André LeFou."

"They also found Kitty and me," Julien said. "We were there because my uncle asked us to be. Uncle Hubert has led British intelligence for years and a number of us who used to work for him find it difficult to disentangle ourselves completely. He was having LeFou followed and got concerned when he got a report that LeFou went into Gresham's rooms and didn't emerge."

Jeremy's fingers had curled into fists. Judith took his hand and pulled him down beside her.

"Uncle Hubert was concerned," Julien said, "because he had

intelligence that LeFou had been hired by someone in the British government."

Lizzy Delaney gasped. "I'd been thinking it was all a misunderstanding until now."

"It still could be," Raoul said. He was sitting on the arm of Laura's chair with his usual catlike stillness.

Kitty looked at Malcolm. "I don't hear you denying Wellington could be behind it."

"Because I can't categorically do so," Malcolm said. "And in any case, my instincts don't matter. We need to be objective about all possible suspects."

"We can't rule people out," Raoul agreed. "Especially based on personal ties. On the other hand, your instincts are keen. And invaluable. I never ignore them and you shouldn't either."

"Are you asking what my instincts are about Wellington?" Malcolm said. His gaze was steady and open, yet Mélanie could tell how he'd armored himself against discussing the past. "He can engender a great deal of loyalty. I wasn't immune to that, though events in the past years have strained the ties. Not so much because he's changed as because I see more clearly. He's certainly capable of being ruthless. I've seen that time and again. And he's a keen strategist. But he's the sort to confront an enemy head on, not stab them in the back. Which doesn't mean he isn't capable of employing unorthodox tactics." He looked round the group. "But I'm not the only one here who knows him."

"I remember him mostly in India," Laura said. She glanced at Hara, lying still beneath the blanket.

"When you were a child," Kitty said.

"Depends upon one's definition. I was only thirteen when he went out to India, but I was two-and-twenty when he left, though I certainly had growing up left to do. Wellington's only fourteen years my senior. I remember my father and him having long talks round the dinner table, which I managed to listen in on more than once. He was very interested in my father's insights into the Indian rulers. Including Hara's mother's father. But he didn't pay as much heed to my father's suggestion that we needed to consider the situation of ordinary Indians. Not only for the sake of common humanity, which mattered a great deal to my father, but also because of the risk of uprising." She looked at Hara again. "And Wellington was quite capable of appreciating Hara's qualities, yet at the same time thinking it would contravene an uncrossable line if he promoted Hara. That sort of compartmentalization can let people justify all sorts of things."

"I only met him once or twice, when I was very small," Lizzy said. "I can't claim to know him. My father likes him, but I'm not sure how much of a recommendation that is. Still—" She rubbed her arms.

"He got frustrated by his superiors," Kitty said. "I remember him cheerfully telling me at a regimental ball that, all things considered, life would be much easier if he could simply kill a guerrillero leader who was causing difficulties. It was a joke, followed by his usual bluff laugh. But there was a look in his eyes that said he was partly in earnest. If he were convinced there was only one way to accomplish something—I don't think it likely, but I can't say it's impossible."

"What can one say is impossible?" Julien leant back against the arm of the settee, where he was perched beside Kitty. "I don't recall hearing that he ever expressed regrets over the five thousand drowned in the Malpoorba. He's the sort who can compartmentalize who are the enemy and who are allies. Though he's sophisticated enough to know those can change. But if he persuaded himself someone was the enemy—"

"It's harder to see him turning on his own," Mélanie said. "But he was angry enough at George Chase I think he'd cheerfully have killed him."

"You think he learnt someone in the British government was a murderer?" Kitty said.

"No. At least, I don't think so. But if he'd convinced himself someone in the British government was the enemy—"

"Of course it's not impossible," Judith said in a quiet voice. "I mean, he's Uncle Arthur. I remember him giving me sweetmeats and swinging me up in the air. But just about anyone is capable of just about anything. Isn't that what you're all always saying?"

"Not precisely," Malcolm said. "But yes, one can never be sure of what anyone might do."

"Exactly." Judith locked her hands together, shoulders backboard straight, gaze agate-hard. "So we can't be sure about Uncle Arthur. And you've all made an excellent case of what he might do."

"You all make a good case for his guilt," Raoul agreed. "What's the case against?"

"Someone could be trying to set him up," Mélanie said. "Wilcox conveniently showed up at the inn where Lieutenant Delaney and his family were staying and dropped the information. Then he promptly disappeared."

"You think it was all a setup?" Lizzy Delaney asked.

"I'm not sure what I think," Mélanie said. "But it wouldn't be hard for someone to learn your husband knew Laura and was likely to come to us with information like this."

"And then?" Kitty said. "What would be the point?"

"What, indeed?" Raoul said.

"To sow distrust," Julien said. "To have us suspecting Wellington, when in fact someone very different is behind this. Even another country, possibly. Which could also be the point behind Josef Hauke's elaborate attempt to make it look as though he was putting Malcolm off the scent."

"Are you saying you think Austria might be behind this after all?" Judith asked.

"I'm saying they could be," Julien said. "Just about anyone could be, based on what we know at this point. For all we've learnt tonight, we haven't really eliminated anyone."

"And Harriet?" Jeremy said. "You think she just happened to be with Gresham when all of this occurred?"

"I very much doubt Harriet just happened to be anywhere," Mélanie said. "She's far too self-possessed."

"But why on earth would she—" Jeremy bit back the words. Discussing why his sister might be entangled with Tristram Gresham was clearly not ground he wanted to explore in front of so large a group.

Lizzy Delaney, who seemed very adept, for all her youth, cast a quick look at Jeremy, eyes warm with sympathy, then turned to Malcolm. "You know Wellington. You've worked with him. Surely there are people you can reach out to."

"There are," Malcolm said. "And I'll do so at first light. What I'll be able to determine is another story."

"I have great faith in you, Mr. Rannoch. Hara told me all the things Laura wrote about you."

Malcolm grinned and cast a look at Laura. "Laura is brilliant. But she is a novelist. She knows how to spin a tale."

"Not about you," Laura said.

Lizzy cast a glance round the group. "You've trusted us with a great deal. Well, me. But Hara will learn when he recovers."

"We don't have a lot of choice," Julien said with a friendly grin. "You're already in the midst of it. We're all going to need to work together."

"But we can't be sure whom else we can trust," Malcolm said. "We'll have to go carefully. All of us."

"You sound like Uncle Hubert," Julien said.

"At times, your uncle has sound advice."

"Perish the thought."

"Darling," Kitty said.

"Oh, all right. I'd be an idiot not to admit we can't trust Whitehall and Westminster. But how is that different from any investigation we've undertaken?"

"We have likely evidence they're working against us," Raoul said.

Julien met his gaze in the candle-warmed air. "You're worried."

"I'm cautious. It's not quite the same thing."

"Christ, O'Roarke, if you're talking caution, this is serious indeed." Julien waved a hand. "No, I don't quite mean that. You're always careful of those you care about. Of collateral damage in general. But surely you know we can never be sure where we'll find adversaries."

"True enough. But I've never seen Hubert as concerned as he was tonight."

"I've worried about the home office," Jeremy said. "I've worried about Sidmouth. But not on this level. It's hard for me to think about anything but Harriet right now, but the larger picture is alarming." He drew a breath.

"You can't," Malcolm said. "You can't take any part in this investigation. You can't tell anyone at Bow Street what you know. In fact, you'd do much better saying you're ill or family issues prevent you from being on duty."

Jeremy drew in and released his breath.

"He's right, darling," Judith said.

"My sister's missing," Jeremy said. "And a man's been murdered. If anyone know what needs to be done—"

"You do," Mélanie said. "And you can tell us. But we're all going to have to be acting outside official channels."

"You're very like my husband," Lizzy said. "Hara hates to be sidelined. But he's had to learn he needs to stay out of the way, so many times."

"He has things to deal with that I don't," Jeremy said. He looked round the group. "Do you think LeFou's target is still at risk?"

A crossfire of glances followed. "Probably," Malcolm said. "In the end. Though this has certainly put a spoke in the plan."

"Unless the plan was a setup from the first," Julien said.

"You mean it was all meant to look as though it was an attack?" Lizzy asked. "Wilcox was setting up and hiring Mr. LeFou, and then killing him was part of the same plan?"

"It's a possibility," Julien said. "Difficult to imagine a person with LeFou's talents being caught in such a net, but we can all make mistakes."

"We know he was seen talking to Karl Augustin," Mélanie said. "I can at least talk to Charlotte Augustin."

Jeremy's gaze swung to her. "You said she's Gresham's mistress?"

"Dorothea Lieven said Charlotte Augustin had been his mistress. Even Dorothea's gossip isn't entirely reliable."

"But in the end—damn it, where the hell is Harriet?" Jeremy scraped a hand over his hair. "I realize we have a murder and a possible plot within the British government. But Harriet's missing, with a man I don't trust, from the rooms where a murder took place."

"Could Wellington have targeted Lord Gresham?" Lizzy asked.

"Possible, but unlikely," Malcolm said. "As we've discussed, I can imagine Wellington involved in a plot to have someone killed. But it was more Castlereagh who saw Gresham as a threat. Wellington isn't as focused on Italy."

"Uncle Hubert's the main one who saw Gresham as a threat," Julien said. "But Gresham's politics certainly don't align with Wellington's."

Kitty set down her coffee cup. "I don't think—" Her voice was uncharacteristically soft. She swallowed, then as everyone turned to her, her gaze swept the group. It was rare to see such uncertainty in her eyes. But typically for Kitty, the uncertainty was followed by resolution. "Whatever Harriet's relationship with Gresham, I think we're wrong to assume she was simply with him in his room for whatever reason, and caught up in his attacking LeFou or running from LeFou. I think Harriet may be much more connected to whatever is happening than we realize."

CHAPTER 16

*J*ulien went still, looking at his wife.

Kitty folded her hands. "I was going to tell you all earlier. But I didn't want to in front of Hubert. And then Malcolm was missing. And then when we got to Berkeley Square we learnt about the attack on Mr. Delaney."

"There's been a lot to take in," Raoul said, gaze steady on Kitty.

Kitty nodded. "And all of it urgent. But this could be important as well. I have an idea of how Harriet might have been connected to Gresham. And why she may have disappeared."

"You intrigue me," Julien said.

Kitty cast a look at him. "We don't—"

"Share everything. Quite."

Kitty's fingers tightened. The ruby ring Julien had given her when they married—upstairs in the Berkeley Square drawing room—stood out bloodred against her whitened knuckles. "Have you heard of *Le Monde Gris*?"

"I read it regularly," Raoul said.

"So do I," Mélanie said. It was a newspaper—or more a pamphlet—filled with reports from Radicals in various countries. Even with her background, she was surprised at some of the data

Le Monde Gris gathered. "Did Harriet write for it?" She wouldn't be entirely surprised to find Harriet writing for a Radical publication. Harriet and Jeremy had grown up with parents who were Radical booksellers and Harriet had made no secret of her politics. But the articles in *Le Monde Gris* were from round the world and clearly rang with veracity. Harriet had never, to Mélanie's knowledge, traveled further than Edinburgh.

"Harriet publishes it," Kitty said.

Mélanie stared at her friend. So obvious. Why was she surprised? And yet—

"My word," Julien said.

"What?" Jeremy said.

"It makes sense, darling." Judith gripped his arm. "She's always writing."

"Of course she is." Jeremy turned to his wife. "She has a wide correspondence and she writes things to teach the boys and—oh, my god."

"She has her own life," Judith said. "She just happens to live with us. But that doesn't mean she shares it with us. She was under no obligation to do so."

"But she's here," Jeremy said. "In England."

"She gathers information from contacts all over the world," Kitty said. "Some of it smuggled out. Much of it smuggled out. She puts it together and has it printed and distributed."

"Edmund Blayney," Malcolm said.

"How did you know?" Kitty asked.

"Partly a lucky guess. But I've seen Harriet at their house and print shop more than once. I assumed it was because she and Pippa have become friends and she takes the boys over to play with Pippa's daughters. Fatal mistake not to think of the obvious. And to assume activities are domestic."

"Especially women's activities," Kitty said.

"Quite."

"How did it start?" Raoul asked.

"I'm not sure." Kitty smoothed her hands over her lap. "I wasn't involved when she started. I know because she came to me asking if I had stories from the Argentine or Spain I wanted to get out. Given the challenges the last time I tried to publish articles smuggled out of Spain"—she cast a quick glance at Julien, but none of them needed reminding of the night she'd been wounded—"having a newspaper with a distribution system already was a lifeline." She looked round the others. "Harriet asked me to keep it quiet. She said it was safer for Jeremy not to know, and therefore it was better his friends didn't know."

Jeremy grimaced.

"You had no reason to tell us," Malcolm said.

"No," Mélanie agreed.

"Certainly not," Raoul said.

"We all assume we have secrets," Julien said. "Things have been quiet enough lately, I think we may have forgot that."

A smile broke through the tension in Kitty's face. "Thank you, darling."

"I must say, I'm impressed with Harriet," Julien added. "I always suspected there was more to her, but I didn't quite envision this."

"She was getting stories from Gresham?" Malcolm asked.

"I think she was," Kitty said. "Our only conversations were about the stories I gave her. She was scrupulously careful not to betray a source. But Gresham had contacts with Radicals in Italy and France. I assumed he was giving her stories. In fact, it seems far more likely to me than that they were lovers. Though I suppose the two aren't mutually exclusive."

"Which makes one wonder if LeFou went there to silence a story," Malcolm said.

"Paid by the British government?" Mélanie asked.

Malcolm folded his arms and leant back against the arm of the Queen Anne chair. "An interesting thought. I can certainly imagine the British government trying to silence a story. Depending on whom and what it touched on."

"You're suggesting someone in the British government hired LeFou to kill Gresham and Harriet Roth because they had information on Radical activities?" Julien said. "Surely the government would be more likely to want to learn about the Radical activities."

"Perhaps Gresham and Harriet had stumbled across something damaging to the government," Kitty said.

"Bringing in a foreign assassin still seems odd," Julien said. "That reeks of something involving another country."

"I think—" Lizzy Delaney spoke up softly, but with determination. "I think I can shed some light on this." All gazes swung to her. Lizzy drew a breath but continued speaking, voice steady. "I know about *Le Monde Gris*. Copies found their way to India. I was impressed. To see what people were doing in countries round the world. Many fighting the same battles we were in India. Or that we should be. There were even articles about India, though written by someone in England."

"Cressy," Jeremy said.

"I suspect so," Kitty said.

"She's a childhood friend of Harriet's and mine," Jeremy said to Lizzy. "Her mother was Indian, her father British. Like Hara. She recently married William Beardsley, who sits in the House of Commons with Malcolm and shares his politics," he added, glossing neatly over the fact that before she married Beardsley, Cressida had been one of London's most successful courtesans.

If tales of Cressida's notoriety had reached India, Lizzy gave no sign of it. "Her articles were excellent. But one couldn't help but want to hear voices from people in India now. It's so hard to find a way to speak out."

Mélanie studied the younger woman, recalling articles from a recent issue of *Le Monde Gris*. "You wrote articles for *Le Monde Gris*."

"I wrote one or two. Hara wrote more." Lizzy looked at her

husband, then back at the others. "He said it was time he found his voice again after being silent for too long." She looked at Laura. "He said you'd always been quicker to speak out than he had."

"It was easier for me," Laura said. "I was the colonel's daughter. And I didn't do it in a very focused way. Not then, at least."

Lizzy nodded. "I think it made Hara feel better to find a way to strike back. But people had started to suspect he was behind the last article he wrote. It made it even more imperative to leave." She glanced round the group. "Could this have to do with why Wilcox found Hara? I can't quite put the pieces together. But we wrote pieces for *Le Monde Gris*. Wilcox warned Hara that Wellington had hired an assassin. And then an assassin supposedly hired by someone in the British government was killed where Harriet had just been, and Hara had been writing articles for Harriet."

"Do you think Harriet is the assassin's target?" Judith asked.

Jeremy stared at her.

"It's a good question," Julien said. "I've heard Uncle Hubert rail against *Le Monde Gris*. And if he is, I'm sure others in the government are."

"Julien." Jeremy stared at him with ravaged eyes. "Did you just suggest the Duke of Wellington might be behind a plot to kill my sister?"

"No," Julien said. "Not precisely. We don't even know for a certainty Wellington is behind this. And the suggestion is that it's a plot to kill someone in the government. Which most certainly wouldn't include Harriet. More's the pity. I mean, more's the pity that she's not part of the government. She's far more sensible than most members of the current government. But anyone who knew Harriet was behind *Le Monde Gris* could certainly see a reason to get rid of her."

"You're always so straightforward, Julien," Judith said. "You're quite right being known as the editor of *Le Monde Gris* would put her in danger. And that's all the more reason she wouldn't have told us about it." She twisted her head round to look at her husband, gold ringlets and diamond earrings swinging in the candlelight.

"I understand," Jeremy said. "That is, the part of my brain that can be logical understands. The part that isn't panicked about where Harriet is, and what she's doing, and what she's facing. The small part that isn't flooded by fear thinks my sister is bloody brilliant."

Julien leant over the sofa table and clapped Jeremy on the shoulder. "Good for you, Roth."

Jeremy gave an abashed smile, though the worry never left his eyes. He turned back to the group. "We seem to be in the midst of an investigation where my ability to investigate is limited. Again."

The echoes of the investigation into his first wife's death hung over them. "I'll talk to Harry first thing tomorrow," Malcolm said. "Today, rather." He glanced at the predawn glow through the windows, then looked at Lizzy. "Harry Davenport used to work in military intelligence. He has connections close to Wellington. And he and his wife Cordelia often investigate with us."

"I'll ask Cordy to help me set up a meeting with Charlotte Augustin," Mélanie said. "It will be easier to try to get her to talk about her affair with Gresham with the two of us."

"Julien and I can tell Edmund and Pippa about Harriet," Kitty said. "And at the same time, see if Danielle has news of Gresham." Danielle Darnault, an opera singer and former agent, was currently rehearsing Gresham's latest opera. Her husband Pierre ran a Radical newspaper with Edmund Blayney, and they shared a house with the Blayneys.

Jeremy leant forwards, hands between his knees. "Gresham was a Leveller."

Malcolm returned his gaze. The Levellers tried to avoid putting their friends in Parliament in an awkward situation by telling them too much. "We know."

Jeremy nodded. "And Harriet goes to meetings with me sometimes."

"I can talk to Simon at the theatre," Mélanie said. "It will take a while for Cordelia to reach Charlotte." Their friend, Simon Tanner, was a playwright and part owner of the Tavistock Theatre, where Mélanie's own plays were performed. He was also a noted Radical and part of the Levellers, a Radical group that had begun at the Tavistock, though its members extended beyond it and included Jeremy Roth. And Tristram Gresham.

Laura looked at Lizzy. "I know you want to get back to your children, but you should stay here until morning."

"And then we should send for them, and you should all stay here until we know precisely what is going on," Malcolm said.

Lizzy smiled. For a moment she looked as young as she in fact was. "Thank you."

"I can see if anyone had wind of LeFou's being here," Raoul said. He didn't elaborate on whom he meant to ask, but it was most likely former Bonapartist agents who'd sought refuge in London. Many of whom he and Mélanie had helped settle. "I'm tempted to talk to Liverpool," he added. "But I think I should wait until we know he isn't involved."

Silence fell over the group. Mélanie gripped Malcolm's hand and looked at Raoul. Because in a level, conversational tone, Raoul had just said that before they could warn the prime minister about an assassination plot, they had to be sure the prime minister himself wasn't part of the plot.

Typically, it was Julien who broke the silence. "Well," he said, "that neatly sums up what we're facing. A lot to do."

CHAPTER 17

"*D*arling?" Kitty tucked her hand through Julien's arm as they walked back to Carfax House. Mélanie and Malcolm had invited them to stay in Berkeley Square for what remained of the night, but they'd wanted to be home to look in on the children and be there when they woke.

"Not the night we were expecting." Julien's gaze drifted round the empty street. Seemingly an idle glance, but she knew he had every sense alert for the least sign of disturbance.

"No. Not in the least."

"Keeps life interesting."

Kitty looked sideways at him as they passed through a pool of lamplight. "Harriet came to me in confidence. She wanted to know if I had contacts in Spain or Portugal or South America who wanted their stories published. Which I did. But she said the only way this would work was to keep it entirely secret."

Julien turned from contemplating the shadows round an area railing to meet her gaze. "She was right. No telling where word will spread. Jeremy wouldn't have been able to stay out of it, and he'd have put himself at appalling risk. Any network runs best on only those who need to know having the information. You couldn't have done otherwise. I'd have been disappointed in you if you had told me. And I'm never disappointed in you."

Kitty pressed her head against his shoulder. "Darling."

Julien touched his fingers to her hair. "Are you going to ask me?"

"About what?"

"Dorothea."

She lifted her head to look sideways at him. "Do you want to talk about her?"

"I thought you might have questions."

"I'd look an idiot if I didn't confess to being a bit interested. But we've always said no questions."

"I think we've always said we'd understand. Which isn't quite the same thing."

"Still. No sense in unnecessary questions."

Julien cast a glance down an alley they were passing. "It wasn't particularly serious. But then, nothing in my life was, before you."

"That sounds like the sort of thing people say in plays."

"There's a lot of truth on the stage. Especially if Mélanie or Simon are writing the dialogue." Julien tightened his grip on her arm as they crossed an intersection. "I needed information on Metternich. She wanted to make Metternich jealous, I think. And perhaps she thought she could get information from me. I was pretending to be French."

"But she knows it was you."

"Mmm. Now. She's clever."

"Which is an attraction."

The gates to Carfax House shimmered through the lamplight down the street. "I like her. Though I can't say I'd trust her. She's quite ruthless. Speaking as one who understands the term."

"Do you trust her tonight?"

"You mean, do I think it's possible that whole story was a farrago of lies to distract us because the Russians—or the Austrians—or, I suppose, both together—hired LeFou and she was

114

trying to gauge how much we knew? Or because LeFou attacked one of them and they killed him? It's possible. She looked terrified, but she's a good actress. We talked when I escorted her to the carriage Malcolm had ready in the mews, and her very frankness made me wonder. That, and the fact that Malcolm was abducted just after he saw her home. On the other hand, if one of her allies killed LeFou, why not tell us? We'd have been relieved, overall. Mystery solved, and if she could have told us who in the British government hired LeFou, so much the better. Instead, we're left with a mess where we can trust even fewer people than we thought. Not that I'm ever much inclined to trust the Russians or the Austrians. Or the British government. But it's a damnable thicket being on guard against all of them."

"Not the first time we've been in a thicket, though."

"Not in the least." Julien unlatched the Carfax House gates. They crossed the half-moon forecourt and went into the house through a side door and up two flights of stairs to the second floor. The boys and Genny were all sound asleep. Kitty went to reassure her maid, Dolores, who had been on call in case the children woke while they were out. Dolores had been dozing, but clearly hadn't slept soundly.

Julien was silent when she came into their bedchamber. He'd taken off his coat and waistcoat and was working on his shirt buttons. He stared at his shirt cuff. "Not a bad thing that my old talents can be put to use. They should be good for something."

Kitty closed the door and moved into the room. "We wouldn't have known how LeFou was shot without you."

"We still don't know exactly where the shot was fired from." Julien started on the other shirt cuff. "Just a good guess."

"More a hypothesis."

"Nice way of putting it."

"Honest way of putting it."

"You're being kind."

Kitty moved to her dressing table. "Rot. I'm never kind."

"You just don't admit it. If—Damn." Julien bent down to retrieve a button that had popped off his cuff.

"Give it to me," Kitty said. "I can sew it on in the morning."

"I can sew it myself. I used to do it all the time. It's amazing how easily we forget we can do things for ourselves."

"I don't think you've forgot anything at all."

He turned to look at her, the shadows falling across his face. "If it weren't for you, I could have been the one hired by Wellington or Sidmouth or Liverpool or Castlereagh, or whoever it was, to assassinate someone. I owe you an incalculable amount, sweetheart."

"That's charming, Julien, and like so many charming things, not in the least true. You were already changing before you met me. And I can't imagine you taking on such a foolish mission as this one, whoever is behind it."

"I took on plenty of foolish missions." He dropped the button in a silver dish on his dressing table and watched it bounce round. "And let's be blunt and call this mission, and so many I undertook, what they were. Assassinations."

"When have either of us not been blunt?"

"Well, then."

Kitty took off her cloak and draped it over her dressing table bench. "It's a good point."

"What is?"

"I can't see you being in LeFou's shoes. But if you had been, it's hard to imagine anyone taking you unawares and managing to kill you."

"Anyone can make a mistake."

"True enough. But you're far less liable to make them than others. And if LeFou was even half as clever as you, I'm rather wondering who managed to take him unawares."

Julien's gaze narrowed. "As always, my love, you've focused on the pertinent facts. I didn't know LeFou well. But from what I've seen of him, and from his reputation, this surprises me."

"You think it was another professional?"

"I've wondered that from the first, honestly. Especially given the apparent angle of the shot. But amateurs can unexpectedly take someone unawares. It could have been a lucky accident."

"You wouldn't fall victim to a lucky accident."

"I hope not. If it was a professional, we have someone else sending an agent after LeFou. Which complicates an already over-complicated situation." Julien pulled his shirt over his head and reached for his dressing gown. "I'm not supposed to have a conscience."

"Not supposed by whom?" Kitty asked.

"My father said so."

"Well, then. Since when have you agreed with anything your father said?"

"This may be one of the few things my father and I agreed on. I've never admitted to having a conscience."

"You've never admitted to a lot of things." Kitty leant forwards on her dressing table bench towards him. "Never admitting to having one is entirely different from not having one."

"You could make a fair case that if I had one, I wouldn't have done the things I've done."

"One could make a fair case that if you didn't have one, you wouldn't have said what you just did."

"That's rather convenient, isn't it? To express scruples after the fact, but not act on them?"

"This is hardly the first time you've expressed them."

"I don't—"

"You don't make excuses for yourself. But when Raoul was wounded, you said—"

"I know what I said." Julien turned to the side, away from the light of the branch of candles they'd brought up. "And Malcolm was the one who ended up running the risk." Their doctor friend Geoffrey Blackwell had transferred some of Malcolm's blood to Raoul to save Raoul's life.

"That doesn't change that you were willing to take it."

"There's little point in dwelling on any of it. And whatever I think is hardly relevant."

Kitty kept her gaze on his own in the shadows. She'd always had to look for Julien in the shadows. "It's understandable if this stirs feelings."

"You expect me to admit to feelings?"

"I rather thought that's what we'd both been doing this past year and more."

"Possibly."

Kitty got to her feet and moved to his side. "Julien. I love you. And you aren't the only one with regrets."

He turned his head. The light fell half over his face and caught his twisted smile. "I assume anyone our age has regrets. And I don't pretend to compare. But when I weigh my actions in the scale—not that I'm admitting I do—"

"That's on your conscience," Kitty said. "To the extent you have one. Which I believe you do. I'll only add that it will do no one any good for you to become lost in regret."

"What a ghastly idea. Can you imagine my doing anything of the sort?"

"I should hope not. But we can all be prey to dwelling."

"Put like that—" Julien gathered her to him. "My darling, you've just found a very effective way to tell me I should stop wallowing and get to work."

Laura closed the nursery door. "I'm not sure which of us had a more eventful night."

"Oh, you certainly. I didn't have to stitch anyone back together." Raoul set the candle they'd brought up with them on the chest of drawers.

"I didn't have one of my children abducted. Well, my stepson was abducted. But I didn't even know about it until Malcolm was back."

"It was a challenging hour or so." From Raoul, that was a large admission. Raoul pulled off his coat. A bit slowly. Which told her his back was acting up. And much as he tried to make them all forget it, it was only two months since he'd been seriously wounded. "Mélanie was terrified. And yes, I was too."

Laura went to him and slid her arms round him. "I wish I'd been there."

Raoul pressed a kiss to the top of her head. "You wouldn't have been able to help the Delaneys if you had been."

"No. I've been hoping to see Hara again, but I never expected him to fall, wounded, on the hall floor." Laura drew back and looked up at her husband. "Hara's always been a good friend. I haven't seen him for years. But I trust him."

Raoul nodded. "Of all the people involved in this, he and Lizzy seem among the most reliable."

Laura rubbed her arms. "I haven't been able to speak to him. I didn't know about Lizzy at all. Or about his involvement with *Le Monde Gris*. So much in his life has changed. Yet seeing him took me right back to the girl I was." She glanced towards the door to the nursery, thinking about her daughters. "I don't really like the way I managed things when I was in India. I spoke out, but mostly because I wanted to shock people. I understood injustice, but it was all wrapped up in rebelling against what was expected of me."

"You were a girl."

"I was older than Mélanie is now when I left. But this feels like a chance. To make up for things I wish I'd done. Things I wish I'd framed more articulately."

"I don't think you have anything to apologize for," Raoul said. "But I do know what it is to feel one has to make up for the past."

Laura tilted her head back to lock into her husband's gray eyes. "You always say regret is a singularly useless emotion."

"My darling. Since when do you expect me to follow my own advice?"

~

MÉLANIE LOOKED at her husband across their bedchamber. Not unusual to be confronting danger like this, at the start of an investigation. Yet a few hours ago, when they'd first retired for the night, this had not been the night they'd anticipated. "Hardly worth going to sleep at all."

"We might manage an hour or two." Malcolm shrugged out of his coat.

"You must need—"

"Being hit in the head doesn't make me need more sleep, Mel."

Images she couldn't quite let herself focus on stabbed through her imagination. "I've been on the watch for danger—"

"Don't I know it." He dropped the coat over a chair back.

"But this isn't where I saw it coming."

"No. It always seems to be a surprise. One way or another."

She moved to his side and gripped his arms. "I was scared, darling. Absolutely bloody terrified."

He touched his fingers to her face. "I'll own to being rather alarmed myself. Once I recovered consciousness enough to be aware of anything at all."

"It's not funny, Malcolm."

"It wasn't at the time. It is a bit, now, considering it was just Hauke wanting to have a word with me. Diplomacy can take some odd twists and turns, but I've never faced being abducted."

She leant her forehead against his cheek. "We face risk all the time. You'd think I'd be used to it. There's risk every time you go out the door. But tonight I felt so utterly helpless."

"I'd have felt the same, sweetheart. No way either of us could have known of the danger. It's part of the risk of our lives."

"That sounds like something I'd say."

"You're very wise."

She drew back. She had to find something else to say. Otherwise she was going to lose the ability to speak at all. "I can't believe I didn't see the least hint of what Harriet was doing. I always knew there was a great deal she didn't share, but I never guessed at anything approaching this."

"You, of all people, should be used to how well a person can conceal a secret occupation, sweetheart."

She managed a smile. "That's the most understated way I've heard espionage referred to, darling."

"It's certainly an occupation."

Mélanie cast her mind back through moments with Harriet. "I can understand why she didn't want Jeremy to know. It's not safe for him. But I'm wondering—"

"If Simon knows?" Malcolm said.

"He'd be a natural ally in this," Mélanie said. "Jeremy said as much. And Harriet could have met Gresham through Simon."

"She could. It's good you're going to see Simon tomorrow. And I suppose, in this case, we can worry a bit less about what Hubert knows."

In addition to being part owner of the Tavistock Theatre, where Mélanie's plays were performed, Simon was also the lover of David Mallinson, Hubert's son. Which complicated things. Though Hubert was much more accepting of the relationship now than he'd once been. "No," she said. "Though we don't want Hubert to know about *Le Monde Gris.*"

"Definitely not. Assuming he doesn't know already. Assuming Hubert isn't actually behind this. Though for once he seems to be an ally, and all the clues point in another direction."

"I'm sorry," Mélanie said. "About Wellington. I know this can't be easy to confront."

Malcolm shrugged. "If I had illusions about him, they started to tarnish long ago. I don't want my personal feelings to interfere, but I'll do my best to be clear-eyed. I'll talk to Harry in the morning." He glanced at the gray light already seeping through the windows. "He can make inquiries among other officers."

Mélanie nodded. She was quite sure there were still things Malcolm could say to Harry Davenport that he couldn't say to her. Such as what it meant to suspect Wellington, who had played such a part in both Malcolm's and Harry's lives. And who had led the army that defeated her cause once and for all.

"We're lucky to have friends," she said.

"Yes," Malcolm said. "And for this investigation, I think we're going to need all of them."

CHAPTER 18

Kitty took off her bonnet in the sitting room above the print shop of the house Danielle Darnault and Pierre Ducroix and their daughter shared with Edmund and Pippa Blayney and their children. "I'm sorry. I know it's early." She and Julien had left Carfax House at hour when they normally wouldn't be awake.

"Don't apologize." Danielle Darnault gave a surprisingly cheerful grin. She rarely woke before ten, but despite the early hour she looked ridiculously lovely, her chestnut hair artfully tousled in a way that would take some lady's maids hours to perfect, a paisley shawl slipping at an elegant angle over the shoulders of her white muslin gown. "It's quite like old times. I must say, I miss getting up at dawn for something other than Ilia having a bad dream." She scanned their faces. "I assume this is urgent. Pippa and Edmund are making coffee, but can Pierre and I help you before they join us?"

Julien leant forwards in his chair. He had known Danielle as a fellow agent for years before Kitty met her. "When did you last hear from Tristram Gresham?"

Danielle's brows rose. "Yesterday afternoon at rehearsal. Has something happened to him?" Her voice was level but Kitty caught the stretched-wire tension beneath.

"He's missing," Kitty said. "And we found a dead body in his rooms."

"André LeFou," Julien added.

"What was he doing there?" Danielle asked. She would know perfectly well who LeFou was.

"I think it's usually plain what LeFou is doing anywhere," Julien said.

"Are you suggesting Gresham killed LeFou?" Pierre asked.

"It's one possibility," Julien said. "But not the likeliest. We think Gresham may have fled first."

"He wouldn't," Danielle said. "Not with the formal opening so soon." Gresham's opera, *Liliana*, had had a few performances in the spring, but the official opening was in a fortnight. "Tristram's a revolutionary and something of an agent, but he's a composer, first and foremost. Ask Mélanie. She wouldn't run off with a play about to open."

"Not unless the danger were extreme," Kitty said.

"You disappeared once," Julien reminded Danielle.

"Because Pierre was wounded and I knew Ilia and I were at risk. And I wasn't about to open an opera then. Not that that would—But only yesterday afternoon, Tristram seemed more concerned with Liliana's third-act aria than anything else. Not that he isn't skilled at deception." Danielle cast a quick glance at her husband, who had gone still. "*Cher?*" she asked. "I can be a bit slow these days, but you know Tristram's secrets better than I do."

Pierre's fingers tightened on the arms of his chair. "In many ways, I know Tristram Gresham less well than my wife does."

"But in some ways, you know him more," Danielle said. "Don't be ashamed to admit it."

"Not ashamed." Pierre cast a glance at his wife. "Cautious."

"You've always been far more cautious than I, *mon cher*," Danielle said. "Don't be ashamed to share the truth."

"The truth is an elusive commodity." Pierre leant forwards. "I have no reason to think Gresham was planning to disappear. He seemed entirely focused on the opera and quite obsessed with Danielle's performance."

"No need to gild the lily," Danielle said.

"I'm not." Pierre looked steadily into his wife's gaze. "Gresham made no secret of his admiration for you. And, as you say, he cares for his work perhaps more than anything."

"But," Danielle said, her gaze not breaking from her husband's.

"But I know he went to Italy last month. And possibly to France."

"For?" Mélanie asked.

"I'm not sure. But he shared our general frustration with the direction of Continental politics." Pierre looked at his wife.

"It's all right," Danielle said. "You have allies I don't. You have your own career as an agent. I should be used to it by now. You'll have to forgive me for being slow. I'm so used to—"

"Running rings round me?" her husband asked.

"Being the one with secrets."

"Could Gresham have been allied with LeFou?" Julien asked.

"Are you asking me if Gresham might have hired an assassin?" Pierre said.

"It seems a pertinent question, given the events of the night."

Pierre met Julien's gaze. "Gresham's angry at events on the Continent. And at home. He isn't the only one."

"Point taken," Julien said. "Everyone in this room is angry at events on the Continent."

Pierre nodded. "He said desperate times called for desperate measures. But I can't imagine him working with a man like LeFou. Failure of imagination on my part, perhaps. But morality aside, it's hard to see what he'd have thought he had to gain from having a particular person killed."

"What about his being a target of LeFou's?" Kitty asked.

"Anyone could potentially be a target. I think we all know that.

Tristram is perhaps more dangerous than most people realize. So that could make him more likely to be a target. But speaking as one who has been imprisoned, I'd be surprised if Gresham were the target of an international plot."

"Did you ever hear him talk about Harriet Roth?" Kitty asked.

Pierre shook his head and looked at his wife.

"You think he talked to me about his affairs?" Danielle asked.

"I think he was more likely to talk to you than to me," Pierre said.

"I didn't even know they knew each other," Danielle said. "That is, as more than acquaintances who attended a few of the same events. She wasn't his type. She's lovely, but for all his reputation, Tristram tended to confine himself to married women who knew the way the game is played." She shook her head. "God, that sounds bad. You know what I mean. Who were less likely to be hurt. He has his own rough sort of morality."

"Emotions can interfere with morality," Kitty said.

"So they can." Memories danced in Danielle's gaze. "I got involved with Pierre quite against my better judgment."

"Could Harriet and Gresham have been connected in any other way?" Kitty asked.

"You mean politically?"

"Harriet takes politics seriously." Kitty wasn't prepared to talk about *Le Monde Gris* yet. She wanted to see what Danielle and Pierre knew, and to wait for Edmund and Pippa. "She grew up in a Radical family."

"Gresham and Jeremy Roth are both involved with the Levellers," Pierre said. "You know that." He made it not quite a question. "But to my knowledge, Harriet didn't do more than accompany her brother to the occasional meeting. And it seems out of character for Roth to send his sister as a go-between."

"She has a keen understanding," Pierre said.

Danielle glanced over her shoulder at him. "She does. What of it?"

126

"It's an attractive quality," Pierre said in a level voice.

"Yes, but—"

"It's part of what drew me to you."

"My darling. You aren't Tristram Gresham. Thank god."

"Gresham may be a roué, but he's not an idiot. Far from it, actually. It's one of his saving graces."

"Pierre, are you saying you knew—"

"No. Not that I'd necessarily have betrayed them if I had known. Not that I know anything was going on between them at all. In fact, I'd be surprised if Gresham had let anything happen. He has his own code."

"Harriet visited here a lot," Kitty said.

"I suppose so," Danielle said, seemingly artlessly. "The children all play together. I've been away at rehearsals so much. I've always liked her, but she's more Pippa's friend."

The door opened on her words to admit Edmund Blayney, holding a coffee tray, and his wife Pippa with a plate of seedcake. "We can leave now we've delivered the refreshments," Edmund said, as he set the coffee tray on the sofa table.

"No," Julien said. "We need to talk to you too." He told them quickly about Harriet and Gresham's disappearance and the discovery of the murdered LeFou in Gresham's rooms.

Edmund and Pippa both went still. But then, the news would be enough to shock anyone.

"You haven't heard from them?" Julien asked.

"No." Edmund glanced round the group. "At least, I haven't. They'd hardly be likely to contact us." He met Kitty's gaze for a moment, eyes dark with questions.

"I told Julien and Mélanie and Malcolm and the others about *Le Monde Gris*," Kitty said. "I couldn't risk it. There's too much of a chance it could be connected to their disappearance." She glanced at Danielle.

"Pierre and I knew," Danielle said. "Difficult to keep anything secret in the printshop. But I quite see why you wanted to ask us about Tristram before you mentioned *Le Monde Gris*. And it doesn't change the fact that we haven't heard from Harriet. Or Tristram. At least, I haven't."

"Nor have I," Edmund said. "Truly."

"Did you know Harriet was connected to Gresham?" Julien asked.

Edmund shook his head. "She never mentioned him in connection with *Le Monde Gris*."

Pippa picked up the coffeepot and began to pour. "I can't claim she confided in me, precisely. But we did talk. If she was involved with anyone, I always wondered about the man in the foreign office who was giving her information. Southart? Southcliff?"

"Southcott?" Julien said. "John Southcott was giving Harriet information for *Le Monde Gris*?"

"I don't think he knew she was running it," Edmund said. "But he'd given her some information. He said there were things about the government that needed to be shared."

Julien sat back in his chair. "To think someone so seemingly dull could hold so many surprises. I'd say I hate it when investigations send us to talk to the least interesting candidates. But it seems John Southcott is more interesting than I credited."

HARRY DAVENPORT REGARDED Malcolm over a steaming cup of coffee in the breakfast parlor of his Hill Street house. "Good god. How much did you all get into while Cordy and I were snug in our beds?"

Malcolm took a welcome drink of coffee. "It was certainly an unusual evening. To say the least."

Harry leant back in his chair. "I hate to say this, given all the implications. But can I confess there's a small part of me that's been thinking things had been far too quiet. Not that I don't like retreating into a classical investigation. But there's something about being pulled out of the first century." His gaze sobered as he looked at Malcolm. "I've heard Wellington's name coupled with some very inventive curses through the years. But this is a new one."

"I could have dismissed it as ravings," Malcolm said. "But if the attack on the Delaneys wasn't enough to convince us, we have Palmerston and Hubert saying someone in the British government hired LeFou."

Harry blew on the steam from his cup. "Hubert and Wellington never got on that well."

"You think Hubert's framing Wellington? Hubert hired LeFou and set up Wilcox to talk to Hara Delaney, somehow guessing he'd come to us?"

"Put like that—no. Though he could have known Delaney was friends with Laura. It wouldn't be hard to guess where he was likely to go with the news."

"Yes, we considered that. But even if Wilcox was meant to send Delaney to us, someone else would almost certainly have had to attack the Delaneys."

"Unless the attack was meant to lend verisimilitude."

Malcolm clunked down his coffee cup. "My god, you have a devious mind, Davenport."

"Thank you." Harry reached for his cup. "Mind you, I'm not saying I think it likely. But it's still something to consider."

"Yes."

Harry took another drink of coffee. "Not easy, is it?"

"What?" Malcolm settled his cup on its saucer. "Suspecting Hubert of this? We're used to suspecting Hubert of just about everything."

"Suspecting Wellington."

Malcolm stared at the tangle of leafy oak branches through the breakfast parlor window. "At this point, I'm used to suspecting just about everyone I ever worked for, of just about anything."

"Fair enough."

Malcolm turned his cup in his hand. Mélanie had asked him about it last night. And he'd felt Raoul's concern. But some things he could only discuss with Harry, who had worked with Wellington as well, and felt the pull of personality, for better or worse. "I respected Wellington. In some things. I liked him. I think we all got caught up in admiring him round Waterloo. Which is rather odd, given where I stood at the end of it. Given that I now question so many of my decisions. But I suppose some of that stuck. Sticks even now. Even when I see him as a Tory politician. Just as obdurate as other Tory politicians. Just as opposed to everything I stand for. More so than a number of them. More so than Hubert, in some ways."

"It's different," Harry said. "Disagreeing with someone and facing this sort of betrayal."

"What do you call what he did to Hara Delaney over a decade ago? And countless other Indians?"

"Unconscionable. But he made no bones about it. Wellington's bluntness has always been one of his saving graces. He never pretended to be other than he was. At least, he didn't seem to. If he was involved in a plot like this, it would be—"

"Surprising, among other things." Malcolm tossed down a swallow of coffee. It burnt his throat. "He never struck me as the sort to stab a colleague in the back. He'd plant them a facer. Or challenge them to a duel. But this would be a completely different sort of intrigue."

"And make him not the man you thought you knew."

"I know he isn't the man I once thought I knew. But not in the way you mean. I wouldn't say I'm disillusioned. I don't have a lot of illusions left."

"My dear fellow. You'll always have them."

Malcolm shook his head. "I was a cynic when I went to the Peninsula. More than I am now. Everything I'd advocated for in Oxford coffeehouses seemed impossible and out of reach."

"You still cared about people."

"Individuals. I'd given up on charging systems. Until after I met Mel. But I was a cynic when I met Wellington. Yet somehow there were moments when I'd get caught up in it. In that—aura about him. That thing that makes one admire him and be willing to go into battle after him, for all he's brusque and never tries to make himself liked."

"I know." Harry reached for the coffeepot and refilled their cups. "I've felt it myself, for all I didn't want to. For all I claimed not to believe in anything, or anyone, at that point in my life. For all I really didn't believe in anything or anyone. It's the sheer force of his personality, I think. All the more powerful because he doesn't try to exert it. At least, not seemingly. So that even when you disagree with him, you find yourself not wanting to let him down."

Malcolm nodded. "And telling yourself that even if you do disagree with him, he's a decent person. Not a conniver like Hubert. Not a cold strategist like Castlereagh. Quite forgetting India. And not considering the way things will seem when one returns to the real, messy world of Whitehall and Westminster. But I suppose some of it still echoes through the years—" Malcolm reached for his cup. "Yes, I'm disappointed. Or, yes, a part of me doesn't want to believe this."

"And so you're going extra far to make sure you aren't biased in Wellington's favor."

"I'm not particularly proud of the fact that I might be biased in his favor. But yes, I'm afraid I could be."

Harry nodded. "I used to like to think I wasn't biased in my research. But then I accepted that there's no way not to be. The simple act of deciding where to focus one's research, which questions to ask, involves a degree of bias. The trick is to try to acknowledge those biases." He pushed his chair back. "I'll learn what I can about what Wellington might have to do with this. And I'll try to be open about how my questions may bias my report. You'll have to decide what to do with the data."

CHAPTER 19

David Mallinson stared at Mélanie in the pale early morning light streaming through the muslin sub-curtains. "Harriet Roth ran off with Tristram Gresham?"

"We don't know that," Mélanie said.

"But they're both missing?" Simon Tanner asked.

"You don't seem surprised that they're missing together," Mélanie said.

"Not…entirely."

"What?" David spun round to look at Simon.

Simon pushed himself to his feet, refilled their coffee cups, sat down again. They were in the breakfast parlor of the house they shared with David's orphaned niece and nephews, whom they were raising, but the children were not up yet. Mélanie had hurried over soon after dawn, while Malcolm went to see Harry Davenport. Neither of them had been able to sleep for more than an hour.

"You knew Harriet was involved with Gresham?" David demanded of Simon. A political Radical like Malcolm, he was intensely chivalrous and inclined to be old-fashioned about protecting women, as Mélanie knew to her cost.

"No. Not precisely." Simon scraped a hand through his thick, dark hair. "Harriet has a keen understanding. She comes to our meetings with Jeremy sometimes. Not a great secret, perhaps. I've seen her talking to Gresham. Also, perhaps, not a great secret. What may be more surprising is that they've met at the theatre at night." He looked at Mélanie. "Jeremy may plant me a facer when he learns that. But from my perspective, if two adults want to find time to be alone together, I have no business interfering."

"Fair enough," Mélanie said. "I'd have probably done the same. Malcolm might have as well."

"Might."

"Probably."

David drew in and released his breath. "All right. I might have done as well."

Simon raised a brow. "Seriously?"

"They're adults, as you said." David took a drink of coffee. "Are you saying they were a couple?"

"Define couple," Simon said.

"Were they lovers?" Mélanie asked. Sometimes one had to be blunt.

"Again, it depends on the definition. I can't claim—nor would I want—to know what went on between them in private. But I do have reason to think their feelings for each other went beyond collaboration between agents."

Mélanie studied her friend. Simon was a fellow writer. He used words with care. "So they were romantically involved."

Simon met her gaze. "I think so. Yes."

"But do you think they've eloped?" David asked.

"Right before a Continental assassin was killed in Gresham's rooms?" Simon said. "That strains belief."

"Coincidences do happen," Mélanie pointed out.

Simon shifted in his chair. "I can't claim to have been in Gresham's confidence. I'm not sure he confided in anyone. I do

133

think whatever was going on with Harriet was different from his other affairs. He said as much to me."

"Gresham talked to you about Harriet?" David demanded.

"He said it was different?" Mélanie asked, almost in the same breath.

"He said he'd never been involved in anything like this. That he wasn't sure what he was doing. That he was afraid of making a mistake. Gresham doesn't talk about his feelings easily. Nor do I." Simon cast a quick glance at David, who had been his lover since they met at Oxford. "Gresham and I were hardly confidants. But I found him drinking across from the theatre at the White Rose one night, after Harriet had been at a meeting at the Tavistock. I think Gresham needed to talk."

"Did Jeremy know anything about this?" Mélanie asked.

"Surely he's told you he didn't."

Mélanie took a drink of coffee and smiled at Simon over the gilded rim of the cup. "I know what he's told us. I'm asking you."

Simon inclined his head. "To my knowledge, Jeremy didn't know. And I can't imagine either Gresham or Harriet confiding in him."

"I can't imagine he did," David said. "I mean, any man would try to protect his sister from—"

"Yes, I imagine that's what made Harriet determined not to let him know about this. Whatever *this* proves to be," Mélanie said. She looked back at Simon. "What brought Harriet and Gresham together?"

"What do you mean?"

"Their politics may align, but they move in very different circles. As you just pointed out, Harriet is very different from the sort of woman Tristram tends to be entangled with. Harriet hasn't been entangled with anyone at all, so far as we know."

Simon raised a brow. "My dear Mélanie. Far be it from me to understand the complexities of the human heart. I can barely make sense of my own romantic life, much less of anyone else's."

David was staring at his lover. "Are you saying you knew Gresham seduced Harriet?"

"I wouldn't say he seduced her. Harriet's always struck me as eminently sensible. And she's past thirty."

"She's a—"

"David, please don't say she's a virtuous woman."

David clunked his cup down, spattering coffee on the pristine saucer. "I wasn't going to say anything of the sort. I'd hope you'd defend any woman against a man like Gresham."

"What if she wanted Gresham?"

David's fingers froze as he reached for his coffee cup again. "What on earth—?"

"He's not my type, but he's undeniably attractive. I don't see why Harriet shouldn't be allowed to choose for herself."

David folded his arms over his chest. "Because, unlike you or me, Harriet could be ruined."

"A point," Simon conceded. "But she's not a girl on the marriage mart. In fact, she's never given any indication she has any desire to be on the marriage mart. If Gresham's what she wants—"

"Gresham could abandon her and leave her with child."

Simon went still and met David's gaze across the table. "Fair enough. I'll own I asked Harriet if she had thought things through. Without really quite admitting what I was asking about. And she told me that at two-and-thirty, she'd been doing little but thinking. That at a certain point, she had to be able to live her life." Simon went still, gaze weighted with questions. He was too uncompromising to dodge questions, whether from others or himself. "I'd have looked an awful hypocrite disagreeing with that."

David sucked in his breath "Why couldn't you—"

"What? Tell her brother behind her back? Lose her trust? Challenge Gresham to a duel?"

"Well, no. But confront him—"

"And he'd rightly ask me what business it was of mine. If he did listen, it would infuriate Harriet and drive her more firmly to Gresham. People need to make their own decisions, whether we agree with them or not. You haven't always agreed with my decisions. I haven't always agreed with yours. But if Gresham and Harriet have run off together, I don't think it's an elopement. For one thing, they'd have no reason to elope. They were managing perfectly well. And if she'd wanted to move in with him as his mistress—"

"Good god," David said.

"—no one could have stopped her. It might have meant a row with Jeremy, but this is worse. So if they've run off, I think it's because they know they're in danger."

"Then why haven't they come to us?" David asked. "That is, to Malcolm and Mélanie and the others."

"There could be a lot of reasons," Mélanie said. "Gresham may not trust us. He doesn't know us that well. They could be concerned about what they're dragging us into. Or more, perhaps, what they're dragging Jeremy and Judith and the boys into. Or—they could have killed LeFou. Quite possibly in self defense."

"You can't think—" David said.

"Someone killed him," Mélanie said. "In Gresham's rooms." She sat back in her chair and took another drink of coffee. "Of course, it's also entirely possible their disappearance has to do with *Le Monde Gris*." She looked at Simon.

Simon returned her gaze. "You know."

"Kitty told us. She was supplying articles from the Peninsula and South America."

David stared from Mélanie to Simon. "Gresham published *Le Monde Gris*?"

"No," Mélanie said. "Harriet did."

"Well," David said. "That explains a lot."

"You can still surprise me," Simon said. "I thought you'd be protesting it couldn't be true."

136

"Why would I? Harriet is eminently capable. I always thought she must have something more to keep her occupied than managing the household and looking after the boys."

Simon gave a faint smile. "Remind me not to underestimate you."

"Did she tell you about it?" Mélanie asked Simon.

He met her gaze without flinching. "I helped her secure some articles."

"Did Gresham know?"

"Not that I knew. It certainly wasn't common knowledge among the Levellers. It wasn't common knowledge among any of us. Harriet swore me and anyone else involved to secrecy. She was very worried about her sources. And about Jeremy and Judith and the children." He reached for his coffee and stared into the cup. "And given what's happened, it seems she had good cause to be."

"CARFAX." John Southcott looked round with a quick, uncertain smile. He always smiled as though he were a bit unsure about how to do it. He had the same round face Julien remembered from childhood, slightly heavier round the jaw, and the same wide blue eyes that took in more than one at first supposed. "Lady Carfax." He got to his feet and bowed.

"Please." Kitty waved a hand.

"We haven't time to stand on ceremony, Southcott." Julien pulled out a chair for Kitty and perched on the edge of Southcott's desk. The only other chair in the small office was piled high with papers. "Uncle Hubert brought us into the situation last night. Palmerston talked with him. After you talked to Palmerston."

"I see." Southcott pushed his chair towards Julien. Julien shook his head. "They think it's serious, then?"

"It seems it may be. Difficult to know whom to trust. Best on the whole to keep quiet about it."

"I'm not in the habit of blabbing, Carfax. Apologies, Lady Carfax."

"No need to apologize," Kitty said. "Julien has a way of bringing out that tone in people."

"I assured Palmerston I wouldn't say anything. And that I wouldn't ask questions."

"But, naturally, you're curious," Julien said. "You'd better sit down, Southcott. We have a lot to talk about."

Southcott frowned, as though tempted to resist, then dropped back into his chair. "Naturally, I'm willing to help in any way I can."

Julien smiled. "We didn't realize you were acquainted with Harriet Roth."

Southcott went still for a fraction of an instant, then settled back in his chair. He was better at this than he once had been, Julien acknowledged. "I've met her once or twice. We frequent the same bookseller in Piccadilly. Charming woman. But I presume she has nothing to do with this?"

Julien leant back, resting his weight on his hands. "You tell me."

Southcott met Julien's gaze, his own focused. "My dear Carfax. I don't know anything about what is going on. I just found some irregular entries in a ledger. Which I took to Palmerston. I'm happy to be of more help. If what you've discovered has anything to do with Miss Roth, I would very much like to know. But I can't imagine how it could be connected to her."

"Harriet's a good friend of ours," Kitty said. "You'll understand our concern."

"Of course. But I assure you I never—"

"No one is suggesting you did." Kitty smiled at him. The smile Julien had seen her use to disarm British officers and Spanish guerrilleros and diplomats of all stripes. Smile with supreme confidence and wait for the enemy to break. It worked almost every time.

"Is Miss Roth in any trouble?" Southcott's eyes opened wide with a guilelessness that just possibly might have been genuine.

"We hope not." Kitty didn't glance at Julien, but Julien felt her tacitly reach out for his consent. "She's disappeared."

"What!" Southcott pushed himself out of his chair again.

"Of course, she's an adult, and quite free to go off on her own whenever she wishes. But naturally, her family are concerned."

"Good god, I should think so. Do you know—"

"We know very little."

Southcott dropped back into his ladder-back chair and wiped his hand across his brow. "I wouldn't for the world have mentioned this. I take confidences very seriously. But if she's in trouble—Miss Roth was perhaps involved in writing articles."

"We've heard as much." Julien kept his voice easy as syrup warmed over a spirit lamp.

"She has a keen understanding and a good heart. She wanted to share injustices with the public. I may not agree with everything she said, but I understand her impulse."

Julien swung his leg against the desk. "That's one of the most decent things I've heard you say, Southcott."

"Don't be clever, Carfax."

"I'm not trying to be."

Southcott passed a hand over his close-cropped dark hair. "I don't know everything she was doing. Is doing. But I know she was publishing articles. And—"

"You gave her articles," Kitty said. "Don't deny it. You can't imagine we, of all people, would object."

"In fact, I've never liked you so well, Southcott," Julien said.

Southcott gave a quick smile that might almost have been genuine. "I'm not a Radical. You know that. You and your friends rather despise me."

"I wouldn't say despise," Julien said in an easy voice.

"But I'd have to be an idiot not to see the idiocy of what the lot in charge are doing. Castlereagh and Sidmouth and Wellington and Liverpool. And my father. Even my uncle Tony. It barely worked at Vienna, and it certainly isn't going to work going forwards. It's a frayed bandage trying to hold the world together, and while we're tugging at the bandage, Russia and Austria will push us out entirely. If you knew the mind-numbing frustration of sitting behind a desk, drafting memos to express their ideas, arguing their points across a conference table—"

"I don't, thank god," Julien said. "But I think Malcolm Rannoch would be in sympathy."

Southcott shifted in his chair. "Rannoch and I don't agree on a lot. But I think we could agree on the madness of working for the foreign office." He shifted in his chair again. "So when I realized what Miss Roth was doing, I couldn't help but think that this was an opportunity to share my ideas."

"You wrote articles for her," Kitty said.

"I prefer to think of them as letters. From a private citizen."

"Who happens to work at the foreign office," Julien said.

"Just so." Southcott folded his arms over his chest.

"When did you last see her?" Kitty asked.

Southcott's dark brows drew together. "Three days ago. No, two. We met at the bookseller's and got coffee in Covent Garden. I gave her some thoughts I'd jotted down. Nothing ready for print. Just something for her to review and discuss with me. We shared coffee and talked for a bit."

"You had no sense anything was amiss?" Julien asked.

"Of course not. Can you imagine I'd have simply let her leave if I had done?"

"I don't imagine anyone lets or doesn't let Harriet Roth do anything," Kitty said.

Southcott shifted in his chair again, putting Kitty in mind of her sons when they were telling half-truths. "Miss Roth is a very capable woman. As are you, Lady Carfax. I meant no disrespect. But naturally, as a friend, I'd have been concerned if I thought she was facing difficulties." His gaze shot between Kitty and Julien.

"I've admitted a great deal by sharing my work with Miss Roth. It goes without saying that you have the power to ruin me."

"You're clever, Southcott," Julien said. "You'd manage to avoid ruin."

"I'm not sure I could manage to do so. I need hardly say that I have only shared this out of my profound concern for Miss Roth."

"As my wife said, we, of all people, are in sympathy with you, Southcott," Julien said, for once keeping the irony from his voice. "I certainly know the impulse to share thoughts at odds with those in power. Did you say anything to Miss Roth about the discoveries you'd made in the war office ledger?"

"Good god, Carfax. You can't think I would."

"You were writing articles about the British foreign office."

"I wasn't sharing secrets."

"It doesn't always seem like secrets with those one is close to. I say things to my wife I'd say to no one else."

"That's the hardly the"—Southcott coughed—"hardly the nature of my relationship with Miss Roth."

"Who else knew about your friendship?"

"I've just told you how at risk it put me. You can't imagine I'd have told anyone, for that reason alone. Let alone my concern for Miss Roth's reputation. Not that there was anything between us that should have damaged her reputation," Southcott added quickly. "But I'm very aware of the risk of gossip."

"Could Miss Roth have told anyone?"

"You know her, Carfax. Lady Carfax knows her. She didn't tell her closest friends what she was doing. Even I didn't realize how involved she was in publishing *Le Monde Gris* until I'd known her for some time. She was very aware of the risks to her brother and his family. And, as you know, she's not the sort to talk idly."

"Did you ever notice anyone hanging about when the two of you met? Following you?"

"I'm not a spy, but I am wary of my surroundings." Southcott's gaze fastened on Julien. "I noticed nothing. Carfax, are you suggesting my association with Miss Roth may have to do with her disappearance?"

"The plot you stumbled upon in the ledger appears to be very serious, and connected to the highest reaches of our government. Someone you were close to has disappeared. If someone knew about your association with Miss Roth, they might have thought you'd told her something, even though you hadn't."

"So you're saying I'm at risk as well?"

"We're all at risk," Julien said. "Did Miss Roth talk to you about others she was collaborating with?"

"No." Southcott shook his head. "She was very protective of her sources. Understandably."

"Did Miss Roth ever mention Tristram Gresham?"

"Gresham?" Southcott frowned. "I knew he was a source of hers. Frankly it was difficult for me to imagine Gresham and Miss Roth having the least thing in common."

"They have politics in common." Julien leant his weight back on his hands. "More than she does with you, I should think."

Southcott frowned. "Miss Roth and I do debate politics. We have quite lively conversations. But I can scarcely imagine her with a man of Gresham's stripe."

Julien let his leg swing against the side of the desk. There were risks in sharing more, but they also had to know what Southcott knew. "What would you say if I told you Gresham has disappeared, along with Miss Roth?"

"What?" Southcott pushed himself out of his chair.

Well, that settled one thing. The fellow was clearly in love with Harriet Roth.

"Are you saying Gresham abducted Harriet?"

"We have no reason to think so," Kitty said. "But we do have reason to think they left together. For reasons we don't understand."

Southcott gripped the back of his chair, knuckles white on the wood. "You can't leave it there, Lady Carfax. You must know more. I understand you have no reason to fully trust me, but trust that I have every concern for Harriet's safety and happiness."

Strategize all one could going into a mission, sometimes one had to improvise. And that could mean rolling the dice. But Southcott was already so far in, he was probably more dangerous with less information. Julien glanced round the office. "Who's in the rooms next to you?"

"No one right now."

"You're sure?"

"I know my colleagues." But Southcott moved to both doors, cracked them open, and glanced out. "Secure," he said, with the seriousness of an amateur on an intelligence mission, as he dropped back into his chair.

"Good. The payments you found in the ledger appear to be to a man named André LeFou, who is a hired killer. Kitty and I found LeFou dead last night in Gresham's rooms. Gresham had fled, apparently with Miss Roth."

Southcott had gone white. "How do you know—"

"We found her earring," Kitty said. Though she didn't add in which room they had found it.

"They were there when this LeFou was killed?"

"We're not sure," Julien said. "But I suspect they left first."

"Because otherwise, Gresham killed him."

"Or Harriet did," Kitty said.

"You can't think—"

"I think Harriet is fully capable of killing in self-defense. Most of us would be."

"My god." Southcott sat back in his chair. "You're telling me Harriet may have been abducted by a killer."

Julien leant forwards, hands locked round his knee. "To begin with, I think it unlikely Gresham killed LeFou, as I just said. But even if he did, it was very likely self-defense or to protect Harriet. And we have no evidence Harriet Roth was abducted. She had clearly gone to see Gresham on her own, for reasons that aren't yet clear."

"It's not like you to be so squeamish about stating the obvious, Carfax. You think Harriet is Gresham's mistress."

"I don't think anything of the sort. It's one possible explanation, but given the things she was involved in, there are any number of other possible explanations for why they might have been allied. And her relationship with you makes the possibility that she was Gresham's mistress even less likely."

"Miss Roth and I didn't have a relationship."

"You were friends. That's a relationship. Kitty and I are friends. Among other things. You could say we were friends before we were lovers. We were also antagonists, which is another story."

Southcott drew in and released his breath. "Har—Miss Roth— means a great deal to me. I hope that she values my friendship. I wouldn't think she would become entangled with a man like Gresham. Every feeling revolts at the thought."

"I can't precisely say I agree," Julien said, "but I think we're agreed in thinking there may well be an explanation other than a love affair for Miss Roth's presence in Gresham's rooms. So what might it be?"

Southcott's brows drew together. "As I said, I know Gresham had supplied information to Miss Roth. His romantic activities are what one is most likely to hear drawing room gossip about. But his political activities are certainly discussed in Whitehall corridors." Southcott flexed his fingers and curled them inwards again. "There's nothing in the least improper in Miss Roth's behavior. But she is impatient of conventions. If she had information regarding one of her sources that she felt she needed to discuss with Gresham quickly, I can imagine her going to his rooms at night."

"Agreed," Julien said.

"But if she and Gresham were attacked—if they felt the need to leave—why not go to her family?"

"Perhaps out of concern for her family," Kitty said.

Southcott's frown deepened. "Surely that supports the idea that Gresham killed this LeFou. He wouldn't want a Bow Street runner to know that. In which case, he could be using Harriet as leverage against her brother."

"Gresham is a number of things," Julien said. "But he doesn't strike me as someone who would use a woman—or anyone—in that way."

"He didn't strike you as a killer either, did he?"

"Fair enough. But if he killed LeFou in self-defense or to protect Harriet, I think he'd have the wit to come forward. At least, to friends."

"Difficult to know what anyone would do under circumstances like that," Southcott said. "I can't say what I'd do myself."

"True," Kitty said. "I don't suppose any of us can."

CHAPTER 20

March 1819
Normandy

*H*arriet looked up from the polished oak table in the sitting room of the Normandy cottage, spread with the draft of an article. "You aren't worried?" she asked.

"Worried about what?" Désirée set down her tea and regarded the woman who had come to seem almost like a younger sister. "If I let myself worry about all the things I have to worry about, I'd go mad."

Harriet glanced at the dark ink of the article, highlighted by the sun streaming through the windows, then sat back on the sofa. "That the duke will learn the truth."

"Oh, I expect he will. Even I can't keep secrets from Tony for too long." Désirée reached for the Wedgwood teapot (just looking at the white pastoral figures on the deep blue brought Tony to life in a way that made her chest ache) and refilled their cups.

Harriet added another spoonful of sugar to her tea. "You don't seem very concerned."

"I'd never have survived a mission if I let myself be concerned.

One has to keep an eye on the future, but mostly the only way to survive is to focus on the needs of the moment." Désirée reached for the milk jug and splashed some into her tea. Before Tony, she'd never put milk in her tea. "We'll quarrel. We always do. I used to worry every quarrel would break us. Even now—" She broke off. Because Harriet was risking enough. She didn't need to be distracted by the thoughts that kept Désirée up at night.

Harriet set down the silver sugar spoon. "Is that why you're doing this?"

"Is what why I'm doing this?"

"Working with me. Publishing articles on the situation in France under occupation by your lover's government."

"I thought it was obvious why I was doing this." Désirée took a sip of tea. Tony's custom blend, created for him by Fortnum's. He kept the cottage stocked with tins of it.

Harriet took a sip of tea and curled her hands round her cup. "Well, yes. I know you think it's important, and I know you want to find a way to take a stand against what's happening. But I was wondering if you were also doing it to test him."

Désirée set down her cup. Harriet Roth was a very astute woman. And for someone who had never been married—or as far as Désirée knew, been in any sort of serious relationship—she had remarkably keen insights into the challenges of being a couple. "Our relationship has stood up to far more than anyone would expect it to endure."

"Yes, it's quite amazing. I just thought—"

"What?" Désirée asked.

"That perhaps you're afraid of what may happen when you and the duke confront your different loyalties. Perhaps instead of waiting, you wanted to force the issue sooner."

Astute indeed. Désirée reached for her cup again. She needed armor. "I have no intention of telling Tony about what you and I are doing. That would be an appalling betrayal of you, and of our work, and of the people we're working with."

"No, I didn't mean it consciously. Sometimes one can subconsciously push things."

Désirée savored a sip of tea. It took her back to the first time Tony had brewed her a cup, in the kitchen of this same cottage. "Your insights are rather frightening, *chérie*. I don't believe in shying away from a conflict. But while it's true I may have fled the field of battle—which I confess I don't much regret, given that I was with child, and there wasn't really a battle I could fight in the wake of Waterloo—I wouldn't have much respect for myself if I avoided doing what was right in order to keep my relationship with Tony harmonious. I suppose that makes me sound a horrid prig. But much as we all get caught up in the game-playing—as intoxicating as the game is—I really do believe in what I'm doing. It would be very hard to justify the very uncomfortable things I've done in the service of my cause, otherwise."

Harriet set her teacup down, sloshing tea into her saucer. "I want to be you when I grow up."

Désirée rubbed a smudge of lip rouge off the rim of her cup. "Oh, *chérie*. I hope you have a much easier life."

❧

July 1821
London

DÉSIRÉE WATCHED Tony carefully as they walked through Green Park. Sophie had run ahead with her puppy, Belle. They were happily investigating the roots of a silver lime.

She and Tony had had this sort of conversation a dozen times. But it was different now. The ground had shifted beneath their feet in the past weeks without her ever quite realizing it. And the thing of it was, she didn't want it to shift back. "I didn't want to tell you under the Mallinsons' roof," she said.

"No, that was wise." Tony scanned the path ahead, watching

148

Sophie and Belle, watching for anyone lurking in the shadows. "With a man like Hubert, one never knows how sound might be designed to carry."

"I did talk to Kitty last night. But we didn't discuss specifics." Désirée tightened her gloved fingers round his arm. She almost hadn't taken his arm at all, because it seemed like an unfair advantage, given what she had to say. But then there was the appearance they presented. One never knew who might be watching. "And I couldn't tell you before." She was on shakier ground here, much like the uneven grass Sophie and Belle were now running over.

"No," Tony said, looking ahead at Sophie as she tossed a stick for Belle. "I realize that."

Désirée turned her head to look at him from beneath the brim of her bonnet. "Do you?"

Tony met her gaze, his blue eyes bright as they caught the morning sunlight. "I was a British diplomat. A British diplomat willing to break rules, but still a British diplomat. You were speaking out on the situation in France and the work my country was engaged in."

"Cogently put. It would have been putting you in an unfair situation. Though you could argue that I should have told you before I came to Britain."

"You could. But I'm still British. I was just beginning to disentangle myself from the diplomatic service. And that could have put people you knew at risk."

"Yes. So it seemed."

Tony hesitated a moment. "When we learnt Harriet Roth was missing last night, what were you afraid I'd do?"

The question she'd known was coming. That she couldn't even answer in her own head. "It wasn't you. I was worried about Harriet. About what she'd want. About where she was."

He watched her for a moment, gaze unreadable, more agate than cornflower, then inclined his head. "I understand."

"Do you?"

"You needed more information before you could decide what to do with it."

She stared into his eyes. Open as the windows of the Normandy cottage on the first day of summer. "My god, Tony. You aren't human."

"Is that a compliment?"

"It's hard to believe how understanding you are."

"I wouldn't call it understanding. I'd call it common sense. Do you expect me to tell you everything?"

"Well, no. You may be officially retired, but you'll always be linked to the British government. And you know damned well what I'd do with information."

"Precisely."

"Still."

"What?" Tony asked.

"We've made promises. That would matter to a lot of people."

"Oh, the promises matter immeasurably to me. I'd be distinctly less understanding now if I learnt you'd seduced someone in the pursuit of information. At one point, I had no right to ask you about such things. But I think that's shifted. For both of us."

She lifted a hand to wave to Sophie, who grinned and waved back, then tightened her fingers round his arm. "Yes, fair enough. We never said so, but I assumed it was understood."

"When you agreed to marry me?" Tony asked.

"Actually, when I agreed to live in the cottage in Normandy. Or, I suppose, when I announced I was going to." When he returned after Waterloo. When the loss of everything she'd worked for for decades warred with her relief that he was safe. The memory was still so raw it cut through her. "And when you said"—even now, she couldn't quite put it into words—"what you said then. There were certain lines we weren't going to cross."

"Agreed. As I told you, since our affair began I hadn't—"

"Yes, my love. My eternal romantic."

"I never expected the same from you. I didn't even after Normandy."

Désirée watched Sophie tug the stick away from Belle so she could throw it again. "I was living in a cottage in the countryside with a small baby."

"You're creative."

"We had a family." A word that had never been in her vocabulary. "I was trying to make sense of what that meant. I still am. But it did seem to mean a certain amount of fidelity. Which I find matters to me more than I ever thought it would. But it didn't mean giving up my work."

"Did I ever suggest it did?"

"No, dearest. As I've always said, you're remarkable." She waved to Sophie again. Sophie spun, her white dress swirling in a circle that caught the light streaming through the trees as Belle ran round her. "I've told you. Now we need to tell the Rannochs."

CHAPTER 21

"*J*'m sorry," Désirée said. "I would have told you last night. But the instinct to not confide things in front of Hubert Mallinson is deeply ingrained."

"A very sound instinct," Julien said.

"And I wanted to tell Tony first."

"Also sound," Kitty said.

"There was no need," Tony said. "I wouldn't tell you before I confided details of a mission."

"You might if it impacted me," Désirée pointed out.

"This doesn't impact me."

"It impacts *us*," Désirée said. She looked at Mélanie, Malcolm, Kitty, Julien, Laura, and Raoul, who were gathered within the pale peach walls of the Berkeley Square breakfast parlor with probably the third or fourth pot of coffee they had all consumed today. "Harriet came to see me in Normandy nearly three years ago. Manon connected us."

Mélanie set down her coffee cup. Manon Caret was an actress at the Tavistock Theatre and a former French agent. Mélanie had helped Raoul arrange her escape from Paris after Waterloo, when anyone connected to the Bonaparte regime was at risk. Though settled in London and married to an Englishman, Manon maintained connections with a number of former agents in France and in exile. Including Désirée, as they had learnt two months ago. Usually Mélanie was good at seeing connections, but she could miss the complex ways her friends were intertwined. "I should have thought of that."

Désirée looked from Mélanie to Raoul, who had been Manon's spymaster. "That's already an admission I don't easily make. But in the circumstances, I think Manon would agree I should tell you."

"So do I," Raoul said. "Though I can certainly understand why she hadn't told us before."

Désirée nodded. "Harriet had an idea to publish stories from other countries. She had already gathered several. But I was able to share more with her." She looked round the room. "I told you Edmund Blayney published some of my articles. But Harriet published more, and helped me broaden my reach. And I helped her reach other sources."

"So you know her other sources," Malcolm said.

"Some of them. I can't claim to know all."

"Was Tristram Gresham a source?" Mélanie asked.

Désirée curled her fingers round her coffee cup. "I introduced them. I imagine Jeremy will never forgive me. And no, I don't know where they are. I didn't know they were meeting last night."

"Were they lovers?" Mélanie asked.

Désirée hesitated. "I don't know. It's not a question one asks friends. And it depends on how one uses the term. They were certainly—emotionally intertwined. I think both were aware of the risks. I'm not sure how far it had progressed. But whyever Harriet went to see Tristram last night, and whyever they ran, I think it was more than a tryst and an elopement."

"Could André LeFou have been giving them information?" Laura asked.

Mélanie frowned. "And he went to them as a source at the

same time he was carrying out an assassination plot on behalf of the British government?"

"Something got him to Tristram Gresham's rooms in St. James's Place last night," Laura pointed out.

"It's an interesting thought," Julien said. "LeFou was never political, to my knowledge. And he made it a point of pride not to betray his employers."

"You used to say you weren't political," Kitty pointed out.

"So LeFou could have changed as much as I did?"

"Or been concealing his true motives as much as you did."

"Possibly." Julien folded his arms. "I hate to think I didn't see it. But it wouldn't be the first time I missed something important."

"Harriet certainly wasn't connected to André LeFou through me," Désirée said. "I only met LeFou a handful of times and I wouldn't call him a colleague. But Harriet didn't share all her sources with me."

"Did she talk to you about Hara and Lizzy Delaney?" Mélanie asked. "They were sending her articles from India."

Désirée shook her head. "I knew she had sources in India, but not their names. How did you learn about them?"

"They arrived here last night," Laura said. And proceeded to update Désirée and Tony on the Delaneys' arrival, the attack they had suffered on their way to Berkeley Square, and their surprising report about the Duke of Wellington.

Tony, who had been sitting by quietly while Désirée explained her connection to Harriet, clunked down his coffee cup. "Good god."

Raoul met his friend's gaze. "I don't count Wellington a friend, but I find it difficult to credit as well."

"I'm not sure I'd call him a friend," Tony said. "He's a difficult man to be friends with. But I considered him—"

"A man of honor?" Désirée asked.

"Anyone who's been a diplomat for far less time than I, has

seen how elastic 'honor' can be. I've seen Wellington cross lines I wouldn't cross. But he's always struck me as the sort to confront an enemy to his face."

"Of course, that was when he was a general, not a politician," Julien said.

"A point," Tony conceded. His eyes were clouded, not with shock, but with worry. "Whatever is going on here, something very much beyond the bounds of accepted behavior is going on in government circles."

"Spoken with true diplomatic understatement," Julien said.

"One learns." Tony gave a faint smile that didn't reach his eyes. "I'll make inquiries. I can explore some different channels from Davenport."

"Speaking of Harriet's sources," Kitty said, "we also learnt that your nephew was one of them."

"John?" Tony's brows rose. "John talking to a Radical journalist is almost as surprising as Wellington being involved in an assassination plot."

"Perhaps not," Désirée said. "The way you've described him, he's no Radical, but he doesn't much care for the current state of things."

"True enough," Tony conceded. "He's made it clear—in the most polite, overly detailed language—that he considers both my way of doing things, and his father's, hopelessly antiquated."

"A frustration with the government seems to be his motivation for helping Harriet," Kitty said. She described the interview she and Julien had had with John Southcott. "Pippa Blayney sensed that he was quite fond of Harriet," she concluded. "Julien and I had the same impression."

"John has been a constant source of surprises in the past ten hours," Tony said. "I commend his good taste. If Miss Roth has had an influence on him, that might account for his broadened horizons." He looked at Désirée. "Did you know?"

Désirée nodded. "She told me he'd approached her, offering information. As I heard the story, he sent an inquiry through anonymous channels that got to Edmund Blayney before Harriet first had her supposedly accidental meeting with him at a bookseller's."

"How did he find a way to get to *Le Monde Gris's* printer?" Raoul asked.

"I don't know," Désirée said. "That worried me. Though Harriet pointed out that the articles he wrote put him at risk far more than either of us. She pointed out that while he might be my lover's nephew, she was the one who'd actually met him, and I needed to trust her judgment. I had to confess she was right. Though I never entirely trust anyone else's judgment." She glanced at Tony. "Even yours, my darling."

This time Tony's half-smile glinted in his eyes. "Miss Roth sounds like an eminently sensible woman. Though if John is competing for her affections with Tristram Gresham, I fear he may find himself considerably overmatched."

"I don't know." Désirée took a thoughtful sip of coffee. "As I said, there was—is—definitely something between her and Gresham. But she's clearly fond of John Southcott, though she hasn't talked to me about him as much. And Harriet isn't a woman to be taken in by rakish romance. In fact, I think what intrigued Gresham about her is that she saw through him so well."

"Nothing like a woman who can do that." Julien reached for Kitty's hand.

"Whyever she's missing, she's missing with Gresham," Kitty said. "And while Mr. Southcott is clearly concerned—and more than a bit jealous—I'm quite sure he doesn't know where she is any more than we do."

"Cordy and I are meeting Charlotte Augustin at Gunter's," Mélanie said. "But I have time to talk to Manon first. We need more information."

"So we do," Raoul said. "Lots for us all to do." His gaze swept the table. "Whether the Delaneys were targeted because they knew about a real plot Wellington is involved in, or because they're being used to set Wellington up, it's difficult to believe the attack on them isn't connected to this. Go carefully."

Julien pushed his chair back from the table. "When do we do otherwise?"

CHAPTER 22

April 1819
Normandy

*H*arriet stood just inside the door and watched the person at the pianoforte as his fingers moved over the keyboard and sound poured from the instrument. Intricate pieces of melody, irresistible on their own, but something much more powerful when they intertwined.

He looked up suddenly at her, brown hair falling back from his forehead.

"I'm sorry," Harriet said. "I didn't mean to interrupt. I was looking for Désirée. I'm Harriet Roth."

"Désirée's upstairs with the progeny." He pushed himself to his feet. "Tristram Gresham, at your service."

"Yes, I assumed as much. Is what you were playing from one of your operas?"

"It may be in an opera. If I can get the rest of it to work."

"I saw *Clarinda* three times."

"Only three?"

"I couldn't afford more." She took a step into the room. "You have a knack for making emotion honest without being cloying."

"Easier to do that in music than in life."

She pulled loose the ties on her cloak and tossed it over the settee. "Are you saying you hide behind your music?"

"Possibly."

Harriet undid the strings on her bonnet and tossed it after the cloak. She could feel strands of hair sticking to the nape of her neck. It was a number of hours since she'd had more than a brief stop at an inn to refresh herself. A good thing she was one of the minority of women who didn't care about the impression they made on Tristram Gresham. "I came here to meet you."

He grinned. "Odd to be meeting in a cottage in Normandy when we both live in London."

"It's easier for me here. No one knows I'm here, so there's no one to notice whom I'm talking to."

"There's no one to notice anything at all in this benighted corner of France. I don't know how Désirée has survived this long away from the glitter of Paris and Vienna." He closed the lid of the pianoforte and walked round it towards her. His hair flopped over his forehead in a way that reminded her of her schoolboy nephews. But the light from the windows caught creases round his eyes and dark smudges beneath them that spoke of hard-lived years since he'd been a schoolboy. "I suppose everyone's warned you about me."

"You needn't say that as though you're quite so proud of it."

"Caught." He gave an abashed grin. "Though I wouldn't say proud."

"I imagine it's the sort of thing that gets you a lot of attention."

He raised a brow. "You think it's an act?"

"Oh no." Harriet smoothed a travel crease from the cuff of her gown. "I mean, Don Giovanni obviously liked attention and it wasn't an act for him."

"I assure you I am a far cry from Don Giovanni. The man is

entirely lacking in finesse." He regarded her for a moment. "It can be useful to have a facade. People are so busy seeing it, they quite fail to notice what else one is doing."

"Are you saying being a rake is good cover for being a revolutionary?"

"Excellent cover. I imagine you know something about that sort of cover."

Harriet's fingers froze on the buttons of her other cuff. "Why would you think that?"

"Quiet, scholarly sister and aunt? Lovely and stylish, but seemingly the sort who spends her time looking after others in the domestic sphere. People aren't likely to guess you're actually exposing secrets across the globe."

"I wouldn't call it exposing secrets. I'd call it bringing issues to light. But I protect my work by staying in the background."

"Pity." His gaze moved over her, though not with the sort of obvious appraisal she was accustomed to from many gentlemen. "You shouldn't be relegated to the background."

"One can get rather a lot done in the background."

"I protect my work by flaunting my notoriety. Mind you, I work rather hard to achieve that notoriety."

"I imagine you do. But you needn't worry about impressing me. Or frightening me. That's not what we're here to talk about."

"No." He glanced round the room. "I'm not precisely the host, but given that Désirée is upstairs, it occurs to me that I am quite remiss in not offering you refreshment after your journey. May I pour you a glass of wine? Or would you rather I went to the kitchen and asked Berthe for tea?"

"Haven't you already seen my English spinster aunt pose for the facade it is, Lord Gresham?"

He grinned and moved to a set of decanters by the window. "Wine it is." He unstopped a decanter of what appeared to be Tokay. "How did it start?"

"What?"

"Your work."

Harriet settled on the settee where she had first spoken with Désirée. "I had to find a way to do something. It drives me mad, seeing so many things crumble, not just in Britain but round the world. If we could at least tell those stories, it seemed a way to strike a blow. To make people think. You can't have change without people thinking. And if people can share their stories, they may not feel so hopeless."

He went silent for a moment, fingers still on the cut-glass decanter. "You're an intrepid woman, Miss Roth."

"Thank you, Lord Gresham."

"Does your brother know what you're doing?"

"My brother works for Bow Street, whose chief magistrate reports to the home office."

Gresham set down the decanter and walked towards her with two glasses of Tokay. "He's also a Leveller."

Harriet accepted the glass he was holding out. "That's Jeremy's decision. A risk, but I can understand why he takes it. I see no reason I should add to the risk."

Gresham settled himself in a chair beside the settee. "It must be hard. Not claiming credit for what you do."

"Safer that way. You don't claim credit for all you do."

He frowned. "I would distinctly dislike not getting credit for my operas."

"But you don't get credit for your other work."

"Well, no." He took a sip from his own glass. "No agent does."

"And you let the world think you a profligate dilettante."

Gresham twisted the stem of the glass so it caught the light from the window, turning the pale yellow to gold. "Who says that's a pose?"

"It's not all you are. At least, from my observation."

"Is anyone all one thing? It would be hard to compose interesting characters if so."

"You can't deny you cultivate your persona for convenience."

"Of course. We all do that. For instance, as I said, you cultivate the pose of quiet spinster aunt. Stylish, quiet spinster aunt."

Harriet took a sip of wine. It was excellent, like everything in the cottage's cellar. She had yet to meet Tony Bamford, but she knew he had excellent taste in wine. "I am a spinster aunt. Who likes fashion."

"Precisely. But that's not all you are. You should get credit for your talents."

"I know. But it's the results that matter. Someday I'd like the boys to know what I'm doing."

Gresham relaxed back in his chair, glass held in one hand. "We're quite alike, I think. Creating a useful persona that plays into what people expect to see."

"Except that you flaunt yours. Mine lets me hide in the shadows."

He lifted his glass to her. "You're remarkable, Miss Roth."

"I'm quite ordinary, I assure you." She smiled. "It's a persona I'm careful to cultivate."

He set his glass down on the table between the chair and the settee. "How can I help you?"

"You know people."

"Many of them quite disreputable."

"You travel. You have connections. To Carbonari. To people in Paris whom Désirée doesn't dare contact now, for their safety and her own. You can get me information. Information I could never get on my own."

"Don't underrate yourself."

"I'm not." She set her glass down beside his own. "I know what I can do. I'm very good at it. I also know my limitations. People don't talk to me as easily as they do to you. It would take me years to build up that sort of trust. And I'm not going to leave my family and travel enough to forge those connections. Besides, if I became that well known, I wouldn't be able to publish *Le Monde Gris* safely."

He reached for his glass. "Cogently put."

"Thank you."

He took a drink of wine, and relaxed back into his chair as though he were lounging at his club. At least that loose-limbed sprawl was how she assumed gentlemen lounged at their clubs. "I can get you articles. There are plenty of people I know with things to say. People who would relish a way to say it. You realize what risk you're running publishing their words, though."

"Oh yes. It wouldn't be very fair if I took no risks myself. Perhaps I should be more careful, for the sake of my brother and his family. But I don't think he'd want me to. If he knew. Which I'm quite determined he won't."

"Protecting people for their own safety can be dangerous."

"Do you speak from experience?"

He took another drink of wine. "My dear Miss Roth. I've never cared about anyone enough to try to protect them."

"You're very good at talking nonsense."

"My child. There's no way you can know it's nonsense."

"No. I'm rather good at judging people, though. My brother even asks for my advice when he's on a case. But we didn't come here to talk about feelings. However determined you may be to prove you don't care about anyone, you quite clearly care about politics. And about your friends, I should think."

"Some people want to change the world without caring about those who live in it."

"Yes, but I don't think you're one of them."

He lifted his glass. It half-covered his face. "My dear girl. You can't possibly know that. You just met me."

"I've seen some of your letters to Désirée. I've heard about the things you've done. I've listened to your music."

"Oh, quite appalling people can write exquisite music. Don't be taken in by that."

"I should think music can also reveal things people won't share in words."

"Possibly." He twirled the stem of his glass between his fingers. "The question is what those things are."

"An interesting question. And I imagine the composer may not even realize everything they are revealing."

"You're a dangerous woman, Miss Roth." Gresham returned his glass to the table. "You must have other sources."

"Oh yes. My parents were booksellers connected to Radical circles. My brother now moves in political circles through his investigations."

"Ah, yes. The Rannochs."

"Do you know them?"

"Mostly by reputation. I've read articles she's written. They're quite brilliant. As are his speeches, though I probably shouldn't let on to having paid attention."

"You've already admitted to political contacts. There's no sense in pretending you don't care about politics."

"It's the persona. Acting dies hard." He studied her face. "What do you want me to do?"

"You collect articles from people you know and pass them to me. I assemble each issue, write the connections between the articles. No one suspects me, which gives me freedom. And makes it difficult to trace anything to me. Which protects us all. Though it's not without risk."

"Well said."

"By the way, you could always write an article yourself."

"If I were willing to take the risk?"

"Oh, I rather think risk is something you relish."

He leant forwards to pick up his glass. The sunlight slanted across his face for an instant before he relaxed back into the shadows. "Oddly, I have the sense I'm taking one of the greatest ones of my life just now."

"You do talk nonsense."

"Do I?" Gresham lifted his glass to her and took a deep drink. "We'll have to see."

CHAPTER 23

July 1821
London

Manon Caret regarded Mélanie across the green room at the Tavistock Theatre. Her blue eyes, which could hold so many secrets, were wide with shock. "I had no idea she was missing. If I had done, I'd have come to you right away."

"There's no way you could have known," Mélanie said.

Manon moved to the tea table and poured Mélanie a cup of tea. "Odd how we've all adapted."

"To drinking tea?" Mélanie accepted the cup Manon was holding out.

"To falling in love with Englishmen. You, me, Jennifer. Désirée."

"Oh, Malcolm's Scottish." Mélanie took a sip of tea. Bracing rehearsal tea, rougher edged than the brew they drank in Berkeley Square.

"Same island." Manon refilled her own cup. "We've all fallen in love with the victors."

They moved to a chipped gilt settee that was an old set piece, like most of the furniture in the green room. "You remember what it was like in Paris after Waterloo," Manon said. "Our friends were being arrested all round. Any comment, any rumor could lead to one being next. I'll own my own focus was sheer survival. I'm still not sure the girls and I would have been able to escape if you hadn't been able to help."

"You mean because I was collaborating with the victors." The familiar bitterness of the tea bit Mélanie in the throat with unexpected force.

"Hardly collaborating. You were a spy."

"I wasn't reporting to Raoul anymore after Waterloo. I was dancing and dining with the victors as they ran roughshod over France."

"You were fortunate to be safe. And that let you help others."

"I had to be doing something." Mélanie curled her fingers round the warmth of the cup, gaze on the pink transferware flowers. She could see herself at a reception at the British embassy, diamonds in her hair and at her throat and ears, smiling at the Duke of Wellington.

"And that's how it was for me, once the girls and I were safe. Oh, it took a bit. A lot to do, settling into a new country. But the news from France was too relentlessly grim. I couldn't sit idly by." Manon took a drink of tea. "The girls and I slipped over to Normandy and visited Désirée after Sophie was born."

"Yes, I know. Or, rather, I didn't, until you mentioned it in May."

"Yes, I wasn't doing the maths when I said that. Of course you'd realize by the time Sophie was born I was in Britain."

"I don't know if anyone else caught it."

"Crispin didn't know. Doesn't know. Our affair had started, but it was over a year before we married." Manon took a drink of tea. "Crispin likes the tea in the green room. He says it tastes more 'real' than the blend he gets from Fortnum's. Of course, much as I love him, and much good as he does, Crispin doesn't really know what 'real' is, for nine-tenths of the world. And he can't. Not having grown up in the world he did. Which is why, after I married him"—she smiled for a moment, as though still amazed and bemused that she had actually married her English aristo lover—"it was even more important to me to do something. But other than send money to friends stuck in France, connect them with Bertrand to escape the country, and help settle them in London, I wasn't sure what else to do." Manon tugged a blonde ringlet free of her pearl earrings. "The first time I talked to Harriet was at a party in Berkeley Square, actually. She asked me about the situation in Paris. She said she'd had letters from friends of her parents who were in Paris, and others in Vienna and Brussels and Berlin, and all the issues were remarkably the same. She wanted a way to share the information. The next time I saw her, she asked me what I thought about the idea of her starting a newsletter. A way to connect all this information and give voices to these people. It would have to be done very secretly, to protect the sources. Nothing as official as publishing a newspaper, even a Radical one. Though Harriet already knew Edmund Blayney, and thought he'd be a good source to help with the printing. What she needed was help broadening her sources. That was when I thought of Désirée. She was enjoying motherhood more than she expected, but also going a bit mad in Normandy feeling sidelined. She'd started writing. And her connections across the Continent were even broader than mine. I thought about going to meet her myself. But Harriet said it would be safer for her. No one paid attention to the doings of a spinster aunt—her words. And she confessed she'd relish the adventure."

Mélanie took another drink of tea. "It's precisely the sort of project I'd have loved to help with."

"You were already writing articles in your own right. But you couldn't have helped with this. Or, you could have, but you'd have been risking Malcolm."

"More than I already do?"

Manon's smile acknowledged the risks they all ran without trying to deny them. "And you were in Italy part of the time all this was starting. And then, when you came back, even though you had a pardon, we knew Hubert Mallinson was tracking you. Harriet was perfect because no one paid attention to her, as she said. It was the perfect persona. Which she carefully cultivates. She'd make a brilliant actress."

"And Désirée introduced her to Tristram Gresham."

"Who was able to broaden her sources still further. Harriet didn't tell me a great deal—she was careful to not reveal more than she had to, to protect everyone."

Mélanie turned her teacup in her hand. "Désirée said Harriet and Gresham were emotionally entangled. She isn't sure how far it had gone."

"I'd say the same. Harriet's guarded about her feelings. Gresham clearly meant something to her. But there was another man who did, as well. A source."

"John Southcott."

Manon's brows rose. "She never told me his name."

"He's a foreign office official. His father is a senior diplomat. Tony Bamford is his uncle."

"Good god."

"By now we shouldn't be surprised at how we're all inter-twined, I suppose. It's one of the things that shocked me most about Malcolm's world when I first came to Britain." Mélanie took a drink of tea. "John Southcott is inclined to be stuffy, according to Malcolm and Julien. But he's the one who noted the anomaly in the ledger that led Palmerston to discover the payments to LeFou."

"Interesting. Harriet said she had a new source, who was from inside the foreign office. She said she'd been hesitant at first and was being careful what she shared with him, but his information seemed reliable, and she thought he was genuine in wanting to speak out." Manon frowned.

"What?" Mélanie asked.

Manon turned her teacup on its saucer. "She said they had very different images of Britain and its power. But that it was interesting to talk so openly to someone with an opposing viewpoint. I know that may not sound like a great deal, but with Harriet, any romantic entanglement was going to involve talking politics. And I could tell she was intrigued."

"Kitty and Julien thought Mr. Southcott was intrigued by Harriet. Kitty says he's quite plainly in love with her."

Manon smiled. "I'm not surprised. I don't think Harriet has any idea how bewitching she is. But she always claimed to have no interest in marriage. She admitted she'd seen some positive examples in our circle. But she'd also seen from Jeremy and Allegra how it could go awry. Even if there was love at the start. And she said it would take a very special man to let her be who she wanted to be. And that even then, it would be a lot of work. And she wasn't sure she had time for it." Manon took another drink of tea. "I must say she has a point. It took a lot for me to agree to marry Crispin. Though I think it may be the best decision I've ever made."

CHAPTER 24

November 1820
London

"Sorry to be late." Harriet stepped into the small room in the basement of the Tavistock Theatre and pulled the door to. Odd how meeting in London, within walking distance of where she lived, could feel more daring than her secret trips to Désirée's Normandy cottage.

"Difficulties?" Tristram got up from the battered pianoforte where he'd been picking out a melody from his new opera. Amazing the sounds he could coax even from an inferior instrument. She'd missed those sounds. He'd been on a secret trip to Austria, and they hadn't met for some weeks.

"I dodged into a milliner's when I thought I saw someone I know through the Rannochs, and then took a roundabout path the rest of the way. Nothing terribly taxing." She undid the strings on her bonnet. "You must be used to secret meetings all the time. Do you bring your mistresses here?"

"To Simon's theatre? That would be a bit unfair."

"So you admit you believe in fairness." She set her bonnet on a chipped gilt-painted chair.

"Call it professional courtesy." He came forwards into the light from the brace of candles beside the pianoforte. The shadows round his eyes were darker and the hollows beneath his cheeks deeper.

"What happened?" She took an involuntary few steps forwards.

"Some unexpected challenges. Things are difficult in Italy right now."

"Your friends?"

"Mario and Foscari are in prison. Savelli died in a skirmish with the Austrians."

She reached out and smoothed his hair from his forehead without thinking, as she would for one of her nephews. "I get so caught up in what we're doing. In the excitement. I forget, at moments, why we started. Because of how bad things are. Because we care."

"You care."

"Do stop pretending, Tristram."

His mouth twisted with familiar mockery. "My whole life is a pretense. Isn't that what you told me when we first met?"

"I thought one of the advantages of our work was that we could be ourselves with each other. At least, that's how it is for me. Not that I'm not myself with my friends, precisely. But I hide parts of myself. I don't have to do that with you." She regarded him for a moment in the flickering candlelight. It warmed his skin, but as always, what lay in his eyes was elusive. "I don't think I've ever thanked you."

"You certainly don't owe me anything. Don't turn sentimental, Harriet. Your lack of sentimentality is one of your charms."

"I don't aim to be charming."

"You needn't aim to be sentimental, either."

Harriet touched his arm, wishing she could wipe the shadows

from beneath his eyes. "Take care of yourself, Tristram. If you go on like this, you won't be able to keep up your pose of cheerful libertine, and then where will you be?"

Tristram gave a quick grin and moved away. Almost, it seemed, pulling away from the touch of her hand, though he went to a table with glasses and a corked bottle. "Oh, they'll just put it down to the excesses of my dissipated lifestyle." He uncorked the bottle and poured two glasses of wine. "As I've said, a rakish reputation can cover for all sorts of things."

Harriet accepted a glass of wine. "I heard a rumor while you were gone. About the Condessa Azevado."

"Oh, yes. Rosalind." Tristram took a drink from his own glass. "Her father's one of Britain's leading diplomats."

"Désirée's duke."

"Oh, lord. Don't let him hear you say that. Or no, I rather think Bamford wouldn't mind being called 'Désirée's duke' at all. But Désirée would be horrified. Yes, Rosalind is his youngest daughter —well, his youngest except for Sophie. Married to a Portuguese diplomat."

"The Duke of Bamford is a friend of yours."

"We work together. He's been very supportive about the situation in Naples. Surprisingly decent for a Tory."

Harriet took a drink of wine. The sort of red they might have drunk in a coffeehouse. If they could go to a coffeehouse together. "Precisely."

"And that means I should have kept my hands off his daughter?"

"No, the condessa is her own person. If she wants to have an affair, that's her choice, not her father's."

"You're remarkable, Harriet. I'll admit it's not my finest moment. Rosalind made her interest plain, and I was in the midst of some complicated work, trying to get aid to my Carbonari friends."

"Looking for cover?"

"Or distraction. Or both." Tristram glanced at the settee. "Do you mind if we sit down? I'm a bit unsteady on my feet."

Harriet moved to the settee, a careful eye on him. "Back to my earlier point. For you to collapse won't help your reputation as a roué."

"Mmm. Might be good for sympathy." Tristram lowered himself onto the settee and sank back against the frayed velvet cushions.

"You've been in a fight," Harriet said.

"A skirmish with some Austrian soldiers." He took a drink of wine. "I like the latest edition. You have a new source. British government?"

Harriet took a careful sip from her own glass. She trusted Tristram as she trusted few people. But the instinct to protect a source was deeply ingrained. "Yes. He sought me out. He says he's no Radical, but there are things he sees that have to change, and he needs to find a way to speak out. It's an interesting perspective."

"Do you trust him?"

"That's always a matter of judgment, isn't it? I'm careful with what I share with him. As I am with all my sources."

"Including me. Point taken."

"I trust you more than most people, Tristram. But we all have to keep certain things to ourselves. For the sake of our sources, as well as our own sake."

"Fair enough."

She took another drink of wine. "He's a bit annoyingly inclined to worry about the risks I'm running. He's—" She hesitated, reaching for a word to describe John Southcott.

"Flirtatious?"

"Oh, no. He's much too serious for that. He—"

"Is interested?" Tristram grinned.

"In sharing information."

"That wouldn't stop him from being interested in more." Tristram rested his elbow on the settee arm. "There's no harm in a flirtation, Harriet."

"Oh, I flirt all the time, in the polite way one does at parties. I've got rather better at it since we started moving in the Rannochs' circles. I haven't got time for anything else."

"The Rannochs and your other friends seem to manage."

"That's different. They're married, and they have each other—though how they all—Malcolm and Mélanie, and Julien and Kitty, and Laura and Raoul, and the others—muddled through to where they are now is rather amazing. But it's not easy to find that sort of relationship, and it seems terribly time consuming. Just look at all the time you spend on your affairs."

His wine glass tilted in his fingers. "I wasn't suggesting—"

"Tristram, did you actually flush?"

"It must be the light. You need hardly behave like me to indulge in romance."

"Tristram, don't you dare turn into one of those people."

He righted his glass and took a long drink. "What people?"

"The sort who go on and on about the joys of romance and what I'm missing. I'll tolerate it a bit from my friends who are so disgustingly in love themselves. It's patently absurd from you."

"Just because I have no taste for domesticity doesn't mean I can't acknowledge that it works for others."

"Quite." Harriet took a drink of wine. "I don't think it would work for me."

"I'm not sure why you're so convinced of that."

"Why are you so convinced it wouldn't work for you?"

"My dear girl. Have you seen the life I live?"

"You seem rather less happy in it than I am in mine."

Tristram frowned and contemplated the candlelight shooting through the red of his wine. "You may have a point."

"Unless you're suggesting I indulge in an affair. That's something else entirely."

"My dear—" He spun round to look at her, sloshing wine over

the rim of his glass. "There are all sorts of consequences. And it's a more dangerous game for women than men. Rail against that all you like—I'll gladly rail with you—but for the moment, you can't avoid the realities."

"Quite. Not that I'd want a legion of lovers, in any case. It sounds more time consuming than a legion of children. Which I don't want, either. Fond as I am of my nephews." She took another drink of wine. "You're getting a bit of your color back. Can we settle to work?"

CHAPTER 25

July 1821
London

"Harry." Fitzroy Somerset looked up from his desk in the Ordnance Office. "It's good to see you." He stood to shake Harry's hand. "I hope Cordelia's well. And your daughters?"

"Delighted with their puppy and trying to catch me out with their knowledge of classical history."

Fitzroy grinned. "Mine aren't quite there yet. But it's hard to believe what distinct personalities they've become. Harriet and I wonder at it every day."

Fitzroy's wife, Emily Harriet, was Wellington's niece. Yet another complication in the investigation. "Harriet's well?" Harry asked.

"Oh, yes. Enjoying the season. Happy that Almack's is still holding assemblies." Fitzroy's brows drew tightened for a moment. Perhaps he'd remembered that Cordelia had been denied vouchers to Almack's when she and Harry were separated.

Rare for Fitzroy to make such a blunder. Enough to make Harry wonder if something was amiss.

"Even I can admit the season has its diversions," Harry said.

Fitzroy smiled, then waved Harry to one of the chairs across from his desk. "What's the investigation?"

Harry raised a brow as he dropped into the ladder-back chair. "What makes you think there's an investigation?"

"These days, when you or Malcolm stop in to see me, it's usually an investigation," Fitzroy said, in the same easy voice in which he'd relayed the most sensitive order during the Peninsula and Waterloo campaigns. Often late at night, by a guttering candle, while the others were passing a wine bottle round. "It's certainly not likely to be to discuss politics," he added in the same tone.

Harry met Fitzroy's steady blue gaze. They'd been fellow aides-de-camp to Wellington. Harry had been seconded to intelligence, and Fitzroy had been Wellington's military secretary. Fitzroy was still Wellington's secretary, but Wellington was now Master General of the Ordnance, and a Tory politician. Fitzroy had sat in the Commons as a Tory himself for two years until he'd lost his seat in last year's general election. Harry was a classical scholar again, theoretically not in the political realm, but there was no question of where his political allegiance lay. "Both Malcolm and I have friends across the political aisle. So do you."

"Oh yes." Fitzroy aligned the edges of a stack of papers on his desk. "But there's no denying we've all moved in different directions. In truth, I'm glad when one of your investigations brings us together."

"I can't really say it's an investigation," Harry said, not quite truthfully. Not at all truthfully, actually, though it was true he hadn't been in on the start of this particular investigation. More's the pity. "And you probably won't want to share it, in any case. But we had a rather preposterous report from a soldier in India that the duke might have been secretly reaching out to some foreign contacts. I thought perhaps I could clear the whole thing up just by asking if you'd heard anything."

He expected a quick denial. In truth, he'd begun his inquiries with Fitzroy because of Fitzroy's close relationship to Wellington, but he'd been fairly certain he'd have to move on to other sources to get any real information. But to his surprise, Fitzroy's eyes widened, not with shock but with what almost seemed to be relief. "No—not that precisely."

"But you've heard something." Harry leant back in his chair, careful not to push. He knew when he had an opening.

Uncertainty flickered across Fitzroy's face. He had lived his life in a world of certainties. He served Wellington, he smoothed over controversies, he maintained a sunny demeanor when all hell was breaking loose, but he rarely questioned. Yet something was clearly eating at him.

"You should know I can keep secrets," Harry said. "But you must also know that if I don't get answers, I'll keep asking questions."

Fitzroy ran a hand through his thick fair hair. "I should be horrified. But all I can think is thank god you've come asking questions. Which I suppose gives me my answer. I've been trying to decide what to do about this. And talking to you makes the most sense, since you're at least a friend of his."

"I don't think anyone can exactly call Hookey a friend. At least, not anyone who served under him."

"Not Wellington." Fitzroy's mouth tightened. He pushed back his chair, crossed to a cabinet against the wall, and tugged open the doors. He fished a key from his pocket to unlock a drawer behind the doors, took out a brass-bound box, and crossed back to his desk. He hesitated again, then unlocked the box with another key and stared down at whatever lay inside. "Not Wellington," he repeated. "Tony Bamford."

"What?" Harry half pushed himself out of his chair.

"It surprised me too. I've been stewing about what to do."

Fitzroy pulled a pair of tweezers from a desk drawer and carefully lifted a charred fragment of paper from the box. "I found this in the grate in the duke's office. I'm always careful when there are fragments left of any papers he's burnt. Usually I recognize what they are and destroy them. Most often, if they're something political, I know about it. And if they're something personal"—his gaze clouded for a moment, not surprisingly, given the state of Wellington's marriage—"I simply make sure they disappear. This was different." He nodded at Harry to come over and look at the paper.

Harry stood and moved round the desk to study the paper. Half of it was burnt away, but the remainder was enough to shake him, even after the morning's revelations.

—secrecy is paramount. Are you sure you can trust the person you've hired? I agree we have no choice but to move. Lionel can't be allowed to continue. Risk—but if we're exposed—treason.

It was signed *Bamford*. And stamped with Tony Bamford's seal.

Harry stared at the paper, committing the fragments to memory. Lionel was almost certainly Lionel Southcott, Tony's diplomat brother.

"I perhaps should have just destroyed it," Fitzroy said. "But I can't help but wonder—"

"What?" Harry asked. His voice came out more sharply than he intended.

Fitzroy scraped a hand over his hair. "If Wellington was involved in something over his head. Or something—"

"That you wouldn't approve of?"

"No. Possibly. When I asked him if he'd heard from Bamford lately, he said Bamford hadn't communicated with him in months. I know there's been a great deal of talk round Bamford, with the divorce. There could be an innocuous reason for Wellington to avoid admitting he'd talked with Bamford. Though it's more difficult to put that together with what's in the note." He drew a breath. "It's difficult for me to come up with any explanation of what's in the note."

Harry met Fitzroy's gaze. "You're worried."

"Very."

<hr />

CORDELIA DAVENPORT MET Mélanie at the door of Gunter's, just down Berkeley Square from the Rannoch house. She greeted Mélanie with a sunny smile from beneath the brim of a straw hat lined with azure satin and adorned with artificial cornflowers. "Wretch. You kept us out of all the excitement."

"I'm sorry." Mélanie leant forwards to hug Cordy in the light way that would make this appear a perfectly usual social meeting to any passing observer. "Everything happened very quickly last night."

"I know. And I'm sorry, I didn't mean to be beastly." Cordelia drew back, and adjusted Mélanie's rose silk bonnet which had been knocked slightly askew. Her blue eyes smiled into Mélanie's own with concern. "I'm sorry we weren't there to help. It must have been horrid."

"I had some bad moments when Malcolm was missing." Mélanie tugged at the ribbons on her bonnet. She'd chosen it in the hope that the deep brim would shadow the dark circles under her eyes. "But we're all right."

Cordy squeezed Mélanie's hand, a seemingly casual gesture that held a world of comfort. "It's probably quite horrid of me to confess a part of me was excited about a new investigation. Harry said much the same."

"I quite understand. Thank you for jumping in."

"We'd neither of us have forgiven you for keeping us out. It's all right, Charlotte Augustin will be here shortly. I can't claim we're close friends, but I know her enough to have asked her. Between the two of us, we can manage to talk to her."

They made their way to a table at the back that they favored because it was a bit secluded. But really, the best security for talking at Gunter's was the buzz of conversation on all sides. Highly effective at drowning out any other noise. It was still early in the day, and the weather was fair. The crowd was thinner than in the late afternoon, and a number of patrons were outside in their carriages in the shade of the Berkeley Square trees, enjoying ices brought by waiters who hurried back and forth, but there were still enough customers in the shop to create cover. A waiter who knew them brought a pot of their favorite tea and a plate of cakes. Both welcome fuel after last night. It was all Mélanie could do to sip the tea and not gobble down the cakes.

Charlotte Augustin arrived a few minutes later, faultlessly attired in a jacket and petticoat of violet sarcenet and a straw satin hat with violet ribbons. Her brown hair was carefully arranged in glossy ringlets that clustered over her forehead and almost obscured her pearl earrings, but beneath the stylish brim of her hat her gaze suggested she had not slept well either.

"Charlotte," Cordelia said, springing up from her chair. "Thank you for meeting us."

"Of course." Charlotte touched her cheek to Cordelia's and inclined her head to Mélanie. "In truth, it's lovely to have an excuse for a chat that's not diplomatic protocol."

"Don't I remember it," Mélanie said.

Charlotte sank into a chair and tugged off her lilac kid gloves. She regarded Mélanie over the gilded plate of cakes and gilt-rimmed teacups. "I remember you from Vienna. You looked fault-less leaving a masquerade at three in the morning, and equally faultless and perfectly attired at a review before noon the next day."

Mélanie reached for the teapot and filled a cup for Charlotte. "Blanca gets all the credit for that. My maid. Companion, really.

She kept my clothes in order for each event and managed to get me into them and arrange my hair, and provide the masks and shawls and gloves and shoes and stockings and whatever else was required. Not to mention keeping track of the invitations and never sending me out garbed as a medieval lady when I was supposed to be a milkmaid. A milkmaid in diamonds, but still." Mélanie handed a cup of tea to Charlotte. "Neither of us could do much about the black circles under my eyes. Though I found a heavy application of eye blacking distracted from them."

Charlotte spooned sugar into her tea. "I've never known whether to regret I wasn't there or be relieved I wasn't."

Mélanie set down the teapot. "What I chiefly remember from that time was wanting more sleep and more time with my son. Not in that order. At least, usually not."

Charlotte gave a faint smile. "The Congress wasn't conducive to family life. Not necessarily such a sacrifice for some of us."

Mélanie met her gaze. Sometimes it was better to say such things directly. "I understand you are acquainted with Tristram Gresham."

Charlotte's fingers froze round the handle of her teacup. "Who said so?"

"Dorothea Lieven."

Charlotte's mouth curved. "Why am I not surprised? Many people in London society are acquainted with Lord Gresham." She reached for a wedge of lemon and squeezed it into her tea. "I'll say no more."

"He's missing."

Concern flickered through Charlotte's gaze. She set the lemon on her saucer and stirred the tea. "He travels a great deal. Often on a whim."

"True. But he doesn't seem to have taken anything with him when he left this time."

Charlotte took a measured sip of tea and set her cup down with precision. "Is this one of your investigations?" Her gaze flickered from Mélanie to Cordelia. "You must know I know you both undertake them. Along with your husbands and others. All of London knows."

"We're concerned," Cordelia said. "As you're a friend of his, we were wondering if you'd heard anything."

Charlotte turned her cup on its saucer, gaze on the tea inside. "Lord Gresham and I were never particularly close, but we haven't been as good friends for some months as we were for a time. Even then I can hardly say he confided in me. But he was—it seems odd to say kind, but he was a good friend. He was understanding in ways one might not expect."

"I'm glad," Cordelia said.

"Are you?"

"You deserve some happiness."

Charlotte gave a sharp laugh. "There isn't much happiness in a marriage that's not what one hoped. We don't all manage to fall back in love with our husbands as you did."

"I was fortunate," Cordelia said with a smile that didn't deny the past, while acknowledging her happiness in the present.

"Do you have any idea who Tristram Gresham's current mistress is?" Mélanie asked.

Charlotte frowned. "It's odd. I haven't seen him much. But he's always friendly when we do meet. We both make it a point not to seek each other out too much. But I saw him at Covent Garden recently. He was coming into Emily Cowper's box as I was leaving, and we couldn't avoid speaking. He said he hoped I was well, and of course I said I was, though I could tell he understood things were precisely as beastly as they've always been. I asked him how he was, and he got an odd look on his face, then said he was—unsettled. He hesitated like that before he said it. Then he said he was in the midst of something he'd never expected to experience. And he was afraid he was making an unforgivable mistake, but he couldn't help himself. Of course, he could have been talking about anything, but I couldn't help but think it was a romantic adventure. I mean, with Tristram that wasn't an odd assumption. Then he laughed and said he was talking nonsense and sounding like a character in one of his operas, and I mustn't take him seriously."

"That sounds like the sort of thing he might say." Cordelia cut a pink-iced cake in half and offered a half to Charlotte. "Do you have any idea whom he might have meant?"

Charlotte took a small bite of the cake, as though she wanted to keep her hands busy more than anything. "No. I didn't see him with anyone that night. Well, I saw him with all sorts of people, but no lady to whom he seemed to be attached. And I hadn't heard any gossip about him lately. Which is odd in and of itself. I know Danielle Darnault is in his new opera, and goodness knows she's exquisite, but everyone says she's unfashionably in love with her journalist husband."

"She is," Cordelia said.

Charlotte reached for her tea. "It could all be my imagination. Though, if he's disappeared, one has to consider that it could be an elopement. Though with Tristram I'd very much doubt they headed to Gretna Green or anywhere with a church."

"Do you know anyone who might wish Lord Gresham ill?" Mélanie asked.

Charlotte's fingers stilled on the gilded handle of her cup. "Do you believe someone has done him ill?"

"It's a possibility we have to consider."

"He hardly lives his life to avoid enemies." Charlotte took another sip of tea, grimaced, as though it was bitter, and set it down. "A number of husbands might be angry at him. That can't be a surprise. And I suppose a number of former mistresses. Though—from my observation—he has a disarming way of staying friends. He never promises anything he can't give." She added another spoonful of sugar to her tea and stirred it carefully. "And then there are his politics. I never knew whether to be shocked or admire his audacity. He says things that need to be said. And he gets away with it because people think he's being outrageous to make a stir. Without realizing he's quite serious."

Mélanie took a drink of tea. "You're an astute observer."

"One learns to be, in diplomatic circles." Charlotte's gaze flickered between them again. "I know the level of activity you usually investigate. Is this more serious than you're admitting? Is Trist— Lord Gresham in danger? Or has he done something?"

"Do you have reason to think either?" Mélanie said.

"Don't toy with me, Mrs. Rannoch. I've learnt to be hard-edged in diplomatic circles, but I'm not heartless."

"As far as we know, he's unharmed," Mélanie said. "But he may have disappeared because he thought he was in danger. Which he may well actually be."

Charlotte nodded, eyes dark. "Thank you."

"Did your husband know about your friendship with Lord Gresham?" Cordelia asked.

Charlotte shot a quick look at her. "You suspect Karl of something?"

"At this point, we don't know enough to suspect anyone of anything," Mélanie said. Which was more or less the truth.

Charlotte added another spoonful of sugar to her tea, stirred it, and tossed down a swallow. "Why on earth are we dancing round this? You know what passed between Tristram and me. Or something close to it. I know something very serious has happened. Is someone trying to kill Tristram?"

"Possibly," Mélanie said.

Charlotte's eyes widened, but she nodded. "And you think it might be Karl. No." She put up a hand. "I'm not shocked. At this point, there's scarcely anything Karl might do that could shock me. As to whether he knew about Tristram and me—I have no reason to think so. But the truth is, Karl is so preoccupied with his own affairs—and I mean that in every sense of the word—that he scarcely even notices mine. I'll even own to trying to get his attention, on occasion. Not with Tristram. Well before. That's why

Tristram was so refreshing. He never pretends to be anything he isn't." She stared into the depths of her teacup. "I can't say what Karl would do if he did know. He's shown little inclination to be jealous. But his pride might be hurt." She picked up her spoon and fished a lemon seed out of her cup. "I actually loved him once. Not Tristram. I was too sensible to let myself indulge in love by the time I met him. Karl. He seemed like the epitome of a girlish fairy tale. It makes me distinctly sympathetic to every fairytale princess. One can't but wonder if every prince proved to be so distinctly self-centered after the storybook closed."

"I know something about that," Cordelia said with care. "Only I didn't marry him. I used to think it was the greatest tragedy of my life that I didn't. Now I think it was my greatest escape."

Charlotte met her gaze across the pink and white and gold of the table. "I used to think being a social outcast would be a dreadful tragedy."

"You mean like I was, for a time?" Cordelia asked with a smile.

"Well, yes," Charlotte said. "But now it sounds rather lovely. Though I imagine as with all lovely things, there are unforeseen consequences." She took a drink of tea, grimaced, and added more sugar. "Are you asking every one of Tristram's former mistresses about their husbands? In which case, you must have a number of other interviews to conduct." She set her cup down with a click. "Or do you know something specific about Karl?"

Mélanie reached for the milk jug. Three ladies at the table to their right were comparing bracelets. To their left, a mother was reading her teenage daughter a lecture. A waiter hurried past with a tray of glistening ices in pink and white and pale green. Two ladies and their young daughters had just come through the door, laden with shopping parcels. Laughter and talk and the clink of teacups bounced off the ceiling. Excellent cover. Because even Cordy didn't know all the details of this. "Your husband was seen in a tavern last night with a man named André LeFou. Has your husband ever mentioned him?"

Charlotte shook her head, with a seemingly genuine lack of recognition. "Is he a diplomat?"

"He's an assassin. And he was found dead last night in Tristram Gresham's rooms. Gresham wasn't there."

Charlotte sat back in her chair, eyes glazed with shock. "You think Karl hired this man to kill Tristram?"

"We think it's much more likely whoever hired him has a motive that's political. But your husband had some connection to him. And you're a connection between your husband and Tristram Gresham."

Charlotte glanced away. "Only if he knew. But I can't—If Karl was jealous, it would only be because his pride was hurt. I could see him challenging Tristram to a duel. Planting him a facer. But not—" She shook her head.

"I realize you have no reason to trust us," Mélanie said.

"Not exactly. I want to know what happened to Tristram."

"But could your husband be involved in anything else? Anything that might have given him a reason to meet a foreign agent."

Charlotte clunked down her cup. "You just said he was an assassin."

"To be blunt, yes."

"Mrs. Rannoch, your husband clearly shares his work with you. Karl barely tells me whom he played cards with at his club. And if he does, I suspect it's elaborate cover for a tryst with a mistress. You can't imagine he'd have told me about anything he was engaged in that might involve an international assassin. The only thing I can say is that from observing how Karl's colleagues treat him, I'd be surprised he was trusted with anything so sensitive as surely this would be."

Mélanie nodded. That fit her appraisal of Karl Augustin. "Do you know anything about your husband's movements last night? What time he came home?"

Charlotte went still. Her gaze fastened on the crumbs of pink icing and white cake on her plate. Then she lifted her gaze to meet Mélanie's own. "Karl didn't come home last night. I wouldn't necessarily know that, but I heard the maids gossiping about it when I went down to breakfast."

"Is that unusual?" Cordelia asked.

"Not unusual in the least," Charlotte said. "Though usually he comes home at some point in the morning. He hadn't returned by the time I left to meet you."

"So you don't know where he is at present?" Mélanie asked.

Charlotte returned Mélanie's gaze steadily. "No."

CHAPTER 26

January 1821
Normandy

Tristram dropped into a chair at the deal table in the cottage kitchen. "She's running appalling risks. You both are. But you're used to it."

"A point." Désirée uncorked a bottle of wine. Tony's favorite Bordeaux. She'd accused him once of becoming an agent just so he could have a safe cottage stocked with French wine without resorting to smugglers. Of course, it took an agent who happened to be a duke to have a safe cottage like this at all. "Did you only just notice it?"

"The risks, or that Harriet's far from used to running them? I noticed both the day I met her."

Désirée poured two glasses of Bordeaux and handed one to him. "Are you suggesting she stop?"

"God, no. I wouldn't presume. And anyway, then she wouldn't be who I—" Tristram took a quick drink of wine. "But I wonder sometimes if she realizes what she's got herself into."

"Oh, she realizes it." Désirée sat at the table across from him.

Much as she and Tony had sat at this table the night they met. "She's worried about her brother and his children. But I think she also feels alive as she hasn't before. I can understand that."

"Christ, so can I." Tristram tossed down another drink of wine. "It doesn't stop me from worrying, though. Damned uncomfortable."

Désirée took a drink from her own glass. "It is, isn't it? It took me years to admit how much I worried about Tony."

"I didn't say I—"

Désirée regarded Tristram over the rim of her glass. "I hope you know what you're doing."

"My dear." He leant back where the light from the brace of candles on the table and the glow from the stove didn't touch his face. "When have you ever known me to know what I was doing?"

For some reason, Désirée thought of Sophie, when she had tucked her in an hour ago. "I've become quite fond of Harriet. She's brilliant. She can run rings round most of us intellectually. But that doesn't mean she can take care of herself emotionally."

Tristram dragged his glass across the table to him, rather like a shield. "Désirée. Are you suggesting that a woman needs to be protected?"

"Perish the thought."

"Then are you suggesting that an unmarried woman needs to be protected?"

Désirée took a drink of wine. "I'm unmarried. If you mean, delicately, am I suggesting that a virgin needs to be protected, I have no way of knowing if Harriet is one or not, and I don't think it matters. If you mean that she's likely never been in love before, I think that's spot on. And precisely why I think she's at risk."

Tristram settled back in his chair, arms folded, glass held between two fingers. "How often had you been in love before Bamford?"

"No comment."

He took a studied sip of wine. "For that matter, you might ask how often I've been in love. Or how much risk I'm at."

Désirée reached for her glass. "My dear. There's no need to ask. You're hopelessly at risk. But you've put yourself in the game more than Harriet."

"Fair enough." He took a drink of wine, holding the glass as though it were the ramparts of a besieged city. "I'm a terrible risk for her. It's quite appalling for me to have let it go as far as I did."

Désirée took a drink of wine. Tony had opened a bottle of the same wine the night she met him, though it had been a far older vintage. God, that had been over two decades ago. "That's a coward's way out, Gresham."

"What are you trying to do? Persuade me to matrimony?"

"Is that such a terrible idea?" She leant forwards and refilled their glasses.

He clunked his glass down, spattering drops of wine on the mellowed wood of the table. They glistened blood red in the candlelight. "Have you gone completely insane? Even you and Bamford haven't gone that far."

"Well, technically, we couldn't. The little matter of Tony's having a duchess."

"Are you telling me you want to marry Bamford?"

She laughed. The life she and Tony were living was improbable enough as it was. "Can you imagine me married?"

"Ha. Not particularly, but better than I can imagine my attempting connubial bliss."

"I have no need to be married."

Tristram glanced from the pink-flowered cup on the table, with sticky jam on the rim, to the doll bed on the floor, to the trail of blocks running under the table. "Come to think of it, you're living a ridiculously domestic life. You might as well be married."

Désirée picked up a satin doll shoe half hidden by one of the blocks. "As I said, I have no need to be married. But I do quite like living with Tony. In fact, I wish he could be here more."

"Hard to believe this is Désirée Clairineau speaking."

She put the shoe on the doll bed. "Waterloo put a number of things into perspective. I realized I didn't want to lose any more time with him than I had to. And that I wanted Sophie to have time with him."

"You aren't suggesting Harriet and I—"

"I'm not suggesting you and Harriet do anything you don't want to do."

"You think she wants—Or I want—"

"I think it's quite clear what the two of you want when it comes to each other. And I think it's clear on your side it's more than you've had with other women."

"You think I want to be married? You just said you don't yourself."

"I think the question is what you might do if Harriet wanted to be married."

"I couldn't—" His gaze shot to the side. "She's not in the beau monde, but she'd be judged."

"Precisely. And for all your reputation, you're not the sort to put a woman in that position."

Tristram turned his glass in his hand. "I like her. I like most of the women I—you know what I mean."

"Yes, I do. It's one of your saving graces."

"But it's different with Harriet. She's more than a friend. She's someone I—It's ridiculously agreeable being with her."

"I think you just described being in love."

"That's a damned odd way of putting it."

"It's actually one of the more sensible definitions of love I've heard."

He tossed down a swallow of wine. "I'd be a disaster at it."

"At what, precisely?"

"Anything approaching matrimony."

"Are you so sure you'd be unfaithful?"

"No! That is, I don't—" He scraped a hand over his hair. "It's not as simple as that. Even I can tell marriage requires a certain amount of focusing on the other person."

"You strike me as very focused on Harriet."

"She's avoided scandal. She has a lot of options." Tristram snatched up the bottle and refilled their glasses. "I'm not even sure what she thinks of me. She has a source at the foreign office she seems quite fond of."

"She's intrigued by him as a source. As am I. That's hardly the same as romantic interest."

Tristram took a quick drink of wine. "Désirée, surely you can tell from her stories that the man is already half in love with her."

"You're sounding more like an opera composer than an agent, Tristram. But yes, I can read enough in her careful accounts of their meetings to sense that his interest seems to go beyond politics. I'm not sure hers does. Of course, perhaps that's my own bias."

"I thought you liked nice Tory aristos."

"A palpable hit, as Tony would say. But Tony's unique."

"Well, perhaps this fellow is too. I wouldn't be so dismissive. It could be a chance for Harriet to—"

"What?" Désirée said. "Marry a nice, sensible man and have a nice, sensible life?"

"Does that sound so horrid?"

Désirée clunked her glass down. "Are you asking me?"

"Doesn't it sound like what you want? Isn't Tony sensible?"

"I told you. I don't want to be married."

"Harriet isn't you."

"No, of course not. That doesn't change what she wants. Or doesn't want."

"You don't think she'd want to be married?"

"I think she would be bored to death by a nice, sensible man who wanted her to have a nice, sensible life. Even one who is passing secret foreign office information. Unless there's a great deal more to him than we know. She thrives on adventure. That doesn't mean she doesn't want to be married."

"Exactly," Tristram said. "And I'm not suited—"

"For someone who plays with artistic form, not to mention being a revolutionary, you seem to have a very narrow-minded view of marriage."

"You're the one who said you didn't want to be married."

"A woman gives up a great deal when she marries. Control over her money, her children, her body even. It's a great risk unless one absolutely trusts one's marriage partner. Even then it's a risk. Not one I care to run. But Harriet may make a different calculation."

"You think she'd trust me, of all people?"

"Tristram, you are many things, but you have a good deal to recommend you when it comes to relations between the sexes. I can't see your becoming a domestic tyrant."

"Plenty of people who don't believe in political tyranny are tyrants at home."

"So they are. But I don't think you're one of them."

"You're a brilliant woman, Désirée. But even you can be prey to delusions. I'm not a romantic hero."

"I should hope not. Any sensible woman would run screaming at the sight of most of those. I'm quite sure Harriet would. But you're also not Don Giovanni. It you were, you'd have seduced Harriet and abandoned her long before now. So there's no sense in pretending that you are. It's shockingly self-indulgent."

Tristram took a drink of wine. "Only you would call admitting one is a rake self-indulgent."

"Depends on one's definition of rake."

"You're a mother now." Tristram glanced at the doll bed. "Is this what you want for Sophie?"

"I want Sophie to be happy."

"But are you going to trust that she knows what that means?"

"We'll have to see. As with many things, I'm managing mother-hood one moment at a time."

"What about Bamford?"

Conversations with Tony echoed in her mind. Conversations that might get more challenging as Sophie got older. "What about him?"

"What does he want for her?"

"Tony's a ridiculous romantic. I suspect he wants her to fall madly in love and marry the man she chooses—who will also be agreeable to Tony and me—and live happily ever after. I adore Tony, but he has all sorts of delusions."

"Or perhaps he's more sensible than any of us."

Désirée felt her fingers freeze round the stem of her glass. "Oh, Tristram. You're more far gone than any of us."

He tossed down the last of wine and stared into the dregs. "Isn't that what you've been trying to persuade me of?"

CHAPTER 27

July 1821
London

Hara turned to look at Laura from his chair by the windows in the bedchamber he and Lizzy were occupying in Berkeley Square. He'd eaten this morning, and though he was still pale, some of his color had returned. The outlines of his bandage showed through the paisley dressing gown of Malcolm's he was wrapped in. "There aren't words to describe how much we owe you."

"Nonsense." Laura set the tea tray she'd brought in on the table by the chair. "I'm quite sure you'd have done the same for any of us."

Hara smiled. "And I'm quite sure you'd have thanked us if we had."

"That's what friends do. Though I have to say, we'd help anyone who stumbled wounded into the house."

Lizzy paused in the midst of tying the strings on her bonnet. "You say that as though it happens regularly."

"I wouldn't say regularly. Not precisely."

"I suppose that puts our crisis in perspective." Lizzy threw a shawl round her shoulders. "I'll leave you to talk. I know you have a lot to catch up on. Blanca and Addison and Laila took the children out to the square garden. I said I'd join them." She bent to kiss Hara's cheek, then whisked herself from the room.

Hara watched the door close behind his wife, then looked at Laura. "You're sure they're safe in the square garden?"

Laura picked up the teapot. "Addison and Blanca are both agents. They know how to be on the watch for danger. I trust them with my own children."

Hara watched her for a moment as she poured tea. "I forget how much you've changed."

"I married into a family of spies. I couldn't help but change." She'd also been blackmailed into being a spy long before she met the Rannochs. In fact, she'd first met the Rannochs because she'd been put in their household to spy on them. She wouldn't have met Raoul otherwise. But she wasn't quite ready to share that with Hara, close as they had once been.

Hara passed a hand over his face. "I still can't credit it. What we seem to have stumbled into the midst of."

Laura handed him a cup of tea. "I've become used to international intrigue as an almost daily occurrence, and I find it startling as well. So did the others." She picked up the milk jug. "Shall I—"

"No, I can." Hara splashed milk into his tea and stirred it. "I'm not an invalid. That is, I suppose I am, but I can still manage to add milk to a cup of tea. We must take our victories where we find them." He took a drink of tea. "Do tell Lizzy I managed that on my own."

Laura poured a cup for herself. "I went through my husband's being wounded not very long ago. I'm sure I drove him mad with my fussing. But it's very hard not to worry."

Hara grinned and took a drink of tea. "I imagine you managed not to drive him mad. You've always been eminently sensible."

"Ha." Laura settled on the window seat with her own tea. "I wasn't sensible in the least when we were young."

"Perhaps it's the wrong word. But you never tried to make people's decisions for them."

She took a sip of tea. She'd brewed it with a blend of cardamon, ginger, cinnamon, cloves, and nutmeg, like the tea his mother had served them on long-ago afternoons. "Easier said than done with someone one loves. But perhaps essential. Imagine how you'd feel if Lizzy were the one injured."

"Oh, terrified. And I do drive her mad with my worrying at times. Lizzy's quick enough to say so. But then she's practically—"

"She's certainly not a child. She's old enough to take excellent care of your children." That had been clear to Laura when Laila, the Delaney children's nurse, brought the children to Berkeley Square earlier in the morning. Hal and Anjali had both run across the hall to hug Lizzy in a way that made their bond with her palpable.

"No. Of course. But—" Hara stared into his cup. "You must think me mad."

"For falling in love? How could I do so?"

"You could call me a fool." He turned his cup in his hand. "It's all very well to run risks for love at twenty. At approaching forty, one should have learnt sense. Not to mention that she's half my age."

"Hardly half. She's about fifteen years younger, as I understand it. I'm fifteen years younger than Raoul."

"But you weren't in your twenties when you met. The gap narrows."

"Yes, but of course Raoul still—"

"He had scruples about marrying you?" Hara caught her gaze.

Past conversations echoed in Laura's mind. "He had scruples mostly because he *couldn't* marry me at that point. He was still married, though he hadn't lived with his wife for over a decade and she wouldn't agree to a divorce. He kept having delusions about the sort of life I should have, married to a nice, settled man. Who would have bored me to tears. I expect you had the same sort of delusions about Lizzy."

Hara choked on a sip of tea. "Damn it, you can't blame me for worrying she'd be unhappy being tied to an old man. Not to mention being cast off by her family."

"You can't be so unchivalrous as to call yourself old when we're the same age. The last time I saw your parents, they didn't seem sorry."

"No. They still adore each other. That's what I reminded myself of when I thought about it. The truth is, most of the time I didn't think at all. I find it damnably hard to think rationally round Lizzy."

"Love will do that to you."

He set his cup down on the table by his chair and watched her for a moment. "You're talking quite like a romantic. You used to disdain the word love."

Laura curled her fingers round the warmth of her cup and breathed in the fragrance of the tea. "Well, I hadn't really experienced it then. And I certainly wasn't expecting to when I met Raoul. Or for rather a long time after we met, if it comes to that. It's amazing how it changes one's perspective."

Hara smiled. "I only know him from your letters, but he strikes me as a remarkable man."

"He is. I've always run risks, but I hadn't really run risks with my emotions until him."

"That's a keen way of putting it. Lizzy turned my life upside down. At a time when I wasn't expecting to love again. And we rather—we had to run off without thinking things through properly."

"Lizzy says she threw herself at you and didn't give you a choice."

"No. That is—I was trying to do the right thing, but I'm not sure I could have borne to let her go." He reached for his cup and took a drink of tea. "The truth is I could have sung with relief when she turned up, insisting we go off together. But at three-and-twenty it's hard to see the life one's locked oneself in."

"It's hard to see that at eight-and-thirty. Not that I think we ever really lock ourselves into a life."

"She's married to me. That closes off a number of options."

"Yes, that's what Raoul said. But being with him opened so many interesting options for my life."

"I can understand his concerns. If I'd known—"

"You'd have wanted to plant him a facer for seducing me?"

"No." Hara flushed. "That is—"

Laura leant forwards to refill their teacups. "Actually, I seduced him."

"Good god, Laura. You always knew how to say the most scandalous things."

"Glad some things haven't changed."

"I'd have been glad to see you happy. Whatever your circumstances. But I would have worried about you."

"Oh, well." She settled back on the window seat with her tea. "I'd have worried about you. I still worry about you. We always worry about the people we care about." She took a drink of tea. "I'm impressed by your articles. I was impressed before I knew you'd written them. I rather think I should have guessed by now."

"I'm not sure how you could have done." He turned his cup in his hand. "Long before you left India, I'd learnt to focus on the needs of the present. To figure out a way to survive, for myself and my family."

"I remember your saying that," Laura said. "I thought it was horrible not to fight. I was much more naive then."

"Meaning you've decided it's better not to fight?"

"No, I think it's more important than ever. But I can understand the complications. That it's not possible for everyone. You have a family to think of."

Hara's smile took her straight back to their childhood. "It changes things, as I'm sure you've discovered."

"In ways I couldn't have imagined. I don't think I knew real terror until I had children to worry about." Which, for the first four years of Emily's life, had meant worrying about a child she was separated from, but she wasn't ready to discuss that with Hara yet either. "But at the same time, I found myself thinking about what my children would think of me."

Hara met her gaze. "That's what changed it for me. Hal and Anjali's starting to notice how I was treated differently. How their grandmother was. How they were. And even more, how the Indian population were treated. That, and Lizzy's remarkably keen comments. She wrote an article for *Le Monde Gris* before I did. I was terrified for her, but I was also in awe of her bravery." He tossed down a drink of tea. "And, by god, it felt good to find my voice again." He set down his cup. "I've never met Harriet Roth, but I admire her greatly. Do you think she's all right?"

Laura felt her cup tilt in her fingers. She righted it. "Harriet is a very intrepid woman. I thought so before I knew about *Le Monde Gris*."

"But you're worried." Hara held her gaze in that way that did not permit deception.

She took a drink of tea and willed her fingers to be steady. "How could I not be?"

CHAPTER 28

ony stared at Harry. "What the devil?"

"I know," Harry said. "That was pretty much my reaction. And Fitzroy's. Which accounts for his turning this over. The fact he showed it to me was almost as surprising as the letter itself."

They were in the Berkeley Square library. Mélanie and Cordelia had walked back from seeing Charlotte at Gunter's, just as Harry returned from his interview with Fitzroy Somerset. Malcolm, Désirée, Julien, and Kitty had already been there. Only Raoul was still out making inquiries. Lizzy was in the square garden with Blanca, Addison, and Laila. And Laura was upstairs with Hara. Tony had gone to speak with contacts, but had returned just after Harry to hear the explosive story Harry had gleaned from Fitzroy Somerset. Mélanie had seen him in a number of crises, but she didn't think she'd ever seen such shock on his face.

Tony looked down again at the charred fragment of letter that Harry had carefully transported to Berkeley Square in a box and placed on the library table. "God knows my brother and I don't see eye to eye on a number of things. The last time we met he—"

"Attacked you for marrying a French agent?" Désirée said.

"Wasn't best pleased by my plans for divorce and remarriage," Tony said. "He used some unfortunate words. The talk did not end well. I'll go so far as to say it may have done permanent damage to our relationship. But I certainly didn't wish him ill." He glanced at the paper again, as though it might bite him. "I never wrote this." His gaze shot from Harry to Malcolm to Mélanie. "Do you believe me?"

"Of course," Malcolm said.

"Good of you, Rannoch. Of course, you're questioning if there's any way it could be true. I'd do the same."

"I've learnt to be sure of few things," Malcolm said. "And few people. And my relationship with my own brother was fraught. I still can't make sense of what we're dealing with here. But I'm almost certain you weren't plotting your brother's death."

"Thank you," Tony said.

"You didn't ask if I believe it." Désirée moved to stand beside Tony.

"Oh, I always take it for granted you don't entirely believe anything I say." Tony flashed a grin at her.

Désirée returned the grin, then looked down at the paper with an appraising gaze. "It's an excellent forgery. But the curl at the end of the 'd' isn't quite right. And it looks like the signer went back over the 'B' to make the lines correct."

"So someone's trying to frame Tony," Mélanie said. "And probably Wellington, as well."

"That would seem likely," Harry said. "If Wellington were really involved in a plot, I can see him or his associates trying to frame Tony, but it wouldn't make much sense to do so in a way that implicated Wellington as well."

"Except that this only implicates Wellington because Fitzroy found it in the duke's grate," Malcolm pointed out. "Fitzroy assumed it was a letter from Tony to Wellington that Wellington burnt. But there's nothing on the fragment to suggest Tony wrote it to the duke. To Wellington, that is."

"My god, Rannoch," Julien said. "That would be devious thinking even from me."

"Malcolm." Harry stared at his friend. "Are you suggesting that Wellington drafted this to frame Tony?"

"Well, not Wellington personally," Malcolm said. "He has many skills, but I don't think forgery is among them. But if Wellington really did hire an assassin, I wouldn't put it past him to hire a forger."

"Hiring a forger is one thing," Desirée said. "Would Wellington implicate Tony?" She looked round the group. "I've only met him a handful of times, and I was in disguise most of them. I've never seen him interact with Tony."

"I haven't seen much of him lately," Tony said. "But it's clear he's not much pleased with the turn my politics have taken. And —" He broke off.

"The turn your personal life has taken?" Désirée asked.

Tony flushed, but didn't avoid her gaze. "He made it clear he hasn't the least interest in anyone's personal life. After all, this is the man who said he'd make damned sure Uxbridge didn't run off with him, and he didn't care who else the man ran off with. But he also made it clear he thinks marriage is a commitment to keep. Which he's done. At least so far as actually staying married."

"But you're friends," Cordelia said. "Sorry, that sounds a bit naive. But surely—"

"I'm not precisely sure I'd call us friends," Tony said. "Colleagues, certainly." His brows drew together.

Désirée touched her hand to his arm. Tony gripped her fingers. "I wouldn't have thought Wellington would frame me. But I wouldn't have thought he'd be involved in an assassination plot either. I don't think we can discount any possibilities."

"Wellington couldn't orchestrate this all on his own." Mélanie thought of the man she'd seen kneeling down to talk to toddler

Colin in Brussels. But then, she'd seen Hubert be quite kind to the children, and look what he was capable of. "Aides of some sort would have to be involved. An aide might have offered up a forgery meant to frame Tony, and Wellington burnt it."

"Or the aide was practicing to get the handwriting right," Kitty said. "As Désirée pointed out, it isn't very good. This could have been a discarded draft."

"Which means another version could surface," Tony said.

Malcolm gave a quick nod. "I think we have to be prepared for it."

"And given that the note was found in Wellington's study, if it was an attempt to set me up, he's likely involved." Tony said it evenly, without surprise or recrimination. "On the other hand, if someone was trying to set up both of us, difficult to see what they were expecting to achieve with this."

"It sounds like Fitzroy looks through Wellington's grate fairly regularly," Harry said. "So they might have expected him to find it. What they expected him to do with it is another question."

"Fitzroy's known to be connected to you and me," Malcolm said in a quiet voice. "However, politics have intervened between us. Someone might have thought both Fitzroy and the Delaneys would eventually get to us with the information that's fallen into their hands recently. Though in both cases, there's no guarantee they would have done so."

"So someone was trying to frame Wellington and me. Or Wellington was trying to frame me." Tony looked from Malcolm to Harry. "If it's the latter, it suggests Wellington really is targeting my brother."

"Does that seem impossible?" Malcolm asked.

"I'm a diplomat, Rannoch. I know better than to say anything is impossible." Tony folded his hands behind his back. "My brother and Wellington have disagreed about policy towards Austria. Lionel thinks Wellington is too influenced by Metternich. Such disagreements are common in diplomatic council chambers.

And in diplomatic ballrooms, for that matter. They don't generally lead to anyone's being assassinated. We're on uncharted ground here. But if Wellington were behind a plot to attack anyone—I have to admit Lionel is a possible target. Likelier than some." He shook his head. "God, I can't believe I said that."

"Even if you and Wellington are both being framed, it sounds like LeFou was hired to target your brother," Julien said. "Who else would target him?"

"Lionel's had his disagreements with Castlereagh and Liverpool. But more than anything, I'd say the Austrians. For the same reason he's disagreed with Wellington. Lionel's been particularly vocal speaking against Metternich's influence."

"And Karl Augustin was talking with LeFou," Cordelia said. "And, according to Charlotte, didn't come home last night."

"Josef Hauke went to great pains to tell me Austria wasn't involved," Malcolm said. "Which could have been an elaborate ruse to cover for his own involvement. Though normally Hauke is subtler."

"Your brother's son discovered the plot," Kitty said to Tony. "And was writing articles for Harriet. I'm not sure what to make of that, but it ties him to two parts of the plot."

"I need to talk to John," Tony said. "Especially with this news about Lionel. I have to admit I've been inclined to dismiss my nephew. But his writing articles for *Le Monde Gris* impresses me. Even more than his finding the ledger entries."

"I think Tristram was jealous of him," Désirée said.

"Given how Mr. Southcott spoke about Harriet, that doesn't surprise me in the least," Kitty said.

"That shows admirable good taste," Tony said. "Though I fear John would find Gresham challenging competition."

"I'm not sure," Désirée said.

Tony frowned. "You said she and Gresham—"

"I said there was something between them. But Harriet isn't the sort to be dazzled. I'd never expect her to do what was expected of her. Including when it came to choosing a romantic partner."

"But you said she and Gresham were in love."

"I said they had strong feelings for each other. Which they evidently do. I'll even confess I attempted to get them both to articulate those feelings. But to be honest," Désirée said, "I'm not entirely sure how to define what's between them."

CHAPTER 29

March 1821
London

*H*arriet pushed her chair back from the table in the Tavistock basement that served as a writing desk and stretched her back. "It's good. I'll look at it again in the morning." She looked up at Tristram. "It helps to work on it together. Thank you."

"Any time." Tristram reached for his coat. "I'll see you home."

Harriet got to her feet and picked up her cloak from where she'd flung it over the settee. "Much better you don't."

"You can hardly go alone—"

"I've been walking round Covent Garden alone at all hours for years." She threw her cloak over her shoulders and quickly did up the ties. "No one will be the least surprised to catch sight of me. I have a carefully cultivated reputation for eccentricity. Being seen with you will give me another sort of reputation entirely."

"I was trying—"

"To protect me. I know." Harriet grinned and touched his arm.

"It's terribly sweet of you, Tristram. And also entirely unnecessary." She reached up to kiss him on the cheek.

He went still. "You make me feel like a doddering uncle."

"Don't be silly. You're only a few years older than I am. And that isn't the least how I see you."

It was meant to be light and teasing. It came out meaning more. His face was inches from her own. She turned, aware of her quickened breathing. Or his own. Or both.

Her hand slid up his arm to his shoulder and then her fingers curled behind the back of his neck. She drew his head down to her own at the same moment his arms closed round her.

Her fingers sank into his hair. His mouth moved over her own, slid to her cheek and the pulse in her throat, returned to her lips. Honestly, it wasn't hard to see why people made such a fuss about this. Why had she waited so long?

"I've wanted to do that for months," she said, when she could speak at all.

"As often, we're in agreement." He drew back with a ragged gasp and held her away from him. "But we should stop."

"Why on earth—" Harriet stared at him, aware of her hair slipping from its pins and tumbling against her neck. "You can't tell me you have scruples."

"Everyone has them sometimes."

"Why now? Why me?"

"You don't know me."

"It seems to me I know you rather better than most people know other people before they embark on an affair. How many people write articles together first? You can learn a lot about people from crafting a sentence."

"Harriet. There's a lot you don't know about me—"

"Please don't embark on the catalogue aria. I already know there've been quite a number. I don't need the details."

"One of them was your late sister-in-law." Tristram watched her steadily, as though waiting for the instinctive recoil.

"Oh yes. I know."

"You—"

"Allegra told me years ago. When we'd gone to one of your operas. She was quite proud of her conquest. Allegra never could resist saying anything that gave her consequence. I didn't say anything to you because Jeremy didn't know, and since it was before she was married to Jeremy it wasn't really any of my business any more than any of your other affairs. Of course, at that point I didn't know she'd been spying on you."

"Nor did I, until recently."

"I assure you I'm not spying on you."

He gave a faint smile. "That's one fear I don't have."

"What then?"

He held her off but kept his hands on her shoulders. "You aren't married."

"Allegra wasn't, when you ran off with her."

His brows drew together. "True. She was—"

"Willing? I am. And I'm over thirty. She wasn't yet twenty." Harriet watched him. "Are you saying she wasn't a virgin? Who says I am? And why should that matter? You're sounding distinctly like the sort of hero I deplore in fiction."

His gaze skimmed over her face. As though he were searching for the words. Or perhaps for answers himself. "I think it would mean something different to you."

"Don't you think I should be the judge of that?"

"You can't blame me for having concerns."

"Because you think I'm not strong enough?"

"I think you're exceptionally strong. I also think you don't take things lightly."

"Perhaps. But are you sure you aren't afraid of what it might mean to you, as well as to me?"

His gaze caught her own and held. He jerked away, then looked back at her. "All right. I've always enjoyed the thrill of gaming. But even I recognize sometimes the stakes are too high. There are some games one can't afford to lose."

"Who says either of us would lose?"

"Given who I am, it's difficult to contemplate anything else."

"But don't we both often say that the inability to imagine the world can change is a failure of the imagination?"

He went still, gaze locked on her face. "What are you asking of me, Harriet?"

"To give this a chance. Give us a chance." She hesitated. "Us" was a fraught word to use. "If I wanted to be married, I could have put my mind to it and found a husband years ago. Neither of us wants that. It's a good starting place."

He shook his head. "It seems I have some vestiges of what we call honor."

"Meaning you've put me in a category of women it's dishonorable to take as anything but a wife, and you don't want a wife. That's rather insulting. And also, perhaps, convenient for you."

He took a step back and turned away. "I admit I'm a coward. But I'm also trying to save both of us from being burnt. And I value what we have too much. I wouldn't want to lose you as a friend."

"None of your former mistresses are friends?"

"Not precisely. Thinking it over, I don't have a great many friends."

She caught his hand. "You won't lose me as a friend. I promise. I can't imagine having a lover who wasn't a friend."

He turned towards her. His gaze smashed open to reveal something she had never thought to see there. She stepped into his arms. His lips brushed her hair. She leant her head against his shoulder. And realized she had stepped into something far more complicated than a love affair.

CHAPTER 30

July 1821
London

Franz Stroheim stepped into the Berkeley Square library and drew up short, taking in the group assembled and, Mélanie suspected, the looks of shock on their faces. "It appears I've interrupted something. Shall I leave?"

"On the contrary," Tony said. "Your arrival could not be timelier. We've had some new information." He and Harry explained Harry's talk with Fitzroy Somerset, the suggestion that Lionel Southcott was LeFou's target, and the attempt to implicate Tony.

Stroheim's eyes widened, but he listened intently without interruption. "And you think this makes it more likely Austria is involved," he said when they were done.

"Lionel is known not to be a friend of Metternich's," Tony said. "So Austrian involvement is one option. A plot involving Wellington himself is another. But we do have LeFou's meeting with Augustin last night to explain."

"Have you learnt anything?" Mélanie asked. She and Cordelia had sent Stroheim word after they left Gunter's that Charlotte

Augustin said her husband had been missing since the previous night.

"No one at the embassy wants to confide much," Stroheim said. "But they haven't seen Augustin either, and there's obviously concern. It's not unusual for him to come in late, but he missed two meetings today. I talked to Hauke. He didn't admit a word of his meeting with Malcolm—his abduction of Malcolm—last night. But he did admit he'd gone to Augustin's house looking for him and spoken with his valet, who'd had no news of him. Which apparently is more surprising than his wife's not having heard from him."

"Understandably," Mélanie said.

"So I gather," Stroheim said. "No one is surprised the countess doesn't know where Augustin is. But they are quite surprised Augustin hasn't shown his face all day. No one knows where he is." Stroheim's gaze swept the group. "No one seems to have seen him since I saw him in the tavern with LeFou last night."

"Does anyone know what he was doing with LeFou?" Mélanie asked.

"If they do, they aren't telling me. Everyone denies knowledge of what Augustin might be involved in or where he might have gone. And of what LeFou might be doing in Britain. Or even that he's in Britain at all. Hauke went so far as to tell me I was making things worse."

"That's what he said to me last night," Malcolm said.

Stroheim nodded. "He told me I was mistaken. But he refused to offer evidence as to why he was so sure, or what the real story might be."

"Do you think he could be involved in hiring LeFou?" Désirée asked.

Stroheim scraped a hand over his hair. "My god. My every instinct screams no. But my every instinct has been screaming no since last night." He looked at Tony. "Your brother isn't the most popular British diplomat among the Austrian delegation."

Tony touched Stroheim's shoulder. "Spoken like a diplomat, Stroheim."

"Former diplomat." Stroheim met Tony's gaze. "How can you be so calm?"

"I'm not calm in the least. Numb might be a better word. Perhaps—"

He broke off as the thud of the front door and a chorus of excited voices indicated the children had returned from the square garden. Blanca poked her head into the library to report that Sophie wanted to remind Désirée she had promised them a story.

"Go," Tony said, as Désirée hesitated. "Twenty minutes won't matter."

Mélanie was about to follow Désirée up to the nursery, when the library door opened again. This time it was Valentin, the footman, which meant it wasn't a guest he felt confident letting in unannounced. "Mr. Southcott has called," he said.

Mélanie looked at Malcolm and then Tony. "Show him in."

John Southcott came into the room with quick, focused steps, paused on the threshold, and blinked. "Forgive me." He bowed. "I did not realize you were entertaining, Mrs. Rannoch."

Mélanie choked. "I wouldn't precisely call it entertaining, Mr. Southcott. We're discussing last night's events. Which I know Julien and Kitty spoke to you about this morning." She probably should have said "Lord and Lady Carfax," but Julien would have bitten her head off if she did.

"Yes." Southcott inclined his head to Julien and Kitty, then looked back at Mélanie. "I came to see if there is news of Miss Roth."

"I'm afraid not," Mélanie said. "But as you see, your uncle is here. And, I believe, wishes to speak with you."

Southcott turned to Tony. "Uncle Anthony. I'm sorry for the circumstances, but it's good to see you again."

Tony inclined his head. "I feel the same. Désirée's gone upstairs with our daughter, but I look forward to introducing you."

"I'd be honored." Southcott swallowed, as though at the realization he'd just said he'd be honored to meet a former French agent. "I wish you both every happiness, Uncle."

"Thank you." Tony gestured to the door. "Perhaps we could have a word in private?"

～

"FATHER IS the target of the plot?" John had been a model of self-control since childhood, but his voice bounced off the ceiling in the parlor across the hall from the library, to which he and Tony had withdrawn. "Someone was trying to assassinate him? *Is* trying to assassinate him?"

"We don't know that," Tony said. God, it seemed not so long since he would have ruffled John's hair in an attempt at reassurance. Where had the years gone?

"But someone was trying to make it look as though you were trying to have him killed. You and Wellington."

"It appears so." Tony found it difficult to speak the words.

"You—" The words seemed to get stuck in John's throat like cotton wool.

"God knows your father and I have disagreed, John. But I wouldn't attack him." Tony held his nephew's gaze. There was a time he'd have been sure John would believe him. Now it was difficult to be sure of anything.

"No. I do understand that."

"I'm impressed that you do."

John passed a hand over his hair. "Is Father in danger?"

"The assassin is dead, whoever his target was."

John clasped his hands behind his back. "That wouldn't necessarily stop the plot."

"No." Tony regarded his nephew. He could see John on the

lawn at his country estates, bent over a book while the other children played. "This seems incredible to ask, but do you know your father's current relationship with Wellington?"

Shock shot through John's gaze. "Surely you know better than I do."

"Your father and I haven't spoken in the past two months."

"Oh." John shifted his weight from one foot to the other. "I see."

Echoes of his last talk with his brother shot through Tony's memory. Words spoken that he could not have alluded to in front of Désirée. Words that would never be forgotten. "I'm not sure what angered him more. The divorce or my marrying Désirée. Difficult to disentangle the two."

John's arms tensed as though he'd tightened his clasped fingers behind his back. "Father's always taken family seriously."

"One might have said my marriage to the mother of my youngest daughter has to do with family. But then, your father and I have always defined family differently."

"Father and I don't always see eye to eye either." John's shoulders straightened, in a posture that reminded Tony of his nephew as a schoolboy, alert and eager to please. "Father thinks Wellington is too inclined to trust Metternich. They've quarreled. But then, diplomats and politicians frequently quarrel."

"So they do."

"There was also—" John scraped his boot toe over the hearth rug and glanced away. "I've heard rumors about a lady. An opera dancer. In whom Father and Wellington both took an interest."

Given Lionel's marriage and what Tony knew of Wellington's, that was not entirely surprising. "Do you know her name?"

John shook his head. "You can't imagine I was anything other than horrified. One doesn't—"

"Want to hear such things about a parent. Quite."

"One doesn't want to hear such things at all."

Comments his children had made when he and Hetty informed them of their intention to divorce echoed through

216

Tony's head. "Understandably. Unfortunately, such issues are sometimes pertinent in intelligence."

"One of the reasons I'm more suited to a desk job."

"You've done admirable work from behind a desk. That was certainly good work finding the entries in the ledger that led us to LeFou."

Surprise shot through John's gaze. "Thank you, Uncle Tony. I know you haven't had the highest opinion of me."

Regret bit Tony in the throat. A frequent experience with the younger generation. "That's not true in the least. You did able work in Vienna."

John met Tony's gaze squarely. "You think I'm lacking in imagination."

Recent events had reinforced how much he had failed with his son and heir, St. Ives, and his daughter Rosalind. He began to wonder how much John had been one of his failures as well. "There are different ways of thinking."

"And you think mine is dull."

"My dear boy. You think I'm a dinosaur."

"No. That is—" John flushed. "Of course, I can't but admire the work you and my father did. But the world is a different place now."

"And you think we haven't kept up."

John's gaze held steady. "My father's still living in the past. And if I'm honest, I sometimes think you are as well, sir. You're still fighting the last war. Which for both you and him puts a strangely romantic gloss on things. The world after Waterloo takes a new kind of thinking. The future lies overseas. South America. India."

"I wouldn't disagree with you. Though we might disagree on what we should pursue overseas. And how we should pursue it."

"We don't have a foe as simple as Napoleon Bonaparte, but we have to find a way to keep our allies pacified on the Continent so we can beat them overseas. We need goods from abroad and secure paths to ship those goods. We need to transport those goods after we ship them. For which the new steam engines show great promise. That's all going to take a different kind of thinking. It's going to take new systems and an organization woefully lacking in Whitehall and Westminster at present. The irony is I only found those entries in the ledger that led to this investigation because it's so damnably hard to find anything in our records that, as usual, I was scrambling about."

"Again, I don't disagree with that."

John shifted his weight from one foot to the other. "Father thinks it's a sideshow. He thinks of me as a paper pusher. So do you, if it comes to that. What you both overlook is the importance of paper pushers."

"I've never underestimated you, John. Though I am impressed you'd share your thoughts with *Le Monde Gris*."

John's shoulders jerked back, as though he were retreating into the wallpaper. "I needed to share them somewhere. It's damned frustrating—" He broke off. "I don't agree with Miss Roth on a number of things. But she's shining a light on parts of the world that need our attention."

"She's shining a light on injustices in those parts of the world. Many of them perpetrated by our government."

John's brows drew together. "You didn't used to talk this way, Uncle."

Tony smiled. "I may be a dinosaur, but that doesn't mean I'm incapable of change." He hesitated a moment. "A lot can be done from behind a desk. But I will say my time in the field broadened my perspective."

"Your time, or whom you met?"

Tony returned the veiled fire in his nephew's gaze. "If that's a reference to Désirée, yes, my getting to know her absolutely influenced my thinking. I imagine your relationship with Miss Roth has influenced yours."

John unclasped his hands and folded his arms over his chest. "Harriet and I aren't—It's not the same at all."

"No, of course not. But I know you respect her, and I'm sure you listen to her ideas. As she listens to yours."

John tugged a shirt cuff smooth beneath his dark blue coat. "I value Miss Roth's opinion inestimably. I listen to her and I flatter myself that she listens to me, though I doubt either of us would change greatly. Her views are obviously opposed to mine in many ways. But she's not—"

"A foreign agent."

John looked into Tony's gaze, this time without flinching. "As your nephew, I couldn't be more pleased that you've found happiness, Uncle Tony. But as an employee of the foreign office, I can't but be aware that you are about to marry a French agent."

"Former French agent. Désirée wouldn't have anything to do with the current French government."

John's brows drew together, "That's not funny, Uncle."

"I didn't mean it to be."

"You trust her." John made it not quite a question, but the disbelief that underlay his tone was palpable.

"That's between Désirée and me. I am no longer in the employ of the foreign office or of the British government in any capacity."

"They still call on you."

"That's their business."

"It's mine too. I work for the foreign office."

"And you've also made your own choices about sharing information."

John tugged his coat smooth. "Fair enough. I fully recognize the risks I've run."

"And you clearly trust Miss Roth."

John's fingers tightened on one of the gold buttons on his sleeve. "Implicitly."

"It's a good foundation to start with."

"We're not—whatever my feelings for Miss Roth, I have no reason to think she entertains feelings of that sort for me."

"Have you asked her?"

"I can't—" John swallowed. "It's plain to me Miss Roth cherishes feelings of a certain sort for Lord Gresham. I can't be sure what those feelings may have led to. It is no business of mine. Though I can admit to you I was more aware of them than I admitted to Lord and Lady Carfax. I can't imagine whatever is between them will last. When it's over, I'll be here for Harriet."

"Cogently put." Tony took a step forwards and touched his nephew on the shoulder.

"But her disappearance complicates things. I've been—I don't wish to amplify the scandal. But to say I'm concerned would be an understatement."

Tony's fingers tightened on the well-cut blue superfine of John's coat. "We're all concerned."

CHAPTER 31

April 1821
Normandy

*D*ésirée refilled the teacups and set the teapot down with care. Keeping her fingers steady took more effort than usual. "I hope you know what you're doing, *ma chère*. You're a grown woman and perfectly capable of making your own decisions. And, god knows, I could never bear anyone trying to make decisions for me. Which doesn't mean I didn't make a number of very bad ones."

Harriet added milk to her tea and stirred with precise strokes. "I'm not as experienced as you. In a number of ways. But I am quite good at taking care of myself." She gave a faint smile. "There's no need to be so maternal."

Désirée flung back her head and laughed. "I've never seen myself as maternal in the least. Well, not until I had Sophie." She set down her teacup. "Good god. I suppose I could be having a discussion like this with Sophie in twenty years or so. And I'll admit I would have the same concerns."

Harriet took a sip of tea. "I may not have seen a great deal of the world—"

"My dear." Désirée blotted a spatter of tea on the tray. "You're writing about the world."

"Precisely. My writing has exposed me to all manner of things all over the world. More about politics than relationships, I'll grant. But I assure you I have no illusions about Tristram."

"Oh, I think we all have illusions, don't you?" Désirée reached for her tea again and breathed in the distinct scent that would always evoke her English aristo lover. "I certainly had them about Tony, much as I told myself I didn't. Some of those illusions rather got in the way. Like the one that he was hopelessly bound by the role of chivalrous English gentleman, and that what was between us could never work."

"All right." Harriet jabbed a loose strand of hair behind her ear. "I'll grant there are probably things I'm not seeing properly about Tristram. But I certainly don't imagine him as some sort of rakish hero who will suddenly turn into a model of domesticity. It's not as though I have a reputation to protect. I want to make sure I don't tangle Jeremy and Judith in anything, but for myself I have nothing to risk."

"My dear." Désirée set her cup in its saucer. For a moment she saw herself ten or fifteen years ago. So sure she understood the world. So secure in her seemingly sophisticated ennui. So blind. "You have everything."

"Oh." Harriet's blue eyes widened. "You mean my heart."

"Call it what you will. You think you're immune, and suddenly you meet his gaze and realize you could shatter in an instant. I've seen the most hardened agents fall. Raoul, when he'd have claimed he'd already been through it and couldn't fall again. Mélanie, who deluded herself it was all part of a mission, until she was in so deep she hadn't a prayer of getting out. Julien, who put on such a good show of being incapable of feeling of any sort. Kitty, who had put on less of a show, but had perhaps had even more barriers to letting herself feel. Even Talleyrand, who was more hardened than most spies. Or so I thought."

"You think my heart will be broken because Tristram will be unfaithful?" Harriet said. "But that assumes I expect him to be faithful. I'll own we have delusions, but I'd never be so deluded as to expect him to be anything of the sort. I don't think I'm in the midst of a romantic tale where a hardened roué falls madly in love and swears eternal devotion and means it. I'd be rather horrified if Tristram did anything of the sort. He wouldn't be Tristram anymore. He'd be something of a bore. For that matter, perhaps I wouldn't intend to be faithful to him."

"It doesn't really matter," Désirée said. "I never intended to be faithful to Tony. I wasn't faithful to him. And I had no illusions he was faithful to me." She frowned. "He actually was, as it happens, but I didn't learn it until years later. Which only goes to show how madly quixotic Tony is."

"Or how madly in love with you he is."

"Possibly. Or simply how mad he is. But the point is, none of that stopped me from feeling jealous. None of that stopped me from feeling as though he could slice me in two with a look. I never intended to let it get to that point. I thought I was safely armored. And then I realized I was hopelessly lost."

Harriet leant forwards, elbows on her knees, gaze intent on Désirée's own. "Are you sorry?"

"For all sorts of things."

"Are you sorry you let Tony under your skin. I mean, I know things have worked out ridiculously happily—"

"For the present." Fears, of what might happen to them and between them, sliced into her brain. Fears of what the future might hold. She hadn't yet told Harriet that she and Sophie were planning to escape to England. In many ways, the escape was less scary than the thought of living in the country she had fought against for so long. "Which is all we ever really have."

"But if they hadn't. If Tony had left you, or died at Waterloo, or something else had separated you, would you regret it?"

"If Tony had died or left me, I'd regret a great many things." The chill of myriad past fears shot through her. "But not the time we had together. In fact, for years I was sure we would separate, one way or another. And that we should make the most of what we had."

"Well, then."

"But when I said goodbye to him before Waterloo, I knew losing him was more than I could bear."

"All the more reason not to have lost what you could have with him. Perhaps I'd rather have what I can with Tristram, whatever my regrets later."

"That's honest," Désirée said. "And I'd like to say it's worth it, no matter what. But the truth is I can't be sure. Tony and I face many uncertainties, but we've been absurdly lucky." She glanced at the corner of the room where Sophie was coloring a picture of her favorite doll with pastels. "I wouldn't want Sophie to avoid risks. But I also wouldn't want her to be hurt."

"And you're afraid I'll be hurt?" Harriet asked.

Désirée reached for her tea. "I'm also afraid Tristram could be."

CHAPTER 32

July 1821
London

Cordelia set down her teacup. "We've investigated all sorts of plots, but this has to be one of the most elaborate."

Harry nodded. "I asked Fitzroy who would have access to Wellington's office. One of the servants could have been paid, but Wellington trusts his staff and vets them well. Fitzroy's getting a list of visitors. Whatever is going on, I think we clearly have people working on the inside at some level."

Mélanie cut a wedge of stilton and added it to a slice of brown bread. Valentin had brought tea and bread and cheese into the library. Without her having to ask. He knew the rhythm and stresses of an investigation. "Setting up the Delaneys is even more complicated. It wouldn't necessarily be that hard for someone to know the Delaneys were connected to Laura, but they'd have had to know which ship they were traveling on and track its arrival at Southampton."

"Not impossible," Malcolm said. "But it would take a lot of

planning. Which confirms we're dealing with someone with resources. Or several people with resources."

Julien leant back in his chair, teacup tilting in his fingers. "Are you suggesting a conspiracy in the British government? Or between British government officials and Austrians diplomats?"

"We've been dancing round that explanation since last night," Malcolm said. "Perhaps—"

He broke off as Valentin stepped into the room. Not with more food but with a sealed paper. "This was just delivered for Prince Stroheim."

Stroheim got to his feet. "Who delivered it?"

"A boy of about thirteen. He told me he works holding horses by the Rose & Crown in Piccadilly. He said a gentleman gave it to him and asked him to bring it here. The only description I could get of the gentleman was 'fair hair, older but not old.' Which could mean anywhere from your age to the Duke of Bamford's age, I think."

Stroheim took the paper. "You're good at this."

Valentin smiled. "One learns things working in this household."

Stroheim moved to a writing desk as Valentin left the room. He picked up a letter opener, slit the seal, and scanned the letter. "It's from Augustin."

"Where is he?" Malcolm asked.

"He doesn't say. And he specifically says not to contact the embassy." Stroheim scanned the paper again. "But he wants to meet. Tonight. On neutral ground."

"What qualifies as neutral ground?" Julien asked.

"According to Augustin, Almack's Assembly Rooms."

Julien groaned. "Good god."

"It's not a bad idea," Malcolm said. "One can scarcely imagine a more innocuous setting. And the Countess Lieven will be there, quite naturally." Dorothea was a patroness of Almack's along with

Emily Cowper, Palmerston's mistress. "I assume Augustin wants her there."

"He seems to," Stroheim said. "He mentions that he's been in touch with the countess, and she'll help us find a place to talk. But that we shouldn't alert anyone at the Austrian embassy. Presumably meaning Hauke."

"We'll all stand out," Julien said. "None of us has been to Almack's in years. We don't even have vouchers."

"Yes, we do," Kitty said. "Emily offered them when we became Lord and Lady Carfax, and I thought they might be helpful."

"But no one would actually expect us to go," Julien said.

"We might go for political reasons," Kitty pointed out. "We go all sorts of places for political reasons. Which, in fact, is what we're doing tonight. We just have to hope no one guesses the particular political reasons at play here."

RAOUL STEPPED into the room Tony and Désirée were using in Berkeley Square. Désirée had gone into the nursery, where Raoul had just been himself. Tony was alone, making a last adjustment to the folds of his cravat. "It's not easy."

"It used to be second nature." Tony ran a finger over a fold. "But a lot of days in the country, I didn't wear a cravat at all."

"I have no doubt of your sartorial skills. I meant having a brother."

"Oh." Tony made another adjustment to the cravat, then turned and picked his black superfine coat from the back of the chair. "Lionel and I haven't spoken in two months."

"My brother and I haven't spoken in years. Of course, we were on opposite sides in a war. Easier in some ways. None of the surface politeness, the attempts to paper over differences. Just a simple break. As I recall, he told me I was destroying Spain."

"Lionel said I was a traitor to Britain." Tony shrugged on his coat. "The things he said about Désirée went far beyond what I could mention where Désirée could hear. The truth is I planted him a facer. Far from the first time either of us has drawn a fist on the other. But the first since we turned fifty. Probably since we turned forty." He tugged at a shirt cuff under his sleeve. "We were on separate paths by the time we left Oxford. But we managed to maintain a relationship. Some things once said can't be unsaid. I could never speak again to someone who used those words about Désirée. But I wouldn't have—"

"No," Raoul said. "Of course not. No one thinks you could possibly have been plotting against your brother. Not even Désirée, for all her teasing."

"Thank you." Tony gave a bleak smile. He adjusted the other shirt cuff. "It isn't easy on John, I don't think. He was more open talking to me today than I expected. I begin to think I haven't paid enough attention to him. Just as I haven't paid enough attention to St. Ives." Of all his children, Tony was perhaps least close to his only son and heir.

"It's never too late for things to change," Raoul said. "Perhaps that's one advantage in this. It gives you a chance to see him in a new light. And vice versa."

"I hope so." Tony frowned at a speck of lint on his cuff. "Whatever Désirée says, I think Miss Roth is likely to disappoint John. I'm not sure how much support an uncle can be in romantic disappointment, but I'll do my best." Tony turned back to the looking glass and ran a finger over the same folds of the cravat he'd adjusted a few minutes before.

"I don't know whether to envy you or pity you," Raoul said.

"You've dealt with being an uncle yourself."

"Oh, yes. I do my fair of share of worrying about Raimundo. These days mostly about the danger he's getting into in Spain. Some of it because he's taken over my networks. But I meant Almack's. I find it a distinct relief not to be able to have vouchers.

But I could tell even Laura rather regretted being out of the excitement tonight."

Tony smiled. "I won't have vouchers myself in a short time. Once the divorce is final. Normally I wouldn't go somewhere Désirée isn't welcome. But she told me not to be an idiot. She'd never stay back from a mission because of me."

"Wise woman."

"Except in loving me." Tony picked up his gloves. "If I'm a target to be blamed for the plot, I did wonder if my being there tonight will be a complication."

"On the contrary," Raoul said "It could draw out some very interesting results."

Tony grinned and drew on the gloves. "Spoken like a true spymaster."

"Some things never change."

MÉLANIE SET down the curling tongs as Blanca came into the dressing room. "You didn't need to come. I've got quite good at doing my own hair. And I'm not going to Almack's to be noticed. I'm going on a mission."

"And to blend in on the mission you have to look your faultlessly groomed self." Blanca picked up the tongs and clamped them round a ringlet Mélanie hadn't been able to get quite right. "The Delaneys are with the children. If I can't be out making inquiries like Addison, helping you dress at least makes me feel I'm part of the mission." She coaxed a curl on the right side to fall symmetrically with one on the left. "People at Almack's are more critical than people at diplomatic soirées."

"You've never been there."

"I've heard stories."

"The stories are exaggerated. Like Julien rolling his eyes

tonight." Though it was true the intrigue at Almack's centered on marriage prospects, and that tended to go with an emphasis on appearances. Even when one wasn't angling for a marriage partner.

Blanca set the tongs down on their stand and stepped to the side to study Mélanie. "Your gown works." She ran her gaze over the spangled amethyst gauze over satin. "And the rubies were a good choice, though I know you prefer garnets. But the hair needs something." She reached for a black velvet bandeau ornamented with diamond flowers. When she wasn't wearing it, Mélanie left the bandeau dangling from the gilded looking-glass frame as a decoration. "Wear this. If you insist on having your hair half down, it lends a bit of dignity."

She settled the bandeau on Mélanie's head and adjusted the ringlets to fall about it. The black velvet blended into Mélanie's dark hair, but the diamond flowers glittered and caught the candlelight. "Now your hair can look a bit wild and it's all part of the look. Diamonds make everything more elegant."

Mélanie twisted round to look up at Blanca, remembering the girl she'd met in a Spanish tavern when they were both teenagers. "I can't remember when you became such a fashion expert."

"We all acquire skills in the course of a mission." Blanca adjusted Mélanie's satin sash. "Hara Delaney looks so much better. When I left the nursery, he was telling Pedro stories about India and putting up with endless questions."

"I'm glad." Mélanie peered in the looking glass and wiped a smudge of blacking at the corner of one eye. "They've both been through a lot."

"I like him." Blanca sat on the edge of the dressing table bench beside Mélanie. "I like Lizzy Delaney too." Her dark brows drew together.

"What?" Mélanie turned sideways to look at her friend.

Blanca closed the lid of the velvet box that held the ruby necklace and earrings Mélanie was wearing and lined it up with the other jewel boxes on the dressing table. "She loves her husband,

I'm quite sure of it. You could see how worried she was. The children adore her and she's very good with them. Not easy to be a stepmother, but they all seem to be managing well. But she was telling me about her brother coming after her and Hara when they left Calcutta. She said he threatened her, and then bit the words back. As though whatever he'd threatened wasn't something she wanted to talk about."

"Well, I imagine it isn't. She's quite intrepid, but I imagine her brother said beastly things to her. However difficult one's family, it can be horrid to be cast off by them."

"No. But there was something in her eyes—" Blanca adjusted the angle of the velvet box. "Perhaps I'm imagining things, but I have the oddest sense Lizzy Delaney isn't precisely who she seems."

CHAPTER 33

$\mathcal{M}$élanie hesitated at the top of the stone staircase, on the threshold of the ballroom in Almack's Assembly Rooms. The first time she'd attended one of the assemblies, fresh off the palaces of Vienna and Paris, she'd been shocked at how simple the rooms were in comparison. The chandeliers had only two tiers, the columns were scagliola, the blue draperies were slightly faded. But at Almack's, the point was not the setting itself. It was the difficulty of gaining entrée to that setting.

Julien paused in the doorway to the ballroom. "I swore I'd never set foot in this place again."

"Genny might want to come someday." Kitty tightened her gloved fingers on his arm.

"Genny's much too sensible."

"Have you even actually been here before?" Kitty asked her husband.

"Oh, yes. The last time I was dressed as a debutante. That was distinctly more agreeable than wearing knee breeches." Julien's gaze swept the dancers, mostly young women almost a decade younger than Mélanie, in gauzy gowns of white or pink or blue, waltzing at a very correct distance with men not so very much older.

"Most of the girls on the dance floor were Livia and Emily's age when I used to come to Almack's," Cordelia said. "I remember how excited I was to get vouchers for the first time." She looked down at the skirt of her gown, flame-colored aerophane silk over cream satin. "My mother made me wear the most insipid colors. It feels like a flash of rebellion to wear this."

"I'm surprised they'll even let us in the door," Kitty said. Her own gold silk gown was more subdued in color, but daringly cut with thin shoulder straps and narrow ruffles running down the close-fitting bodice to the skirt.

"No one actually knows we lived together," Julien pointed out. "At least, they can't prove it. It's not like divorce. O'Roarke's lucky. Bamford soon will be. Pity we were never divorced."

"Oh, well. We could always try it and get married again. But we'd be cutting off our investigative options. Not to mention your political prospects."

"Holland does all right. But even to avoid Almack's, I have no intention of letting you go, my sweet. Even for a short time." Julien lifted her white-gloved hand and kissed her knuckles.

Tony scanned the ballroom and went still. "Good god."

"What?" Cordelia asked.

"Lionel. Of all people. I haven't seen him at Almack's since his daughters married. But then I've scarcely been at Almack's myself. It's timely. I was going to call on him tomorrow. I can only hope the setting keeps our interactions civil. Wish me luck."

"Difficult to imagine Tony not getting on with anyone," Kitty said.

"Difficult to imagine Tony putting up with anyone who criticized Désirée," Julien said.

They moved further into the room, prepared to circulate, but before they could, Emily Cowper swept up to them in a stir of peacock silk. "Thank goodness. It's been far too long since we've seen you here. Why do I think this has something to do with one of your investigations? There's a story running through the ballroom that a man was found murdered in Tristram Gresham's rooms and Gresham has disappeared."

"We've heard," Malcolm said. "But Bow Street haven't asked for our help." Both of which were quite true.

"Not surprising to find Tristram Gresham the talk of London," Emily said, "though this isn't precisely the sort of scandal I'd anticipate from him. No one seems to know who the murdered man is, but everyone in the ballroom is speculating it's a jealous husband."

"I don't believe Bow Street have identified the victim," Mélanie said. Also true. Jeremy had sent them an update on what he knew about Bow Street's investigation just before they left Berkeley Square. Bow Street had yet to identify LeFou, as far as he knew. Raoul, on the other hand, had discovered the rooms where LeFou had been staying hours before, but had failed to unearth any clues.

Emily shivered. "It's ghoulish. But one can't but be curious." She looked round the ballroom. "Didn't I see Tony Bamford with you? Until this news about Gresham, everyone was talking about the Bamford divorce."

"We were dining with Tony Bamford and Désirée Clairineau tonight," Julien said. "Bamford came with us, but of course Désirée couldn't."

Emily sighed. "I sometimes—often—regret that strictures keep the most interesting people out of Almack's. I confess I've been hoping to meet her. Mademoiselle Clairineau. You'll have to introduce me if they're back in London. I must say, a ducal divorce will liven things up."

"Even if you can't invite the participants anywhere," Kitty said.

"Oh, I wouldn't say not anywhere." Emily unfurled her peacock lace fan. "One can be much freer at private parties. I don't really worry about whom I invite."

"You've always been very tolerant inviting us," Julien said.

"Julien." Emily tilted her head to the side, her jade earrings stirring beside her cheek. "You've always been clever. You're Earl Carfax. You're invited everywhere."

"So long as I'm not divorced. Or neglect to wear knee breeches."

Emily tossed her head back, dark ringlets cascading over her shoulders. "I know, we'll never quite get past not letting Wellington in that night he arrived in trousers. But if one sets standards, one has to uphold them for everyone. Isn't that what you'd say from a Radical viewpoint?"

"More or less," Julien admitted.

"Well, then." Emily frowned and tapped the sticks of her fan against her white-gloved fingers. "I must say, the one who really surprises me in the Bamford scandal is Hetty Bamford. I'd never had thought she'd give up so much."

"Perhaps she doesn't think she's giving up that much," Mélanie said.

Emily, who was a younger version of the beau monde queen Hetty had once been, pursed her lips. "I can't imagine—I mean, it's all very well to say the world is well lost for love in a play, but it wouldn't really be, would it? In the world we're living in?"

"That rather depends." Kitty tightened her fingers round Julien's arm.

Emily cast a quick glance at Cordelia.

"It all depends on the love," Cordelia said. "One can certainly be let down." She leant into Harry, who was regarding the ballroom with a studied air of nonchalance.

"But I don't think one should have to choose," Emily said. "Not when there are perfectly agreeable arrangements that don't require giving up anything." She cast a glance round the assembly rooms. "Oh, look, there's Prince Stroheim with his fiancée. They do look happy."

"I'm quite sure they are," Mélanie said.

Emily smiled across the room at Stroheim and Lisette. "One

forgets. What a betrothal can feel like." She frowned. "You may not have anything to do with this Gresham scandal, but Harry—my Harry—says there's something afoot that brought you all here tonight. At least, he implied that when I saw him earlier tonight. He seemed to think he should give me a warning without being able to expand on details. It was at once quite fascinating and thoroughly provoking. I won't pry—whatever Harry didn't or couldn't say is between Harry and me—but do tell me if I can help. And if somehow your latest intrigue has brought you all to Almack's, I can't help but be pleased."

Emily moved off, her attention claimed by her fellow patroness Thérèse Esterhazy. A minute or so later, Lisette and Stroheim joined them.

"I've always wondered about Almack's. Even in France I'd heard of it. I never understood what all the fuss was about," Lisette said. She was gowned in peach tulle over white satin, and looked more like a girl in her second or third season on the marriage mart than a seasoned veteran of the spy game. She glanced round the room. "I confess I still don't."

"It's the exclusivity," Cordelia said. "If one has to intrigue as much for an invitation as on the average spy mission, one doesn't scan the decor or the refreshments."

"I'm sorry." Mélanie looked from Lisette to Stroheim. "We didn't mean to drag you into this."

"We've dragged you into so much," Lisette said. "We're glad to help."

"I'm still a diplomat," Stroheim said. "Whatever I said earlier today. Glad to do what I can."

"And, I must say, this is just innocuous enough to be the perfect setting for a secret meeting," Lisette said. "I'm not sure what's better—a disreputable tavern that's too dark to see much, or a quiet assembly where no one expects anything to happen. Or, at least, they're all on the lookout for another sort of scandal."

"Quite," Cordelia said. "Honestly, everyone's too busy right now wondering how I got vouchers to get through the door to be paying the least heed to anything else. And, of course, the only reason I could do it is because, for all the scandal of my life, I didn't actually get divorced. Just about the one scandal I never indulged in. Which is only because Harry was the only person I had the sense to marry. Though I'm afraid I can't claim a great deal of sense was involved." She looked up at her husband. "Except that a part of me knew he wouldn't place strictures on me. I was too foolish then to see the rest."

Harry put his hand over her own. "I was too foolish then to see anything."

Lisette cast a glance round the ballroom. "How are we supposed to know when Augustin arrives?"

"Countess Lieven will alert us," Stroheim said.

Lisette frowned. A former Bonapartist agent, she was inclined to see Dorothea as the enemy. Mélanie could sympathize. "You trust her."

"Not precisely," Stroheim said. "But we need to find out what Augustin has to say. Whether or not we believe him—or the countess—is another question."

"Well put," Julien said.

Malcolm held out a hand to Mélanie. "Nothing to do but wait. Dance with me?"

"Is that your idea of cover?" She put her hand in his own.

"We are at Almack's."

"Husbands and wives don't dance together at Almack's. Husbands and wives don't dance together most places in the beau monde, if it comes to that. We'll stand out."

"Yes, but people are used to our being eccentric. It will give them something to talk about that has nothing to do with our real reasons for being here." Malcolm smiled at the others and drew her onto the dance floor.

"Half the people here still think I married you for your money." Mélanie stepped into his arms.

"Surely not, at this point."

"The people here are the people who don't see us often."

"Well, then." He took her hands for the promenade that began the waltz. "All the more reason to give them new fodder for talk."

"BAMFORD." Lionel's eyes widened with surprise and then narrowed in appraisal. He hadn't called Tony "Tony" since they were in the nursery. He'd been "St. Ives" and then "Bamford" once their father died. Lionel was taller than Tony and broader shouldered, though Tony had always been quicker. He had, Tony had to admit, the same fair hair and blue eyes that characterized so many of the Southcotts. These days Tony didn't much care to share anything with his brother. "Didn't expect to see you at Almack's." Lionel glanced at the couples swirling on the dance floor. "Haven't seen you at the assemblies since Rosalind got off the marriage mart. Thought you were rusticating."

"Hiding out in the country, you mean?" Tony said. "We were spending some time in Richmond. A way to enjoy the country but still be in easy distance of town for business matters." Meaning the divorce.

Lionel grunted in acknowledgement. "That's what brought you to town?"

"Yes, business brought us up to London yesterday," Tony said, not clarifying what type of business. "We're staying with the Rannochs and they were coming here tonight, so I thought I'd look in and catch up with some friends." Which was also more or less true. It just didn't specify why he wanted to look up friends.

"Why on earth are you staying with the Rannochs—" Lionel broke off. "Oh."

"Quite," Tony said. "Hetty and I will always be good friends, and she and Désirée get on quite well, but it would be a bit much for us to descend on Bamford House."

"You all stayed together at Sawden Park." Lionel's lips thinned. He'd been horrified that Tony and Hetty had told their children about the divorce at a house party.

"That's different. Large groups always gather in the country. And Sawden's always been mine more than anyone's. Bamford House has always been Hetty's domain."

"You don't intend to set up residence there? You and—"

"Her name is Désirée," Tony said, before Lionel could use a worse word and bring them to blows again at Almack's, of all places. Though if the Rannochs needed a distraction, that would certainly serve as one. "I'm not sure where we'll live. Or how much we'll be in London. We obviously won't be going out in society much. If at all. I expect this is my last visit to Almack's. I wouldn't have come somewhere Désirée wasn't welcome, but she wanted to stay in with Sophie."

Lionel's fair brows rose. "Soph—"

"Our daughter. Your niece."

"Oh." Lionel coughed.

"I saw John today. He called to see Rannoch about some foreign office business. I must say, I'm quite impressed with how he's grown into his role."

"That wasn't what you said in Vienna."

"He was younger in Vienna. And we disagreed about a number of matters of policy. We still do. But we talked more openly today."

"John's not an idiot. But he's always been too obsessed with numbers and charts. A diplomat needs to be good with people." Lionel met Tony's gaze for a moment. The weight of past confrontations hung between them, a counterpoint to the lively strains of the Écossaise in progress. They'd partnered their sisters in dances like that in the schoolroom long ago. "You are, for all our differences."

Tony returned his brother's gaze. "For what it's worth, so are you. Good we can find something positive to say to each other."

Lionel grunted in acknowledgement. "I understand why you drew my cork the last time we met. I can even admire your standing up for the woman you love. But it doesn't change my opinion that your present course is madness."

"Noted."

"But I don't suppose my opinion changes anything?"

"Can you imagine it would?"

"No. You always were damned stubborn."

"I'll take that as a compliment." Tony looked out over the dance floor. The Écossaise had come to an end. Malcolm and Mélanie Rannoch were walking onto the dance floor as couples formed for a waltz. "Talking of wives," Tony said, "how's Gertrude? Is she in town with you?"

"No, she's at Brighton." Lionel smoothed his shirt cuff. "We find it easier, all things considered, to be in different cities most of the time."

Not surprising, given what Tony had seen of how his brother's marriage had evolved over the years. "You should understand my choices then," Tony said. Not that he'd ever had any trouble being in the same city or even the same house as Hetty.

"What I don't understand is your solution."

"As with so many things, we must attempt to accept that we disagree. John said something about an opera dancer."

Lionel's fingers froze on a button on his cuff. "Good god, what does he—It's none of his business. Or yours."

"Of course not. I think John was rather embarrassed by how much he'd stumbled across."

"I certainly would never follow your course of action in a love affair." Lionel coughed. "Did John say anything about—"

"A rivalry? He mentioned the lady in question had perhaps also caught Wellington's eye."

"How the devil does he—These things can be complicated. As I'm sure you know."

"Don't I just. There were endless challenges to Désirée's and my relationship."

"I have no intention of marrying—oh, never mind."

"I do understand how political rivalries can complicate romantic rivalries."

"Wellington and I've never—I had no notion he had also taken an interest in Clarissa until I encountered him the green room. Difficult to be in competition with the hero of Waterloo. But however unaccountable one could call her taste, Clarissa appears to have chosen me." Lionel tugged at his cravat. "And that's all I'm going to say on the matter."

"My felicitations."

"It's not—"

"It's a relationship." Tony touched his brother's arm. For the first time in years. "There's a great deal afoot right now, Lionel. Do me a favor and have a care."

Lionel's gaze snapped to Tony. "What the devil is that supposed to mean?"

"It means you're still my brother."

CHAPTER 34

The strains of the waltz swept through the room. A melody Mélanie and Malcolm had danced to in Vienna, but somehow it felt very English here, surrounded by pastel gowns and dark coats. Which weren't so very different from the garments at the Congress—if one discounted the lack of uniforms. For all some of the patronesses had been at the Congress. And two, Dorothea and Thérèse Esterhazy, were married to Continental ambassadors.

Mélanie glanced at Thérèse as Malcolm twirled her under his arm. She'd been so focused on Dorothea's role she hadn't thought about Thérèse's being married to the Austrian ambassador. Of course, Dorothea was the Austrian chancellor's mistress.

"What?" Malcolm asked, just before he spun her back to back.

"Only that, for all we're at Almack's, we have a number of interested parties present."

"Almack's has always been a center of intrigue. Though when I was younger, I confess I avoided it like the plague. Of course, I never got to dance with anyone remotely like you." He spun her back towards him just in time for her to smile into his eyes.

When the dance came to an end, Julien came up to them on the edge of the dance floor. "The punch is just as undrinkable as it always was."

"More fool you for trying it," Malcolm said. "Haven't you learnt some things never change?"

A rustle of silk sounded behind them. "What are you all doing here? There must be an intrigue afoot."

Lucinda Mallinson, Hubert's youngest daughter, slid between Julien and Malcolm and cast an inquiring look round the three of them.

Julien smiled at his cousin. "What are you doing here, infant?"

"Oh, that's easy. Mama dragged me." Lucinda nodded towards her mother, Amelia, talking with Lady Castlereagh—Lady Londonderry—on the sidelines. "I may not be in my first season anymore, but she hasn't given up on finding me a husband, and she still thinks Almack's is essential to the search. I've tried to tell her I'm only interested in marriage if it's to an interesting man, and the odds of finding an interesting man here are slim to none, but she doesn't listen. I must say, I'm not sorry she dragged me here tonight if all of you are here. Is it to do with the man who was killed in Tristram Gresham's rooms?"

"Bow Street haven't asked us to assist," Malcolm said.

"That doesn't mean you aren't looking into it. I should have guessed something was up when Papa came with us."

Julien stared at his cousin, eyes alert to a hitherto unforeseen danger. "Uncle Hubert is here?"

He didn't look at Mélanie or Malcolm, but then, he didn't need to. This could change everything.

"Yes." Lucinda glanced round the room. "He's over there, behind the column, listening to Lord Grafton, who's probably telling a hunting story. Or maybe something bawdier. But Papa never goes anywhere for that sort of talk. Are you on the same side or different sides tonight?"

"That's always the question, isn't it?" Julien said.

"Shall I cause a diversion?" Lucinda asked. "I'm quite good at it."

"I have no doubt you're brilliant," Malcolm said. "In fact, I've seen you be brilliant. But tonight we need everything to appear as normal as possible."

Lucinda sighed. "I never thought I'd say this, but I don't see why I can't take after Papa rather than Mama. I'd so much rather be an agent than a wife."

"You can be both," Mélanie said.

"Only if I could find a man like Malcolm. Or Julien."

"By all means, find a Malcolm," Julien said. "I'd do my cousinly best to protect you from the likes of me."

"You wouldn't. You're much too decent to be interfering, Julien. Don't you dare change into one of those people. You wouldn't have liked anyone trying to protect you."

"And look where it got me."

"Married to Kitty."

Julien smiled. "A fair point. You'll have to excuse my parental instincts. I came to parenting late and abruptly, and it brings on concerns at the oddest times."

"I'll forgive you. Provided you don't hover the way David does. I'll say this for Papa. He doesn't tend to hover." Lucinda smiled at Malcolm. "I know you're concerned, but you always try not to let it get in the way of things."

"High praise indeed." Malcolm scanned the dance floor. The musicians in the gilt-railed balcony were striking up another dance. "Actually, there is a way you can help, Lucy."

Her eyes brightened. "Anything."

"We need to appear to be here simply to see friends. Such as a good friend who was dragged here by her mama and is in need of support. Appearing to be entirely normal is one of the greatest challenges an agent faces. Dance with me, Lucy?"

"Of course." Lucinda took Malcolm's arm with the smile of

one going on a mission when she had thought she had simply been dragged to a dull evening of dancing.

"She has excellent instincts," Julien said, watching his cousin move off with Malcolm. "I wish I could train her. I have a feeling she could be as formidable as Gisèle."

Malcolm's younger sister Gisèle had become a remarkable agent while still a teenager, with Julien's support. "She wouldn't have to go undercover like Gelly," Mélanie said. Lucinda was curt-seying as Malcolm bowed at the start of the dance. She already looked happier now the dance had a purpose. "But there are things she could learn. Even with the right husband, she won't be happy simply as a wife and mother."

Julien shot a look at her. "That's a new way for you to talk."

"It's not a new thought. But perhaps it's one I find easier to express. Only look at what we've learnt about Harriet in the past day. She's an excellent example of a woman finding something to occupy her abilities." Of course, Harriet was also likely in danger now.

"Good, you're all here." Hubert Mallinson materialized out of the crowd beside them. He may have been behind a desk for over two decades, but he still had a field agent's ability to move from one spot to another without detection. Even by fellow spies.

"Uncle Hubert," Julien said. "You'll give the game away. Your attendance at Almack's fairly screams there's intrigue afoot."

"I came with Amelia and Lucinda." Hubert smiled at his youngest daughter as she moved through the quadrille with Malcolm. "It's not Lucinda's favorite way to spend the evening, but Amelia insists on it. Anyone who pays attention would know they're here regularly."

"How often do you accompany them?" Julien demanded.

"More often than you'd think, my boy. Especially lately."

"How did you know there was reason to be here tonight?" Mélanie asked.

"I have my sources."

"An understatement if we ever heard one, Uncle Hubert," Julien said. "Just make sure you stay on the sidelines or you'll scare off our contact."

"Don't worry. I know how to lie low."

"Ha," Julien said. "Go do something non-agent. Like dancing with your wife."

Hubert's brows rose above his spectacles. "That really would draw attention."

"Yes, but of a very different sort. It would reinforce that you're here for personal reasons. And get people gossiping about your marriage."

Hubert pushed at the bridge of his spectacles. "Amelia and I aren't the sort to be the subject of gossip."

"There's a first time for everything. We need a distraction. Be a good fellow, Uncle Hubert. Cause a diversion."

Hubert frowned at his nephew for a moment, but then turned and moved off towards his wife.

"Just the distraction we need," Mélanie said. "And it may actually do their marriage some good." Hubert and Amelia's marriage had never quite recovered from the revelation that Hubert had had a long-ago affair with Malcolm's mother. In pursuit of a mission, but every marriage had its limits.

"Possibly." Julien watched through narrowed eyes as Hubert touched Amelia's arm and Amelia turned towards him. "Not that Uncle Hubert's happiness is any concern of mine."

Mélanie hid a smile. "Of course not."

"Though Aunt Amelia's always been quite kind to me."

Amelia turned to Hubert with apparent surprise, but took his arm and moved onto the dance floor.

"Well done," Mélanie said.

"Uncle Hubert, or me?"

"Both of you."

Julien gave a faint smile, then went still as he caught Kitty's gaze across the room. She was standing with Dorothea Lieven and lifted her black-and-gold fan in an agreed-upon gesture. "Uncle Hubert's distraction is timely. It seems Augustin is here."

~

DOROTHEA GLANCED round the sitting room tucked away off the ballroom and supper room, and in an instant went from lady of fashion to international agent. Which wasn't such a very great transformation in some ways. Diamond earrings swung beside her elaborately dressed hair. The bronze-green satin of her gown shimmered in the light from the brace of candles on a low table beside the sofa. But then, Désirée often presented just such an image as well. A lady of fashion could look very like an international agent. "I'll bring him in in a moment. You should be quiet here. No one uses this room. And everyone at the assembly has other interests."

"Thank you," Mélanie said. "You've risked a lot."

Dorothea met her gaze and smiled, gaze level. "So have you."

Mélanie pressed Dorothea's hand. "We haven't always been allies. Or wanted the same things. But alliances have a way of shifting, these days."

Dorothea inclined her head. "He can't suspect you're all here until he's in the room. He wrote to Franz. He isn't expecting all of you. We can't have him bolting. Not only would you lose the information, it would disrupt the assembly. Which could lead to all sorts of chaos."

"Point taken," Malcolm said.

Dorothea met his gaze, white-gloved fingers tight on the ebony sticks of her fan. "I know caring about such niceties must seem an absurdity. But diplomacy is built on such absurdities."

"I am very familiar with just such absurdities," Malcolm said.

"Do you know where he's been?" Mélanie asked.

"I know no more than you," Dorothea said. Which might or might not be the truth.

247

Dorothea left the room. They moved to the sofa and chairs by the fireplace. Mélanie, Malcolm, Julien, and Stroheim. Kitty, Tony, Lisette, Harry, and Cordy had stayed in the ballroom to try to divert attention. Malcolm poured wine from a set of decanters on a console table.

Julien lifted his glass and stared at the candlelight through the rich red-gold. "I didn't know you allowed anything so strong at Almack's."

"Don't be difficult," Mélanie said.

"After all these years, you expect me not to be difficult?" Julien asked.

Mélanie arced a brow and took a drink of wine.

A light rap sounded on the door.

Mélanie went still, and felt the others do the same. Except for Stroheim, they were all sitting out of the sight line from the door.

Stroheim got to his feet as the door opened to admit Dorothea and a tall, fair-haired man. With the air of one used to commanding his surroundings. And yet, at the same time not entirely secure in these particular surroundings. Mélanie had danced with Count Augustin once or twice in Vienna. He was a decent waltzing partner, though his hands had a tendency to wander to uncomfortable places. He wore an evening coat and the required knee breeches, but even in the soft candlelight, his cravat and shirt collar were a bit dingy. Mélanie suspected he was in the same clothes he'd disappeared in last night, though he appeared to have retied his cravat. His eyes were red-rimmed and slightly unfocused. She doubted he'd slept much, and he'd likely had a lot to drink and not much food.

"Count Augustin," Stroheim said. "Thank you for speaking to us."

Augustin inclined his head. The candlelight caught sweat glistening on his forehead. "Stroheim." He took a step further into the room. And went still as his gaze shot to Mélanie, Malcolm, and Julien.

"The Rannochs and Lord and Lady Carfax are undertaking the investigation into André LeFou's death," Dorothea said. "They need to know what you have to say."

Augustin's shoulders straightened. "I put myself at great risk by coming here."

"And we'd like to help you," Malcolm said. "But to do so, we need to understand why you disappeared."

Stroheim smoothed a crease from his coat sleeve. "I can't claim to have any knowledge of how LeFou died."

"You met with him yesterday," Stroheim said.

"A chance meeting in a tavern." Augustin moved to a chair, lurched, and gripped the chair arm to steady himself. He dropped into the chair with a thud. "I had encountered him in Vienna, and we recognized each other. I had no notion what he might be doing in Britain."

"Do you know how LeFou might have been connected to Tristram Gresham?" Malcolm asked.

Augustin settled back in his chair and accepted a glass of wine from Dorothea. "Gresham is a Radical reprobate. I had nothing to do with him except occasional attendance at his operas, which one can't avoid."

"And yet you left town last night," Mélanie said.

Augustin passed a hand over his damp forehead. "I wouldn't say I left town. I didn't return home."

"Or put in an appearance at the embassy this morning," Stroheim said.

Augustin took a drink of wine. "I had reasons to be gone from both. Reasons that have nothing to do with politics. I do not lightly share them, but you are a married woman, Mrs. Rannoch. As are you, Countess." He cast a quick glance at Dorothea. "I assume you both understand the complexities of the married state. I'm sure Rannoch does. And Lord Carfax. My reasons for leaving town last night are entirely personal."

"Your personal life is your business, " Malcolm said. "But why return in such secrecy then?"

"Because I realized what was being suspected and whispered." Augustin ran a finger round the inside of his collar. "We all know where whispers can"—he coughed—"lead." He coughed again.

"Would you like some water?" Mélanie asked.

"Please." Augustin's fair skin had flushed red.

Stroheim went to the console table and poured a glass of water, which he handed to Augustin. Augustin gulped down a swallow. "Whatever's going on, you're on the wrong track. This is nothing to do with Austria." He gulped down another drink of water, then tugged at his cravat again, disrupting the elaborate, if grimy, folds. "You must know how things can be set up to create fal-false appearances." He gripped his left arm with his right hand. "I can't claim I know wha-what's going on, but you're being pushed on the—wrong—" He coughed, the words caught in his throat.

His face had turned beet red. Mélanie leant forwards and put a hand on his back. "Count Augustin—"

"I'm all—" Augustin broke off and gasped. Mélanie gripped his arm and felt a spasm run through him. He went still and then tumbled to the carpet.

CHAPTER 35

*M*élanie sprang down beside Augustin and put her hand to his throat.

Stroheim moved to the door. "I'll get a doctor—"

Mélanie shook her head. She could feel no pulse at the base of Augustin's throat, and his eyes were clouding.

Franz glanced at Augustin's wine glass. He'd hit it with his elbow as he fell to the floor. Red wine spilt over the polished wood of the table.

"There wasn't time," Mélanie said. At least, she didn't think there had been. And surely Dorothea wouldn't—

Well, if she forced herself to be as detached as possible, she couldn't be sure what Dorothea might or might not have done. And either this was a coincidence, or someone had intervened.

"At least it's not at the embassy," Dorothea said. She was sitting bolt upright in her chair, eyes wide with horror but also with appraisal. "But—"

Mélanie sat back on her heels. "Julien?"

Julien was already on his feet. He knelt beside her and bent over Augustin.

"We can't just leave him here," Dorothea said.

"We have to, for the moment," Malcolm said "Until we learn more."

"But surely—" Dorothea stared at Augustin, then at Malcolm, then at Julien and Mélanie. "You think someone killed him?"

Mélanie looked into the gaze of her friend. They'd shopped for gowns together. Pored over seating arrangements. Shared tea and cakes at Gunter's. Taken their children to Astley's Amphitheatre. "It must have occurred to you."

"Yes, but I can't imagine who might have—"

"That's generally true when it comes to murder," Julien said. His gaze had focused to onyx. "And we already couldn't imagine who our enemy might be." He put his fingers to Augustin's throat, as Mélanie had done. Tugged back his eyelids. Picked up his hands. Turned them over, stared at his palms.

He sat back on his heels, gaze hard, face paler than usual. "Something with digitalis, I think. A large dose."

"You're sure he was poisoned?" Mélanie asked.

"Definitively? There's no way I can say with a certainty. But one has to look at the preponderance of evidence. That's what Davenport would say."

"How long ago?" Malcolm asked.

"Depends a bit on what he ate. And I suspect he had an underlying condition for it to have induced such a strong heart attack. That might have made it occur more quickly."

"But it didn't happen here." Dorothea's voice was harsh.

"Unlikely." Julien's gaze shifted to meet Dorothea's own. "Assuming he really did arrive here within the last half hour."

"A footman told me the moment he arrived," Dorothea said.

"Well, then. I suppose that rules out some suspects, but only those who couldn't have known he would be talking with us in this time frame."

Dorothea's fingers tightened on the satin folds of her gown. "You think someone poisoned him because he was going to talk to us?"

Julien met her gaze. Whatever might have passed between them of a personal nature, it was wiped from his expression. He was an agent. Looking at a target. "It's difficult not to wonder if there is a connection, Countess."

"But surely—I don't really understand how these things work —but could the murderer have known when he would succumb to the poison?" Dorothea said. "How could they have been sure he wouldn't talk to us first?"

"An excellent point," Julien said. "They couldn't. Poison is notoriously unreliable in terms of timing. They might have estimated wrong and thought he would collapse before he got here. Or they might have thought at least they'd be rid of him. Even if he revealed information to us, he couldn't reveal it to anyone else."

"But we could have shared the information," Dorothea said.

"Perhaps they were counting on our not being believed. Or just not counting well at all."

Dorothea shivered. "You sound so matter of fact. As though it were something normal."

"There's nothing normal about it. But it is a matter of fact now."

Dorothea's fingers bit into her arms through her white gloves.

"He didn't reveal any information," Stroheim said. "We can't know what he might have said if we'd had more time, but while he was here, he denied any knowledge of anything to do with LeFou beyond what he claimed was a chance encounter in a tavern."

"A fair point," Malcolm said. "But the killer couldn't have been certain he'd do as much. And who knows what he might have said if we'd had more time to talk to him."

"You think the same person who poisoned Augustin killed André LeFou?" Dorothea asked.

"We can't be sure of anything," Julien said in the same steady voice he'd been using since Augustin collapsed. "But I think it's highly unlikely there's no connection. Don't you?"

"I'd be a fool to deny the connection, Lord Carfax. Though for the sake of my country, I'm going to have to deny everything. Even that I was in this room tonight."

"He asked to meet." Stroheim's gaze was fixed on Augustin's body. "He claimed not to have any information when we spoke, but he asked for the meeting. And he'd wanted to meet in secret. He must have had his reasons."

"Yes." Mélanie shifted on her heels. Her skirt was tangled over Augustin's legs. There was a bright red smudge on one of her gloves. It must be the wine. He hadn't bled. "And also his reasons for disappearing last night and lying low. I don't for a moment believe it was merely a love affair. That's far too convenient."

"So is his simply stumbling across LeFou in a tavern," Stroheim said.

"Are you saying you think he hired LeFou?" Dorothea demanded.

"I'm saying there's a great deal we don't know," Stroheim said. "And while Augustin was a victim, I also think he was a liar."

"And he quite certainly knew something that got him killed," Malcolm said. "Even if he wasn't willing to share whatever that was."

Julien unbuttoned Augustin's coat. "Probably too much to hope he has something revealing on him, but we should look."

Mélanie pushed back Augustin's coat and helped Julien go through his pockets. A purse with banknotes. A card case. An enamel snuffbox. The usual belongings of a gentleman. But then, in the pocket in his coattails, she felt something unexpectedly heavy. Not the right shape to be a pistol. She reached into the pocket and pulled out a heart-shaped diamond pendant on a white-gold chain.

"Interesting," Julien said. "Somehow I doubt it was a gift for Charlotte Augustin."

"Unless he felt he had a lot to atone for," Malcolm said. "But I doubt he spent his missing twenty-four hours at the jeweler's."

Mélanie watched the diamond heart catch the light from the

candles. "He could have been on his way to meet someone he meant to give this to last night. Or he could have taken it from someone he saw in the past twenty-four hours."

"Which raises some interesting possibilities," Julien said.

Dorothea cast a glance at the door. "If this becomes public—"

Julien pushed himself to his feet. "None of us wants that. On that, we can agree." He spared Dorothea a brief smile and exchanged a look with Malcolm. "We'll move the body."

"Why?" Dorothea's words were unusually blunt. "I mean, why are you willing to help? You could all just walk out of the room."

"Because none of us has anything to gain from his being found here. And a great deal to lose. And whatever my opinion of our relations with Austria and Russia, I don't much care for our countries falling out over an incident like this. I don't imagine Malcolm does either."

"No," Malcolm agreed. "But while we aren't working with the British government—"

"We're working against them," Julien said.

"We're dealing with a murdered diplomat on British soil. Before we move Augustin we need to apprise someone."

"Not Hubert," Julien said on a note of horror.

"No," Malcolm said. "Someone actually in the government. Palmerston."

CHAPTER 36

itty moved to Mélanie's side as she re-entered the ballroom. A waltz was in progress and the crowd had grown thicker. Two ladies with almost identical diamond clips were gossiping nearby, loudly enough to create excellent cover. "Why do I have the feeling something unexpected happened?" Kitty said, tone conversational enough not to alert anyone. "Did Augustin run?"

Mélanie closed her fingers round her fan. Gripping something steadied her. "No, he's dead."

"Well." Kitty's eyes widened. "Even I wasn't anticipating that. I'm glad Julien was there. Unless Julien killed him?"

"No, he was poisoned. Before he got to Almack's. Or so Julien thinks."

"And Julien and Malcolm are tidying away the evidence?"

"They're going to. But first, I've sent for—"

"I must say, all these disappearances this evening have me distinctly curious." Emily Cowper moved to stand beside them with a swish of silk and a waft of Floris scent. "I'd ask questions if I weren't sure the most helpful thing I can do is stay out of your way and provide cover." She looked between Mélanie and Kitty.

"Why do I think this has something to do with why Harry—my Harry, not Cordelia's—has been so secretive lately and looking so haggard?"

"No comment," Kitty said.

"And with why I saw him with Dorothea in the park this afternoon. With their heads close enough together it felt like a dagger cutting through my stays. Don't tell Harry I said that."

"Emily." Mélanie caught her friend's white-gloved hand. "You must know that only something political would pull Palmerston's attention to Dorothea."

Emily's finely arced brows drew together. "I can't say I entirely agree with you. But I do think it's most likely something political. Harry is rather more focused in these things than I am, all things considered." She looked from Mélanie to Kitty. "How else can I help?"

"Distraction would be splendid," Mélanie said. "And be kind to Dorothea. She's had a difficult night."

Emily frowned. "You intrigue me. But I promise not to tease Dorothea. Oh look—there's my Harry. This must be serious indeed if it's brought him to Almack's."

"Emily." Palmerston bowed over her hand. He was faultlessly attired with the correct knee breeches and silk stockings, though his cravat appeared to have been hastily tied, and his black superfine coat was rumpled. "Seeing you would be reason enough to attend. But I confess I also have business. Mélanie sent word."

Emily sighed. "It's not that I mind intrigue at Almack's. But I rather detest intrigue I'm not involved in. I still can't believe this doesn't have something to do with Tristram Gresham. No, don't worry about niceties." She put up a hand as Palmerston started to speak. "Go off and do what you need to do. I'll cover for you. That, at least, gives me the illusion I'm involved in the intrigue."

Palmerston kissed her hand again and held it for a moment, gaze locked on her own. Then he moved off with Mélanie and

Kitty, head tilted towards them as though he was engaged in flirtatious banter. He'd make an excellent agent.

Julien and Malcolm turned to the door as they came into the sitting room.

"We have a problem, as you see," Julien said.

Palmerston went still, staring at Augustin's body. "He's dead?"

"Most definitely," Julien said.

Palmerston nodded, shock giving way to focus in his gaze. "And—"

"Julien thinks he was poisoned before he got here," Dorothea said. "Whatever information he wanted to share at our meeting, he never had the chance to share it."

"In fact, he was denying all knowledge of anything to do with LeFou when he took ill," Stroheim said.

"Damnable." Palmerston looked at Augustin. "He can't have died here."

"No," Malcolm agreed. "I'm thinking a few streets over. Near a tavern."

"The Red Lion in St. Martin's Lane," Mélanie said. "We can alert Jeremy to discover the body."

"I thought you were trying to keep Roth out of this," Stroheim said.

"At this point, we need an ally investigating," Palmerston said. "Not an outsider who'll go running to god knows whom."

"Sensible," Julien agreed. He looked down at Augustin. "We'll need a diversion when we move him."

"Who's going to move him?" Palmerston asked.

"Julien and I will," Malcolm said.

Palmerston looked between them. "You're willing to do this?"

"Someone has to," Malcolm said. "We started this."

"Actually, I think I started it," Palmerston said. "By bringing the information to Hubert. Or, rather, Southcott did, by bringing the information to me."

258

"But it wouldn't be good for you to be entangled in this," Julien said. "And Southcott's the last person we want involved, frankly."

"There's no need for you to rescue me."

"Oh, yes, there is," Julien retorted. "We need an ally in the government. Besides, it's what friends do. I think. I'm still getting used to having friends."

"Someone has to let Charlotte Augustin know," Mélanie said.

"Somehow I don't think she'll care much." Julien's gaze was focused on Augustin.

"No, but he was her husband. The father of her children."

"At least in name," Kitty said. "And I can say from experience, that does mean something. To the children, if not the mother."

Julien met her gaze and nodded.

"How are you going to get him out?" Dorothea asked. "You can get to the street without going through the main assembly rooms, but there's no way to avoid people entirely."

Malcolm studied Augustin. "Wrap him in a greatcoat. Carry him between us. It will look like he's drunk and we're shepherding him out."

Dorothea frowned. "We don't serve alcohol." She glanced at the console table with the decanters. "I mean, not in the main rooms."

"Don't I know it." Julien said. "But he wouldn't be the first person to come in here drunk."

"But if someone sees—"

"If you're worried about the scandal of a drunkard being escorted off the premises, I'd worry more about the scandal of a murdered Austrian diplomat," Julien said. "Metternich wouldn't like that. A lot of people wouldn't like that."

Dorothea folded her arms. "Point taken."

"Can we find a greatcoat?" Malcolm asked.

Dorothea frowned, then nodded and swept from the room.

"How long ago was he poisoned?" Palmerston asked.

"Impossible to know for a certainty," Julien said. "If we could trace his movements, we could learn something. It would have to have been disguised in some sort of meal or drink."

"My sense is Augustin drank rather a lot," Palmerston said. "But we don't know where he's spent the past twenty-four hours."

"No," Malcolm said. "We don't. One of many mysteries."

Dorothea came back, an olive-drab greatcoat in her arms. She handed it to Julien without explanation.

"This is rather ghoulish," Palmerston said, as Malcolm and Julien wrapped Augustin in the greatcoat and hoisted him to his feet.

"As opposed to what else about tonight?" Kitty said.

Palmerston sucked in his breath and nodded. "What can I do?"

"Go back to the ballroom and create a diversion," Malcolm said. "Stage a quarrel with Emily. That always creates a distraction."

"Rannoch." Palmerston gave a half smile that didn't reach his eyes. "I didn't think you noticed."

"Professional expertise. Harry and Cordy are there. And Tony. All heroically staying out of things. They can help. Hubert may help too. Though I wouldn't tell him too much."

"You should go too," Mélanie said to Dorothea. "You can keep watch better than anyone. And the point is to keep you and Palmerston and anyone official out of this."

Dorothea frowned, then gave a quick nod.

"And you." Mélanie touched Stroheim's arm. "Find Lisette and help create a distraction. We don't want this linked to either of you."

Malcolm and Julien moved towards the door, Augustin balanced between them. Stroheim hurried to open the door. Mélanie and Kitty followed.

Following Dorothea's instructions, they started down a side passage. They'd only made it a few feet when a door burst open in front of them. Four girls in various shades of white and pink spilt into the passage in the midst of a high-pitched conversation which stilled abruptly as they took in the group in the passage.

"Good heavens!" one of the girls said. "Is he ill? Or drunk?"

"The most tiresome thing. He seems to have been three sheets to the wind before he got here." Mélanie quickly moved in front of Augustin, Malcolm, and Julien, skirt held out to hide Augustin. Kitty did the same.

"Who is it?" Another girl leant forwards, peering between Mélanie and Kitty. "I must know. Is it someone's brother? Or someone's father? Perhaps—"

"Lydia! Mary! I've been looking for you everywhere. And Edwina and Louisa. Thank goodness you're all together." The voice was Lucinda Mallinson's. She pushed past the men and Kitty and Mélanie and seized one of the girls by the arm. "Do come back to the ballroom with me. I have such a story to tell you. You'll never guess the latest rumor about whose husband was found dead in Tristram Gresham's rooms. And why!"

Uncertainty flickered in the girls' gazes at abandoning one scandal for the prospect of another. Lucinda grabbed two of them by the hand. "Do come now. It won't be nearly as good a story if we wait."

She half pulled the girls down the passage, past Mélanie, Kitty, and the men, too quickly for anyone to see anything. The other two girls ran after, as Mélanie and Kitty adjusted to conceal Augustin as best they could. Lucinda cast a quick smile over her shoulder at Mélanie.

"You're right," Julien said to Mélanie. "She has the makings of an agent. Far too skilled to be allowed to languish as a debutante. Shall we?"

The coast clear, they made it to a green baize door at the end of the passage and down a narrow flight of stairs lit only by a couple of lanterns hung on the wall. Mélanie and Kitty went first. It was fortunate, Mélanie thought, that she implicitly trusted Malcolm and Julien, because the thought of their losing their grip on Augustin, and his body hurtling down on top of her and Kitty, was too ghastly to contemplate.

They emerged into a narrower passage lit by subdued wax candles in gilt wall sconces. Quiet. Was it too much to hope they could make it to the door to the outside undetected? Malcolm and Julien moved slowly, dragging Augustin between them, keeping him upright. In the dim light, he could plausibly be an inebriated friend. A door that seemed to lead to the street was tantalizingly close when a figure lurched in front of them.

"Here now, who's there?"

"Steady on," Malcolm said. "He's had too much to drink."

"At Almack's?"

Mélanie recognized that voice. Reginald Featherington. A Whig MP from the back benches, always on the fringe on things.

"Before he got here," Mélanie said. "Do keep this quiet, Mr. Featherington. We wouldn't want to create a scene."

"If you ask me, Almack's could use a scene. Dashed dull place. Who is it?" Featherington peered through the shadows.

"Do come with me and I'll explain." Kitty slipped past the men and gripped Featherington's arm. "It's been the most shocking mess. I count on you to help me smooth things over. We can't have news get back to his wife." She cast a look at Mélanie over her shoulder and drew Featherington away.

They slipped past while Kitty spun whatever fairy tale she could. Mélanie opened a door that she profoundly hoped led to the outside. It did.

The night air was a welcome blast of cold after the close, candle-warmed air inside. Malcolm and Julien paused for a moment, struggling under the burden of Augustin's—literally—dead weight, then moved forwards, both affecting a casual slouch in keeping with two gentlemen helping an inebriated friend. They moved slowly towards Piccadilly, keeping to side streets. Mélanie could see the swinging sign of the Red Lion, scarlet and gold glittering in the lamplight. Almost there.

"Here now. What are you doing?"

"Don't be difficult," Julien said in a slurred voice. "Had a bit too much."

"Who did?"

A night watchman. Mélanie hurried to intercept him. "Oh, please. It's the most awkward thing." She smiled up at the night watchman with wide eyes. Far from the first time she'd disarmed a night watchman in the course of a mission. "He's never able to lay off the claret—or the port or the madeira or the brandy, if it comes to that. Before we knew it, he was making quite improper advances to Maria, in front of her husband, no less. So of course we had to get him out. Otherwise, they could have come to blows or even pistols at dawn, and my husband might have been asked to be a second, and then where would we be? He sits in the Commons and so does Maria's husband, and just because Castlereagh and Canning survived a duel doesn't mean others would, does it? We're just taking him somewhere where he can cool off without anyone knowing. You won't tell, will you?"

The watchman looked down into her eyes. Her best beseeching expression. "Of course not," he said, seemingly quite forgetting that he wasn't possessed of enough facts to tell anyone anything.

"Thank you." Mélanie pressed his hand. Julien and Malcolm had already taken advantage of her diversion to pull Augustin past.

The watchman smiled into her eyes. "Anything I can do to help, madam," he said, in the tone of a knight offering to embark on a quest.

Mélanie gave him another smile and hurried off after Malcolm, Julien, and the very dead Count Augustin.

CHAPTER 37

*J*eremy stared down at Augustin's body, slumped against the smoke-blackened brick side wall of the Red Lion in an alley next to the pub. Lamplight from the street beyond just caught the sheen on Augustin's polished black shoes. Jeremy had arrived only a few minutes after Mélanie caught up to Malcolm and Julien. "I thought you wanted to keep me out of this," he said.

"Change of tactics." Malcolm leant a hand against the brick wall. He and Julien were both breathing hard after dragging Augustin from King Street. "We're now trying to avoid an international incident. And this doesn't necessarily have anything to do with Harriet."

Jeremy swung his head round to stare at Malcolm in the murky light. "This man, Augustin, was seen with the man who was killed in Gresham's rooms. Hours before that man was killed. And just before or after Gresham and Harriet ran."

"Yes," Malcolm acknowledged.

"And he disappeared that night and then asked to meet with you in secret tonight."

"Yes again." Malcolm kept his voice and gaze steady. Though

Mélanie could tell he was exerting every ounce of control to recover his breath.

"And someone poisoned him before he could talk to you."

"Someone seemingly poisoned him," Mélanie said.

"Quite." Jeremy pushed his hair out of his eyes. "You're better than this, Malcolm. So are you, Julien. And you, Mélanie." His gaze shot to each of them. "Don't ask me to think there isn't a connection to Harriet."

"Accept cover when you've got it, Roth," Julien said. "The point is Augustin was found here, as far as anyone knows or should know. For the purposes of the investigation, there's no reason to think his death has anything to do with Harriet or LeFou or anything else to do with last night. Do you want to investigate?"

Jeremy let out a rough breath. "By god, I do." He scraped a hand over his hair again. "I haven't thanked you yet, have I? For bending the rules." He looked back at Augustin. "Do you think the same person who killed him killed LeFou?"

"Possibly, but not necessarily," Malcolm said. "The person who killed him could be the same person who hired LeFou. But if so, that person may not have killed LeFou. LeFou's death could still be an act of impulse."

Jeremy's gaze shot back to Malcolm. "You mean Gresham or Harriet killed LeFou in self-defense."

"Or someone else did."

Jeremy's brows tightened. "You realize we won't be able to keep this from Sidmouth, once it goes to Bow Street. Murder is a rare occurrence. The chief magistrate will hear about it and Conant will tell Sidmouth. Who will tell others in the government. Especially in the wake of the LeFou affair. They still haven't identified him yet, but there's a search on for Gresham. They were giving odds in the Brown Bear on whether or not he was guilty of the murder of the unknown man found in his rooms."

"We've heard," Malcolm said. "At least, about the search for Gresham. But no one's connected it to Harriet."

"Not yet." Jeremy stared at a tattered playbill on the brick wall advertising their friend Manon in *School for Scandal* at the Tavistock. "You did a good job of removing the only connection to her. But if I start investigating Augustin's death, there'll be no keeping the news of the murder from Whitehall and Westminster."

"There wouldn't be, in any case," Malcolm said. "The death of a diplomat would draw attention even without LeFou's murder last night. But it will be very interesting to see the government ministers' reaction."

Jeremy's eyes met his own, a glint in them. "You're treading on dangerous ground."

"When aren't we?" Mélanie asked. "By the way, there's a diamond pendant in the pocket of Augustin's coattails. Heart-shaped. We think it may have something to do with where he spent the past twenty-four hours."

Jeremy gave a quick nod. "We'll have him moved. I'll get a medical examination, and we'll try to narrow the time of death. We'll first have to find a way to determine who he is, since we can't claim to know. And then the foreign office will have to be alerted and his embassy informed. We'll need to talk to his wife. Were this an unconnected investigation, I'd ask you to assist, and perhaps ask Mélanie or Kitty or Cordelia to talk with her."

"I don't see why you shouldn't do that," Mélanie said. "We'll have time despite the other things we're working on. And there's no reason anyone should think there's any connection between this man's death and those other things we're investigating."

"My thoughts exactly," Jeremy said.

"Charlotte Augustin knows Gresham is missing," Mélanie said. "While others may not connect Augustin's death to Gresham's disappearance and LeFou's death, Charlotte is likely to do so the moment she learns her husband is dead. But if Cordy and I talk to her, we can keep that speculation away from the official investigation."

"A good plan." Jeremy drew a breath. "My god."

"What?" Mélanie asked.

"Just that it feels good to be back in the game. I was going a bit mad."

Julien clapped him on the shoulder. "I know the feeling."

~

"Well," Désirée said. "I never thought not being able to get vouchers to Almack's—which I hadn't even heard of until I came to England—would keep me out of the action. I'm sorry about Augustin," she added. "I can't say I liked him very well, but it seems an unnecessary waste."

"Sadly," Cordelia said. "Though I suspect Charlotte Augustin may be happier in the long term."

They were gathered in the Berkeley Square library. The group from Almack's, Laura, Raoul, and Désirée. Laura and Raoul had had coffee waiting when they all trickled back.

"Why do you think Augustin wanted to talk to you?" Raoul asked, reaching over to refill the cups.

"Technically, he wanted to talk to Stroheim and the countess." Malcolm looked from the Queen Anne chair where he sat with Mélanie to Stroheim on the sofa beside Lisette. "He didn't panic when he saw Mel and Julien and me, but he was wary. I'm wondering if that changed what he was going to say."

"He has to have known I was working with you," Stroheim said. "From the description, I think he gave the letter to the lad who brought it to Berkeley Square himself. Even though he didn't explicitly ask for all of us, he must have suspected I'd bring you."

"He was claiming not to have any connection to LeFou besides a chance meeting." Mélanie curled her hands round her coffee cup. "And that he was being set up. He might have been launching into a story meant to put us off the scent—"

"By saying he stumbled across LeFou in a tavern?" Kitty said. "Not very scent off-putting."

"No, but having had the dubious privilege of knowing Augustin in Vienna, I find it a bit more likely." Mélanie drew her legs up onto the edge of the chair. She'd pulled off her satin slippers when she got back to Berkeley Square. She could feel the imprint of the cobblestones on her feet. "I wouldn't precisely say he's keen with anything. Except a pistol."

Julien took a drink of coffee. "Phrased with exquisite diplomacy."

"On the other hand, the part about being set up could have been a lead into a real story," Malcolm said.

"Yes." Mélanie turned to look at her husband beside her in the chair. "Which brings us to the question of what story he might have told."

"Whatever it could be, it doesn't involve Countess Lieven, apparently," Kitty said.

"No," Stroheim agreed. "Unless—"

"What?" Lisette turned to look at him. "You think Countess Lieven and Augustin were working together to lay a false trail?"

"Think it?" Stroheim said. "No. At least, I can't say I think it likely. Precisely. But we do have evidence that other false trails have been laid. The story Hara Delaney was told. The burnt paper Fitzroy Somerset found. Difficult to see reality when one is in a hall of distorted mirrors."

"She's clever enough for it." Julien stared into his cup. "And ruthless enough."

Kitty turned to look at him. "You don't want to believe it of her."

"My dear. When have you known me to allow personal feelings to intervene in an investigation?"

"When? My darling, let me count the times. Starting with that night in Hyde Park—"

"Those all involved you. Dorothea is another case entirely." Julien settled back in his corner of the settee. "But I will possibly admit to not being entirely unbiased."

"Oh, well," Kitty said. "None of us is free of bias."

"Well said." Raoul set down the coffeepot.

"Even if Dorothea and Augustin were working together," Julien said, "it still leaves the question of who killed Augustin. Not to mention who killed LeFou."

"Lionel admitted his rivalry with Wellington over the fair Clarissa quite readily," Tony said. "Readily enough that it's difficult for me to imagine he suspects anything. Of course, Lionel's always been good at misleading people across the negotiating table." He frowned into his coffee. "I did my best to warn him without giving the whole game away. Lionel would never believe the story. Ten to one he'd go to Sidmouth or Castlereagh, and then everything we know would be everywhere in the government."

"Including with whoever is behind this," Mélanie said.

"That's my fear," Tony said. "But I can't but—"

"He's your brother." Désirée touched his hand. "Of course you're worried about him."

Tony swung his head round to meet her gaze. "It was all I could do to get through twenty minutes of conversation with him and keep things civil. But yes, I'd prefer that he not come to grief."

"My darling." Désirée gripped his hand. "If your qualification for holding on to friends is going to be their accepting us, you are going to severely limit your social circle."

"I'd be perfectly happy with our social circle being confined to the people in this room. And a few others. But this isn't about you."

"No?" Désirée's voice was gentle but even.

"Lionel and I've always been at loggerheads. It's odd that we both went into diplomacy, given how different we were from boyhood. I think he thought I should give it up and focus on being a duke and leave the field to him. Which I suppose I've done now."

"You'll never leave the field, my love," Désirée said. "I think the last twenty-four hours proves that."

"The diplomatic field's a bit different from the intelligence field."

"Ask Uncle Hubert," Julien said. "He isn't a diplomat at all."

"No," Kitty said. "But—"

The doorbell clanged through the house. In an instant, everyone in the library was on their feet. They tumbled into the hall, Malcolm leading the way, a candle in his hand.

"I'm so sorry." A familiar voice rang through the hall as Malcolm tugged open the door. "But all things considered, I thought it was better to come here before I went home."

Mélanie let out a shriek of sheer relief and ran to hug Harriet Roth.

CHAPTER 38

"*J*'m sorry." Harriet hugged Mélanie and drew back. She was wrapped in a dark blue cloak and smudges of fatigue showed beneath her eyes, but her gaze was bright as she glanced round the crowd assembled in the hall. "Good god. Are you having a party? You aren't all here because of me?"

"Not entirely," Mélanie said. "We're in the midst of an investigation."

"The dead man in Tristram's rooms? Is Jeremy—"

"He's out on a case," Julien said easily. "But not the man found in Gresham's rooms. What do you know—"

"That's what we have to explain. I wasn't sure where Jeremy was and how much he knew. That's why we came here before we went home."

"We?" Mélanie said.

The door opened wider. Tristram Gresham stepped over the threshold with uncharacteristic diffidence, hatless, hair disordered, coat rumpled, a day's growth of beard on his face. He met Mélanie's gaze and gave a faint familiar smile, though his expression was unwontedly serious.

"It's all right," Harriet said. "Lord Gresham and I are—"

"Literary allies," Malcolm said.

"You know." Harriet's gaze flickered to Désirée.

"Actually, I told them," Kitty said.

"Though I would have," Désirée said. "I don't lightly betray a confidence. But in the circumstances—"

"No, I quite understand," Harriet said. Her gaze moved to Tony, standing beside Désirée. "You're Désiré's duke."

"Eternally so," Tony said. "That's the most agreeable title anyone's ever given me."

"Tristram told me Désirée wouldn't like it."

"I can accept it," Désirée said. "Now."

Harriet smiled. Then her face went serious. "We have a lot to explain."

"So do we," Mélanie said. "I think we'd best go back into the library."

"We didn't mean to alarm everyone," Harriet said in the library a few minutes later, her hands curled round a brandy-laced cup of coffee. "I got word that friends of mine were in danger. A message saying they were at Southampton and needed help. They'd just come from India."

"Hara and Lizzy Delaney?" Laura said.

"Yes." Harriet's widened. "You know them, of course. Have you heard from them?"

"They're upstairs. With their children. They came to find us last night. But—"

"Oh, thank goodness," Harriet said. "I was so worried. I went to see Tristram, and we left together."

"I could hardly let her go alone," Gresham said, cheeks faintly flushed.

"Any more than I'd have let you go alone," Harriet said. "But we checked on the road because we thought the Delaneys might already be on their way to London. And then we got a description at a posting house that made us think they'd already passed us. So we turned round and came back."

"And on our way back, we heard someone had been murdered in my rooms," Gresham said. He looked round. "Is it true?"

"I'm afraid so," Malcolm said. "Apparently not long after you left. You didn't know anyone was in your rooms?"

"No. My valet was off visiting his family. Harriet and I left down the back stairs so we wouldn't be seen." Gresham took a drink of coffee. "I hate to seem inquisitive, but do you have any idea who this man was who broke into my rooms and then was killed?"

"A French assassin," Julien said.

Gresham sputtered on a sip of coffee. "And to think I thought I was beyond surprise."

"Have you ever heard of André LeFou?" Raoul asked.

Gresham's fingers closed round his cup. "And I also thought I was beyond shock. I've heard the name mentioned. In Italy. Are you telling me he not only broke into my rooms, he was murdered there?"

"We're sure of very little," Malcolm said, "but we are sure of both those things."

"He was trying to kill Tristram?" Harriet inched closer to Gresham on the sofa.

"We're not sure," Malcolm said. "That's one theory."

"And another was that I hired him?" Gresham said. His face was scored with exhaustion, but the old humor was there.

"No, we think someone in the British government did that," Julien said. "Or possibly the Austrians. Or maybe the Russians. Or several of them working together."

Gresham held out his cup. "I think I need some more brandy. And a lot of explanations."

They recounted the events of the past twenty-four hours, holding nothing back.

"John found this?" Harriet said. "In a war office ledger? That was quite clever of him."

Gresham shot a look at her. "I never said he was without wit."

"Is he all right?" Harriet asked.

"He's very worried about you," Tony said.

"He must be worried about his father as well. You must be worried about your brother."

"There's plenty of worry to go round," Tony said.

Harriet shook her head. "I can't believe Hara and Lizzy have been caught up in this. I've never even met them, but I feel I know them so well from their letters and articles. Do you think whoever targeted them knew they were connected to me?"

"Not necessarily," Malcolm said. "It would have been easier for someone to know Delaney was connected to Laura and expect the Delaneys to come to us. Assuming the warning Delaney received was a setup."

"You mean assuming the Duke of Wellington didn't really hire an assassin," Harriet said.

"In a nutshell," Malcolm said.

"To kill John's father."

"That's a theory," Tony said. "But there are a lot of false trails in this."

"Count Augustin's death is very real," Harriet folded her arms, hugging her elbows.

Gresham turned his cup on its saucer. "You know about Charlotte and me?" He turned to Harriet. "She and I—"

Harriet cast a quick look at him. "I suppose I shouldn't be surprised. I don't know the names of half your mistresses."

"Mélanie and I talked to her today," Cordelia said. "She more or less admitted it. She was worried about you."

"Poor Charlotte," Gresham said. "Augustin was a brute of a husband. I won't rejoice in anyone's death. But she's well rid of him." He frowned.

"What?" Harriet said. "If you mean the affair wasn't over—"

"It was over months ago," Gresham said. "Charlotte was entangled with Josef Hauke."

Julien let out a whistle. "That changes things."

"You're sure?" Malcolm said.

"As much as one can be about such things. She came close to admitting it to me the last time I spoke with her."

"Which could have interesting implications for Hauke's pulling Malcolm aside," Kitty said.

"Not to mention giving both Hauke and Charlotte Augustin a reason to get rid of Augustin," Julien said.

Gresham cast a sharp look at him. "I can't imagine Charlotte —" He broke off. "I'm sure you hear that all the time in an investigation. I'm sure you've been asking yourselves questions about me." He looked round the group. "I'm going to have to answer questions from Bow Street. What do you think the odds are that I'll be arrested?"

"Tristram," Harriet said.

"I'm quite serious. I mean, I'd certainly bring me in for questioning if I were in charge of the investigation." He looked round the group again. "Wouldn't you?"

"I'd have questions," Mélanie said. "I certainly wouldn't jump to arrest you."

"But you aren't Bow Street."

"Jeremy wouldn't arrest you," Harriet said.

"Your brother," Gresham said, "will probably want to plant me a facer and challenge me to pistols at dawn. But that's another matter."

"Jeremy doesn't believe in dueling."

"Beliefs will have nothing to do with it, my sweet."

"You're going to face questions, no doubt about it," Malcolm said. "There's no evidence to tie you to the crime—"

"Except the little fact of the dead man being found in my rooms."

"A point. And Bow Street, under the home office's direction, may be looking for someone to blame. All things considered, I think it might be advisable for you not to appear in public."

"Are you suggesting I leave London again?" Gresham asked.

"Too risky," Malcolm said. "It might be better for you to stay here."

"Rannoch. Are you proposing to hide a fugitive from justice?"

"It wouldn't be the first time," Mélanie said.

"No," Malcolm agreed. "Perhaps—"

The doorbell clanged through the house again. Malcolm pushed himself to his feet. "That's probably Jeremy." He looked at Harriet. "I sent word. He's been going mad."

"I'm glad you did," Harriet said.

"So am I," Gresham said. "Though I suspect I'm not long for this world."

Harriet ran to hug her brother when Malcolm brought him into the library a few minutes later. Jeremy's arms closed tight round his sister.

"I'm sorry." Harriet drew back to look at her brother. "It all happened so fast."

"Never mind. You're safe." Jeremy's gaze shot past her to the rest of the group. Gresham had pushed himself to his feet.

"I'm sorry," Gresham said. "I can imagine what you've been through."

Jeremy inclined his head, face stripped of expression. "It was up to Harriet to tell me."

"I was worried any message I sent would be traced," Harriet said. "I was desperately worried about the Delaneys."

"The Delaneys?" her brother asked. "You knew—"

"Yes, I had word they were in trouble, but I didn't realize they were already in London."

"So someone sent you a false message."

"It looks that way. Do you think they wanted to lure me out of London? Or Tristram?"

"Could someone have guessed you'd leave together?" Jeremy's voice was even.

"Possibly." Harriet drew her brother over to the sofa where

Gresham was sitting. "Have you learnt anything about Count Augustin's death?"

"Not much yet. Though one of my constables did find a report of man in rumpled evening clothes who matches Augustin's description in a coffeehouse in Covent Garden earlier this evening. He was talking to another man. My constable couldn't get much of a description beyond 'dark hair', which with dim light could be just about anyone."

"That could be when he was poisoned," Julien said.

Jeremy nodded. "That's my thought."

Harriet turned to look at her brother. "Tristram thinks he's going to be arrested. Do you think he is?"

"I'm not sure." Jeremy met Gresham's gaze again. "There's a lot of speculation. They haven't even identified LeFou's body yet. I have heard—" He bit the words back.

"Speculation that the victim was a jealous husband?" Gresham said.

"Something of the sort."

"We think Gresham should lie low," Malcolm said.

Jeremy studied the man seated beside his sister. The man his sister had disappeared with. Myriad conflicting emotions raced through his gaze. "All things considered, I think that's probably a good idea," he said.

CHAPTER 39

*A*njali Delaney looked at the glistening white currant ice. "It's too pretty to eat."

"No, it isn't." Her brother Hal dug his spoon into his pistachio ice.

"You have to try the coffee ice," said Colin, Mélanie's eight-year-old son.

"And the elderflower," Laura's daughter Emily added.

"Raspberry." Sophie bounced on the bench. The Rannoch children had introduced her to Gunter's last month.

"Currant's my favorite." Jessica, Mélanie's four-and-a-half-year-old daughter, tucked her hand into Anjali's.

Mélanie had seized a moment from the investigation to take the children to Gunter's with Laura and Lizzy Delaney. Experience had taught the vital importance of snatching moments with the children in the midst of investigations. No use saying the investigation would be over soon. There always seemed to be another one. Besides, Blanca's words yesterday had left her curious about Lizzy Delaney.

Lizzy smiled at the children. They had carried the ices into the square garden and were sitting on benches beneath the shade of the plane trees, Berowne the cat and Sophie's puppy Belle at their feet. "My father brought me to Gunter's once when we visited London. I never forgot. That or the cakes at Fortnum's. It almost made up for being cold all the time."

"It's not so cold now." Anjali looked up at the sunlight filtering through the thick canopy of green leaves.

"It's July," Colin said. "Winter's colder."

"Have you seen snow?" Anjali asked.

"Oh yes. Sometimes in London. But there's lots in Scotland."

"We have snowball fights," Emily said.

"Papa says he'll teach us how to make snowballs in the winter," Anjali said. "When we go to the country with Grandmama and Grandpapa." She looked at Lizzy. "Did your father teach you?"

"Not to make snowballs." Lizzy swallowed the last spoonful of her cherry ice. "I was never in England in the winter. I only came the once."

"Will it be safe then? To go to the country?" Anjali asked. She looked from Lizzy to Mélanie to Laura. "I mean, that's why everyone's being so careful, isn't it? Why Papa was hurt?"

"They won't let anything happen," Colin said. "Everyone's used to danger. My parents and their friends know how to take care of it."

Mélanie drew her breath to respond when the shadow of someone approaching fell over her lap.

"Mrs. Rannoch."

Cold shot through Mélanie despite the warmth of the day. At the voice, even before she turned from the shadow on her pin-tucked lilac muslin and looked up from beneath the brim of her chip straw hat to meet the mocking gaze. Before she saw the sleek dark hair and sharp-boned features. He was a stone or so heavier than she remembered, his skin more flushed, but still unmistakable.

"Colonel Radley." No sense in avoiding the unavoidable. Unfortunate the children were present, but as Colin said, she knew how to protect them. "It's been a long time. I trust you are well."

"A long time indeed. I should have known we'd encounter each other again."

"Diplomacy is a small world." If the word diplomacy could be used to describe a spy mission that had led to a hurried affair, followed by a blackmail attempt at the Congress of Vienna that she had feared would end her marriage. And then a revelation Radley had made to Malcolm three and a half years ago that had unraveled her masquerade and very nearly ended their marriage in truth.

The glitter of unsheathed knives echoed in Radley's eyes. "So it is."

Mélanie turned to Laura and Lizzy, who were sitting quietly beside her. Lizzy had gone stone still, in fact. Any new arrival was a potential threat. "Colonel Radley, an acquaintance from the Peninsula and Vienna. My friends Mrs. O'Roarke and Mrs. Delaney. Mrs. Delaney's husband was also a soldier. We brought our children to Gunter's for ices." Normally she would have introduced the children, but she had no desire to have them interact with Radley any more than strictly necessary.

"Mrs. O'Roarke." Radley inclined his head. "I've met your husband. Charming, if unexpected, that he gets on so well with the Rannochs. And Mrs. Delaney and I have also met." Radley's gaze settled on Lizzy in a way that made Mélanie want to put her arm round her friend. And tightened the knot of chill in her throat.

"Colonel Radley." Lizzy's voice was steady, though Mélanie could feel the effort, palpable as frayed rope. "Colonel Radley worked with my father in India," she added to Mélanie. Her voice caught, but didn't break. The rope caught on a rock.

"Mrs. Delaney wasn't Mrs. Delaney at the time," Radley said. "Odd where life takes us all."

Laura met Mélanie's gaze for a moment. Mélanie inclined her

head. She needed to learn what Radley wanted and what he knew about Lizzy, and better with the children out of earshot. "The children and I were just going to have a game of hide and seek," Laura said. "If you'll excuse us."

She caught Jessica and Anjali by the hand. Colin scooped up Berowne. He and Emily sent Mélanie worried looks, then linked arms with Sophie and Hal. Sophie grabbed Belle's lead. Mélanie smiled at them to indicate she was quite all right and acting like normal children was a way to help with the investigation. Which was true.

Radley watched Laura and the children move off, then looked back at Mélanie and Lizzy. "Remarkable to see you both as devoted mothers. But then, you both have formidable acting talents, as I know to my cost. I must say, the last time I saw you, Mrs. Rannoch, I didn't expect to still greet you as Mrs. Rannoch the next time we met. Or, at least, not as Mrs. Rannoch living with your husband. He obviously cares more for scandal than I realized."

"You may take it whatever way you wish, Colonel Radley," Mélanie said.

"And living with O'Roarke, of all people."

"Mr. O'Roarke is my husband's father," Mélanie said. That should at least throw Radley off his stride.

Radley's eyes widened, which was a quite agreeable reaction.

"It wasn't commonly known until recently," Mélanie added.

Radley's brows rose. "One would think that would make Rannoch's reaction to what you and O'Roarke did all the worse." His gaze moved over her, saying more clearly than any words that he remembered precisely what she looked like undressed. "Rannoch always had a soft streak."

Mélanie smiled into the gaze of the man she had once gone to great efforts to seduce. "My husband is one of the strongest men I know."

"You would see it that way." Radley's gaze shifted to Lizzy. "I suppose I shouldn't be so surprised to see you together. You're both expert at pulling the wool over men's eyes. Whether it's cheating at cards or selling secrets to the French. It's still deception."

Lizzy had gone as pale as cream laid paper, but she gave an artless smile that even glinted in her eyes. "You do say the oddest things, Colonel Radley. I can't imagine what you suspect me of doing. Or suspect Mrs. Rannoch of doing. Really, the life of a military or diplomatic wife is much tamer than you imagine. I don't blame you for your fairy tales—I've always found fairy tales quite amusing and I love telling them to my children. But I'm quite sure you're much too sensible to share them with anyone."

Radley flung back his head and laughed. "Mrs. Delaney. You should know better than to think I'm the least bit sensible."

Lizzy's gaze sliced into his own. Steel cutting steel. "I wouldn't presume to know you at all, Colonel Radley."

"Interesting, Mrs. Delaney. I feel I know you quite well. But then, I imagine the future will offer insights into that."

Lizzy's smile dazzled like broken glass. "One can never tell what the future holds, Colonel Radley."

Radley inclined his head and moved off.

The wind ruffled the tree branches and shifted the shadows. Shouts and laughter, the voices of their children, and a bark from Belle carried on the breeze. A game of hide and seek was underway. Laura was apparently "it." The children were hiding behind trees branches, lost in a world where the only danger was their hiding place being discovered. But then, that was a world Mélanie had lived in for a very long time.

She stared at her hands, gloved in decorous ivory thread net, on the sprigged lilac of her gown. Then she turned her gaze to Lizzy. Because for both of them, the mask had been stripped away.

CHAPTER 40

"Sometimes the most public places are the safest for talking," Mélanie said.

Lizzy nodded. Now that Radley had left, she was visibly shaking, but she didn't seem about to collapse. At least, not for a few minutes.

Mélanie linked her gloved fingers together. All these years and she wasn't above tricks to keep her hands steady. "How much do you know?"

Lizzy folded her own hands in her lap. "I'm not sure there's anything I need to know."

"I'd have said that." Mélanie kept her gaze steady on Lizzy's own in the shifting shadows of the plane trees. "But now we've both been privy to each other's secrets."

"Are you sure you want to say more?" Lizzy asked, gaze direct and open beneath her dark brows.

"My husband wouldn't want me to. But despite being an eminently sensible man, he's ridiculously protective. And I have a pardon. So does Raoul. That makes things safer." Mélanie smoothed a snag in one of her gloves. "Though not entirely safe, as Malcolm would say."

"The war's been over a long time. And you're still married to him."

"Much to Freddy's surprise. I used to call him Freddy. God, that seems a long time ago." Mélanie studied Lizzy, searching for the right words. She wasn't ashamed. Not precisely. But the words stuck in her throat. And then there was the matter of trust. "Frederick Radley and I were close. For a time. In the Peninsula. I went into it to spy on him. Which is the same reason I went into my marriage." The admission that defined who she was. Or, at least, who she had been for so long. "Raoul was my spymaster."

Lizzy's eyes widened. "And Mr. Rannoch—"

"Suspected Raoul was his father. Had done since he was a child. Didn't know Raoul was a French agent."

"But Mr. Rannoch was a British agent."

"Yes. He'd say we were all playing the same game. But Raoul and I played it differently from Malcolm. We made compromises he never would."

"Somehow I think Mr. Rannoch would argue with you."

"Probably. Malcolm's ridiculously hard on himself. And ridiculously forgiving of everyone else." Mélanie's fingers tightened, pulling on her gloves. "I fell in love with Malcolm. I didn't with Freddy." She met Lizzy's gaze through the shadows. "I love my husband. And I think you love yours."

Lizzy swallowed, cast a quick glance towards the game of hide and seek, then looked back, chin held high. "Much of what I told you the night we arrived was true. Most of it actually, one way and another. My father was—is—a captain. Only he had gaming debts when he went into the army, and never quite seemed to get over them. So he had to turn to other ways to recoup his fortunes. Or simply to stay afloat. And while cards got him in debt, he was also rather frightfully good at them. Cards, that is."

"And he taught you."

"Yes." Lizzy dragged the reticule in her lap closer, like armor.

"For all his qualms about other things his daughter should do, he was quite proud of my skill at cards. He was always saying that I could play rings round Gerald. That's my brother. Which I could. Run rings round Gerald. Practically before I could talk. I can't say I'm proud of what we did, precisely, but it did make life much more interesting than needlepoint or watercolors. And truthfully, the way we lived, I didn't think much beyond the moment. Not until Hara, actually."

"What changed things?"

Lizzy folded her arms over her chest. "You mean besides just meeting Hara? It would be too much if I just fell madly in love and changed my life, wouldn't it? Papa thought Hara would be an easy mark. And he said"—she shuddered, her shoulders hunched, pulling at the puffed shoulders of her moss green gown—"he said an Indian wouldn't understand how the game was played. In any number of ways. Which was wrong. Hara's quite fearsome at cards. And he's brilliant at reading people. Papa didn't mind my flirting with him to get closer and gain a tactical advantage. But then one night he saw us dancing together. We'd stayed late at a regimental dance after most people had gone home, but the band was still playing and we were waltzing closer than one would normally. Nothing one could really call improper, I swear it. I've seen the most sheltered girls dance much more closely with gentlemen while their mamas watch with eagle eyes on the side-lines and don't see anything amiss. But it was one of those moments the ballroom seemed to fade away and it was just the two of us. I'll own I was a bit dizzy when we stopped dancing. I looked over and saw Papa watching us. Though I'm not sure if it was more that our dancing got to him, or the fact that I'd made sure Hara didn't lose a hand of whist earlier in the evening. In any case, he berated me in the carriage going home. Papa said I was going soft and he'd never known me to be so addlepated. Then he said I couldn't actually be in love with the—well, I won't repeat it, because I can't bring myself to say such words." Lizzy's gaze fastened on her stepchildren for a moment. Hal had his hands covered to count, and Anjali was hiding behind a tree with Emily. "But it was clear how he saw Hara." Her fingers dug into her elbows, knuckles white against the gauzy green of her gown. "He forbade me to see Hara. But I knew then. I knew he'd never accept Hara. And I knew I could never forgive him."

"Not an easy thing to face about a parent." Though for all the things Mélanie had faced in her life, that was one challenge she'd never confronted.

Lizzy shrugged. "In some ways, it made it easier. There was no point in trying to work things out with Papa. Or with Gerald. He's just as pigheaded as I made it sound in my cover story. I knew I'd have to run with Hara to have a life with him. And I knew a life with Hara was what I wanted. I only had to persuade him of that. Which I did by giving him no choice." Her dark brows drew together. "Which may have been a bit unfair. Was a bit unfair. But I convinced myself it was what he wanted, and I was justified in doing anything to push him past his scruples."

"I can understand the impulse."

"Can you?" Lizzy's gaze fastened on Mélanie's own, granite hard and yet at the same time searching. "Is that what you did with Mr. Rannoch?"

"Not precisely. But the circumstances weren't the same."

Lizzy regarded her, words trembling on her lips.

"It's hard," Mélanie said. "Having secrets from one's spouse."

"I didn't tell Hara," Lizzy said. The words came in a rush, like the pop of a champagne cork. "I meant to. But at first, persuading him that we had to leave together seemed paramount. And then Gerald showed up and that complicated things. And I had to simply focus on all of us getting on the ship for Britain safely."

"Sometimes one has to put one's family's safety first."

"So one does. All those months on the ship I told myself there was no point in his finding out while we were at sea. It wouldn't be fair. So for all the cramped quarters, we could simply enjoy being together. Those months were heavenly, in a way. I could forget for hours—days at a time—"

"I know," Mélanie said. "For me it was sometimes weeks."

Lizzy's eyes widened in recognition. "But I realize it's still there. Between us. Or, at least, on my side. And if—when—Hara learns, it could change everything."

Mélanie drew in and released her breath. It hurt her chest. "For a long time, I thought that if Malcolm ever learnt the truth about me, it would end everything between us. I was so focused on the need to keep the truth from him, I didn't spend nearly enough time considering what might happen if he did learn the truth and how we might muddle through. So I was woefully unprepared. And yet we did manage. In far more challenging circumstances than you face."

"I'm not sure. You had far greater justification for your actions than I did. Hara's a man of principle. He won't think much of cheating at cards."

"He'll understand the need to make a living."

"Not a very honest one."

"He'll also understand a rigged system."

Lizzy reached up and pushed a lock of hair beneath the brim of her bonnet. "You're kind, Mrs. Rannoch. And I think we both have reason to fear Frederick Radley."

"He's entirely too willing to do his worst, and he means what he says with his threats." Mélanie hesitated. Difficult to ask, but it had to be said. It was another layer of risk they'd have to guard against. "Did you—?"

Lizzy met her gaze without blinking. "He flirted with me. It never went further. Well, it went as far as Papa and me both winning rather a lot off him. For which I suspect he's never forgiven me." Lizzy tugged the green ribbons on her bonnet tighter. "I'm going to have to tell Hara the truth, aren't I?"

"There could be worse things."

"I never thought of myself as a coward. I hate the idea that I am one. But I suppose the only thing to do is face up to the consequences of my actions." Lizzy straightened her shoulders. The square neckline of her gown pulled taut. The ribbons on her bonnet snapped against her throat. "I've done an awful thing to him. I didn't really think it through properly. I couldn't get past the idea that I had to push him past his scruples so we could be together. I didn't think of it as manipulating him, because I was quite sure he wanted to be with me. And obviously, if he'd known the truth about Papa it would only have muddied and complicated things. I didn't consider that I was trapping him into marriage to a cardsharp, whom he might not want to be married to at all if he knew the truth. I didn't think about his feelings. Or if I did, I simply looked past those thoughts. That's how I grew up, after all. Focused on the main chance." She stared at a knotted tree trunk. "I can't say Papa thinks about other people's feelings. Including mine. It was only after we got here and I started realizing I was going to have to tell Hara, sooner or later, that I started realizing how hard it would be. And then before I knew it, we were worrying about an assassination plot by the Duke of Wellington. I don't think it fully hit me until just now. After Colonel Radley confronted us."

Mélanie looked into the younger woman's face. This was not something she talked about. Not even to Malcolm. Or Raoul. Perhaps especially not to them. She was so accustomed to compartmentalizing it that she didn't often think about it herself. But it was always there. The confusion in Lizzy's eyes cut through to a place deep inside her. "It often doesn't," she said. "Until one's faced with a choice. For years, I thought my only hope of a life with Malcolm was his never learning the truth. That was after the first few years when I didn't think about the future at all. And if I did, I didn't think we could be together."

"But you told him."

"He found out. Because Frederick Radley let something slip."

288

Mélanie loosed her clasped hands and gripped her elbows. "I recommend telling Hara."

Lizzy nodded. "Hara's far too good a person to throw me over. He feels protective. It's one of the few things we argue about. I'm perfectly well able to take care of myself. Perhaps when he learns the truth he'll recognize that more. That might be the one advantage. And he won't want to disrupt things for the children. So he'll be stuck with me. Stuck in a marriage where we can't tell the truth. I'm sure he'd be faultlessly polite. But the thought of looking into his eyes and having him not able to be truly open—"

"Malcolm and I went through that." Mélanie's fingers tightened on her elbows. "The first anger was over the fastest. But I could tell there was a part of himself he couldn't share with me for some time after. Understandably. He didn't want me to see what he was feeling. He had to have some part of himself where he could be angry with me."

"What changed it?"

"You'd have to ask Malcolm. But time, I think. There was a moment I looked at him and knew we'd left the past behind." In fact, she'd gone to bed with him and known it from the way he'd made love to her, but she wasn't going to quite say that.

"So you're back to where you were?"

"Oh, I don't think we'll ever be that. Thank goodness. I mean, I wouldn't want to be, precisely. I wouldn't want to go back to where we were living with a deception. But I think what we have is stronger. I won't say there aren't challenges. But then, there always are, in a marriage."

Lizzy nodded. "I just hope we can survive this one."

Jessica came running across the garden, kicking up a spray of dust, and hurtled into Mélanie's legs. "Can we come back now? Is that man gone?"

"Yes." Mélanie pulled her daughter onto her lap. Really, it was folly to try to keep anything from the children.

"I don't like him," Jessica said. "Are we supposed to like him, Mummy?"

"No," Mélanie said.

"It's serious, then." Jessica swiveled her head round to look up at Mélanie. "You tell us to like everyone."

CHAPTER 41

April 1821
Normandy

"How did you do it?" Harriet asked.

"Do what?" Désirée set down the teapot and glanced at Sophie, who was coloring on the floor of the cottage sitting room. "Be an agent? One step at a time. Be a mother? I'm still learning."

"Keep going." Harriet's fingers tightened round her blue-flowered teacup. Désirée had told her Tony ordered the pattern exclusively from Wedgwood, who kept it specially for him. Not because he insisted they do so. Because that was the way they treated a duke. "After Waterloo. All those years and it must have seemed everything was going backwards. Or hurtling full-scale backwards, more like."

Désirée set her cup down. "You could say I didn't keep going. I left. I left Brussels almost as soon as I knew Tony was all right. I came here. I retreated to a safe nest owned by my English aristo lover." Her mouth curved with typical irony, more than a bit touched by self-derision.

"But you didn't. Not really."

"I'm here. In this so-called cottage, with ridiculously luxurious comforts, while my former comrades are facing imprisonment."

"Well, you couldn't very well have stopped the imprisonment if you'd stayed in Paris. You'd just have ended up imprisoned yourself. And you were pregnant."

"Yes, that was my excuse." Désirée tossed down a sip of tea. "I rather hate myself for using motherhood as an excuse."

"But you didn't. You did what you needed to do to protect Sophie and yourself."

"Which rather sounds like an excuse for escaping to safety."

"The thing is, you escaped to safety, but you kept going. You could have turned your back on it all because it was too unutterably depressing."

Désirée turned her cup on its saucer. "It was indeed unutterably depressing."

"And yet you didn't. You found a way to keep fighting. How you summoned up the willpower to do that—"

Désirée got to her feet and moved to a cabinet against the wall. She opened a lacquered door painted with flowers and took out a decanter. "This calls for something stronger than tea." She moved back to the table and splashed generous measures of calvados into their tea. "Odd. I loathed tea when I first met Tony. Of course, I don't think I'd ever had a properly brewed cup. He made me one in the kitchen here. A bracing and fragrant way to wake up. And no, the circumstances were not what you'd be pardoned for assuming. It was the morning after the night we met. At loggerheads on a mission. I got a jump on Tony and had a knife to his throat. But then he patched me up after a colleague tried to kill me. I came away with the papers we both wanted. Tony was a gentleman, tucked me into bed alone, and helped me get to Paris the next day."

"And you've been fond of tea ever since?"

"Along with other things." Désirée set the decanter down. "I learnt to appreciate calvados from Talleyrand." She returned to her chair and took a deep swallow of calvados-laced tea. "It was hard after Waterloo. Harder perhaps than I've ever admitted to anyone."

"Well, I don't imagine you could to Tony. The duke."

"Not entirely. He understood. After Waterloo, he said he'd understand if I couldn't bear to see him. But of course there were limits to what we could talk about." Désirée took another drink of tea and calvados. "I've never been the sort to give way to despair. But I think I might have done then, if I hadn't been so worried about Tony. And if I hadn't been pregnant. Those gave me a reason to hold on. We said things to each other before and after Waterloo that we'd never said before."

Harriet took a drink of the calvados-laced tea—supple and aromatic. Lethality encased in elegance. "But you could have just focused on Sophie and forgot about the world. No one would have blamed you."

"No one except myself, perhaps." Désirée curled her fingers round her cup. "I've seen a lot. I remember the excitement of the Revolution. I remember the horrors. I remember the fear of going backwards, and how Bonaparte seemed a shield against that. We put up with a lot. It's always one thing at a time. Sometimes that can keep one from seeing the bigger picture. But sometimes it helps to find a way to keep going. To take one step against injustice." She set her cup down. "God, I sound maudlin. Don't let Tony know I spoke like this."

"From what you've said about him, I think he'd wholeheartedly agree with you."

"Probably. Tony's an idealist, god help him. I just can't bear somehow for him to know I've let my guard down and joined him in the delusions I've scoffed at."

Harriet set her cup down. "Are they delusions?"

"You'll have to work that out for yourself."

"To you, I mean."

Désirée reached for her cup. "No. They never have been. Or I wouldn't be where I am now. But we all have to be permitted our defenses. Not that those defenses did much in the face of loss. Perhaps it's madness, but I have to believe there's a possibility of change if we keep going." She glanced at her daughter. Sophie had a brown pastel in her hand and appeared to be drawing a puppy. "Oddly, I have to believe it even more now I have Sophie. Retreating into motherhood completely wouldn't help me get the world I want for her. That's what we all have in common. Even people as different as Tristram and John Southcott. We want to make the world better."

"I hope so," Harriett said.

CHAPTER 42

July 1821
London

élanie found Malcolm in his study, papers spread on the desk before him. Laura had taken the children into the library and Lizzy had gone up to talk to Hara. "No sense in delaying," she'd told Mélanie with determination. She'd hugged Hal and Anjali before she went upstairs.

Malcolm looked up from the papers. "Rupert sent round some questions on the debt relief bill. I didn't want to leave him hanging, despite the investigation. Everything all right?"

Mélanie closed the door behind her. Her fingers were not quite steady. Delayed reaction. "Lizzy and I ran into a mutual acquaintance today."

Malcolm's brows rose. "Not surprising, given your connections to the military. But—"

Mélanie walked forwards to the desk. "It was Frederick Radley."

Malcolm pushed himself out of his chair. "Bloody hell, Mel—"

"Honestly, darling, I've been thinking for ages that it's been far too long since we've seen him."

"Far too long—"

"He was bound to turn up again, sooner or later. Knowing him, probably at the worst moment. But really, there's very little he can do to us now."

Malcolm folded his arms and regarded her over the desk strewn with papers that defined his career. Which, she conceded, one could argue she was threatening.

"He was surprised to find us still together," she said.

"More fool he. But then I never credited Radley with more than crude sense. If that."

"He's more of a threat to Lizzy and Hara." Mélanie hesitated a moment. Lizzy had told her she could tell Malcolm, but she knew better than most the risks inherent in sharing secrets. "There's more to their past than we at first realized. Which isn't entirely surprising."

"No. But—"

"Lizzy told me I could tell you. Her father is a card sharp. And Lizzy worked with him. Hara was one of their marks. Until Lizzy fell in love with him."

"It does happen." Malcolm's gaze was steady in the sunlight slanting through the window.

"So it does. In all sorts of circumstances."

Malcolm reached across the desk and touched his fingers to her cheek. "I take it Delaney doesn't know."

"Not yet. Lizzy's upstairs talking to him now. I tried to give her advice. I'm not sure how well I did."

"He quite clearly adores her."

"That could make it better or worse."

Memories shot through Malcolm's gaze for a moment. "He'll be angriest at her father."

"That will annoy Lizzy. She'll think he isn't giving her credit for the person she is and for making her own choices."

"She didn't marry him to fleece him."

"No. Much easier, in many ways, than our situation."

He held her gaze. The past hung between them, and neither of them tried to deny it. That was progress. "There are differences. He may not see himself in her."

"You can't see yourself in me, darling."

"If so, it's because you had the courage of your convictions."

"You wouldn't have done what I did."

"Perhaps not. But I can still admire you."

"I looked at her across the bench in the square garden today. She looked so young."

"She can't be so very many years younger than you."

"It's not the years. She can't have had an easy life, based on what she said. But I couldn't help thinking—I don't want her to go through what's ahead."

"We got through it."

Mélanie rested her hands on the edge of the desk. The wood was cool and substantial beneath her fingers. "We're getting through it."

"He's a good man. He won't want to lose her."

"There's a difference between a marriage lasting, and the feelings it's based on lasting."

Malcolm didn't pretend not to know what she was talking about.

"You must be so angry with me." Harriet looked at Mélanie across the sofa in the library. Mélanie had left Malcolm in the study to find Harriet had just arrived in Berkeley Square, along with Kitty and Julien and their children. Kitty and Julien were at the other end of the room, along with Tony, Désirée, Raoul, and Laura, organizing a game of lottery tickets. The strains of piano music drifted from across the hall. Gresham had said if he had to miss another day of rehearsal, at least he could work on the score.

"No!" Mélanie said. "Not angry in the least. Tremendously impressed. I wish I could have helped. But I also understand why you needed to keep it secret. I know better than anyone that the more people who know about a mission, the more dangerous it is."

Harriet's brows drew together. "I didn't think of it quite like a spy mission. But I suppose it is, in a way."

"Certainly in the secrecy it requires. And in the network you built." Mélanie regarded Harriet for a moment. "Jeremy will understand."

"Yes, I think he does. He told me he did last night, when we got home. And that he understood my keeping him out of it—for his own sake and because I had to limit the number of people who knew. Jeremy doesn't care for being protected any more than I do, but he does understand the need for secrecy. And Judith said she understood. Goodness knows they've both had to confront the need for secrecy since they've been a couple. I think they both have questions about—" She hesitated.

"Lord Gresham?" Mélanie said.

Harriet met her gaze. A minor chord echoed from the music room. "They don't want to ask. But they don't understand our relationship. I'm not sure I understand it."

"That's between you and Lord Gresham. I don't think any one of us, including your brother and Judith, expect all relationships to follow a conventional path. Certainly most of us haven't followed a conventional path ourselves." Mélanie looked at the group round the lottery tickets game. Laura and Raoul, Julien and Kitty, and Tony and Désirée had all lived together before they were married. Judith and Jeremy had been lovers. Cordelia and Harry had been separated for years. In fact on the surface, Mélanie and Malcolm had followed the most conventional path of all of their group.

Harriet glanced at Julien as he swung his daughter Genny onto his lap. "But you are aware of the dangers."

"There are dangers in any relationship," Mélanie said. "And in the world we live in, relationships can carry more risks for women."

Harriet's gaze shot back to Mélanie's own, her gray eyes clear and steady. "I know that all too well. I see examples round me all the time. I saw it growing up with my parents' friends. It's all very well for free-thinking Radicals not to believe in marriage, and it's quite true that legally, marriage is appalling for women. But it's also true that women pay a far heavier price than men for defying convention."

"You haven't mentioned Mr. Southcott," Mélanie said.

"What about him?"

"He's obviously very fond of you as well. You must be aware of it."

"Well—yes." Harriet tucked a loose strand of dark brown hair behind her ear. "And I'm fond of him. But I hadn't thought—I'd drive him mad. He wouldn't want a wife who writes articles and communicates with Radicals all over the globe. He enjoyed having a forum to voice his thoughts about the foreign office. And he genuinely does want change, but it isn't the sort of change I want."

"You may be doing him a disservice."

"I think I understand his politics."

"Politics can change." Mélanie glanced at Tony, who was helping Sophie and Kitty's son Timothy lay out the mother-of-pearl fish. "His uncle's certainly did. But I was thinking more that he may be able to appreciate a woman who doesn't agree with him on everything."

"And I could have a nice stable life with him? Stability sounds rather ghastly."

"I'd have said the same once," Mélanie said. "But it doesn't have to be a trap."

Harriet spread her hands over her lap, smoothing the pearl-gray sarcenet of her gown taut. "Are you asking me if I want to be an unstable rake's mistress or a sensible man's wife?"

"Is that what you're trying to decide?"

"I'm not sure it's an option, precisely," Harriet said. "That is, Tristram and I aren't—He has scruples."

A phrase repeated from the piano. Gresham, trying to work out a problem in the score.

Harriet smiled. "But if I put my mind to it, I think I could be his mistress. As to John—I'm not sure what he wants. But I think anything between us would have to involve marriage."

"I think the issue is to sort out what you want."

Harriet met her gaze. "I'm not sure of that at all."

As if to punctuate her words, the door opened and Valentin stepped into the room. "Countess Augustin and Baron Hauke have called, Mrs. Rannoch. They're asking for a word with you and Mr. Rannoch in private."

"JOSEF TOLD ME. That Karl's been found dead," Charlotte Augustin said. She was seated on the sofa in the parlor, a very correct distance from Josef Hauke. Mélanie, Malcolm, Julien, and Kitty had joined them. The four of them had started the investigation, and Charlotte seemed accepting of their presence. "He heard it at the embassy. He was told Karl was found in the street by a tavern. And it appeared to be a heart attack. But it wasn't, was it?" Her gaze skimmed between them.

"We don't think so," Mélanie said. "He had offered to share information with us just before he died."

"And he didn't die by the Red Lion," Hauke said. It wasn't a question.

"No," Malcolm said. "But he collapsed before he could share information."

"My belief is he was poisoned," Julien said.

He didn't elaborate on why he believed that, or why he had the expertise to judge. He didn't need to. Hauke met his gaze and nodded.

Julien turned his gaze to Charlotte. "It was very fast. I don't believe your husband suffered."

Charlotte gave a quick nod. "Karl and I weren't—Our marriage had been broken for a long time. But the memories are there. And he was my children's father."

"I lost my children's father in similar circumstances," Kitty said. "It's beastly. But don't let the circumstances interfere with your ability to be happy later on."

Charlotte met Kitty's gaze for a long moment and nodded again. She didn't move any closer to Hauke or even look at him, but the bond between them was palpable. "That isn't why we came, though. Josef—Count Hauke—has information about Karl. We think it may be relevant."

Hauke stared down at his hands for a moment, then met Malcolm's gaze squarely. "I told you the night before last that Stroheim and Countess Lieven were mistaken to think Austria was involved in LeFou's being in London. What I didn't say is that Augustin had come to me earlier in the day with intelligence that someone in the British government had brought an assassin to London to kill one of their colleagues."

"'Someone in the British government'?" Malcolm asked. "Or someone specific?"

"Someone specific." Hauke's shoulders straightened. "That's why I tried to warn you," he said. "I was hoping you'd be able to work out the truth for yourselves."

"Why not simply tell us everything you knew?" Malcolm asked. "Why not name this person?"

"Because I didn't think you'd believe me." Hauke held Malcolm's gaze the way he would across a counsel chamber. "I know you'd reached out to me. We've worked together, Rannoch. We've faced each other across the negotiating table. We've shared intelligence. We also run missions against each other. I respect you. I think you respect me. But I can't say I'd believe you against one of my own, and I wouldn't expect you to do the same. It would be my word against his. And you have a personal connection to him, after all. Or one of your friends does."

Wellington's name hung unspoken in the air. The sound of the piano from next door echoed through the room.

"Who?" Malcolm asked. He scarcely moved, but his voice was taut as a bowstring.

Hauke drew in and released his breath. "Lord Lionel Southcott."

CHAPTER 43

A piano chord crashed through the room, breaking the stillness that held all of them. "Augustin told you Lionel Southcott had hired an assassin to kill someone in the British government?" Malcolm said.

"Yes. I know it sounds improbable." Hauke ran a hand over his hair. "I was tempted to ignore it all. But when I got reports that LeFou was in London and that Countess Lieven and Stroheim were talking to you, I started to take it seriously."

"Did Augustin say where he got this intelligence?" Malcolm asked.

Hauke's mouth tightened. He cast a quick glance at Charlotte, then looked back at Malcolm. "From an opera dancer he was— acquainted with. Who apparently was also entangled with South- cott. Clarissa. I didn't get a last name."

"At least we have evidence she exists," Malcolm said. "And was —is—entangled with Lionel Southcott. As well as the Duke of Wellington."

"Augustin and I were not—on good terms," Hauke said. "But in this case, I think he may have had good intelligence."

"Why do you think he disappeared?" Mélanie asked. "And what did he want to tell us last night?"

"He may have thought his knowledge put him in danger, especially if he'd got wind LeFou had been killed."

"Are you suggesting his encounter with LeFou the night of the murder really was the accidental meeting he claimed it was?" Julien said.

"I'm not sure," Hauke said. "Even if he encountered LeFou accidentally, I suspect he was trying to draw him out." He looked at Charlotte.

Charlotte shook her head. "I'd like to say I could tell Karl was upset about something the last few days, but the truth is I scarcely saw him. We passed each other in the hall once or twice. And if he looked preoccupied, it never occurred to me it was over anything more than an appointment with his bootmaker or a quarrel with his mistress." She frowned. "There was one thing. Two days ago. I happened to be in the hall when a letter was delivered for him. I didn't hear who it was from, but I happened to notice the seal. It had the imprint of a laurel leaf. Karl came out of his study and fairly snatched the letter. As though he was afraid I'd see it. I assumed it was from a mistress. But now…"

Her voice trailed off. She looked from Malcolm to Mélanie to Julien to Kitty, with questions none of them could answer.

"It makes a sort of horrible sense," Tony said. "Lionel could have tried to set up Wellington and me."

They were back in the library, sharing the news with the others, while Harriet and Laura entertained the children.

"But presumably your brother wasn't planning to have himself killed," Julien said.

"No." Tony frowned. "The point would have had to be to have the plot uncovered, with him the hero, and Wellington and me blamed. Which would have improved his standing. Not that I'm much of a threat to him at this point, but he seems to have a hard time believing I'm as retired as I am. And he certainly might have been himself benefiting from Wellington's disgrace."

"So who would LeFou's target have been in that case?" Kitty said.

"I'm not sure. Perhaps the point was simply for the plot be uncovered, leaving Lionel a hero. Or perhaps the attack was supposed to go awry, killing someone else."

"There's another explanation," Malcolm said. "As Stroheim said, we're in a hall of mirrors filled with false trails. This information Augustin had could be one more false trail."

"Fed to Clarissa the opera dancer, or laid by her?" Mélanie said.

"I'm not sure," Malcolm said. "But I don't discount that she was entangled with Wellington as well as Lionel Southcott."

"We should talk to John," Tony said. "At this point I'd like his perspective on Lionel. And I know he's anxious about Miss Roth."

"Harriet sent word to him just after she got here," Raoul said. "I expect—"

He broke off as the door opened and Harry and Cordelia came into the room.

"I've just had word from Fitzroy," Harry said. "He thinks he's worked out who had the best chance of planting the burnt note in the fireplace in Wellington's study. An officer visited three days ago. Lately returned from India. He had served under Wellington in the Peninsula and had done work for him in Vienna." Harry looked round the group. "Do you know a Frederick Radley?"

CHAPTER 44

February 1815
Vienna

*D*ésirée cast a glance round the tavern's walled garden. Rare late winter sun dappled the tables, and a crowd had gathered to enjoy the open air. Soldiers in the uniforms of at least five countries, along with numerous people whose nationality—and loyalties—couldn't be determined. "Just how many agents do you have here, Tony?"

Tony raised a brow in that way only he could. "If you can't tell, they must be well disguised."

"Don't flatter yourself, my dear. Since you're here, I assume you've brought agents."

He cast a sideways glance at her, leaning against the stone wall of the tavern with his glass of beer. "You'd only say that if you knew there was a reason to have agents present."

"Dearest. Don't insult me. Why else would we both be here?"

She glanced across the courtyard as two uniformed Austrian officers grabbed a fair-haired man as he got up from a crowded table.

"Metternich." Tony took a sip of beer. "Nothing to do with us."

"Say whatever you like, my darling."

Tony took another swallow of beer. "Excuse me, Désirée. I'm late to meet friends."

"That's a tired excuse, Tony."

He touched her arm. Lightly. She'd never let him see the shiver it sent through her. "You'd see through a better one, so what's the point? A pleasure as always, my dear."

~

"HAND IT OVER, TONY." Désirée put a hand against the wall of the passage out of the tavern courtyard to block Tony

"Need I remind you that we are on Austrian soil and you have no authority here? Besides, hand what over?"

"The papers that the charming girl with the nut-brown hair passed to the fair-haired young man whom your Austrian friends arrested. And then let you interview."

"Even if you were correct that I have papers, why on earth would I hand them over to you?"

"Because my people are holding your friend Folyat—who I fear will never master the art of disguise—two streets over. They'll release him as soon as they know I have the papers. Also, because I have a pistol pointed at you under my cloak."

His gaze glinted at her in the waning sunlight. "You wouldn't use it."

"Interesting question." Her gaze slid over the garden beyond him. It wasn't as crowded as it had been earlier. Most of his people were gone. But a dark-haired man she was quite sure was British was talking to a man in gray. Light brown hair. Anonymous features. Good god, was that André LeFou? "Shall we put it to the test?"

"I'm not talking about your feelings for me. A shooting in

public would be far too messy. You're a lot of things, my love, but your work is never messy."

"You don't think I could slip out in the chaos as everyone screamed and swarmed round your body?"

"Planning to shoot to kill, are you?"

The dark-haired man who looked British and André LeFou had been joined by another man, also dark-haired, in a British uniform. "If I simply wounded you, they'd be scrambling to help, and I'd have an even better chance of escaping."

Tony's gaze shifted over her face. "I'd quite like to see you try."

"You'd be flat on your back bleeding on the paving stones and straw. You'd miss the whole thing."

"Mmm. You might miss."

"Folyat, Tony. You might play games with yourself, but with him?"

"I could run. You're a good shot, but I'd be dodging through the crowd and you wouldn't like to hit bystanders."

"Folyat."

Tony sighed. "The perils of agents whose parents went to Eton or Harrow and have delusions about what their sons can accomplish. Perhaps I want to get rid of a long-standing problem."

"That would be sensible. But it's not you."

"I could run. I may not be the man who bowled for Eton anymore, but I'm not wearing a gown and corset."

"You could try it. But as you know well, there are any number of things I can do in a gown. And as you also might know, I'm not wearing a corset."

Tony sighed, reached into his coat, and handed over a sheaf of papers.

Désirée glanced through them. "Where's the fourth sheet?"

"Who said—"

"Don't play games, Tony."

"My darling. Our interactions have been a game since the night we met in Normandy. We both of us work in a game."

308

"The fourth sheet."

He reached into the other side of his coat and held out another sheet of paper.

Désirée tucked the papers inside her cloak and into the bodice of her gown. "Thank you for being sensible, Tony."

"You wouldn't have used the pistol."

"Probably. But then you've always made dangerous assumptions about me."

"The Metternich masquerade tonight."

"What about it?"

"I'll be there."

"Good to know. I imagine I'll see you there."

DÉSIRÉE DROPPED her crystal-beaded shawl on the dressing table bench and reached for the brandy decanter. "All the masquerades tend to blur together."

Tony unhooked his domino and pulled off his mask. "The themes change. At least, I think they do. I'll own to being a bit confused on the details. Tonight seemed to have something to do with peacocks. Or was it butterflies?"

"Laure Metternich would be so sad to find her careful planning went to waste."

"I'm not the audience she has in mind. I think a plain domino and mask are the best answer to the situation in most cases."

"It's much easier for gentlemen. I couldn't possibly wear the same gown each time." Désirée filled two glasses with brandy. "When I think of what I've spent just on gowns at the Congress—" She handed him a glass.

"I'm sure the intelligence you've come up with was more than worth it."

"Mmm…" She lifted her glass to his own. "By the way, who

was the British agent who was talking to André LeFou this after-noon while I was recovering the papers from you?"

"Who's André LeFou?" Tony asked.

"You expect me to believe you don't know?"

"I've not been as well informed as you."

"He's a French assassin. Though at the moment I suspect he works for the highest bidder. I saw him talking with two men. Both dark-haired. One was in a British uniform."

"That doesn't guarantee either of them were British."

"No, but something about them seemed British. Of course, that could simply mean they were very good at their masquerade."

"You should know all about that."

"Any repercussions for this afternoon?"

"Give a man some pride. Do you think I'd tell you?"

"Not much I could do with the information."

He took a drink of brandy. "The truth is, so much information is being stolen and bought in Vienna that there's hardly more fuss when any is taken. I'm not sure anyone's keeping track, overall."

"It could get you in trouble if your superior knew what happened this afternoon and then saw us now."

Tony looked at her over his glass. "Are you suggesting I leave?"

"You're an adult. I hate it when anyone doesn't let me make my own decisions. I trust you prefer the same."

"Wise woman."

"It doesn't mean I don't worry about you." It came out more softly than she intended. With Tony, there had always been more times than she intended when she spoke the unvarnished truth.

Tony closed the distance between them and brushed his fingers against her cheek. "It's appreciated. I'd say not to let it get in your way, but I know full well you won't."

"Just make sure you do the same."

He slid his fingers into her hair, in a very distracting way. "You think there's any risk I wouldn't? I'm an agent."

"And a brilliant one. But you also have old-fashioned ideas

about chivalry that you take far more seriously than most people who are far less clear-eyed about the aristocracy than you."

"You wound me." His fingers slid behind her neck.

"Whose favorite poet is Lovelace?"

"I'd say it's a tossup between him and Marvel."

"Precisely."

"And I'm fully conscious of the irony in both."

"Ha!"

His eyes smiled in her own in a way that definitely counted as unfair tactics. His fingers tightened behind her neck as he pulled her to him. She closed her eyes. Enough for scruples. Time to let go and enjoy what they had. For as long as they had it.

She went still seconds before her lips met his own. She couldn't have said which sense alerted her to danger. A sound that was off, a flash of light through the curtains? She just knew something was not as it should be. And from Tony's stillness, he did as well.

He released her and moved soundlessly to the window. He flattened himself against the wall and slid two fingers behind the closed curtains. Just enough to glance out with his head pressed against the paneling. A glimmer of lamplight from the street shot into the room.

"We're being watched," he said without moving.

"Your or ours?"

"No way to tell. Dark greatcoats have a way of blurring. I don't recognize any of ours. Folyat's all too likely to give himself away. At a guess, I'd say Austrians. But could be anyone."

He inched away from the window and let her take his place. She glanced down at the murky figure just on the edge of the glow from the street lamp. "No significant tells. But they could have followed you here."

"Or they could simply be watching you. Even your friends could be doing that."

"True. But you need to careful, Tony."

He caught her wrist and drew her away from the window. "We're here now. Safest thing for both of us is to stay put. At least until morning."

She smiled up at him. "We've been here before."

"So we have. Source of some of my most treasured memories." He pulled her to him.

She slid her arms round him but leant back and said, "This can't last, Tony."

"Us? It's lasted for decades."

"What we've got in Vienna. It's a moment out of time. The whole Congress is a moment out of time. More fool those running it if they really think they can turn the clock back. And more fool the rest of us if they can and we stand by and let it happen. But the fever will break one way or another, and we won't be able to live in this gilded haze."

"I don't need to live in a gilded haze. I just need you. Haze or not."

"Worthy of Lovelace. Or Marvel."

His arm tightened round her. "I'm not a schoolboy, Désirée. I wasn't long before I met you. Happily-ever-afters are in a different world. That's quite divorced from espionage. Let's enjoy what we have. For as long as we have it."

She leant into him and drew his head down to her own. "For once, my love, we are entirely in agreement."

CHAPTER 45

July 1821
London

𝓗arriet, who had been staying on the sidelines with the children, got to her feet when Valentin showed John Southcott into the library. "Mr. Southcott. Thank you for coming."

"Miss Roth." Southcott went to her side with quick steps, then drew up short and bowed. "It's a great relief to see you well."

"I'm sorry to have scared everyone. I had no notion what was happening while I was gone."

"No," he said. "You couldn't have done."

Harriet took his arm and drew him towards the others. "Come and have some tea. There's a great deal to talk about." She looked round the group. "Oh, you haven't met Désirée yet, have you? At least, I don't think you have. John Southcott, who has contributed articles to *Le Monde Gris*. Perhaps against his better judgment. Désirée Clairineau. Who helped me make *Le Monde Gris* what it is."

Southcott went still at the sight of Désirée, rather like a man who has suddenly glimpsed a panther lying amid the garden furniture, "Mademoiselle Clairineau." He regarded Désirée with the caution of a knight approaching a sleeping dragon. "I wish you and my uncle very happy."

"You're too kind, Mr. Southcott."

Désirée settled herself on the settee beside Tony. She was unusually quiet while Tony outlined Hauke's story about Augustin's report on Lionel Southcott. But then this concerned Tony's family, and in some ways she was still an outsider. Mélanie knew the feeling.

"I can scarcely credit it," Southcott said when Tony had finished.

"Nor can I," Tony said. "But I think we have to at least consider it. It's difficult to fit any of the pieces together. And as Rannoch pointed out, we know we're dealing with a great deal of false information."

"Does your father have any connection to a Colonel Frederick Radley?" Harry asked John. "We think he's the one who planted the information in the grate in Wellington's office."

"Radley?" John blinked. "It's odd. I was at school with a Frederick Radley who went into the army. I've seen him occasionally since, but I wouldn't say we're great friends. Father's met him, but they don't know each other well. At least, I wouldn't have thought they do. You think Father engaged Radley to plant evidence that Wellington and Uncle Tony were trying to have him killed?"

"It's entirely possible Augustin's evidence against your father was manufactured as well," Malcolm said.

"By Augustin?"

"Possibly. Or by someone who planted the evidence with Augustin." Malcolm didn't mention Wellington's name.

The conversation continued on, with various theories, none of which quite held together. Mélanie got up at last to see about more tea and some seedcake for the children. Désirée, who had scarcely said a word for the past quarter hour, offered to help her, and suggested Malcolm and Tony might help with the tea tray. Once they were in the hall, she paused and gripped Tony's arm, rattling the teacups.

"John. I've seen him before. In Vienna."

"He was in Vienna," Tony said.

"He wrote good reports," Malcolm said. "Though we disagreed on almost everything. He had his own frustrations with Castlereagh and Wellington, but they were over style, not policy in general."

"It's where I saw him." Désirée was uncharacteristically pale. "In the garden of a tavern where Tony was arresting an agent and I took papers from him. From Tony. While I was confronting Tony, I saw André LeFou talking with a man in a British uniform and another man who struck me as British. That man was John."

Tony went still. "You're sure?"

She nodded. "It doesn't prove anything."

A host of thoughts shot through Tony's gaze. "It's suggestive."

"Very suggestive." Julien appeared in the hall, a pale Harriet beside him. "Something about Southcott's been bothering me. Southcott's talking about Radley with Harry. I seized the opportunity to take Harriet aside and ask a key question."

Harriet locked her hands together, but her gray gaze was steady. "John uses a special seal on communications he wants to keep secret. At least, he used it when he wrote to me. It has a laurel leaf."

Désirée settled back in a corner of the sofa, a fresh cup of tea cradled in her hand. "I didn't realize you actually knew André LeFou, Mr. Southcott."

"LeFou?" Southcott's eyes widened. For all his formality, at times he could look like a disingenuous schoolboy. One forgot he was almost Malcolm's age. "I may have crossed paths with him without realizing it—it sounds as though he was everywhere—but we never formally met."

"You were more than crossing paths when I saw you in Vienna," Désirée said.

"During the Congress?" Southcott's eyes widened further. A pulse was beating above his tightly tied neckcloth, but he gave no other sign of not being in complete control. "My dear madam, that was over six years ago. You obviously have keen insights and a good memory, but you can't possibly be sure—"

"Believe me, Mr. Southcott. I may hold a book further from my face to read these days, but there's nothing wrong with my long-range vision. And I wouldn't have survived this long if I couldn't recognize faces."

"She's right." Tony perched on the arm of the sofa where Désirée was sitting, a hand on her shoulder. A gesture of solidarity. And protection.

"Are you saying you believe her, Uncle?"

"That she saw you in Vienna with LeFou and a British soldier? Who I suspect was Frederick Radley? Yes."

"Radley?" Southcott passed a hand over his hair. "I told you I went to school with a Frederick Radley who went into the army. I've been talking to Davenport about him, trying to work out any connection he might have to my father. But I wouldn't say Radley and I are close."

"I've strategized missions with plenty of people I wasn't close to," Harry said.

Southcott sat back and surveyed the company. "I thought we were talking about my father."

"The suspects in this case keep shifting," Malcolm said. "Which is the whole point, I think."

"The point of what?" Southcott clunked his teacup down. "What are you accusing me of? Killing LeFou?"

"No, I think Augustin did that." Julien swung his foot against the sofa leg. He was sitting at the opposite end from Désirée and

Tony. "I've been trying to work out the shot that killed LeFou. If I'm right about the angle, it was a tricky one. But Augustin could have done it. I remember watching him practice at Manton's. Shooting was one of his few real talents."

"I can't speak to that," Southcott said. "But what would Augustin have been doing in Gresham's rooms?"

"You sent him there," Julien said, with a smile as deadly as a dagger. "Or, rather, LeFou did at your instigation."

"Excuse me?" Southcott shook his head as though to clear it. "LeFou sent Augustin to Gresham's rooms and then Augustin killed him there? Did they go together?"

"No, Augustin was supposed to arrive first, but LeFou was delayed, as Stroheim saw, and got there later than anticipated. I think Augustin really was ignorant of his wife's affair with Gresham. LeFou apprised him of it when they met at the tavern that night. With the goal of sending Augustin to confront Gresham. Gresham was supposed to be alone in his rooms. You'd probably ascertained that his valet was away. LeFou was supposed to follow and kill Gresham and Augustin, making it look as though they killed each other. Or if Augustin had managed to kill Gresham, LeFou would have taken care of Augustin. Only Miss Roth went to see Gresham earlier. She'd received word that her friends the Delaneys needed help—I suspect you sent that message to get her safely out of the way while all this was going on. But you didn't bargain on her going to Gresham—I don't think you realized quite how close they'd grown. So Augustin arrived at Gresham's rooms—broke in—and found Gresham gone. He was angry and waited. And when LeFou came in, Augustin shot him from across the room, thinking he was shooting Gresham. When he realized his mistake, he panicked and fled down the backstairs from the bedchamber. The same way Gresham and Harriet had left earlier."

Southcott stared at Julien with a wide, steady gaze. "You're

317

very clever, Lord Carfax. A bit too clever for me. Why on earth would I have wanted Augustin and Gresham dead?"

Julien's gaze flickered to Harriet, who had moved to a seat across the room from John when they returned with the tea. "Anyone who's seen you round Miss Roth can understand why you'd want Gresham dead."

Southcott flushed. "That's hardly—"

"And I think Augustin had become a liability."

"To whom?" Southcott said. "His government?"

"To you. He'd been working with you."

"Working with me on what?" Southcott struck a perfect tone of aggrieved confusion.

"Your plot to bring down the British government," Mélanie said.

"*What?*"

Mélanie glanced at Malcolm. They were still piecing this together based on a hasty conversation in the hall and kitchen, but she was quite sure they were lining up the pieces in the same way. "It was quite clever. I'm still not sure if LeFou was actually supposed to kill someone, or if the plot was meant to be uncovered in advance. But you set up the pieces to cast suspicion throughout the government. In the end, no one would have trusted anyone. What a perfect way to shake the government to its core and let you pick up the pieces."

"That's what you've always wanted, isn't it?" Tony said. "To get rid of the dinosaurs?"

Southcott's gaze locked on his uncle's own. For a moment, the disingenuous look of the past hour was gone. "I've always been very open that we can't keep operating on the ideas of the last century. Even Metternich doesn't seem to realize the world has changed, and he can't force it back to what it was fifty years ago. But if you think I could set all this up—"

"Oh, I think you could," Malcolm said. "We kept thinking the plot was so elaborate it involved a vast conspiracy, possibly between countries. But in the end, it was you, with some help from Radley and Augustin. You used Radley to plant the evidence implicating Wellington and Tony. Augustin set up the evidence implicating your father. But the planning was all you. I'll say this for you, Southcott. You're efficient at getting things done."

"I don't deny being efficient. I do categorically deny the rest of this. It's a preposterous story. Given that Mrs. Rannoch is a play-wright and Mrs. O'Roarke writes novels, perhaps I shouldn't be surprised." Southcott hesitated a moment, hands on his knees. "Though I will say, if the war office records weren't such a tangled mess, whoever hired LeFou wouldn't have been able to get away with hiding the payments. Perhaps that, at least, will bring about some needed change."

He looked at Harriet. "You're making dangerous choices."

"Coming from you," Harriet said, "that sounds a bit odd. But I've come to realize I like danger. I think perhaps you do too."

Southcott returned his cup to the tea table and pushed himself to his feet. "Every game has many gambits. Any good player must be prepared to lose more than a few of them. Thank you for the tea, Mrs. Rannoch. It's been a very edifying afternoon."

CHAPTER 46

"Are we simply going to let him get away with it?" Julien asked.

"He hasn't got away with anything." Hubert, whom they had summoned to Berkeley Square along with Palmerston, looked round the group gathered in the library. "LeFou's dead. All Southcott's carefully laid trails of evidence designed to make the government ministers chase their tails suspecting each other have been tidied away. So efficiently that I think we're the only ones who actually chased our tails."

"And Southcott gets away with murder." Frustration sharpened Julien's voice. Mélanie shared that frustration, though she'd already realized how limited their options were.

"Are you suggesting I ask you to eliminate him?" Hubert inquired of his nephew.

"I wouldn't do it," Julien said. He hesitated a moment. "And I wouldn't be happy if you had someone else do it."

"Oh, darling." Kitty reached for his hand.

"We can't bring him to trial," Palmerston said. "The story's convincing, but it would never hold up in a court of law." He frowned. "And if it could hold up, we wouldn't want it told. For the family alone—"

"That shouldn't stop you," Tony said. "But the implications of a foreign office employee being charged with killing an Austrian diplomat are distinctly complicated."

"We can find a way to remove him from the foreign office," Palmerston said.

"We could," Hubert said. "Though I think it might be more interesting to leave him in place and watch what he does next."

Tony glanced from Désirée to Raoul. "We did that once. The person we were trying to watch came damned close to killing Raoul and me."

"Actually, it was the woman he loved who did that," Désirée pointed out.

"Well, then," Hubert said. "There's no woman in Southcott's life we have to worry about."

"Southcott's clever," Désirée said. "Far cleverer than St. Pierre was."

"True enough." Hubert glanced round the group in the library. "Which is why it's fortunate the rest of you are so much cleverer than he is. I have every faith in you."

"Uncle Hubert," Julien said. "You don't have faith in anything."

"There's a first time for everything."

TRISTRAM GOT up from the piano as Harriet came into the music room. "If you knew what it's cost me to focus on my score for the past few hours—"

"Truly heroic." She managed a smile and closed the door behind her.

"I'm sorry," he said. "I've been doing my best to stay out of the way, but Kitty came in and told me. About Southcott."

Harriet moved to the piano. Fragments of her memories of John still churned like broken glass in her brain. "I liked him. I can't believe I was deceived in him. But I never—I couldn't but be flattered that he contemplated a future with me. But it was the fact that he contemplated it, not the future itself that intrigued me. If that makes any sense. I wouldn't—John was never what I wanted."

"That doesn't mean it doesn't hurt."

"It does, in a way." She touched her fingers to the warm wood of the pianoforte. "But mostly because I feel the most unutterable fool."

"My dar—dear girl. That's the last thing you are."

Harriet gave him a quick smile. "Jeremy and Judith are here. Jeremy came to get a report on the case."

Tristram nodded, face contained. "Your brother and I need to talk."

"Oh for god's sake, Tristram. There's no reason for you to talk to Jeremy—"

She broke off because the door opened and, predictably, her brother and Judith entered the room.

"Oh," Jeremy said. "I didn't realize—"

"Come in, Roth," Tristram said. "I'm sure you have a number of questions. Is the Augustin investigation wrapped up?"

"Officially, Karl Augustin's death is being ruled a heart attack." Jeremy pushed the door to. "So the investigation is over. There are a number of things we'll never learn. I think we can assume Southcott is the dark-haired man Augustin was seen with in the coffeehouse, and Southcott managed to slip him the digitalis. But I still can't make sense of the diamond pendant."

"Augustin had a diamond pendant on him?" Tristram's gaze sharpened.

"It was in one of his pockets when he was killed," Jeremy said.

"I saw it." Judith moved into the room and settled on the settee, by far the most comfortable of the four of them. "I must say Augustin had good taste in jewelry. I've always liked heart shapes."

Tristram took a step towards her. "With a white-gold chain?"

"Yes." Jeremy's eyes narrowed. "Do you know something about it?"

Tristram swallowed. For a moment, Harriet had the oddest sense he was embarrassed. "There's one like it in my rooms. Or there was when Harriet and I left. If Augustin was prowling about in a rage before LeFou got there, I wonder if he decided to help himself to it."

"That sounds very like the sort of thing Augustin might have done from what I've heard about him." Jeremy said. He hesitated a moment. "I'll see it's returned to you."

"Thank you," Tristram said. "I—it's rather important." He regarded Jeremy. "I'm sure you have questions. Not about the investigation."

"I told you I—" Jeremy drew a rough breath. "Damn it, how could I not?"

"Stop it, both of you." Harriet ran between the two men. "Jeremy, this isn't anything to do with you."

Her brother stared at her. "It isn't—"

"I'm not a girl of eighteen who needs to be protected. I'm a woman of two-and-thirty. What I choose to do with my life is my own business. I wouldn't need your permission to marry. And I have no intention of marrying Tristram."

Jeremy stared at her. "You don't—"

"I should think you'd be relieved. You needn't have any worries about lasting stability now."

Jeremy swallowed. She could see him bite back a dozen words that sprang to his lips.

Judith got to her feet and gripped her husband's arm. "Careful, darling."

Jeremy drew a measured breath. "You can't think I'm—"

"Oh for god's sake, Jeremy," Harriet said. "I'm not allowed to have a lover? You did."

"For what it's worth," Tristram said from the sidelines, "I understand your brother's concerns."

Harriet rounded on him. "You stay out of this."

"If you like. Though I think your brother and I can agree that I'm involved."

"If it were up to the two of you, I'd be wrapped in cotton wool and you'd go off thinking you loved honor more. Which is all nonsense."

"I never said anything about honor," Tristram protested. "I never uttered the word."

"We made our own decisions," Judith murmured to Jeremy.

Jeremy looked from Harriet to Tristram. "All right, I'll admit it. I'm not living up to my ideals. I'm concerned about my sister."

"So am I," Tristram said.

Jeremy turned back to Harriet. His gaze was open and steady. "The boys will miss you."

"I'm not going anywhere. Not unless you throw me out. I wasn't going to be so brazen as to actually live with Tristram. Besides, he hasn't asked me. He hasn't agreed to any of this."

"No," Tristram said. "No one's asked me anything. You're all assuming a lot. Including that I don't want to marry you."

Harriet spun towards. "You said—"

"I said I didn't believe in marriage. In the abstract. That's an entirely different question from marrying someone in reality."

Her throat had gone tight. "Only you could talk such piffle, Tristram."

"I never claimed to be logical." He took her hands and moved to face her. "I want to be with you."

"And marriage is the only way you think you can be? I keep telling you—"

"And marriage is what I want. I don't want to hide. And I don't want anyone else."

"For now." Her fingers tightened involuntarily over his own.

"It's true I can't guarantee it. But I've never wanted to risk this

324

before. On the other hand, I'll fully admit taking me on is a risk. I quite agree with your brother in that. I've been trying to tell you as much almost from when we met. You're much better off turning and running."

"But if I want you, you'll only succumb to marriage?"

Tristram smiled into her eyes in a way that most unfairly made it hard to think. "Precisely."

"You've only just realized that?"

"No, I realized it some time ago. But a lot's happened to keep us from talking." He hesitated a moment. "The pendant was a gift for you. There was a great deal I was going to say when I gave it to you."

"Oh," Harriet said.

Judith clapped her hands together. "Well, I think it's splendid."

"That's because you're a romantic," Jeremy said.

"I was right about us, wasn't I?" She looked from Harriet to Tristram. "Far be it from me to interfere in your domestic arrangements. But we have a rather ridiculous amount of space. And the boys are very attached to Harriet. We could quite easily take one floor and make it yours."

"What a splendid idea," Harriet said. She looked at Tristram, still holding his hands. "That is—"

"I have no desire to separate you from your family. And my own domestic arrangements are hardly what one would call suited to a family. Though someone should probably ask Roth what he thinks."

"You don't mind, do you, darling?" Judith said. "You're always saying we have more space than you know what to do with."

"No," Jeremy said. "That part actually sounds like one of the more sensible suggestions of the past hour."

"It's only a suggestion if Tristram and I get married," Harriet said. "Which we haven't agreed to yet. In fact, he hasn't asked me."

"Do I need to?" Tristram said. "I thought you were a liberated woman. Surely you aren't holding me to such distinctions. But if you must—Harriet, I love you to distraction. I admit I have very little to offer you, but I will do my best to make you a good husband. Will you marry me?"

"Thank goodness. I thought you'd never say it." Harriet released his hands and linked her own hands behind his head. "I was quite prepared to not get married. I never felt that I needed to. But all things considered, I do agree it will be easier this way. And I suppose—I'll admit I'd like to." She pulled his head down to her own and kissed him, heedless of Jeremy and Judith. Heedless of anything. Except the possibility of happiness.

CHAPTER 47

Désirée shut the door of the room she and Tony were staying in in Berkeley Square. Sophie and Belle were happily settled in the nursery. But the events of the day had far more reverberations for the adults. "I'm sorry," she said.

"I keep remembering him as a child," Tony said. "I'm going to have to get used to seeing him as an adult. And a formidable opponent."

"At least Harriet and Tristram came to their senses."

Tony gave a welcome smile. "Is that what you call getting engaged now?"

"If it's what the people in question want." Désirée moved to Tony's side. "Oddly I thought I had a sense of what Harriet and Tristram wanted long before I could admit what I wanted myself."

Tony regarded her, an odd look in his eyes.

"What?" she asked.

"I remember your telling me you valued your freedom more than anything."

"Did I? That sounds like me being defensive. When?"

"The morning after the first night we spent together."

"Ah." She slid her arms round him. "Well, I was rather aware of how much I was at risk. I needed to do something to protect us both."

"From you?"

"Well, you were showing signs of giving way to romantic delusions—which you were already obviously prey to the night I met you, but by that night you seemed to be developing romantic delusions about me. Which I suspect you have about every woman you sleep with."

"You wound me."

"Deny it if you will, Tony. Anyway would you rather be callous and heartless—"

"Well, it's not as if I've slept with so many—"

"Precisely." She reached up and smoothed his hair off his forehead. "You were in danger of being hurt. And I was at risk of feeling things that were entirely too complicated. And that could interfere with what I had to do. Besides, politics were battering me enough. I couldn't risk my heart getting battered as well. It wasn't as though you were—"

"It wasn't as though I were free? Are you telling me you thought that way?"

"It wasn't as though it was going to last."

His gaze stayed steady on her. "Wasn't it?"

"So I thought. Caring for you would be complicated. Spying is messy enough without being in love with someone on the other side. I was bound to betray you—"

"As I recall you left with papers that morning."

"You see? I'd betrayed you already."

"We made our own rules."

"More or less. We broke them often enough." She glanced at Sophie's favorite doll, Cendrillon, propped up on her dressing table bench. "I was bloody terrified when I left that morning. Life wasn't simple anymore."

"Did you think it was before?"

"Not at the time." Désirée pressed her forehead against his

own. "But in retrospect, I had a remarkably simple view of things. I didn't have the least understanding of the emotional messiness of life. Though I had encugh of an inkling to try to push it away."

Tony laughed and wrapped his arms round her. "Thank goodness I was too stubborn to let you do so."

~

JULIEN CLOSED the door of the Carfax House nursery on the sleeping children. "To think a man like LeFou was felled by a jealous husband."

"A jealous husband catching the wrong person." Kitty dropped her shawl on her dressing table bench. It seemed a long time since they'd been home.

"Yes, I suppose it's oddly appropriate that Karl Augustin pulled off a brilliant shot only to shoot the wrong person." Julien moved into the room and pulled off his coat. "While Gresham, who everyone thought would succumb to a jealous husband, has instead succumbed to matrimony."

Kitty bent to pick up a shirt of Timothy's, which had somehow wound up on the floor beneath her dressing table. "You should know something about that."

Julien moved to her side, a lazy smile on his face. "You once told me you wanted to be free more than anything."

"No."

"Yes."

Kitty looked up from folding Timothy's shirt. "Not before anything. Not before my children."

"Well. You might have been over emphasizing to avoid undue dependence on me."

Kitty turned to face him. "I never didn't want to be dependent on you, Julien."

"No?"

329

"Well, not precisely." She set the shirt down with care and smoothed the sleeves. "I wasn't sure how long you'd be with us."

"You thought I was going to bolt at any moment."

"All right, yes. I thought you were enjoying playing at family life but at any moment you'd want to go back to being the Julien St. Juste you'd always been. I knew I had to be ready to be on my own if you did. To keep the children safe." She tilted back her head and watched him. "I've never minded being on my own. In fact I quite relished it. Life was much simpler without Edward. I quite like being the only one to make decisions. Easier than trying to make one with someone with whom one disagrees. Or trying to persuade him to one's view when he doesn't agree. Which involved all sorts of tiresome wiles. I quite liked parenting on my own."

"And you were good at it."

"I think so. I wasn't looking for someone to share my life with." She put her hands on his chest. "But once I realized you were—"

"Not about to turn craven and run?"

"That you actually wanted to stay. When I realized that—when I accepted it—I wanted to share it with you. Sharing can be complicated, but sharing with you was worth it. More than worth it."

"Worth the distraction?"

"Being on one's own may be easier. But being with the right person is more fun."

"You made a great sacrifice for me."

"My darling." Kitty slid her arms round his neck. "It wasn't a sacrifice in the least."

"LIZZY AND DELANEY looked happy at dinner," Malcolm said. "Did she say anything to you?"

"Only that it had gone better than she hoped," Mélanie said. It had been a quick whisper in the drawing room after dinner, in the midst of so much else, including celebrating Harriet and Tristram's engagement. "But the real test is living with it."

"Delaney did say he had a brilliant wife tonight," Malcolm said. "That says a lot. Including that he's a very sensible man and knows what he has to hold on to. I don't think Lizzy need worry he wants to be anywhere but where he is."

"Nor do I." Mélanie moved to her dressing table. "Harriet said she spent so long telling herself she didn't need to be married that it took her forever to admit she wanted to marry Gresham."

"Not surprising, perhaps." Malcolm moved to the bed to pet Berowne. "Sometimes marriage doesn't make sense until one finds the right person."

Mélanie pulled out the combs she'd used to hold her hair back on the sides. Blanca's careful ringlets from last night fell about her face. "Odd," she said.

"What?"

She turned, leaning against the dressing table. "I used to not want to be tied to anyone. Not even Raoul." She cast a quick sideways glance at Malcolm. "Sorry."

"It's all right."

"I thought that was freedom. But it wasn't, really. I was so determined not to be tied that I boxed myself in. I didn't realize that until years later."

Malcolm rubbed Berowne behind the ears. "You didn't realize you wanted to be tied to anyone at all until years later."

She met his gaze for a moment in the tapestry of candlelight and shadow between them. "Well, no, that's not true. I admitted I was tied first. And that you were tied to Colin. And I realized some ties can't be broken."

"So you knew you'd trapped yourself."

"Darling. No."

He raised a brow. "It doesn't change what we have now to

admit how it started. You've as good as said you first decided you couldn't leave because of Colin."

"Well, yes. Because, without Colin, the fair thing would have been to leave and let you have your life back."

"My darling." Malcolm moved across the room to stand beside her. "You may have been single-mindedly focused on the mission, but surely you realized I wasn't ever going to have my life back. That I didn't want my life back."

She folded her arms. "There were times I wondered if you'd be happier with your old life back—when you forgot to tell me where you were or to send word home. But mostly I thought you'd want your old life back when you learnt the truth."

"Mmm. That wasn't going to happen."

She met his gaze. Her own gaze felt as though it was stripped raw. No defenses left to hide behind. "I've always been good at accounting for different scenarios. An escape route being blocked, a picklock not working, a disguise being seen through. And improvising to handle each. I completely failed to take emotional scenarios into account. Largely because I didn't consider them at all. Some people say spies need to be detached, but if you're too detached it can cause all sorts of problems. You can miss countless risks."

"The risk of being trapped by your own feelings? Or someone else's?"

"The risk of hurting someone. And the risk of being hurt oneself when one realizes not being tied seems unbearably lonely."

"You think that's what Harriet and Gresham realized?"

Mélanie saw Harriet and Gresham laughing together at the dinner table. "I think they realized they were in love."

"Oh well." Malcolm grinned and drew her into his arms. "That makes all the difference."

A READING GROUP GUIDE

The Gresham Scandal

About This Guide
The suggested questions are included
to enhance your group's reading of
Tracy Grant's *The Gresham Scandal*.

1. Harriet and Tristram both talk openly about how they cultivate a persona to conceal what they are really doing. Which other characters do the same?
2. What do you think lies ahead for Tristram and Harriet?
3. What common themes run through the three scenes at the end of the book?
4. Several characters worry about how marriage will change them. Which character do you think is the most changed by it?
5. What do you think lies ahead for Lizzy and Hara?
6. How might Harriet and Tristram's story have played out differently if the book were a romance rather than a mystery?

7. Do you think Tony will really be able to retire from the beau monde and the diplomatic world? How might that impact his relationship with Désirée?
8. How does the book shift Hubert's relationship with the central characters?

ALSO BY TRACY GRANT

Traditional Regencies

WIDOW'S GAMBIT

FRIVOLOUS PRETENCE

THE COURTING OF PHILIPPA

Lescaut Quartet

DARK ANGEL

SHORES OF DESIRE

SHADOWS OF THE HEART

RIGHTFULLY HIS

The Rannoch Fraser Mysteries

HIS SPANISH BRIDE

LONDON INTERLUDE

VIENNA WALTZ

IMPERIAL SCANDAL

THE PARIS AFFAIR

THE PARIS PLOT

BENEATH A SILENT MOON

THE BERKELEY SQUARE AFFAIR

THE MAYFAIR AFFAIR

INCIDENT IN BERKELEY SQUARE

LONDON GAMBIT

MISSION FOR A QUEEN

GILDED DECEIT

MIDWINTER INTRIGUE

ACKNOWLEDGMENTS

It takes the help and support of an amazing number of people to bring a book into the world. My amazing agent, Nancy Yost, has been a wonderful support to the Rannoch Fraser Mysteries from the start. As always, huge thanks for her insights and brilliant eye for framing the story and editing cover copy. Thanks to Natanya Wheeler, a fabulous Director of Digital Rights, for shepherding the book expertly through each stage of the publication process. Natanya also designs the covers for the series. For this book, she brought to life a key scene with a brilliant cover image that actually inspired a plot twist. To Sarah Younger for helping the book along through production and publication, and to Sarah and Christina Miller for superlative social media support. To Emma Barbour for another great set of character and quote cards. And to the entire team at Nancy Yost Literary Agency for their fabulous work. Their creativity and dedication make all of them a dream to work with. Malcolm, Mélanie, and I are all very fortunate to have their support.

Thank you to Eve Lynch for the meticulous and thoughtful copyediting. I love sharing the Rannochs with you and so appreciate your care for getting their story right when it comes to everything from historical usage to series continuity.

Thank you to Kristen Loken for a magical author photo. Your brilliance never fails to amaze me, Kristen!

I am very fortunate to have a wonderful group of writer friends near and far who make being a writer less solitary. Thanks in particular to Lauren Willig for sharing the joys of historical research and the challenges of juggling life as a writer and a mom. To Penelope Williamson, for sharing adventures (including wonderful writer escapes to the Oregon Shakespeare Festival), analyzing plots from Shakespeare to *Scandal* to *Miss Scarlet & the Duke*, and being a wonderful honorary aunt to my daughter. Thank you to the #momswritersclub on Bluesky for bimonthly chats that are energizing and inspiring, and especially to Shay Galloway, with whom I now co-host the chats, and to Jessica Payne for starting the group.

Thank you to the readers who support Malcolm and Mélanie and their friends and provide wonderful insights on my website and social media, and especially on the Goodreads Discussion Group for the series.

Thanks to Gregory Paris and jim saliba for creating and updating a fabulous website that chronicles Malcolm and Mélanie's adventures.

And thank you to my daughter Mélanie, for brainstorming *The Gresham Scandal* (including ideas for a couple of key action scenes, plot points, and character names), proofreading, and supporting me all the way through the process. I am so proud she is now writing her own books. From the time she could touch the keys, Mélanie has contributed something to each of my books. This is Mélanie's contribution to this story – "It's the most amazing thing ever that my mom can write endlessly amazing books. My mom is so incredible, and I strive to one day be as amazing as my mom. I hope that you enjoyed another incredible book in the best series ever written, by the best person and mother to ever live."

ABOUT THE AUTHOR

Photo by Kristen Loken

Tracy Grant studied British history at Stanford University and received the Firestone Award for Excellence in Research for her honors thesis on shifting conceptions of honor in late-fifteenth-century England. She lives in the San Francisco Bay Area with her daughter, four cats, and a gecko. In addition to writing, Tracy is Executive Director of Cantare, an organization dedicated to sharing the power and beauty of choral music through adult choirs, youth programs, and concert performances. Her real-life heroine is her daughter Mélanie, who is very supportive of Mummy's writing and has become a writer herself. Tracy is currently at work on her next book chronicling the adventures of Malcolm and Mélanie Suzanne Rannoch. Visit her online at www.tracygrant.org.

www.ingramcontent.com/pod-product-compliance
Lightning Source LLC
Chambersburg PA
CBHW060227100726